I0826214

The Treasure of Cocos Island

by

Mike Riley

THIS IS A LIMITED FIRST EDITION

PUBLISHED BY MIKE RILEY

PRINTED ABOARD THE KETCH *BEAU SOLEIL* WHILE SAILING THE SEVEN SEAS

THIS IS A WORK OF FICTION

ISBN # 978-0-9828247-5-7

sailingbooks@rocketmail.com

WRITER'S NOTE

The Treasure of Lima exists. It is the largest, most documented, unrecovered pirate treasure in history. All treasure maps and treasure locations in this book are quoted directly from history books and the internet. Only the language was changed to improve comprehension. There is absolutely no doubt that the Virgin is still buried on Cocos Island. It has never been found (Despite rumors to the contrary). The descriptions of the pirate's battles are as accurate as I could make them. The internet is full of misinformation. This book contains the truest version I could find. I hope you enjoy this book, I had a great time writing it!

Mike Riley
Sea of Cortez

DEDICATION

This book is for the spirits of fellow cruisers who's eyes shine at the hint of adventure. Especially, I dedicate this book to the spirit of Karen, my wife, who joins me whole heartily in whatever hare-brained idea creeps into my head. Eventually.

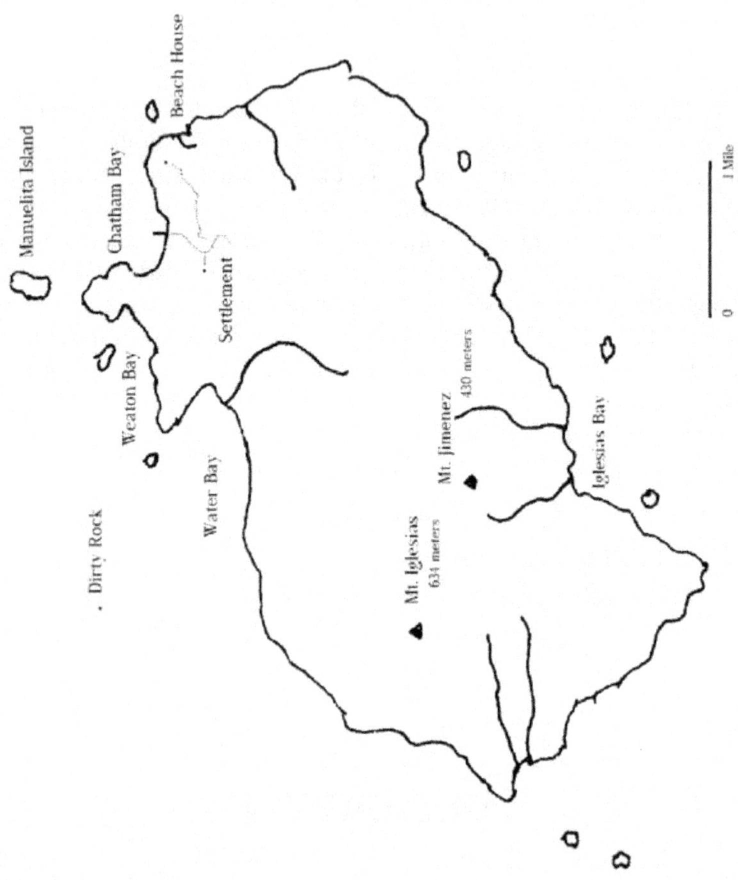

Cocos Island

Book I

How it all Started

Beware of all endeavors requiring the wearing of shoes.

Robert A. Heinlein

It had all started with a kiss. It had gotten inside of her when she kissed him on the lips. She tried, oh how she had tried, to get rid of it, but it wouldn't come out. It was there to stay. Wherever she went, it was with her, changing her, telling her, instructing her, forcing her. For a while, she was tempted to kill herself just to finally, finally get rid of it, but then she realized that it was also a magic fence she could erect in a moment against an unwelcome world. Once in a rare while she loved it, most of the time she hated it and fought it every way she knew how. But it just wouldn't leave her alone. No matter what she did, it wouldn't allow her to be alone, ever. Ever. For every moment of every hour of every day.

It had happened that day, not so long ago, in a dusty little town in Baja, California. He had saved them from a fate so bad, a terrible death that no one should ever be doomed to carry down the tunnels of eternity; she hadn't even thought he liked her, in fact, she thought he hated her, but he had saved her and her daughter and her husband. And he hadn't even broken a sweat doing it, or so it seemed. He had just saved them, just like that, like a snap of his fingers, and then, after, he had driven out of their lives forever. But before he left, she had kissed him. Just a friendly, no harm, no foul, thank you kiss. An innocent kiss. She had kissed him and then, somehow it had gotten inside of her. From him to her. Through his mouth, carried by his tongue, his breath, his spirit. It had gotten inside of her and grown like a baby.

Like a little baby getting bigger every day, and she worried what would happen when it was big enough to be born. What would happen to her, to her sanity, to her family, to her mind, to her soul. What would happen when it came out, when it saw the light of day, when it took over, when she could no longer summon the will to fight it, when it came into the power that its master had injected into her. When it made her become like him. When she was just like him. Powerful like him. Spawn of the devil, guardian angel, good and bad combined, when she would be hated, feared and loved like he was, by everyone. By the world. By her family. By herself.

She was so very scared.

The sharks were circling down below him. They were between him and the strange shape he had seen on the depth sounder. It looked like a small ship shaped lump. It could be a Spanish treasure galleon from the late 1500's. It was about the right size. If it was it would be the answer to all his hopes. To all his dreams.

He was a tall, well built man, not that you could tell under water. Down there perspectives change. The eyes invent things, normal things that the brain expects to see. A clump of seaweed turns into an evergreen tree. A bit of coral, skull mountain from the children's book, Peter Pan.

But his eyes weren't inventing the sharks between him and the lump. They were real. It was a pack of over fifty sharks. The biggest one was slowly rising up, using the underwater thermals, saving its strength for a lethal dash towards its prey. Maybe towards him. The man's eyes never left the shark. He projected in his mind the thought that he was hungry, and that he was particularly hungry for a large shark. He wasn't telepathic but the man hoped the shark was. He didn't want to kill the beautiful, graceful animal. If he even could kill it.

His right hand grasped the bangstick tighter as the shark approached. He tore his eyes off the shark which he could now identify as a bull shark, a man-eater and of the same family as the tiger shark. The man noticed to his horror a pack of hammerheads coming towards him from above, between him and his boat. Hammerheads definitely had a reputation for liking human flesh. He had been told that Cocos Island had a reputation for the number and ferocity of its sharks, but it had to be seen to be believed.

He wasn't supposed to be here. The Costa Rican government restricts visits to the Cocos Island World Heritage Site, including the entire island and surrounding ocean. That was just to visit. To get a permit to look for treasure took years and thousands of dollars in application fees. And currently, they weren't even allowing treasure hunting. He wasn't the kind of man that waited for anyone, certainly not some faceless paper pusher. He didn't care that he was doing something illegal. He didn't care at all.

'Damn, if I worried about every little law there is, I would never get any sleep. Plus, it ain't a crime if nobody saw it,' he thought to himself, as the bull shark got closer. It was starting to hunch its back and flare its gill slits, dead giveaways that it was planning an attack. It swirled its tail faster now, as if it was trying to decide which part of the man's body to eat first. It came closer and closer. When it was only fifteen feet away it charged forward in a mock attack. The man knew that sharks never attack on the first contact. They hadn't survived for 200 million years in their present form by being rash or careless. Before they attacked something they always checked to make sure their prey wasn't playing possum and was going to attack them, instead. Unless they were in a feeding frenzy, then the sharks became mindless killing machines.

As the hammerheads approached, the pack of sharks down below moved away. Other sharks always feared a large group of hammerheads because their heads acted like a forward rudder giving them an unfair advantage in maneuverability during a fight, and because in general, sharks had poor to pathetic vision, hammerhead's binocular eyesight gave them an bio-technological advantage. They all moved away except for the big bull shark just below the man. It wasn't thinking about hammerheads, it only had thoughts on lunch, a grab and rip and gulp lunch.

As the bull started his test run, the man brought up his bangstick into the ready position. It was a five foot fiberglass pole with a twelve gauge shotgun shell on the end. As soon as the shark was close enough, he jabbed it in the belly. Even though the shark's body absorbed most of the explosion, the man was thrown backwards. He flipped around and started to swim as fast as he could away from the wounded and dying bull shark and sideways from the rapidly approaching hammerheads. He raced as fast as he could, trying to do an end run, around the line of sharks to get back to his boat. He didn't think he was going to make it, but he kept trying. He took a quick look behind him and saw twenty hammerheads tearing at the bloody body of the bull shark he had shot. There wasn't much left of it. A few of the sharks were coming straight at him looking for more lunch. More were following. Many more.

He took a quick look at his air gauge. Damn, 700 pounds left. Enough for five minutes at this depth. He took a chance and sank down into the seaweed and coral below. Maybe if he didn't move they wouldn't find him. He would use his air up faster the deeper he went, but if he didn't panic his air would last longer. As if panic was something he could turn off. Once on the bottom, he grabbed some sea fans and pulled them around his body, and tried to relax and to be as calm as he could. He knew that the calmer he was, the less air he would use. Through the ferns he could see sharks crisscrossing above him, looking, searching, smelling, hunting. He chanced a quick look at his air pressure gauge, 200 pounds. He flipped the lever on his J valve on his tank, opening his reserve air. His gauge read 600 pounds now. He could see his boat on the surface forty feet up and a hundred yards away. Too far. Way too far. If he waited too long, he would run out of air and have to pop, blow and go. To inflate his life vest, vent his lungs on the way up and go for the surface. He had to be sure not to go too fast, to go faster than his bubbles, or he would get the bends. Tough choice, live the rest of his life with excruciating pain in all of his joints, or to be eaten alive by a pack of sharks. Above him the hammerheads crisscrossed above his sea fan patch. He tried to ignore them, thinking that his awareness of their existence was attracting them, keeping them near. Just a few minutes later, he didn't have a choice any more. His gauge read zero. He released his hold on the seaweed, dropped his weight belt and sped for the surface. He didn't inflate his PFD as the last thing he needed was to be more visible. He circled as he rose keeping a wary eye on the feeding frenzy which was now looking for dessert. One big hammerhead suddenly spotted him and raced at him. Its eyes were black, black like the lower depths of hell. It must have been all of fourteen feet long and its gaping wide open mouth was huge. It was just feet from him. The man shoved the depleted bang stick's fiberglass shaft straight into the shark's mouth and down its gullet. He gave it a last hard shove for good measure, and turned quickly to continue to swim for the surface, air and his boat.

The other sharks noticed the shaft sticking out of their former pack member's mouth and were on him in a flash. Tearing, biting, ripping, if a shark in a feeding frenzy didn't have time to swallow, it didn't matter. It was the killing, the destruction of another living thing that mattered. Dessert didn't last long and the man was still too far from his boat. He made one last, heroic effort, thrashing his fins as hard as he could, the hell with the bubbles and the bends, and hooked a hand around the gunnel of his boat, spit his regulator out of his mouth, took one huge gulp of air, and kicked his feet to propel himself into the boat. Something was wrong, he wasn't rising. He looked down past his hips in the crystal clear water, both feet were missing. Two hammerheads were fighting over the remains of one foot and the attached fin. The man pulled himself up with his arms alone and suddenly, very easily, plopped into the bottom of the boat. Little wonder, all of him was missing, all of him below his waist. His last thought was of the lump under the sand off the treasure island of Cocos Island. It could be solid gold and gems.

The boat's automatic bilge pump sensed the increase liquid in the bilge as the torso bled to death and pumped the blood overboard. The sharks went crazy. Crazier. They rammed the boat, tore the outboard off of her, severed the anchor line, and pounded holes in the thin fiberglass. One shark forced his head through a larger hole, grabbed the remains of the man in his jaws and gulped madly, eyes wide open, staring blindly, its head stuck up through the bottom of the boat, eating before his meal could be torn away from him by his pack mates, and then, finished, it sank back into the silence of the deeps. The other sharks quickly demolished the remains of the boat looking for the smallest morsel of human flesh.

An hour later, if someone had been looking out to sea, it would have been as if nothing had ever happened. It was a quiet, clear, peaceful, Pacific afternoon on a island where nothing had happened for generations, or so it would seem.

The sun eased down towards the horizon, taking its time, making everyone wait, breathlessly, hoping for a green flash. The colors went through every hue of the rainbow, faded and changed, flared and then dissolved into blackish blue. The fluffy clouds slowly became grey night, then black, and the first stars glittered, quasar-like, blinking messages to the threesome far below.

"That was like the most awesome sunset I have ever seen. It even beats that one we saw on the cliffs of Acapulco. Don't you think so, Daddy? It was totally rad. Why, if we could put that on a movie screen we could be millionaires over night! Isn't this just the best, Mom? Being here all together, having fun?"

"Honey, would you please sit down and stop jumping around next to the cliff, please, Baby, just for me and your Dad. Sit down and start acting your age."

"Aw, let her have some fun. After all we have been through, we all deserve some fun in our lives, right, Jill? And besides we were really hoping for a green flash. Maybe one of these days, we'll get lucky."

"Yessiree, Bob! I'm going to see lots of flashes in my life. And I am going to have the absolute most fun of anyone! Anyone in the whole world. And I can cuz I saved us! I bagged me a pirate, I did. Then the pirate saved us all." Jill smiled with a happy, irresistible smile and raced over to a flag pole and for no discernable reason, started to climb it. For a moment she had a confused look in her eyes, but it soon faded in a spirit of youthful abandon.

"In fact you can start calling me, 'The Green Flash' right now. It is my new name. Much better than Jill. And you better keep your eyes open, cuz I'm as fast as anything and you might miss seeing me in action! Watch me now!" She shimmed her way up to the top of the pole where she shaded her eyes with one hand and scanned the horizon. Then she slowly started back down, sliding slowly, her eyes on a group of kids playing soccer on a field down the road. She watched one boy in particular.

"Now see what you have done, Harv. Sometimes I wish she wasn't so active, it really gets on my nerves. Wait I take that back. I didn't really mean it." Two plus years ago, Jill was a shy introverted child who refused to even think of sailing, much less crossing oceans, fighting pirates and desperados, and getting rich, in experience if not necessarily money. One day, two and a half years ago, she woke up and experienced a sea change. She became a tomboy deluxe. Instead of playing with dolls, she wanted to help her father fix the diesel. She wanted to help her mother stock the boat for long sea passages. She wanted to do anything that was new, different and adventurous. Especially climbing flag poles and walking along steep cliffs.

"Just ignore her and she will come back in time." Harv looked up at her as 'The Flash' inched her way back up the pole with a silly grin on her face. "Let's go get some ice cream," he said in a loud whisper.

"Well, OK. But give her a few more minutes." Janet knew she should give Jill more independence, but whenever she was out of sight, her mind brought back the image of Jill laying dead in the stern cabin of their boat, with the knife she had thrown stuck in her heart. Again, the agony she had felt then, returned to her, luckily in a slightly dulled and muted form.

By a miracle Jill had lived. But then they had run into some desperados in a small port in Baja. It was only by the intervention of the criminal who had pirated them that saved their lives. They all had suffered multiple

traumas, physical and psychological. It was only the love they felt for each other and the closeness of the family that got them through the experience and the so far partial recovery.

But now things had changed for Janet. And to the good. Suddenly everything seemed to start going her way. She found that if she wanted something, that if she really thought about it, if she could visualize it, then it came true. At first she thought that it was just the music of the spheres playing her song after ignoring her for so long, but then she started to realize that it was coming from within her. Somehow. She thought about that, and then threw up her hands in disgust while walking to the ice cream parlor.

"Who do I think I am, a Messiah or something? What am I going to do next, start raising the dead? I am so full of it, it is incredible," she whispered to herself while walking down the street. She looked quickly out of the corners of her eyes to see if anyone had noticed her talking to herself, or if they had, if they thought she belonged in the loony bin. "Ranting and raving while walking down the street. People will think I am a bag lady pushing my grocery cart down the street with all my worldly belongings in it." With a blush she realized she had done it again. She vowed to stop thinking about any newborn talents or demons that might be within her. 'I just want to be a mom, that's all.' This time she made sure she just thought the words. She kept her lips tightly closed. She made very sure her lips stayed closed by pushing them against each other, hard. She didn't see the lines forming and radiating around her mouth with the effort of pressing her lips together.

"I think you are a Messiah, I do. I think so everytime we make love." whispered Harv, coming up behind her after a last ditch attempt to talk Jill down from the flag pole. "I mean, first you bring the dead back to life, and in a erect position, no less, then as tired as I might have been beforehand, I feel rejuvenated afterwards. So in my books, that makes you at least a saint!" Janet just kept her lips pressed together as her face reddened in embarrassment. "Here's the ice cream store," he whispered trying not to move his lips, "I told Jill we would wait for her here. And I told her that there probably wouldn't be any ice cream left if she took too long." He looked back along the sidewalk and was happy to see Jill waiting impatiently for a red light several streets back.

"Here comes Jane, AKA, The Green Flash! Let's pretend we already finished our cones and are standing outside waiting for her. What do you say, Janet? Want ta torture our kid, not having anything more fun to do at the moment?"

"If I thought for one minute that you were serious, I would kick you on the shin. Men!"

"Aw, come on, Babe! We can always tell the judge that our religion uses torture as an educational tool to make it easier to get into heaven,

"Oh, Hi, Jill. We, uhm, your mother has something to tell you." He pretended to jump a few paces away to avoid a sudden fist to the biceps, a smile slowly spreading over his face.

Later on as the threesome sat happily on the seats outside the parlor, filling their tummies, watching the people of the sleepy little Mexican resort town, and at a policia car as it drove by. Harv glanced at it with equanimity. There had been a time when he would look away in fear or nervousness at the sight of a cop, after being traumatized in jail. Later, in a little town on the Pacific coast of Baja, a cop had died trying to save him and his family. After that he developed an increasing respect for anyone who stood up against the decline of society as we know it.

"Dad, do you think I can do a headstand on the top of that parking meter? I think I can. It's just a body lift, a leg lift, a double handstand and then a headstand. What do you think?"

"Personally, I think that my head is too sore from watching you all day long on top of a metal flag pole. Besides, if I tried it, I'd throw up all that ice cream I just ate." Harv raised his eye brows at Jill. "But I am an acrobat, I am; I can stand on just one finger! Right here on the sidewalk!"

"Dad, we learned that one in first grade! See?" She bent down and put one finger under a bare foot and pushed it into the sidewalk.

"Oh, yeah, well I can poke my head right through this hole," her father held up his thumb and forefinger of his right hand, digits just touching.

"No way. Impossible. You and what army?" Her father held his right hand next to his head and inserted his left finger through the circle formed by his right hand and poked his head.

"Cheap. That was so cheap. Dad, I expected more of you. But I gotta remember that one."

"If you two would stop messing about, we still have to decide if we are going to spend the summer hurricane season here in the Sea of Cortez, head back to California or sail down to Panama or Ecuador to get out of the possible tracks of named storms. We can't wait for the last second before we decide. We have to stock up the boat, make sure we have the right charts and try to find some cruising guides." Janet raised a finger in the air. "I for one don't want to experience the 'thrill' of a hurricane while at sea."

"Aw, Mom! It would be fun! I could climb the mast and con the boat from up on the spreaders! I could warn you about any great big greybeards coming to get our sweet little *Rose Marie*!"

The family's sailboat wasn't a yacht. It was an older boat, built back in the late sixties, in the last millennium. Back then, they built the boats stronger as the builders didn't realize what a good boatbuilding material fiberglass was. However, they also built the boats with the same designs as the wooden boats that had preceded them, instead of the modern world cruiser designs with multiple cabins, exotic galleys, and nav desks with hundreds of circuit breakers controlling as many electronics as a jetliner. Not the *Rose Marie*. She was seaworthy. But she was also, to put it kindly, camping in style. Her family didn't care. They dedicated serious time to the maintenance of her, keeping her ready to take on the worse the sea could throw at her. Anything less than a hurricane, that is. Especially a full blown, Category 5 hurricane with winds exceeding 250 knots and seas towering high over their masts. Seas that could best be seen by looking straight up, up fifty or sixty feet, as the tops of the waves curled down and crashed on top of any helpless little toy-like boat wind and seas that could destroy and sink any boat that ever floated. It wouldn't take many such waves to make matchwood of the *Rose Marie*.

"Well, girls, what do you say? We already have the charts for the Sea of Cortez and the upper gulf usually doesn't get hurricanes. And if it does, there are plenty of hurricane holes. Let's go there? What do you say, ladies?"

"Yay, let's go there, yippee!"

"The only problem is that we are still in the hurricane zone. In San Diego or Ecuador, we would be totally out of danger. And at least in San Diego, Jill could return to school if she wished. We are kind of forcing home schooling on to her, aren't we? And she really doesn't have any long term friends, does she."

"I think we should go to the upper gulf or Ecuador, for sure. But only if they have flag poles. We just got away from San Diego, and besides, where would we stay? In that same marina? Those same showers?" A haunted look briefly passed over Jill's face. She had been almost raped and killed in those showers just before they departed San Diego. "Let's go see someplace new! That's what I say. Besides they have silly rules about not climbing the flag pole in that San Diego school."

Her mother looked at her with concern. 'The poor child,' she thought, 'She shouldn't have to relive that kind of experience.' She opened her mouth to ask Jill if she still had bad dreams, but then snapped it shut again. 'Of course, she would still have nightmares. How could she not? Best not to upset the cart. Upset it even more.' Janet thought. She reached over and gave her daughter a warm hug and little lines formed around her mouth as a twin pair of drops appeared in the corners of Janet's eyes.

"Ok, San Diego is out. Of course we could take the big jump and head across the puddle to Hawaii! Are we ready, Harv?"

"Yeah, are we ready, Sir Daddy? Ready to cross the big puddle. The Pacific Ocean!" Jill jumped up and did a cartwheel on the sidewalk. "The big puddle! The Green Flash is going to cross the Pacific! Yippee! I am so going to be a surfer girl! Forget flag poles, I am going to ride those big 100 foot monsters on the North Shore! Oh, yeah! This is going to be so much fun!"

Harv gazed down at his left hand. He had dislocated every bone in it during his attempt to save his family from the man who had pirated their boat. He had gained use of it again and continued rehabilitation by daily squeezing a rubber ball 500 times a day. But still, could he do a one hand pull up with his left arm? What if he broke his right arm during a knockdown, could he pull his daughter back on board with his left? Harv wasn't sure he was ready to cross oceans yet, to be beyond help from rescue teams, beyond the backup of civilization.

"Or, if your Sir Daddy agrees, we could sail from Cabo down to the Marquesas and Tahiti! To go on down to the South Seas! To the land that time forgot, to the seas the *Bounty* and Mr. Christian sailed! Why, Jill, that is the beauty of a sailboat, we can go anywhere we want, anywhere in the world!" Janet's eyes were gleaming. Her teeth were glistening through slightly open lips. "Oh, I do love this life so much!"

She glanced over at Harv and was saddened to see the doubt and confusion in his eyes. The caution and the fear. When he was younger, when they were first married, he had wanted to sail around the world. Where was that man now? She wondered if she could somehow reignite the love of adventure that she was sure lay just below the horizon in the world of his soul. She had loved Harv so much back then. He had such a spark of life. A spark that had changed her humdrum boring life into an exciting adventure. But then he had changed as he grew older and as the responsibilities of fatherhood annealed his spontaneity. Then being pirated and not being able to do anything about it didn't help.

"I still love him, I do, I do." With a shock she realized she had whispered aloud again. With her cheeks turning pink, she quickly glanced over at Harv. It didn't seem like he had heard her ranting and ravings. 'Thank God. Thank you, sweet Jesus.' She touched her index finger to her lips just to be sure that she thought the last.

"I suppose, girls, that instead of flying off the handle and going off sailing wherever, we should be mature and do the responsible thing. I think we should go on down to Central America. We have already been as far south as Acapulco. The rest is just more of the same. More of the same except for crossing the Tehuantepec and the Papagayo." A tic formed in the muscle of the outside of his right eye. It spasmed every couple seconds. Harv rubbed his temples trying to ease the tension, but the tic remained.

"Yay, Sir Daddy says we are going to Tehuantepec! I've always wanted to go there! Uhm, Daddy, where is this Tehuantepec anyway?"

"It's nothing to worry about, my little flash of green, it is just this big bay in the southern part of Mexico where the Rockies and the Andes meet. It is the bigger of two low spots in the entire Western hemisphere's spine of mountain ranges that abut the Caribbean. You know how the wind is lazy? It hates to go up and over something if it can go around it?

"Remember how wind races around the ends of islands and escalates around major points of land? It is the same in Tehuantepec. The entire winds of the Caribbean and Gulf of Mexico try to get through that one little low spot all at once, but just on some days. We just have to watch our weather, pick a good window of opportunity and when the time is right, go for it. Nothing for little girls to worry about, Ok?" He reached out and rubbed the hair on top of Jill's head, messing up the mass of tangles and curls that seemed to accumulate there everyday as if by magic irregardless of the time Janet spent brushing them out.

"Papagayo is much the same. There is a big lake in southern Nicaragua and there are low mountains facing the lake on the Costa Rican side. Sometimes the winds develop over the lake, aided by the Caribbean winds and blow with huge gusts. We just have to watch our weather, right, Green Flash?"

"Right, Sir Daddy! And the best place to watch for those evil winds is up the mast, at the very tippy top!" She started jumping around, eyeing the ice cream parlor. "We are going to Costa Rica! We are going across the Tehuantepec! We are going on a great adventure cuz my Big Daddy says so!" She gave Harv a hug, wrapping her arms around his neck. "Sir Daddy, can I have another ice cream cone? A chocolate one?" Her eyes were shining in anticipation and adoration for her father.

"Alright, guess I have to keep your tank topped off. Janet, babe, do you want another?" Janet just smiled her secret smile. She shook her head and whispered,

"I'll just take a bite and a lick of yours, you big sexy hunk!"

The three of them walked back to the dinghy dock hand-in-hand, back to the sea, back to the *Rose Marie* and back to their world, eating their cones little realizing what fate was planning for them. The poor innocent family.

People thought he was an actor sometimes, he had the looks and the presence. The charisma. Then after they got to know him, well, the truth was he never knew what they thought, not that he cared. In fact, he couldn't even remember asking what anyone thought of him. He hadn't let anyone get to know him, the real him, for decades. He didn't let anyone inside his guard. It wasn't that he didn't like people or was shy of them. It was just a habit. The way he figured it, if no one knew what he was doing, it was that much harder for anyone to stop him from doing it. And he liked doing whatever he wanted. It was like a religion or something to him. A reason to be. A reason to live. A reason to wake up in the morning. A reason to exist, to warrant breathing oxygen. To be able to do whatever the fuck he felt like doing whenever the fuck he felt like doing it.

Exactly. And woe be to any asshole who tried to stop him. Oh, yeah. Goddamn woe be to all the assholes. And you can write that up on the wall in blood.

Like the other day, he parked in his favorite spot, next to the hydrant in front of the city hall. When he came out after screwing some little sucker in the real estate biz, there was some stupid flatfoot writing a ticket on his car, his car! Boy, did he lay in on that dumb kid. Rules were for other people. Little people. That's right. Rules weren't for him. What did they teach these kids in cop school? He grabbed the kid by the ear and pulled him into the Mayor's office. Stupid kid tried to struggle, tried to pull out his gun. He just slapped it away. No wonder they had him writing tickets.

"Damn it, Ralph. I can't have these, wet behind the ears, kids going around writing tickets on my car. Can you talk some sense into this boy's ears? I got a shopping mall to build, a wife to divorce, her kids to screw, and I have to decide who I am going to fund in the next election. I just can't do it all if I have to put up with all these little annoyances. I have half a mind to sell out and move up to Miami. They understand power over there. Power and money. Ain't that right, Ralph."

"Hawkins, look Hawkins. I really appreciate the funding you have given my campaigns. But really, Hawk, you have to follow the rules the same as everyone else. It is what civilization is all about." He ushered the 20 something cop out the door with a pat on the shoulder and a whisper, 'We'll talk, later, Ok?"

"Fuck you. Who is running against you next year? Whoever. I think I will support him, her or it to the tune of a million big ones. How do you like them apples, Mr. Soon to be Mr. Ex-Mayor?"

A sweat broke out on the chubby face of Ralph McHenry. He visibly swallowed. The rolls of fat around his belly vibrated. His cock didn't work without Viagra anymore but even if it did, right now it was so shriveled up that any girl would laugh at it. He pulled out a bandana, a nice common touch that had won him one election all by itself, and mopped his face. He had been living well on the public trough for quite a few years and really liked it. But one thing he had definitely learned about politics, was how to suck up to the big money guys. Without them, no one could win an election these days. No how. The television and newspaper ads were just too expensive.

"Look, Hawkins. Look, I am really sorry. You are absolutely right. You really do have the right to park right in front of city hall. With all the good you do for this city, we can't have you wasting your time walking here and there, and everywhere." He mopped his face again then stuck the soaking cloth into a back pocket.

"Hawkins, I am going to have to square away our bumbling police department. Sorry for all the inconvenience. Can I buy you lunch as penance?"

"Up yours, Ralph. But I'll mark it down as one you owe me. And you know I always call in my markers."

"Sure, Hawkins, sure. Whatever you want, whenever."

Yeah, people thought he was a nice guy. The thing was, he did look like a nice guy. Kindly looking blue eyes, a bit of a pouch since he turned forty, a bit of grey around the temples, and he walked, normally, like a nice guy. You know, like he had no place to be and had time for everyone. That kind of walk. Hell, maybe he was a nice guy, after all, kind of like Santa Claus. Unless someone got in his way and didn't move quickly out of it. Then, really, it was their own fault. It was their fault when he screwed them. You'd think people would realize that they should just sit down or something when he appeared, or at least get the fuck out of the way. People can be so stupid. He might walk nice when he didn't want to screw someone, but when he was on the warpath, no one would ever think he was anything but bad dog, mean. His eyes flared with blue sparks of anger, his pouch disappeared as his body produced massive amounts of adrenaline which tightened up his stomach muscles and, then, he certainly could never be described as kindly. Not then. No way. No how.

He certainly could not be described as kindly last week when he was, for some fucking unknown reason, waiting for a happy meal at the drive thru for his grandson. He took the kid out once or twice a year to show him the ropes. Make sure he was growing up Ok. Anyway, there was this old Chevy ahead of him and they couldn't find the right change or some fucking, idiotic thing. So he eased up to the Chevy and pushed the car out of the way and into the street with his Hummer. He laughed as the driver applied his brakes, as if that was going to stop his car. Ha. Damn Hummer had so much power, it was mind blowing. But then, when he backed up to window, the stupid girl in the stupid window got in his face. Saying he had to go to the back of the line for being mean. Mean? Him! Ha! She fucking sure quieted down fast when he stuck his black 45 in her face. God, what did they want him to do, let some little person go first? Shit. What's the world coming to?

But he was a nice guy. When he got into this new gig, this treasure thing, he called up all his pals to see if they wanted a piece of the pie. He didn't say how big a piece. Fuck, what did they expect? Let 'em cough up and if he felt good some morning after it was all over, he might give 'em some of their stake back. They all knew better than to stiff him. They all coughed up. They better. He was not the kind of guy to get on the wrong side of. Some guys had little black books with chicks names in it. His little black book had the names of guys that tried to screw him or refused to back him, or didn't smile at him, or didn't send his grandson a birthday card, or didn't send his soon to be ex-wife flowers and candy at Christmas. Fuck, what is life without respect? Nothing, that's what. Shit.

He really liked this new gig. There was this island out in the Pacific, somewhere, who the fuck cared, that was loaded with treasure. Totally fucking loaded with treasure. Not any stupid little chest with a couple gold pieces and cut pieces of colored glass in it, like Hollywood. Real treasure. Including, just as an example, a life-sized solid gold statue of Mary, bestudded with emeralds and rubies, and she was holding that brat Jesus, who was wearing this halo of massive great big diamonds. Now that was treasure! Stuff had been there on that island for centuries but no one had ever found it. Oh, they tried! Oh, yeah! Even old Teddy Roosevelt sent his nephew, Franklin, to blow the shit out of the island with his Great White Fleet's guns on his world tour trying to have some adventure and solve the nation's financial problems all in one go. Sounded like something old Talk Softly but Carry a Big Stick would do. They had books written about this treasure. Lots of 'em. But no one had ever found it, ever. It had been waiting just for him. It knew who its daddy was. Fucking A.

He was a nice guy to let his pals in on this deal. But that was what pals were for. Just what was he supposed to do, hold back and not take their money? What kind of pal would that be? Hell, he might even let some of them come with him to do the dirty work. He could see 'em now. Hands all dirty from washing dishes as he laughed at them from his deck chair. Then he would reach over and finger their wives right in front of them. Them with their hands all dirty with his castoff, filthy food. And they would just have to take it. They owed him respect, that's why. That, and his 45, his temper, and his bodyguards.

He didn't have to have bodyguards. He was tough enough. More than tough enough. He might not look it but he was. Thing was, it was just expected for a guy like him to have a few bodyguards around. Like driving a Hummer around the city. It was like, expected. So anyway, he had the best bodyguards money could buy. One was this ex-seal who was thrown out of the service for being a homicidal maniac. Hell, all seals were maniacs, homicidal or otherwise, what with their endless exercises and drills. Christ, a man had to be one bad dude to get thrown out of that bunch. The damn guy was up every morning before dawn doing push ups or some damn thing. Fuck. Another was this Arab who got on the outs with the Taliban. Seems no one was allowed to kill except on Bin Laden's orders. This guy invaded a whole city, all by himself. Shit, took the damn thing over in a couple of days. All alone. When Bid Laden made him give it back, he quit. He didn't blame the guy. He wouldn't have given it back, either, no how. Fuck Bin Laden. Guy didn't know how to lead real men. Not like him. He knew how. He let his boys terrorize a little now and then just to keep them happy. Cost of doing business, that's all. If some of the little people got hurt? Fuck, that is why there are little people in the world.

To be messed with, to be fucked with, to live or die at his will. Shit, they are all going to die eventually, anyway. He was just helping them on their way a little. Being a fucking boy scout. Helping them cross that damn river he could never remember the name of between this world and Hades. They should give him a medal. Fucking A. Solving the population problem.

When he went to fundraisers to help save civilization as we know it, everyone told him what a nice guy he was. Donating so much money. Shit, if they only knew that it all was money he had just screwed out of them that morning. Hah, what a laugh! And then, they were all listening so earnestly when he gave his little speech. All about how they were saving the world for their children by donating their money to his companies. Yeah, right, but they all said he was a nice guy. He was being nice only cuz of thinking how much more money he was going to screw out of them. Assholes. Little people. Fuck 'em. Stick it in 'em and twist it. Twist it and spit in their eyes and watch as the light faded as they died. Fuckers. Just taking up oxygen. His oxygen.

Anyway, he had gotten himself a boat, hell, he guessed it must be a ship. Had one hell of a great owner's cabin. Damn right. If you want respect, you have to demand it. Had to show why he deserved it. Show off his wealth. Cost him a pretty penny, them ships don't come cheap, and then the repairs! The damn ship thing was always breaking something. Not that he cared. He had a crew to fix whatever. And he could always sell it after he had finished playing Captain Bligh. Now there was a guy who knew how to get respect. Only thing he did wrong was not shooting that Mr. Christian the second the guy acted up. Damn right. Yeah, he could sell the damn ship after fucking around with it for a while. Like all nice guys do. Just like a wife; get tired of her and sell her off, or fuck, just kill her and get rid of the body. Hell, the world was full of holes. He was just being nice. Anyway, what the fuck was he supposed to do? Stay married? Live with the same broad his whole life? Hah!

Then he had hired himself some treasure people, to do the diving and shit, and to look around on the island. Do the digging, look in little caves. Whatever. The island had been a pirate hangout for centuries, no telling how much loot there was buried here and there. What? They expected him to go looking for it, himself? Hell, he was going just to add up the loot and watch out for Mr. Christians.

This Key West place was full of these treasure people. All he had to do was say he was going after the Cocos treasure and the people just lined up. Just lined up! He had Mary, his present temporary, soon to be ex, squeeze, interview them first, just to get rid of the dreamers. Not that he minded dreamers, but he just wanted focused people. He had to chase after a couple of guys that were good at what they did. No problem, he could take the expense he had incurred out of their pay after they had finished their work. Figure out some imaginary government tax. He needed the focused people. No way he was going to go all the way over there, wherever the fuck it was, and not come back with any treasure. No fucking way. Absolutely no fucking way. And, fuck the blood, you could write that in guts and brains and shit up there on the wall.

Erhart lived for buried treasure. Ever since he was just a little kid reading stories of Treasure Island, he knew that he was going to spend his life looking for the treasures forgotten by everyone except Hollywood and children. His parents tried to steer him into a respectable job as a lab technician, hoping that would lead him into a medical career, anything that would take him away from his fascination with pirates. They would have planned for something more exalted but Erhart had average grades in school, mostly because he never read anything that didn't have something to do with pirates. Erhart loved his parents. He really did. And he wanted to please them. But some secret siren song sang to him while he lay in his bed after their nightly lectures and guided him to a Life Exceptional, as he called it. He wanted so much to live, even vicariously, the life of a buccaneer. It didn't matter that he was well under six feet and on the low side of a 150 pounds. Ok, Ok, so maybe he weighed 138 and stood at five feet four inches. But so what? It was the desire in the heart that should matter, shouldn't it?

He took scuba lessons at a junior college and he learned that his small size was a blessing underwater. His body required much less oxygen to stay alive than a tarzan of a man. He could stay down longer and think clearer while performing his required tasks, like hauling up pieces of eight! He was so much happier in his dream world than walking the streets. The modern world just moved too fast for his eighteenth century brain. And the modern world of checks, credit cards and credit ratings was woefully lacking in gold bullion.

He spent his free hours on the internet and had built one of the best buccaneer sites on the web. It included the histories of all the famous pirates, the supposed locations of where they stashed their booty, and all the many attempts to search out and recover the treasure. People from around the world visited his site and joined in on his forum. He hadn't written any books or magazine articles, but he was rapidly becoming a recognized, world-wide, authority on the subject of piracy.

And now this guy sent him a letter and wanted to hire him on a treasure hunt! Wow! Him! It was like a miracle. It was like, the best dream of all his dreams. Erhart liked to dream. He kept a log book by the side of his bed and he wrote down as much of his dreams as he could remember when he woke. It all started when he was a little kid, about seven, when he had a reoccurring dream about being abducted by aliens. Considering that he had the dream so often, it was strange he couldn't remember that much about it. Of course, it all happened so many years ago, long before he started his log book. He could still remember the twenty year old searing image of being tied to a stainless steel table in the woods and surrounded by aliens. He guessed they were aliens. They looked awfully much like women but with weird eyes. And, of course, he remembered seeing the spaceships, while peeking between trees in the forest. That's all he could remember. He wished he could remember more. He had the dream so often as a kid. He hoped it would come back again one day so he could write it all down. It must have been one hell of a great dream for him to still remember it so many years later. But he also had another even greater dream, a real one, a daylight dream. A dream of waking intention, not of sleeping aberrations. He dreamed of becoming the discoverer of the Cocos Treasure. Especially now that he was hired as an expert on just such an expedition!

Erhart opened his log book that he bought just for this trip. Sometimes he didn't have internet access. He imagined this would be the case out in the middle of the ocean. He didn't want to lose any data. He started with a brief summary just to put himself in the mood. He wrote:

"Cocos Island is 300 nautical miles due west of the southern coast of Costa Rica. It had been a pirate lair for decades, all during the Spanish conquest of present day Columbia, Ecuador, Peru and Chile. In those days the pirates were just small time operators. No one could survive long against the naval might of Spain, even though it was on a downward spiral from which it would never recover, which was still one of the mightiest nations on Earth. Oh, for sure, Sir Francis Drake in the Golden Hind, whom the Spanish labeled a pirate, captured and sank many Spanish treasure ships, but his ship was there for only a few months before it left to return to England. Anyone who stayed, who stayed in the waters of the Eastern Pacific to get rich beyond their wildest dreams, were eventually captured, tortured, and killed as gruesomely as possible. It took a while to get the Spanish military into action, but once moving, they were invincible. No one could stand up to the trained armies and navies the Spanish could muster. Even in the last days of the Spanish conquest of the Americas, when Simon Bolivar was freeing the continent from Spain, the Navies of Spain ruled supreme in the Eastern Pacific, challenged only by the smaller, quicker ships of England, their oft-time mortal enemy.

One of the last countries Bolivar freed was Peru. The loss of present day Columbia and Ecuador had given the British navy friendly ports to reprovision and effect repairs. The Viceroy of Peru hadn't been able to send the normal annual galleon of treasure to Panama to be unloaded and transshipped to Portobello on the Caribbean side of Panama, then part of Columbia, for two long years. And this year was the third. The treasury, huge by any standards, was bursting at the seams, loaded with gold, silver, gems and incredible statues meant for the grand cathedrals of Madrid, all made out of solid gold and bestudded with gems. The worth of the cathedral treasury in Lima was calculated to exceed 60,000,000 dollars, that is what it was worth in 1823 dollars, the year Simon Bolivar conquered Peru. The value of the state treasury was unknown but measured in tons of gold and silver consisting of all the workings of the mines for three years. In addition, in those days the Spanish Cathedral walls were covered in gold leaf. In Lima the entire church's interior was lined with beaten gold. Today, if it was all found it would be worth well over 100 trillion US dollars in just the raw materials. In the inner treasury, in the most guarded room in the world, lay the statue of the Virgin Mary. She was beyond compare. Priceless. If she was ever found, she would eclipse the Mona Lisa. Of all the incredible masterpieces created by the Inca gold wrights, the statue of the Virgin was by far the best. Reportedly, it erased original sin to any who kissed the Madonna's gold feet, thus ensured entrance into heaven. Plus it was made of solid gold and encrusted with millions of dollars worth of gems.

In 1823, the Spanish didn't know what to do. Bolivar, and his equally talented assistant Sucre, were ravenous when it came to pillaging Spain's treasure houses, and they were just days away from Lima and its seaport of Callao, and Argentinean San Martin was invading Peru from the south. They were trapped. The city fathers had to do something about the treasure they were responsible for, but they didn't know what to do. The only ship in port big enough to carry the treasure was an American Brig which made a living resupplying whaling ships offshore in the lucrative South Pacific whale trade. The Mayor of Lima opened negotiations with Captain Thompson of the *Mary Deare*. They designed a plan to save the treasure. Their idea was to load all the treasure on board the vessel which would then sail over the horizon and wait for the eventual battle. If the Spanish won, the ship would return to Callao, the seaport for Lima. If Bolivar won the Captain was to sail to Panama and hand over the treasure to the authorities there. The priests and bishops liked the idea. Normally the conqueror of a city always ripped the gold off the walls when they got to the church. The Bishop of Lima had all this gold taken down and also place aboard the *Mary Deare*, along with all the thousands of gold chalices, crucifixes, and candlesticks.

Erhart smiled at the thought of how full the internet was of misinformation. It was commonly thought that the *Mary Deare* was British. While it was true that after the defeat of Napoleon, peace, or at least the lack of war had returned to Europe, Spain had its back up against the wall. Its economy was crumbling and England, who had exited from the Napoleonic Wars in much better shape, was trying to snap up the remains of the Spanish Empire. Spain needed every Sou. The last thing they would do would be to trust a British ship with their gold. England never trusted Spain after Napoleon conquered it and put his brother on the Spanish throne, even though it was Spanish rebel resistance to French command that led to Napoleon's defeat as much as anything that Wellington did at Waterloo.

They liked the idea of putting the treasure aboard an American vessel as Lord Cochrane (who later became the inspiration of Patrick O'Brian's Jack Aubrey) was cruising the area and at the moment the British and Americans were at peace. The *Mary Deare* could not be attacked or boarded by the British. Spain and England while not at war, were economic enemies and they feared putting the treasure on a Spanish ship would be just giving it to Cochrane, who had been thrown out of the British Navy after a stock scandal, and was working for Chile and San Martin, who after liberating Argentina from Spain brought his army over the Andes, one of the great military feats of all time and was readying to attack Peru from the south. Cochrane, the year before had attacked Callao and cut out the Spanish flagship *Esmeralda*, effectively making the English flag unwelcome in Peru. Plus the only Spanish vessel large enough in the area had just been taken in a three day battle with the British. The *Mary Deare* was a great plan, too bad it didn't work.

The Spanish were worldly men and knew how much a temptation the treasure would be. They wanted to fill the vessel with guards, but who would guard the guards? The guards would be just as tempted as the sailors. Finally they decided on six of the most trustworthy guards, and two priests to keep an eye on them. The guards and the priests were locked up with the treasure with more than enough supplies to last for either voyage. Another six guards and two more priests were set to guard the captain and make sure he didn't try to steal the loot. Being careful administrators they also sent another ship, a smaller, more powerful one, named the *Espsigle* which wasn't big enough to hold the treasure, but was armed to the teeth, to guard the *Mary Deare* or to retake her, in case she scampered off with the skull and crossbones flying high.

One dark night at sea, the greatest treasure the world had ever seen was too much temptation for the crew of the *Mary Deare.* They overpowered and killed the captain, the priests and the guards. Afterwards they bored small holes through the walls of the treasure room, stuck muskets in and killed the other priests and guards. The ringleader was a bosun named John Keating.

During the night, Keating directed the *Mary Deare* on a northerly course hoping to be over the horizon by morning. They almost made it. A lookout atop the *Espsigle's* main mast just made out the flash of the *Mary Deare's* sails at first light and the chase was on. Keating soon had his crew throwing the great guns overboard. They were worthless against the heavier armed *Espsigle.* Soon spare anchors, extra water, months of provisions followed the guns. The *Mary Deare* was a very fast ship but the tons and tons of gold bullion were slowing her down.

For five days and five nights the chase continued. Keating sighted and ignored the Galapagos islands. They were Spanish owned and fortified. He would find only a rope's end there. He continued to race northward towards a little known pirate hangout named Cocos Island. Named so, not because it had so many coconut trees, but because after the arid Galapagos islands, even the few coconut trees lining the shore were a cause for celebration.

All was not well aboard the *Mary Deare.* Some of the crew broke into the treasure room and then the grog room. Soon sailors were prancing around the decks festooned in gold crowns and necklaces of pearls, drunk as a skunks. Keating shot the main trouble makers and soon things turned nasty. God must have been on their side as they somehow kept the wind in their sails while the surging *Espsigle* fought for every mile trying to close the gap.

Aboard the *Mary Deare*, things were tense indeed. The crew had little doubt of their fate if they were captured. The best they could hope for was to be hanged, but they feared that the holy fathers would hand them over to the Inquisition, and death would be but a hoped for miracle. They anchored in Chatham Bay on the north side of Cocos early in the morning. They quickly buried the treasure, somehow, before the *Espsigle* appeared at last light. A battle started with small guns. The priests on board the *Espsigle* refused to allow the great guns to be used lest they harm God's treasures. The two ships fought for most of the night and by morning only three sailors were alive on the *Mary Deare*. On seeing the Spanish ready to board and hungry to kill, the three sailors swam desperately for the shore. One was shot in the leg and was soon eaten by the many sharks in that area. Keating and another man made it to the beach and quickly disappeared into the jungle. The crew of the Espsigle searched for a week, but neither man was ever found. This was not unusual. Many documented cases relate that castaways or pirates hiding their treasure got lost while exploring the island of Cocos and were never seen again.

Erhart put down his pen and rubbed his eyes. There was so much else to tell but he thought he was getting writer's cramp. It was so much easier to write on a keyboard. He marveled at the thought of all those Irish monks penning the great works of ancient civilization in dark and drafty castles during the dark ages, keeping alive the glories and tragedies of Greece and Rome, Egypt and Palestine, of Alexander and Helen of Troy. They must have had terrible writer's cramp using those quills as pens.

He would continue his log book later. Not that he really needed it. He had a great memory. However he hoped that if he was instrumental in the finding of the Treasure of Lima, and that he would be able to record every detail. He owed that much to those ancient Irish monks.

God damn cave. He hated small tiny places. Small bathrooms, closets, elevators, attics, any place that made him feel trapped and helpless. But he hated caves most of all. He really didn't know why he became a prospector. Stupidity or self degradation he had always guessed. Either that or the universe had it out for him. Like that cop down in that hick town at the bottom of the mountain who always was hassling him, for no good reason. He wasn't breaking any laws. He didn't like breaking laws. Breaking the bank down at the casino in Denver, well that was a different story. He loved to gamble. Maybe that was why he was in this tight cave.

Thing is, all those prospectors back in the last millennium didn't have any scientific background or the proper tools to do a bang up job. They just dug a hole in the ground and hoped for the best. Dug and dug and dug and hoped they would strike a vein. Hoped for the best, that's what it was. Not that they had any choice. Not like him. He was a scientific prospector. Not that he liked calling himself a prospector. Gold gatherer, maybe. Picker of nuggets off the ground, definitely.

Them nuggets were just laying there ready to be picked up, ready to be picked up if you were a scientific prospector like him.

Back then they didn't have anything going for them except luck and lots of it. God, some of those old boys must have been killers at the craps table. There must have been some pure luck running hot and heavy in their veins. Probably made more money in the casinos than down in those holes in the ground. Kind of like him, he was a scientific gambler, too. Not that he wasn't lucky, but he had a system. Not as great a system as his prospecting gig, but what the hell, got to go with what you got. Those old guys did as good as they could. Can't say any fairer than that, but they just didn't have the tools.

He did. He had himself the best metal detector ever made. It could select the metals or the ores that he wanted to find, it could sense through 3 feet of solid rock, more on looser ground. It gave him a strength reading that guessed at the volume of the target metal when it found it, it was good on power usage, damn batteries lasted for days and days of prospecting. Not that he was prospecting. He was just gathering. All these old gold mines that were played out years and years ago; weren't. Played out, that is. There was still a lot of gold in them. Millions of dollars worth. Especially considering the value of gold in these days of financial uncertainty. There was plenty of gold in them caves, back then it was just too hard to find. The truth was them claims were anything but played out.

But they were still on the books as mines. He just wandered around the old mine country, exploring them old caves. Some might call them mines. Not him. They were caves. Mines had a inner structure holding the dirt up so it couldn't fall on some poor old guy's head. Mines had wooden beams holding up the ceiling, studs holding up them beams, and some kind of track making it easy to get in and get the gold out. If all of that had rotted and rusted out, then they was caves. Pure and simple.

He kept track of which mines still had veins of gold just a few feet sideways from the tunnels, he picked up a few nuggets as proof and to pay expenses and once a month went into Denver and bought the old claims, the ones he wanted. They went for a dollar for a year. If a year went by and he didn't show any improvements, or show a strike, the state took the claim back. He wasn't worried. All of the claims he applied for had yielded nuggets that he carried around in his pocket. He didn't worry about the dust. That required too much work. He wasn't a miner, he was just a scientific prospector, a gatherer of nuggets; nuggets and greenbacks. He didn't work his mines, he sold the information and the claim. There were lots of wheelers and dealers in Denver who sat on mines and were waiting till gold hit $2000 a troy ounce. Till all the gold was in the hands of investors, till people were begging for more, till they could sell knowledge of gold sitting there in the ground just waiting to be picked up. Well, kind of. He had already picked up all the easy stuff. But if you didn't mind investing a few bucks to shore up the caves and lay in a rail, then you could have yourself a gold mine. $2000 for 31.1 grams came out to $29,000 a troy pound. A lot of money for an element that wasn't that hard to find. Not really. Not if you knew where to look.

He went after silver for a while, but his heart just wasn't in it. He was a gold man. He loved the touch of it, the weight of it, the way it looked around a beautiful woman's neck, the way it swung when that same woman was atop making love to him, all for a few hours looking around in caves. It almost made up for being in the caves in the first place. Almost. Once, he gave up caves and went bouldering. Placer deposits in stream beds always collected nuggets of gold and gems and were most often found under massive boulders. His metal detector was so advanced it could look under water and spot the nugget to within a few inches. Then he just had to reach under and pull out a couple of thousands of dollars. Problem was he didn't like getting his feet wet either. He was sure you could get a cold that way, especially in the cold mountain streams. Then one day he realized while looking up at a massive dam that a lot of old stream beds had gone dry, all to make lakes and electricity. He didn't really have to get his feet wet. All he had to do was walk along old arroyos swinging his detector this way and that till he found a strike. Then it was dig under the boulder, easy work in the dry sand, and pick up the diamonds, the zircons and the gold. But still, it did require digging and he always worried about a boulder rolling on top of him. So he went back to the holes in the ground, to caves. Besides, it was the selling of the claims that was his real money maker. That and he liked looking at how
all those rich cats sat up when he walked into a room. They sat up at attention and wanted to talk to him. Him! Then they wanted him to go out and find some more caves, mines they called them. He knew better. They were caves. And he really was getting scared of going into them, a little bit. Last month one dropped on him. Luckily, he was on the way out when the cave-in occurred and he could dig his way out in only a few hours. But still.

Maybe that is why he said yes when another rich cat offered him a thousand a day to come with him to some island out in the Pacific. Looking for some treasure, pirate loot. Sure, a thousand a day was a cut in pay, but he didn't have to go into any caves and he got his own cabin on this fancy luxury ship this dude had. He always did want to go on one of those ships, but he was always too busy prospecting. Time to start enjoying life, relaxing a bit. That is what this rich dude said anyway. Guy came to him, himself. Must have really wanted him. Well, he was known as the best prospector still alive.

Yeah, it would be a nice change to get away from those caves. Nice to get some peace and quiet for a change. Not that caves weren't quiet, he could hear his heart beat faster and faster as he crawled down into the ground, into the cold hard hole in the ground. Into a death trap of a cave. It had him worried, had him more worried than about that idiot cop the township had, that they couldn't get rid of. The one that had a hard on for him. He must of known where bodies were buried to not get fired, no doubt. Yeah, maybe a boat trip, far away from Colorado, was just what the doctor ordered.

The water rushed past the sides of the *Rose Marie* in a rustling harmony of bubbles and joy. When the boat reached a crest of a wave, the music eased momentarily only to yet again reach a crescendo of dancing life as the boat surfed down the far side of the cresting wave. Harv was at the helm singing aloud all the different sea chanties he almost knew. He made up the words for the lines he had forgotten. Usually the words referred to his stalwart crew.

"One night as I was sitting on the rail, fishing I was for a bit of tail, a voice on the starboard shouted ahoy, and there was me Janet sitting on a buoy.

"What has become of my evening dishes, me Janet inquired of me. One was washed with a scrubbing brush, the other was covered with an apple pie crust."

Down below Jill was holding her hands over her ears as she tried to study her algebra textbook. Every few minutes she cast her eyes upwards towards a hopefully, merciful redeemer with an exasperated look.

"God and the Virgin Mary won't blame me if I put arsenic in his coffee. I just know they won't," she muttered to herself. "There has to be some justice in the world." She rammed her iPod earphones into her ears even tighter and revved up the volume. "It doesn't matter if I go deaf, at least then I will have some peace and quiet around here."

On the paper in front of her were some halfhearted attempts at solving quadratic equations from the questions at the end of the chapter, none of which had gone past a few lines of proof before they bogged down in pictures of tall cliffs and flag poles. At the bottom of the page was a vague attempt at the likeness of a young man she had seen on another boat in La Paz. She hadn't had the nerve, or to be honest, the desire to talk to him. She had seemed content to just watch him from a distance, satisfied somehow that just knowing of his existence made life worth living, except, of course, for chantey singing fathers.

On the foredeck, Janet sat on a spinnaker bag reading a book on yoga. She had gone to a cruiser potluck where sailors gathered on deserted beaches, shared food, books and stories for a few hours. The lady on that big catamaran that was anchored way out took one look deep into her eyes and pressed this yoga book into her hands.

"This book will change your life. It changed mine," she had such an intense look on her face as she said it that Janet bit back the repartee she was going to blurt out, 'Actually, I don't want to change my life. I am incredibly happy.' And instead just mumbled her thanks. She thought about trading the book to someone else but was afraid the lady would notice it and be upset. 'I can always trade it in some other port, later on down the coast,' she thought to herself absently as she tried some French fried breadfruit chips brought in by a far ranging sailor while she passed around a rather mundane bowl of Fritos. Back on the boat she shoved the book into a bookcase and forgot all about it, that is, until this morning.

The book was filled with photos of a rather hunky guy and a washed out blond, who definitely needed breast implants. They were twisted into different painful looking positions and were trying, vainly, to smile. The text was filled with references in Hebrew or Sanskrit or some weird language. She didn't really pay attention until as she leafed through the book, her eye fell on a position called the lion. The blond had her mouth and eyes wide open like a lion growling and then squished her eyes and mouth shut like she had just stepped on a pointed rock while running on the beach. The book said she wouldn't ever have to have a face lift if she practiced this position every day. Janet tried it out. She opened her eyes and mouth for all she was worth and the squished them shut feeling very silly.

"Mom, are you having fits or something?" Janet slammed the book closed and glanced over at the curly haired head sticking out of the fore hatch with eyes sparkling with laughter. "I can get you an aspirin or something." The mouth below the laughing eyes was now trying to disguise the amusement bubbling inside of its pre-teen mind.

"And how is your school work going, young lady?" Janet tried to put a stern look on her face, what she called her school teacher look, but her pupil was still trying to suppress a fit of giggles. "Do you want to try it?" she asked loosing her teacher look. Jill just nodded and climbed out of the hatch and sat down on the sail bag with her mother. Janet reopened the book and found the right page.

"It says here that you will never need a face lift if you do this every day, how about them apples?"

"Mom, don't be silly. You are the most beautiful woman, ever. You will never have to have a face lift. Why, you are like gorgeous! When we walk down the street, every man we pass stares at you. Really!" Janet felt a thrill of delight sweep through her. Then she had a momentary moment of dread. Harv was her man. And she was a one man kind of gal. Why should she react to the thought of other men who were interested in her? What if Harv found out? She didn't want other men noticing her. Better to think of her daughter. What was best for her. That's what her job as a mother required of her.

"Aw, my sweet baby, how much I love you! But we women have to keep up appearances for ourselves, we have to use sunblock every day, especially now that we are getting so far south." Janet lightly touched Jill on her freckled nose. "Beauty is one of the secrets of being a successful woman." She loved Harv with all her heart. Forever and ever. She had since she first met him, there by the harbor where she was feeding vaguely interested seagulls. True, he hadn't been as active in bed since he had hurt his hand trying to rescue her from that weirdo in Baja. But she was sure he would come back into his former stud like performance. He was just channeling all his energies into repairing his hand, that's all. That was it.

"I don't want to have to be beautiful, just so some guy might like me more. No way. Besides, I don't even like boys. I want to live my own life, my own way. I want to do whatever I want to do, not obey some man, just because he has a bat and a couple of balls." Jill looked closely at her mother to see if she would react. She was not disappointed.

"Jill, what did you just say? Where did you hear that?" Janet's voice spiraled upwards. "Really, Jill, some things ladies just don't say." Janet stared at Jill who was smiling back at her smugly, and knew that she had been had. She didn't know how, but she was sure she was going to find out. "Tell me who you have been talking to."

"Oh, Mom, it was just something I heard at the market in Mazatlan. You know the one in the center of the city that has a roof over it? Just a couple of old ladies talking. Why? Does it bother you? Is it something very bad to say?"

"People will think you are cheap if you say things like that. And really, Jill, do you want people to think badly of you?"

"You mean cheap like I don't cost as much? I could be had for less? Is that what you mean, Mother?" Janet looked closely at her daughter. Her smug look was even more pronounced now, enhanced by a superior look around her eyes.

'I think my little Jill is growing up very quickly,' she thought to herself. 'Very quickly indeed.' She thought for a minute and then said, "It sounds like you are becoming a woman right now, Jill. I admire that about you. If you are going to become a woman, it is time for you to start taking care of yourself. Time to be more serious about your sunblock. Time to think about using make up." Jill squinted her face in disgust. "Jill, women dress and adorn themselves mostly for other women. Men, men don't know anything. The make up and perfume we wear are a mask so no one really knows what we are thinking, especially other women. And young lady, you just might change your thinking about men and balls in a couple of years when your hormones start kicking in."

"What hormones? I got plenty of hormones already, whatever they are. And I don't need any mask, that's for sure. If anyone wants to know what I'm thinking, I'll tell them right out if they can beat the Green Flash to the top of a flag pole!"

"Hormones are wonderful things, Jill, they change our bodies so that we can become mothers. Don't you want to become a mother when you become much older? To have your own little baby? A little baby you and your husband create all by yourselves?" Jill seemed to become suddenly seriously interested.

"Created how? Do you order it on line? Like from eBay?"

"You grow it inside of you, in a special place that the hormones make ready. A place just right for babies to grow. Isn't that exciting? But that is all in the future. Nothing to think about now." Janet's lovely face suddenly became sterner. "Now how is that algebra work going?"

"Oh, Mom. Stop trying to be a school teacher. I like talking to you more than doing stupid math. Anyway, I like you much more as a mom than a school teacher. Why don't I do my work, at my own pace and if I get stuck, why then I'll come running to you? Ok? It will give you much more time to pursue your own projects and desires." Janet looked closely at her daughter. Jill was so young and yet so mature. She recently seemed to be able to understand so much about her daughter. Sometimes she wondered if she had become psychic or something. If she was, was it really true she was interested in other men? She couldn't be. She loved Harv. She did. She really did. She was so sure she did.

From the cockpit in the stern, they heard Harv break out in a new chantey. At least his version of one.

"Hi ho and up she rises. Hi ho and up she rises. Hi ho and up she rises early in the morning.

"What do you do with all the girls in port, what do you do with the gals in port, what can you do with all the lovers in port, so early in the morning?"

Elena, come in here. Bring your dictation pad, Chica." A beautiful young woman appeared in the doorway in a few seconds. She glided across the floor, demurely sat in the chair next to the desk and crossed her legs. Inadvertently, she raised the hem of her short dress and exposed her right leg up to within a few inches of her panty line. She sat with her back straight, not touching the back of the chair, pen ready, eyes politely on her boss.

"Si, Jefe. For you, I am ready." The man didn't seem to notice her dress or scarcity of it. He was a large man, sweating slightly despite the air conditioning. He was well dressed in the uniform of a Lieutenant of the Costa Rican Police Force.

"Take a letter for the Commandant of the Isla de la Cocos Detachment. Send copies to all relevant offices.

"Honorable Sergeant Alberto,

"We have information that indicates that an expedition is being organized to look for the supposed treasure on Isla Cocos. We have authorized no expeditions for this year. No monies have been paid. No permissions have been given.

"If a body of treasure seekers lands on the island you are commanded to eject them with any and all forces at your command. The national treasure of the beauty and uniqueness of Isla Cocos is in your hands. The biodiversity of the island is unique in all of the world. As you know the Nation of Costa Rica maintains the largest percentage of its lands in National Parks of any nation in the world, and the queen of that system is Cocos Island. Keep it safe.

"I am sending two additional rangers with the supply boat to assist you in any way you see fit.

"As always, repel any newspaper people with extreme prejudice They always lie and incite the populace."

Lieutenant Dominic Ferer

"Did you get all that, Chica? Good. When those rangers come in, send them to me right away, the one's El Presidente wanted us to hire."

"Si, Senor El General. You're wish, Commandant, is my command." Elena made a production of straightening her dress before returning to her desk, leaving the office door slightly ajar, giving the Lieutenant a view of her slim, beautifully manicured toes, adorned with red glowing polish, that projected into his view from under her desk.

Dominic wondered for a moment about the symbolism of the red nail polish and red lipstick. Was it to show the female had made a kill and was inviting him to share? Or luring him into her cave? He wondered why he was attracted to his secretary while his interests waned in family matters.

His wife was very obedient and very properly brought up. She was a wildcat in bed when he first met her, even now she would obediently perform any sexual act, no matter how deviant that he asked her to perform. But her heart wasn't in it. He could tell. She never started any coupling in bed, and if they did anything, once it was finished, she fell off to sleep, or seemed to, once her work was finished. He imagined his wife had la amore with him from a sense of obligation and duty than as a display of her love for him. As part of her job as a wife. Like sweeping the floor or washing the dishes. Of course, she insisted he pay everytime they made love. Not in money. In the back of her mind, she must have a computer to keep track of such things. Whether it was dinner at a nice restaurant or a bouquet of flowers, she made sure she got paid.

Elena, she was different. She wanted to do it with him purely for lust. She wanted to get herself off, using his body, because he turned her on so much. He did! The whole idea appealed to his sense of machismo and egotism. Elena stared at his body with a hungry wonder that time and the tree of knowledge had erased from his wife's eyes.

He wondered if that was what had happened in the Garden of Eden. When Adam and Eve had eaten of the Tree of Knowledge, had they lost all their spontaneity? All the wonder and joy of being with each other? Did the tree give them knowledge of their mate, dissolving any need for continual discovery of the wonderful person whom they had married?

With a sigh, Dominic Ferer closed the file on Isla Cocos. He wondered if he would ever go out there, to such an island of enchantment, to such a Garden of Eden. He stared again through the barely open door at Elena's slim ankle. Her toes were curled and as he watched she straightened them and curled them languidly, over and over again. She started to increase the pace of her toe movement. Faster and faster, then suddenly they straightened as far as they could and the heel lifted off the ground. The whole foot vibrated slightly and then fell to the floor, spent.

Dominic found himself breathing heavily. He would have to phone his wife again. Tell her that he had to work late. She would understand. She didn't care. It wasn't like she really wanted him in her bed, except as someone to talk to and to make her feel that she was successful as a wife. She wasn't waiting at home, racked with desire to have him in her arms. When he was in bed with her she always had a headache, or she was too tired, or it was the wrong time of month, but she would do it, she said, just for him. He tried forcing himself on her, his right as a husband in Latin countries, but he didn't enjoy it. He wanted a wife who wanted him. Who loved him and proved it dramatically every night of their marriage. Sure, if he asked, she would perform. But he wanted a partner, not a slave. A wife, not a whore.

A single tear ran down his cheek. Dominic angrily brushed it away. He had more important things to worry about than wives and secretaries. He had his responsibilities to the Nation. He had his job and his career. Things that mattered, mattered much more than happiness between a husband and a wife. The phone rang. It was Elena. She was only ten feet away. Why did she have to use the phone? Women, they were strange and wild creatures.

"Jefe. The hombres you wanted, the rangers. They are here. Should I bring them in?" Ah, that is why. He should have trusted Elena.

"Yes, show them in." The door opened and Elena entered first swinging her long hair this way and that, her hips echoing the movement, languidly. Following her were two men. He guessed they were men. They resembled rocks or huge trees more. There wasn't an ounce of fat anywhere on their bodies and their faces were as hard and craggy as the bark on the giant mahogany trees found high up on the Costa Rican mountains. Their eyes weren't like the eyes of normal men. At first glance, he thought they might be blind and had glass eyes, there was so little life in them. But then he realized that the eyes were just aware, they weren't judging, weren't feeling, weren't even thinking. They just were.

Dominic stood up and shook the men's hands. Their grips were like iron. No, he thought, that wasn't right. Not like. Their hands were iron. He had seen a lot of action in his career, arresting Pre-Columbian artifact thieves. He had been shot twice on duty and considered himself a brave man. However, his belly quivered a little when he looked into the first man's eyes. It was like looking into an angel's eyes, there was such purity in them, purity or experiences that had burned all need for judgment out of his mind.

"Gentlemen, we believe an attempt will be made to infiltrate Isle de Cocos and to search for the supposed treasure. As you know, the island represents a unique biosphere in the world. The island is home to hundreds of life forms that exist nowhere else in the world, any one of which might contain the genes for curing cancer and other diseases. Every treasure hunter who has gone to the island has destroyed large sections of the island, one even attempted to set the entire island on fire trying to clear the land of vegetation. This cannot be allowed. The island is itself a treasure in its beauty and biodiversity.

"In addition, we believe this effort to be well funded. One of these days, someone will find a treasure of some kind. I want you to realize that all artifacts, gold or not, found on Isla de Cocos are the property of the Republica de Costa Rica. If anyone finds anything, you are to seize it, radio this office and we will send a helicopter to the island to remove the artifacts.

"Do you have any questions?" The men shook their heads. Their eyes still never changed expression. The men shook hands and departed without ever having said a word. Dominic watched them file out. They never looked back. He turned to Elena.

"What do you think of those men?" She was surprised. Her boss had never asked her opinion before about other people. About office procedures and inter-department politics, yes; people, no.

"Jefe, they are muy mucho hombres. I am glad they are on our side." It seemed for a minute she was going to say more.

"Si, that is the question. Are they really on our side? They certainly were not very communicative." He thought for a minute. "Elena, I wonder if I could ask you to do a service for your country. Do you have any friends that you trust who would like to make a trip out to Cocos as my representative? I can promise some pay as, let us say, a grant for biological studies. They would just have to keep an eye on things and radio me if anything strange is going on. I am a little concerned that our rangers might have an agenda of their own. I have never seen such self contained, self confident men. We don't usually get men like that working for the government."

"Where will they stay? In tents? Will they have to cook for themselves? Are there beaches?" Elena's eyes had a wild, excited look.

"I can arrange for them to stay in the barracks. There are a few beautiful beaches and they could eat with the police detachment or they could make their own arrangements, at the department cost, of course."

"I will check around, Senor. Ask my friends. See what I can find. I'll let you know tomorrow."

Dominic watched her walk out of the room, for once she forgot to be sexy. Her feet were barely touching the floor. He hoped she would pick the job for herself. She would be perfect. Everyone knew she was his mistress, everyone except his wife, he hoped. It would be assumed he was giving her a present as a thank you, a trip to a far away place where there was no chance of her meeting anyone related to him. He would miss her, of course, while she was gone. But he could do with a rest, that woman could wear out a tiger of a man. She was so insatiable. And if he got lonely, there was always that typist down the hall. The one with the long legs, glasses and the red nail polish.

Dustin Horner gently took off his glasses and rubbed the top of his nose. The world around him became a blur of color and chaos. He snorted in an unobstructed breath with a sigh of pleasure and then regretfully put
the coke bottle bifocals, back on his nose. The world became ordered again, a blessing, but at the cost of a quarter of a pound of weight pushing on his nasal passages and ears. Dustin looked around at the mess his laboratory had become and tried to think of what he might have forgotten. How could he be expected to organize an expedition in just a few hours? He was a methodical man, used to thinking before acting and resented this rashness he had been compelled to perform. It went against everything he believed in and trusted. For a minute he didn't know why he had agreed.

With a secret smile he remembered. He hugged his overweight body with delight. It had happened so fast. First he had published his findings with a brief, very brief, description of his new invention, the Sonic Microwave, a device that could find anything under ground, under water and even behind concrete, steel or lead. He could control the strength of the waves. He was sure it could out perform the MRI, but he hadn't the funding for human trials. After he published, there was silence in the halls of science as if no one cared, no one was in the slightest bit interested. Then out of the blue, a private investor expressed his desire to fund his research, completely, for another year. And all he wanted was to use his machine for a couple of weeks with Dustin as an operator on a search for dinosaur bones. The investor did not want to license his machine or to merchandise it. He didn't seem at all interested in it, except to find a couple old bones on some island out in the Pacific. Cocos Island, that was the name. And he didn't even want to be cited as a member of the expedition. He said he was a very private person and would like to keep it that way. Horner could have all the glory for himself.

With a flip of his remote, Dustin booted up his main frame over in the corner and chose a geography program with a short cut. After a few minutes of fussing with an underwater sensor, trying to get it to fit into its case, he gave up and walked over to the computer. It didn't offer him much in information. Cocos Island was a few hundred miles off the coast of Costa Rica, which owned it. He searched for dinosaur bones in a sub-routine and the only hit he came up with that wasn't porn or stupid was a movie where live dinosaurs were recreated in part from frog DNA. He wasn't a biologist but he stared at that for a whole two seconds, an inordinate amount of time for someone with an IQ of 186. He shook his head again and he understood why he didn't go to movies. He hoped the director had the dinosaurs croaking, hopping and eating flies with long quick tongues.

He was allowed to bring one lab assistant to help set up the machine and to do odd jobs but he still didn't know who to ask. He was sure any of his assistants and students would jump at the chance of joining such an expedition, but it was made clear to him that his assistant would have to bunk in his cabin. Apparently it was a luxurious cabin on a very large yacht, but he was used to exaggeration from expedition leaders. He asked for photos and they were in his inbox within hours. It certainly looked like a beautiful ship. He tried to discover signs of a fish eye lens in the photo of his cabin, but it looked genuine. Dustin wondered again if he dared ask Mary, if she would like to go. Not because she was a beautiful woman. Of course not. Absolutely not. He would ask her because she was conscientious in her work and tireless at taking notes, an important part of any scientific inquiry.

He had wanted to ask her out on a date for some years now, but never had the nerve. It was unfair. He was her boss. She wouldn't be able to say no. He knew that. And it would cause jealousy among the other assistants. But this was different. He would be able to get to know her better, hopefully much better. It was off campus, it was a private expedition instead of being state run and he would be able to control any info exported from his files, he could squelch any rumors before they got started. Mary would gain invaluable experience on a major expedition. Experience that would help her with the university. Bunking together might be awkward at first, but he was sure it would work out. With a start he looked again at the photos of his cabin. There wasn't a door to the small bathroom, but just a curtain on rings, like a shower curtain. He was surprised for a minute that such a luxurious yacht wouldn't have doors but he was side tracked by noticing that the curtain was too small to close all the way. She would be able to see the entire small bathroom from the double bunk bed. She would be able to see his body during his ablutions, but on the other hand… With a smile, he made up his mind and took out his cell phone.

Within a few hours, Mary was busy creating order out of his attempt to pack his instruments. Her eyes shown with excitement as she worked, fingers flying. She was indeed a good looking woman, even at 39 she outshone many women much younger than herself. Her blond hair was pulled back into a long pony tail that slightly smoothed the few wrinkles around and between her eyes. She was dressed in jeans, de rigor in labs around the world, and a matching denim jacket opened to display a white pleated blouse with the top button undone. A ring was around the middle toe on her left foot framed with open leather sandals but her fingers were naked.

"Dr. Horner, this is going to be so much fun! And on a yacht! Is it going to be just you and me from the department? Oh, I just can't wait!" She briefly hugged herself as a shiver of excitement ran down her spine. She grinned a happy, blossoming smile at Dustin and then inserted the underwater sensor into its case in seconds.

"Mary, please, let's not be formal. We are not going to be in the classroom. Please call me, Dustin. Would you be so kind? It will remind me that this is a great adventure we are going to be sharing, an adventure I have been looking forward to for a long time."

"Sure thing, Doctor, I mean Dustin. When do we leave? I do have a few minor things to clear up, but nothing I can't do on the phone."

"As soon as we are packed, then. I talked to our benefactor, and we can board the yacht at any time. I believe the ship will leave as soon as all are on board. It is too big, I believe, to be at a dock, so they will ferry us out on a shore boat."

"I do hope that I won't get seasick. Is it really a very big yacht? Is it stable? Where do we sleep? In a dormitory, in the forepeak?"

"My, so many questions, Mary. Not to worry. I believe the yacht is 176 feet long, we sleep in suites with attached baths. As I understand it, the vessel is very stable but if you do get some mal de mer, I have packed some special pills, just in case." He patted his pocket where he had tubes of anti-motion tablets, tranquilizers for tension, and for some reason a couple of Viagra tablets.

"Now, is there anything else to pack? We really don't know what to expect. I have been on these types of expeditions before and unexpected problems always come up. But I think as long as we are flexible, then I am sure our adventure will be a success. I also want to say, Mary, that if you perform as well as I am sure you will, then I want you to share credit in the paper that you and I will write on our no doubt enormous success at proving the flexibility and durability of the Sonic Microwave."

"Oh, I agree, Dr, I mean, Dustin. You can count on me. Whatever you need, just ask," she said with a serious face as she secured another box with packing tape. "And thank you for wanting to give me credit, but I doubt I could write as good as you, sir. As well as you, Dustin." She turned facing him, her head bent to one side, the opposite leg bent at the knee and the same side shoulder angled slightly towards him. He stared at her for a moment, enormously attracted, but he didn't know why.

"We'll cross that bridge when we come to it, Mary. Best thing to do is to help each other out and do our best, Ok?" He blinked his eyes and took a step towards her. Somehow he seemed to be irresistibly attracted to her. He always liked her. To be true, he had daydreams about having her in his bed to do with what he wished. This was something different. Something much more powerful. Just the way she stood opened some deep primitive urge that called to him from a previously untouched abyss inside his psyche. His powerful brain wrest control of his personality back again. He turned slightly and smiled at her. "We don't have much time, Mary. What else do we need to pack?" He forced himself to look away from her even though every atom of his more primitive side was calling out to her. Wanted to be with her. Wanted to be inside of her.

'Now what brought that on?' he wondered to himself.

Hawkins's great grandfather had been a captain of a whaler out of New Bedford way back when and had fallen in love with a girl in Hawaii while his ship was there. She was a member of the Alii, the royal family of the Hawaiians. He snuck her onto his ship when he left against her will, got her pregnant and made her into his concubine. He kept her on his various ships through out his career, far away from his wife and family but he did love her deeply and promised to bring up her children as his own. They had various offspring over the years but his grandfather was the only one who inherited the unique Hawaiian royal family's trait of huge hands, hands easily twice the size of a normal man's. The trait had missed a generation in his father, but had returned in him. He loved his huge hands. He felt they made him special. When greeting his competitors, he instantly had them at a disadvantage as they felt like children when their hands were engulfed by his in a handshake.

He liked to use his hands on women. His fingers were huge, yes, but his thumb was twice the size of a normal man's thumb. When he met a girl he used his fingers on her first. Then his thumb. It curled in just right to lightly rub her g spot with the tip of his thumbnail. They always came in a screaming orgasm, a full, mind-blowing 15 to 20 minute long, gut wrenching climax. Unfortunately his cock was normal size, not a problem for most men but after his thumb had stretched a girl to the limit, his cock felt like it was in an airplane hanger in there, there was so much space. So he flipped her over into the doggie position and entered her in the ass. After he was fully in, all the way in, he pushed her down and lay on top of her prone body, not moving. The after spasms of her orgasm from his thumb were so strong they caused his cock to pulsate which brought both of them into the ecstasy of heaven again. All this while one hand covered her entire face and his fingers held her hair above her head as his teeth sank into her neck to hold her in place.

He wasn't interested in women now. He was looking at his ship. She was a thing of beauty. Long, stately lines made her the queen of the town as she lay to anchor off the old sub base in Key West. Hawkins glowed in pride as tourists next to him on the boardwalk oohed and awed and snapped pictures by the hundreds of his yacht backlit by the sunset. He had never owned a ship before. He didn't think he had ever been on a yacht before. Sure, ferries, cruise ships and the like, but a thing of beauty like this, never. He started getting a hard on just looking at her, knowing she was his, knowing he had just to give a command and her crew would jump in obedience and she would be off to a destination of his choosing. What a feeling. He felt a light start to glow within him and his breath start to quicken as his nostrils expanded and then the girl next to him spoke.

"Hawk, love, do I get to get a tour of your boat? I really want to. Especially the owners cabin. Can I, Hawk? Please?" The girl was cute enough. She had all the parts in the right places. But like all girls, she talked when she should have been quiet. Like now. She did have great legs. Like his ship. In seagoing parlance, his ship had great legs if she had the fuel capacity to cross oceans without refueling. This girl had the stamina to go all night and to be ready for more, come morning.

"Hawk, Honey, Earth to shuttle, hey, you up there tall man, Hawk babe, can we go see your boat?" The damn squeeze just wouldn't shut up. Well, whatever, he wasn't tired of her yet. Not yet. Couple more days, then he would find something new.

"Anything you want, darling," he whispered to her, his eyes hardening, "as long as you rub my cock right now."

"Right here in front of all these people?" She tried to look shocked the truth was, the idea excited her. She always was something of an exhibitionist, the people were all strangers, if any of them said anything, she was sure Hawk would bite their heads off. He was good at that, she knew, unfortunately, by experience.

"Right here and right now. This instant if you ever want anything from me again." He didn't look like a friendly Santa Claus anymore. He looked hard and mean and cruel and very sexy.

She snaked one slim hand down the front on his trousers and found his meat. He didn't wear underwear. She slowly ran her fingernails down his organ, all the way onto his balls. He began to respond and grow larger. She raised her mouth and as he bent down to kiss her she began to stroke his organ up and down, occasionally reaching down to cup his balls. Comments resounded around them.

"What is that woman doing to that poor, sweet, innocent man?"

"Come children, it's time to get ready for dinner. Look at that beautiful tree over there. The tree, children, look at the tree."

"I think someone should call the cops. Such public display of lewdness shouldn't be allowed. Women like that shouldn't be allowed to exist in the same world as the rest of us. Something should be done."

Both of them ignored the comments, if they even heard them. Finally Hawkins couldn't take it any more. He was ready to come in her hand. He tore her arm out of his pants, gathered her into his arms and carried her down to the finger pier where his shore boat was patiently waiting.

"*Steel Balls* and don't spare the diesel," he ordered the sailor at the controls. The boat had come with the name *Steel Balls.* At first he was going to change it but after awhile he found the name grew on him. A month after buying her, he wouldn't have changed it for the world. Who would have guessed that a boat could be an aphrodisiac? It was, though. He could go on all night on his boat. He could have girl after girl after girl. He could go around the world on his boat in more ways than one. And, aboard, his balls were made out of steel. Absolutely.

He walked up the ship's gang plank carrying the girl over his shoulder. He struggled for a minute to remember her name, then gave it up as he entered his cabin and tossed her onto his king size bed. He nipped her throat with his eyeteeth, tore her blouse off of her in one motion and then flipped her skirt up over her head. She wasn't wearing any panties. This was the kind of girl he liked, always ready for whatever he wanted. He didn't bother with his hands or thumb, he just smeared some lubricant over his cock to protect it and took her in the ass. The girl, what ever her name was, really liked it in the ass. Some girls do. The feeling of being penetrated, of being filled up, of feeling the guy's thrusts all the way up in the back of the throat was much more intense in the back door. He screamed like an animal as he came. The force of his orgasm was so strong it brought the girl to ecstasy along with him as her ass pulsated with his cock in perfect unison.

When he awoke at first light and after a shower, he ignored the girl still lying on the bed, ass slightly in the air, every muscle relaxed, the slight lines on her face had disappeared as she softly snored. Her orgasm had been so strong she looked like she was a teenager again. Intense pleasure took away the aches and pains of life and left one ready to see the world in a new light in the dawn of a new day. It made today, as they used to say, the first day of the rest of her life.

As he dressed in black slacks, black loafers and a white open neck shirt, he decided to take a tour of his ship, see if she was ready for his treasure expedition. When he was ready to leave, the girl was still asleep on the bed, comatose from such an intense night. As he put on his captain's hat with all its gold braid, he felt a stirring between his legs.

"Damn ship is an aphrodisiac," he muttered to himself. He toyed with the idea of taking the girl again. He wouldn't have to undress her or spread her legs. She was arranged in perfection for him. The stirring in his groin was stronger now. He fought the sensation. "Time enough for that later," he thought. "Besides it is better if I can hear her scream." Either from pleasure or from pain. It didn't seem to matter to him.

He turned and surveyed the luxurious stateroom. Subdued, indirect lighting easily overcame the early morning sunlight in the plate glass windows that covered an entire wall. A massive stereo system and a built in bar covered one wall, Bose speakers hiding tiny TV cameras were hanging from the ceiling in every corner. A walk in closet shared another bulkhead along with a bathroom complete with bidet, sauna, jacuzzi and a wall to wall set of mirrors. On the last wall of the cabin was a control panel covered with led TV screens. He sat down in the chair and played with a few buttons. Several screens came to life and he saw a couple of empty cabins. He found a toggle switch and found he could swing the cameras this way and that. He flipped a few more switches. He could see every cabin on the ship. He found a switch where he saw himself looking at the console. Feeling stupid, he waved to himself. A red switch showed him the bridge where he could see a couple of officers looking out the windows at something. Another switch allowed him to see what they were looking at, a big sailboat. A feeling of power came over him. He felt almighty, all knowing, fuck, he felt like a god. His cock erupted out of the top of his slacks. He looked down and saw it pulsating.

"Can't waste this one. Besides, she is all ready for me, greased up with her ass in the air." He glanced over at the girl. She looked so innocent, so relaxed, almost like a virgin. "God, I love this boat," he muttered as he tore off his clothes.

It was another day on the beat. Another fucking day on the streets. He was solo today. Not that he minded. They always saddled him with newbies, hoping they would learn something, anything, from him.

Damn newbies. One of them was sure to get him shot, if not killed. Especially now that they demoted him back to patrolman, again. He knew newbies were always looking at him. Him, with all his years of experience. Couldn't blame them. There he was, the best cop ever. If he could stay alive. Fuck. He could see it now. Newbie pulling his gun in a hostage situation, looking over at him, gun following his eyes, perp makes a loud noise of some kind and bang, newbie fires automatically. Right in his leg, or worse. Shit. This is what he got for spending his entire life defending the great state of Colorado? He should be running the whole bang up show by now. Would be too, if he'd had a few lucky breaks. Seems everytime he came up for a promotion some do-gooder stood up and told a pack of lies.

All lies. He was a damn good cop. If he saw something that needed to get done, he did it. Why call for backup? He didn't need no fucking back up. Especially when dealing with some no good, fucking speeder. He hated speeders. Didn't matter to him if they were only going 5 miles over the speed limit. Didn't matter if they were doing one mile over the limit. Speeding is speeding. Downtown, they asked him why did he always just pull over the cute sexy girls for speeding? Fuck. He pulled over every damn ass who speeded. Couldn't be helped if young chicks were terrible drivers. They needed someone to teach 'em a lesson. Fuck downtown. Couldn't they see the truth?

They asked about how he ordered the girls to get out of the car and frisked 'em. Frisked 'em everywhere. He told them he wasn't about to get himself shot by some gun toting Annie Oakley hiding a gun strapped to her upper thigh. They asked him about recording addresses, visiting the girl's houses after hours and forcing himself inside. They asked him about accusations of rape. He said that no one had ever made a formal complaint against him. He was innocent, but they demoted him anyway. Fuckers. God damn fuckers.

Another fucking day on the beat. God how he hated it. It didn't help that this morning his wife was on the rag, or the PMS had control of her brain, or maybe he should have taken that shower. Whatever. He sure didn't get any. And that put him in a seriously bad mood. Down in the station, everyone took one look at his face and walked the other way. He was definitely not in a good mood. By the time his beat took him out towards mining country, he had already given out five moving violations, three for speeding and two for reckless endangerment. Having a taillight out was endangerment, and on his beat it was certainly reckless. Fucking drivers. Why couldn't they all just stay home and watch the boob tube like the nice little zombies they were supposed to be. Who the fuck gave them permission to drive on his beat? Assholes. Just ahead he saw a rattletrap of a vehicle pull out of a dusty side road and slowly build up speed, heading towards Denver.

"Fuck. A miner." he muttered to himself. "Ten to one he doesn't even have a license." He reach down an flipped on the siren and smashed the accelerator to the floor. He was doing ninety by the time he braked viciously behind the '57 Chevy pickup and flashed on his lights. As the pickup slowed and stopped on the side of the road, he released the lock on the car's shotgun and chambered a shell.

He didn't bother to call in the license plate, it was like backup, he didn't need it. If the car was stolen, he would be able to smell it. He approached the vehicle, stood behind the driver side door and ordered the driver to get out of the vehicle keeping his hands insight at all times, and then stepped back a step. There was only a single man in the car. He came out obediently, which proved nothing. Nothing at all, especially when it came from miners, especially, if he was right, this miner.

"Alright, mother fucker, up against the car and spread them feet wide. Real wide." The bastard did as he was told, which proved nothing. He jammed the business end of the shotgun barrel in the small of the fucker's back and ran his other hand up and down his body. Didn't seem to be carrying, which proved nothing.

"Open that tool trunk keeping one hand behind your neck at all times." Inside of the silver box mounted just behind the cab, was a pile of strange looking instruments. "What the fuck are these things?" He jabbed the shotgun harder into the perp's spine to emphasize his words.

"Mining tools, nothing else, sir. Metal detectors and the like, that's all, Sir."

"Fuck that, asshole. Them ain't no mining tools. Don't even see a single decent shovel. What are you, a fucking terrorist?" With that he rapped the guy across the temple with the barrel of his shotgun. The fucker fell to the ground, hands to his head, covering his eyes and face. He reached in and grabbed a handful of terrorist stuff and threw it to the ground. "Ain't no mining tools in here."

He started stomping on the instruments as they lay on the ground, feeling pleasure as glass dials and fancy doo-dads crushed and cracked under his feet. He got both feet into it. Stomping and breaking. Fucking asshole miners. He really got into it and started to laugh. Fucking stuff up was so much fun. God, he loved it.

The first hint he got that something was wrong was when he saw a moving shadow on the ground. He tried to move but by then it was too late. He felt something hit him across the back of the head and all went blank. He was still vaguely conscious, conscious enough to feel continuing blows crashing down on his head and back. The ground below him seemed to be changing color. It was slowly becoming red. Iron oxide? Might be rich in bauxite? His mind slowed down as it died from lack of blood borne oxygen. His face no longer resembled anything human. His last impression was the fucking miner's car leaving in a spray of rocks and dust. That was his burial, a spray of rocks and dust from a getaway car speeding away on his beat.

The wind fell light as the *Rose Marie* coasted down the Mexican mainland, the Riviera, as it is called. Harv brought the boat in closer to soundings past Isla Grande just as the sun's first light lit the clouds on the eastern horizon with a dazzling display of vivid colors predominated by reds and pinks. The wind lasted a bit longer and he kept sailing, getting the most he could out of the dying shore breeze. Finally he brought her into the small cruiser hangout of Z-town, still trying to decide if a red sky in the morning was good or bad, or if it was just a story to scare children. Janet and Jill woke up when he turned on the engine and dropped the sails.

"Where are we, Sir Daddy?" Jill rubbed her eyes and peered around the boat with sleep crusted eyes. "Are we there, yet?"

"Depends where there is, little one. The wind died and I don't want to use up our diesel. Damn stuff is just too expensive these days. This is Zihuatanejo, a little town where we can get some rest and relaxation while we wait for the wind to fill back in. It is tough to make any progress with these light temperamental on shore, off shore breezes." Janet stuck her head out of the main hatch and gave Harv a lewd look and licked her lips. "Unless, of course, you don't want to stop for some ice cream?" He winked at Janet, smiling.

"What? Me? Ice Cream? Sir Daddy, I love Z-wat-in-a-ho. I do, I really do. Thank you so much for bringing us here. Wait one minute till I get my anchor clothes on and I'll drop the hook for you, Sir Wonderful and Kind Daddy who loves me so much!"

The town wasn't quite the dusty, quaint coastal town the cruising guide had depicted. The cruise lines had discovered it and Z-Town had become tourist central, but it still retained a bit of its friendly, carefree Mexican attitude. The streets were lined with tiendas selling all manner of souvenirs. However, the shopkeepers sat in relaxed attitudes, smiling at the passing tourists. Some strummed guitars, others struck up conversations full of smiles and good will. Not many seemed overly concerned with making sales or even talking about their wares.

Jill and Janet sat on a park bench licking their ice cream cones as Harv scouted the town for a NGKBP7H-10 spark plug for their dinghy's outboard. Harv and his fellow captains on other cruising boats seemed to spend all their time ashore looking for odd parts for their boats that had broken, were about to break or were needed for spare parts, just in case they broke. Janet was used to Harv's slightly desperate but determined look as he wandered all over every town they came to. He always had company, captains from all the other boats in port. They traveled in packs, invading small hardware stores, often returning with very interesting items but not the thing they had gone looking for.

While sitting on the bench, Jill spotted a teenage girl from a boat they had met up in the Sea of Cortez and was gone in a flash to eye the statue in the center of the park with her friend. Just as Janet was finishing her cone, a local woman sat down beside her. Janet was used to the wide smiles from all the town folk. They seemed to gravitate towards her, to truly like her. This woman was not smiling. In fact, she seemed desperate. Her cheeks were streaked with dried tears and her eyes red from sleepless nights.

"Please, por favor, Senora, you can help me? It is my child, she is very sick. If you could only touch her, Maestra, you could save her. Please, Senora, it would be a great kindness. Just a little touch, please."

"Me? I am not a doctor, I'm sorry but I am not. I know very little about medicine, Senora. Perhaps I can give you some change to help pay for the Doctor, the Medico?"

"Por favor, do not insult me. I can see the power within you. Everyone can. It glows. It, how you say, it comes in waves from within you. It is all around you as you walk. Please, all you need do is touch my little Alica. Please, Maestra, please. Help me. My Alica, she is just over there." The woman indicated a side street.

Janet didn't know what to do. She didn't have any powers and she didn't glow. She had looked in the mirror this morning and all she saw was more crow's feet around her eyes and a new black hair growing from her chin. She certainly wasn't glowing, growing older, yes, glowing, no. But the woman was staring at her with such desperation, and such confidence, she couldn't find it within herself to refuse her. Maybe there would be something she could do. Give some advice, or something. Help somehow. She rose to her feet and followed the woman to a curb on a side street.

The little girl was laying on a dirty sheet on the side of the road. She was very pale and was hardly breathing. Tourists, on the backs of donkeys, passed by with only a casual, absent look, if they even saw her at all. Everyone seemed to be ignoring her. No one acknowledged her existence, thinking if they ignored her, the made up world they carried around in their heads would gain more strength, over stark reality.

"Please, Maestra. The medicos say there is nada they can do. They say it is her time. Please, please, Senora, just lay your hand on her." The woman started to weep. Her body was racked with her sobs. Her eyes were feverous with her desperation. She wrung her hands together, pleading. Her unbrushed hair hung around her face, partially hiding it, making the visible parts more gut wrenching. Janet didn't know what to do. It seemed easiest to squat down and smooth the poor girl's hair off her forehead. Her skin was burning up, she was so hot. Janet was suddenly worried that she might catch some strange tropical disease. But she steeled herself and brought her hand down, for some reason and touched the girl above her budding breasts and below her throat, the palm of her hand resting, for a moment, over the small bone protruding there in the center of her chest between the collar bones. The mother instantly fell on her knees, sobbing and crying.

"Thank you, Senora. Thank you so much. Mucho gracias, Maestra. May the Lord and the Virgin always guide your path." She picked up her daughter in her arms and in a rush, disappeared into the crowd.

Harv soon returned to the park bench they had designated as their rendezvous spot, eyes happy with achievement, a spark plug in his hand. He gave the waiting Janet a quick kiss and a warm hug then dragged her over to a table at a local restaurant where all his fellow captains were bragging about their successes at acquiring parts for their boats. Harv bought her a beer and they sat down to a table of laughter and good cheer. Little dying girls were soon forgotten.

"Harv, where is Jill?" Janet asked with a tug on his sleeve. Harv just smiled down into her eyes with all the love in the world and pointed to the top of the statue in the middle of the park across the street where Jill and her girlfriend sat sneering at local boys far below. Janet smiled back.

"At least it is a step up from flag poles!"

The next morning when Harv and Janet rowed ashore, leaving Jill to struggle, fighting her war with the quadratic equation, they found a delegation waiting for them on the beach. In the front of the crowd was Janet's acquaintance from the day before, Alica's mother. The woman's eyes were filled with tears, and she held something in her arms. Janet' fooled for a second. You don't get the kind of money needed to own a boat like the *Steel Balls* without being one hell of a mean mother fucker.

"Sir, this is Charlie Ross," Jim indicated his first officer standing by the radar. "If you ever need something and I am not available, Charlie knows the boat inside and out." The three men shook hands. Jim was surprised. The new owner had a hand of iron. A huge hand, sure, but most big handed men were very dainty with their grip, not wanting to hurt, to crush. Not this one. 'What other surprises were in store?' Jim thought to himself

"How long are you able to stay with us this time, Sir," Charlie asked timidly.

"Quite some time. I am taking some guests over to an island off the Costa Rican Pacific coast. Cocos Island, I believe it is known as. My guests will be arriving this coming week and I want to leave as soon as the last guest is on board. Do you men perceive any problems? I suppose I should say, 'Make it so.'" Jim looked at him in surprise.

"I wish you had told us sooner, Sir. We will have our work cut out for us to be ready in time."

"I think I pay you men well enough to get the work done." Jim saw the owner's face change slightly. His eyes became steely, his chest seemed to enlarge and his neck seemed to stiffen.

"No problem, Sir. You will have to send in the Panama Canal fees ahead of time to avoid a delay. Our last transit cost over $750,000." The new owner didn't even blink.

"Let me know if you need any other petty cash. Give me the exact amount and I'll give you a check for the Canal."

"I'll let you know about the cost of stocking up for your guests, sir, if you inform me of any special foods that might be required. However, the Panama Canal only deals in cash. You are required to submit the funds to City Bank in Cristobal. I'll get the routing number for you." Jim kept his face neutral. The last thing he wanted was to be responsible for three quarters of a million dollars. Captains were blacklisted for loosing much less. Or after being framed for the supposed loss by a new owner.

"Now, Sir, would you like to take a tour of the yacht?" He wanted to end this conversation about money while he was still ahead. Why couldn't he at least once, have a great owner that just wanted him to drive the boat, to keep it running and to make sure she got to where they wanted? And when they wanted. Why did he have to be a nursemaid? Somehow he always expected the Captains of Industry to act like, well, Captains. Instead he got tyrants who believed their temper tantrums were a proper way to lead men.

"Show me a couple of cabins and the galley. I trust there is an Owner's galley on board." At the first cabin, Hawkins ran a finger along the combings along the door and windows. He seemed surprised when the cabins were sparkling clean and he could have shaved in his reflection from the windows. The varnish and paint were first quality, as were the furnishings which were done in a different style in each cabin.

"Sir, every owner likes to redo the cabins. If I may be so bold to offer some advice, if you wish to change the appearance of the boat, start with
just one cabin and see how it turns out. The appearance of many furnishings on the showroom floor, don't translate to shipboard cabins. But I am sure you know best, Sir."

"Why are these flimsy shower curtains masquerading as bathroom doors? How can you talk to me of doing only one cabin when you have such crappy doors?" Jim Banks looked straight at the new owner for a couple of seconds, wondering how far to go. Should he tell the truth? Finally he decided the truth was a good place to start.

"The previous owner demanded we install these curtains, Sir. You might notice they all are a bit too small." Jim turned and pointed out several small cameras hidden about the cabin. "He had cameras in the heads, too, but the moisture from the showers kept fogging them up and then eventually ruining the electronics. He had these curtains installed to monitor the heads from the cabins. You are up to date on the 'security system', Sir?" Hawkins nodded, giving nothing away.

"We still have the original doors down below. It would be a simple matter to re-install them. It would make the crew happy. They don't have any doors either." Jim was careful to keep his face as neutral as he could.
It wasn't his job to take sides. The owner paid him to drive the boat. That was what he was going to do.

"Would you like to have them reinstalled, Sir?" Hawkins thought carefully. He could always have the shower curtains put back on. If he wanted to. He felt a little chill go up his spine at the thought of spying, of watching naked girls. Then he thought, watch them do what? Wipe their asses? He was going to need a certain amount of loyalty from the crew if he was successful in recovering the gold. And in transporting it to somewhere safe. He supposed Costa Rica would think it was their gold, especially that the Virgin was theirs. Ha. If they wanted it so bad they should have gone and picked it up. Yeah, the crew might be the key to success. Mutinies have happened for less than a king's ransom and more for something as simple as a shower curtain.

"I don't need my guests or crew spied on. Put them back. I'm sure the rest of the cabins are in equally beautiful condition. Please thank your crew for me, Captain." Jim Banks smiled for the first time since Hawkins had come on board.

"No problem, Sir. And thanks."

The fucker was sweating right through his shirt. And the smell of fear was intense. He spun the cylinder of his revolver again, loving the clicking of the pawl, watching the panic in the fucker's eyes. He hadn't even asked him any questions yet. He didn't want to; he had been told to grill the suspect to try to discover the hiding place of the money, but Joe didn't care. He just wanted to kill. He wanted to smell, to taste, to feel the brassy, salty fresh blood, arcing in a beautiful stream from the asshole's fucking neck. He held the gun up to the thief's temple. He stared into his eyes as he slowly pulled the trigger. He loved the fear emanating from the guy. Fear of him. Fucker was frightened of him, as well as he should be. The gun clicked once and then the hammer dropped.

"Joe, you ain't supposed to off him, till he squawks. The Don, he won't like it, he don't squawk. He won't, Joe. He'll be royally pissed. You'se knows he won't like it. He don't even like you playing Russian roulette like dat." Joe swung on Tugs, grabbed his fat neck and forced his gun deep into his bulging gut.

"Fuck what the Don wants. Fuck what anyone wants. I do what I want to do. You got a problem with that you sloppy asshole?"

"Joe, the Don, you got to keep him happy, Joe. He don't like it, you mess with him." Liquid started to squeeze out from the folds of the man's fat. "Joe, he'll come after me, too, Joe. Being as how I is here. We got to ask him about the money, make him talk. The Don, he don't care about this punk. He only care about his money. He don't get it, he gonna take it out of our hides, Joe. Out of my hide, too." Tugs was emanating fear now, too. Not that it was hot in there. It was just something that Joe did to people. All the hell in him was just too hot to handle.

"Fuck it all. Fuck the world. Fuck the Don. Fuck you." It wasn't anger in Joe's eyes, it wasn't disgust of his life as a torpedo. It was an insanity, a glare not meant for one man, a glare meant, in a way, for all humanity. A glare that fed on itself, that required no victim, no aggressor. A glare that was a window on a diseased mind feeding and consuming itself. A glare that was a time bomb with a hair trigger just waiting to go off. A glare without logic or reason. A glare of walking death looking at the world straight from the lowest dungeons of Hades. A glare that was as scary as hell.

Joe broke open the revolver and loaded the empty cylinders with bullets. He snapped the gun closed and without a wasted movement, raised the gun and shot the fucker right in the middle of the right eye, then the left eye, and without a pause right between the two, then in the mouth that was sagging open in astonishment and them he buried the gun in the guys crotch and blew off something down there too. He turned and aimed the gun at Tugs' right eye.

"We asked him but he didn't know nuthing. Got it? If you don't, I got one more bullet, just for you." Tugs dramatically agreed and he slowly sat down on a blood sprayed couch.

"Sure, Joe. Sure." He slowly wiped his sweating face.

The Don hated gringos. He wanted his cartel to be manned totally by his local countrymen. But the truth was that even with Europe's increasing demand for drugs, America was by far his number one customer. And that meant working with the criminal syndicates that controlled the distribution of drugs in the United States. And that meant that he had to employ some thugs from the syndicates just as they employed some of his men. They were non-secret agents. Both sides recognized they needed a conduit into each other's camps to try to avoid unnecessary bloodshed and to stop turf wars before they started. Once, a long time ago, the Don had tried to set up a small distribution center in Miami. Within two weeks, all of his men were dead and he received their electro-shocked balls by postal express. Since then, the Syndicates always kept an eye on him. And he only sent disposable people up to El Norte.

But he still hated the gringo spies. They were coarse, stupid, vain men. He hated having them in his house, or even talking to them. So he gave them shit jobs. If there was something idiotic to be done, he preferred to give the job to idiots. Like these two, these Joe and Tugs. Such stupid names. Such stupid men. He knew the American syndicates sent men they didn't care about, in case he killed them. Just as he sent worthless men to America. And now they stood in front of him, telling him that they didn't screw up. Assholes. Stupid assholes. They couldn't even grill a chicken shit informer. They lost him tens of millions. Sure, it was a drop in the bucket, but it was his bucket. He could have bought another piece of Waikiki Beach with that money. He had a dream that one day he would control all the land from the Honolulu Zoo to the Ala Wai Marina. A man had to have a dream. He already owned five percent of the land and controlled ten percent more. The properties made almost as much money as his grass plantations. Of course, his main interest was in cocaine, which had the added advantage of being tax free, unlike his Honolulu property. But not without expenses. He spent millions in gifts to senators and congressmen to keep drugs illegal in America. Why would they want to legalize such drugs, anyway? They should come to his country, he could show them what suffering such drugs caused. But there was no worry. The men in Washington, they understood the power of money. Just as the syndicates understood the power of fear.

He hated those two gringo spies. He had them brought before him. They smelled. He wondered when they last bathed. It didn't matter. They would soon be gone. And he would make sure they would not be buried on his land.

"So, you two screwed up. You didn't find my money. Did you?"

"Don, your Honor, we tried but he didn't know anything. We asked and tortured, we did, Jefe, but he knew nothing. He knew nothing, Senor."

The Don threw photos of the dead man at them. Joe looked at them in confusion. They had buried the body under a new concrete road that was being built outside Cartagena. They had dug a hole just in front of the pavement, late at night. They shared a bottle of booze on a hill top as the workmen started their road building machines and paved over the burial site. Where had these photos come from? Only one possibility came to mind. Tugs had informed on him. Tugs was trying to get the Don to eliminate him. Tugs was trying to take his place. He looked over at Tugs while wishing they hadn't taken his gun before he was allowed to enter the room. Tugs was looking back at him. He looked like he thought. Tugs looked like he thought he, Joe, had talked.

Joe wasn't the smartest rat in the maze but he could smell a con with the best of them. They were being set up. Someone was trying to get the two of them to take each other out. And for his money, the Don was the someone.

"The two of you owe me ten million dollars. Find it, steal it from someone else, I don't give a rat's ass. I give you two weeks. Give me my money by then or I will put a contract out on you. I already have talked to your syndicate. They have okayed my actions, so don't go crying to them. They said they were sorry they sent, how do you say it, bozos? Yes, bozos like the two of you." He reached into his desk drawer and pulled out a thin long stiletto, and proceeded to clean his already spotless fingernails with it. "Why are you still here? You have not much time."

With a jump, Joe was on his feet, dragging Tugs with him. He backed out of the door, keeping his eyes on the stiletto, once outside they grabbed their weapons and ran for their car. Once behind the wheel, Tugs turned to his partner.

"Joe, what are we going to do? The Don, he is going to kill us. I just know it. I do." His shirt was icy wet from sweat and fear.

"Fuck the Don. Let's get the fuck out a here. Go, go, go."

Tugs always drove. He had a natural talent as a driver. He didn't have much else going for him. He lasted in school till the third grade when he ran into the multiplication tables. His personal war with math lasted a few weeks until he was beaten into a mental pulp. From then on, he let others do his thinking for him. His life as a young man was one of petty crimes and prison sentences. When he was 21 he heisted a torpedo's car. It was a 1967 Camero, one of the better muscle cars of that era. Tugs loved that car and took great care of it. He personally bored out the cylinders to take a larger piston. When he was eventually caught by the mafia, the torpedo after inspecting his car, instead of torturing him to death, gave him a job as a mechanic and a chauffeur.

The mafia took care of him. If the cops caught him, he was out on bail within hours. When he went to trial, the prosecution's witnesses never showed up. Life had never been better for Tugs. The mafia turned him into a wheelman. He excelled at it. He seemed to have an innate sense of how a car would react when it drifted around corners, all four tires skidding, rubber burning, smoke billowing up from the rims in concentric spirals. He seemed to know just when to ease off and allow the tires to grab asphalt again. At some subliminal level he knew just how much to brake into a curve and how much to accelerate out of it. He was respected in the mafia, as much as an idiot savant could ever be respected.

Then he screwed up. He was the wheelman for a job, waiting outside of the bank, motor running, making sure his racing gloves were on just right, listening to the sound of the pistons humming, when a passing cop made him. He didn't know what he should do. When his partners came out of the bank, what would they do if a cop was right there? So he took off, racing around the block, hoping that when he returned to the bank, his partners would be ready for pick up. They were, but so were the pigs. The first cop had called in for back up and the streets were filled with black and whites.

The mafia got him out of the clink and sent him out of the country. When he asked what he was supposed to have done, they told him he should have shot the first cop in both kneecaps as he walked up to his car.

Tugs wasn't a violent man, he just liked to drive. And here he was driving in Columbia, in trouble, again. Shit.

T

The sea is a great cleanser. There is little wonder that Jesus chose fishermen as his apostles. The lessons they learned from childhood while fishing the sea were to hide and wait when the weather was too nasty, to never give up bailing the boat as eventually the storm would pass; that the only way to survive in a small place like a boat was to care for each other and that it didn't matter if the fish weren't biting today, maybe they will tomorrow. At sea, land's problems are left behind. At sea life is pure. Pure and simple. Keep the water on the outside and the people in the inside. The pointy end goes towards the next island. The stick stays up pointed towards heaven, and the keel stays down in the water, balancing all on board. That is all there is to it. Simple. People, however, end up adding complications to their lives.

"What do you mean my algebra is wrong?" Jill was livid. She had her hands on her hips and was automatically bracing herself against the rolling of the seaway. She had become enough of a sea dog that she didn't have to hold on all the time. "Everyone of those answers are right. You must be reading the answers wrong or something. I'm right, I'm telling you, I'm right!" Her eyes were very angry, sparks seemed to fly out of them.

"Honey, Baby. I'm not trying to make you wrong. I love you. I really do. So does your Dad. I'm not a teacher. I'm just a mom trying to do the best job I know how. And to tell you the truth, I wasn't all that good at algebra, either, in High School. Listen, let's look at the answers at the back of the book together. Maybe the author of the book made a mistake. Will you try with me?"

"Well, maybe. But Mom, you really have to have more trust in your own flesh and blood. Who else do you know who can climb flag poles as well as I can? Doesn't that tell you something?"

"It tells me that you are a special girl who likes challenges, like algebra." Janet gave Jill a wink. Jill gave Janet a pout and sat down at the table resignedly.

On deck, Harv was reading a book, occasionally looking up to make sure they were still on course, there weren't any ships on the horizon and there weren't any logs or entire trees floating in their chosen path. This part of the world had massive rivers that discharged flotsam of all sizes and types. Once in a while, there was a tree out there floating that was so scary that it had to be shared to lessen its impact, like pointing out a car wreck to each other on the freeway.

"Hey, you guys, come on up and see this one. It's awesome! Ya got ta see it. Wow!"

"Where is it, Dad?" Jill was instantly on deck, scanning the horizon. "Mom, come and look. Dad, where exactly is it?" Harv held out a finger and Jill sighted down it.

"Mom, you are not going to believe this one," she shouted down the companionway. "Dad, you are too close, edge away." She grabbed hold of the wheel and tried to turn it.

"It isn't your watch, Flash, it's mine. I am in command of driving the boat for my watch. It will be your turn, soon enough."

"My turn! I get to be in charge? You two are going to be below and I am going to be on deck all my myself?"

"All by yourself, yes."

"Oh, this is too cool! When is my turn? When? When?" Jill was bubbling with excitement. Her eyes flashing with the prospect of recess. Janet stuck her head up the companionway hatch.

"Just as soon as you finish your algebra."

"Oh, Mom!" Jill rushed below and finished her math in record time accepting her mother's pointers with good grace and without complaint. She was soon up in the cockpit dressed in a foul weather jacket and boots, with binoculars around her neck and a flare gun in a cowgirl holster at her side.

"Ready for duty, Sir Daddy! I relieve you of your watch." Harv stared at her for a moment, looked out at the cloudless sky and felt the heat of the intense tropical sun, but decided that discretion was the better part of family feuds.

"She's all yours, Flash-person Jill. Call me if anything exciting happens." He made a mock salute towards Jill and went below trying not to break out in laughter while still in Jill's hearing.

Not knowing any sea chanties, Jill went through what she remembered of her nursery rhymes. Her voice wasn't any better than her father's and, apparently, her huge enjoyment of singing, equaled his.

"Do I really sound that bad?" Harv whispered to Janet down in the salon where she was tiding up and Harv was doing his best to not get in the way. A tough job on a small boat.

"Worse. At least Jill can say she doesn't know any better!" She smiled at her husband. "Now will you please get your big feet out of my dust pile?"

"I don't know why you have to sweep the boat every day. She just gets dirty again. Maybe the boat attracts dirt and resents you stealing it. If you gave the boat a little dirt, maybe she would stop attracting it?" He arched his eyebrows in his practiced, male superiority look. "Maybe it is like women. Take some of their dresses away and the first thing they do is go and buy some new clothes. Maybe it is a female thing?" Harv drew a finger downwards in the air. "Sizzle, score one for me!"

"Men! If it wasn't for taking out the garbage, I don't know why us women keep them around. Right, Jill!"

"I can't hear you two whispering down there in loud voices cuz I am up here on watch. I am keeping a good watch so stop trying to distract me, you two! And you have to obey me cuz I'm at the wheel and in command! And Daddy, better do what Mom wants or she will make you sit at the table until your work is done. I know!"

Harv sat down on the foreward corner of the settee in the salon as Janet finished cleaning. After she washed her hands, she sat down next to him and lay her head gently against his shoulder. She closed her eyes and tried to relax, if only for a moment. If she could just rest for a moment. If she could only ignore that endless, mindless something inside of her, pushing her, driving her to who knew where?

"Harv, Babe?" She asked timorously, her eyes opening just a crack, her left hand reached out and found Harv's right.

"Yeah, Honey?" His hand was rough and calloused from handling the lines and sails of the boat and the chain of the anchor.

"What do you think happened in that dirty little hut?" She liked his rough hands. Her finger tips made little circles around some of the rougher spots.

"With the cowboy with the machete?" She tried to nod without moving her head from his shoulder. "I don't know, Janet. It was like something weird came out of you. It was very eerie, all the hairs on my neck and arms stood straight out from my skin. It was something white and yet not white, something full of energy or light or, I really don't know. What did it feel like to you? Can you remember?"

"It was very strange. I don't know what to think. It wasn't like any force or anything took over my body. It just came and did it's thing and left. It didn't take over my mind or hurt me. It is really hard to remember now, what exactly did happen." She turned her head slightly so she could see his eyes. "Tell me exactly what you saw." He smiled down at her and slipped his right hand around her body and his left took over holding her hand.

"Well, we went in and he raised the filthy sheet off the woman on the ground. You looked very surprised and I tried to pull you out of the hut as you looked unhappy about the whole thing. As I pulled you to the door, the cowboy pulled his machete and tried to stab me in the ribs. I was just about to toss him out of our way when you reached over and put your hand on the woman's belly. It seemed like your hand was glued to her. The woman screamed something, I'm not sure what. Something in English, which was weird, too. I was pulling you towards the door with your other hand." He bent his head and kissed her lightly on the cheek and hugged her with his arm.

"Janet, your hand I was holding, was getting so cold. Almost like a stone, you know? Then something happened. Your other hand started to almost glow. Glow isn't the right word. The cold in your arm was gone and a light that wasn't a light was bursting out of your skin, just here and there, not everywhere. I saw a burst of light go down the length of your other arm and enter the woman. Juanita, right? It was like she was having one of those shock treatments. Her body was vibrating from head to toe. Then she burst to her feet at the same time as your hand pushed her away and she ran from the hut. Then it was like a fire, white fire, burst from your hand, from your fingertips and lit up the whole hut, just for a second. It seemed to sanitize everything, cleaned it of anything bad, you know? Then I finally got you out of that little hut and we ran back to the beach and the boat and safety." He lightly rubbed his forehead against hers. He thought about asking where the white light had come from but was afraid of the answer he might get. Was his Janet possessed? Was there something else inside of her? How did it get in there?

He bent down and kissed her on the lips. She didn't feel any different to him. The lips were so connected to the soul that he felt he should feel it if there was something else, someone else, living in there. Her lips were soft and parted for him. Suddenly he wondered if a white light would come out of her and get him. Attack him. Shock him. He pulled away from her, confused.

"Honey?" Her voice was plaintive and tiny, like a little girl's. She edged her lips back towards him and then fell back in dismay when he didn't respond.

"I better check how our little Flash is doing." He disengaged himself from her arms and walked away without looking at her. Janet's body deflated slightly, as if she were a balloon that just lost some of its air. A single tear seeped out of her left eye. She ignored it. And then the dam burst and she ran into the head, the little bathroom, slammed the door so she could cry her heart out in private. So she could cry in loneliness, in sadness and in fear. And in the end, it didn't matter at all if her boat was clean if her soul was polluted with who knows what, and if she was to be left alone, eventually, all alone, with no one to love or to love her.

Dustin Horner wasn't afraid to fly. He knew flying was the safest way to travel, as far as survival was concerned. Healthwise, he considered flying incredibly dangerous. He thought being locked in a closed container with hundreds of strangers, none of whom were required to disclose a health report to the authorities, who were breathing the same air as he, who were often touching other people in the aisles, who were sharing the same bathroom facilities, was incredibly unintelligent.

When he had to fly, he always boarded last, turned off the overhead fan immediately before it recycled every other person on board's germs into his nostrils 'all for his personal pleasure', sat just in front of a bulkhead so no one would be breathing down his neck, sat in a window seat to be away from aisle traffic, wore an air purifier around his neck, wore disposable gloves when using the facilities, and always sucked on a candy or antiseptic cough drop. The body's first defense against airborne germs was the salvia in the mouth and throat, and sucking on something, even a rock, produced saliva. Salvia was very effective in killing and eliminating all types of pathogens and then recycling them in the stomach by swallowing. It only made sense that the body would develop such defenses. Horner thought that there was no doubt such effective saliva was developed back in the days of cavemen. He could imagine them huddled together for warmth in cold, damp, drafty caves as saber-toothed tigers raged outside. Survival would have demanded they develop resistance against colds and flus of all types, effective in all weathers, all in close company. Those who didn't, died and their inefficient genes died with them.

But when he could, he didn't fly. He drove himself or took the train. He liked the train because the passing scenery helped him to enter into a reflective state. He often thought about his past and what might be his future. He reflected on the problems he was facing in his work and how he could solve them. It was on a train that he first developed the idea of what eventually would become the Sonic Microwave. It was the noise of the track and the vibration of the rails that got him thinking about combining two types of energy that could hyper-dyne with each other to discover abnormalities.

Now, as the Amtrak was click and clacking him across America, he was thinking about Mary. He thought he could feel her presence sitting next to him. He didn't turn his head, preferring to try to sense her presence, her essence, whatever it might be labeled, that which was her. He thought he did feel something after a few minutes of introspection, but doubted that it was anything but his brain supplying what it thought he wanted. His brain did that. He didn't think he was his brain, or that his brain was him. His brain was a tool he used, a great, magnificent tool, but a tool nonetheless. He didn't know where his being, his personality, dwelled, neither was he overly concerned about it. He didn't worry if there was a God or not, after all, the question would resolve itself in just a few years, one way or the other. Many questions that weren't going to be solved in the near future were more worthy of his time. Not many people were granted his analytical abilities, neither were many people determined enough to train their brains to a high enough pitch, high enough to see around corners.

To see past roadblocks was his personal skill. Where others reached a dead end, he usually found a way to proceed. He thought he developed this skill by playing computer games as a child. Often the game designers put the hero in a totally impossible situation, but he knew there was a way out, somehow, someway. They designed it that way but made it next to impossible to discover. He always found it. Such games became boring after a few months. They were too easy for him. They did, however, waken in him a latent talent. Modern day physics, where quarks and mesons had turned Newton's world upside down, where everywhere one looked was a question mark, was a world of roadblocks. In such a discipline, he developed his mind to the utmost. Most of the time, he chose to use his intellect to develop solutions to mankind's problems, and to get payed for it. He considered being paid for his work the highest compliment there was.

The rest of the time when he might be on a train, he thought about his personal life and how he could increase his personal happiness. It was an interesting problem. For a time he searched up a blind alley. He tried to increase his happiness using the least amount of effort from himself, always a good place to start. Kind of like being paid with happiness for just being alive. It didn't work out. He found he became less happy when he didn't work very hard for it.

So he determined to make a lot of money to buy happiness. It didn't work. Making money was fun, but it didn't increase his happiness. Something was very puzzling about happiness. No wonder the Founding Fathers made such a big deal about the pursuit of it.

He decided happiness might come from love. It didn't work either. He fell in love with the high and mighty and the girl next door, he experienced love in all its splendor, but it wasn't enough. At the best it kept boredom away for a few hours, that's all.

He decided to dedicate himself to his fellow man, he found out most men were very satisfied living the life they found themselves in. They really didn't want rescuing, no matter how much they might plead for it.

Now he was experimenting with loving just one person, ignoring himself, being happy only if she or he was happy. So far it wasn't working out. It really couldn't, seeing as how he hadn't found the one girl to fall in love with yet. He had thought of Mary as his test subject. Of course Mary was a special girl. She would be easy to fall in love with. Would he be able to maintain his analytical distance in such a relationship? Would being in love compromise his ability to think clearly? He tried to feel her presence again as she sat next to him. Wouldn't it be great if he could read her thoughts. He could give her exactly what she wanted. Tell if she was happy? So far he couldn't do it. His brain kept getting in the way. How could he hear his feelings when his brain was throwing thousands of ideas a minute at him?

Was being smart a detriment to attaining happiness? He didn't think so. He guessed he could pretend to be non-smart, as a test. But that would be unintelligent. And his brain, definitely, did not do stupid.

Tiring of his thoughts, he stood up and walked up to the club car. There was a football game on the big screen TV. In high school he was too small to make the team, in University, he was still too small and far too busy, but he still loved the game. For a moment, while watching the TV, he amused himself with developing a mathematical formula for determining the next play either team would attempt. It was too easy to hold his attention for long. In this particular game, each team was either ineptly coached or couldn't be bothered to learn more than a few dozen plays. He dabbled on a napkin. Several variables instantly came to mind. Points behind or ahead, next opponent, injuries, incompetence and or prejudices of referees, weaknesses of the opponent, and perceived team strengths. As he started to formulate an equation, a hand touched his shoulder.

Normally smaller men don't like to be touched unannounced, but this hand that touched him was so gentle, so feminine, so soft, he didn't immediately react. He turned and looked up. A beautiful woman stood behind him, smiling, smiling at him. She was dressed in a basic black short dress, black silk bellbottoms, a black ribbon around her neck and a red ribbon in her hair. She kept her dainty hand on his shoulder.

"Is there anything you require, Sir?" A dozen quick ripostes came to his mind instantly, but his mouth was frozen. She didn't seem upset. He guessed that with her looks she must be used to stunned, verbally challenged men by now. "Anything at all, Sir? I am ready to comply to your every demand, Sir."

Instantly, a picture of Mary came zooming into his mind. It faded as his own private genie lowered her other hand and started massaging his neck. Her hands were so knowing, they found the knots in his neck within seconds. Quickly they banished them and moved over onto his shoulders. He looked back at her. Her lips was slightly open as she massaged him. He could not stop his mind from wondering if her mouth was as knowing as her fingers. Slowly he managed to get himself back under control. With a smile he acknowledged to himself how very little mankind had matured past the origins of their distant past. He stood up and turned.

"Thank you my dear lady, that was a delightful experience. I hope I will get a repeat performance one day." He smiled at her. "Can I expect to meet you again? And perhaps I may have your name to complete a unique memory?" She seemed a little put off by the relative ease he had resisted her charms but she just smiled and looked sexier than ever.

"I'm going all the way to Key West and my name is Mary." His mind would never let him alone. The micro-second she said Key West, his mind blasted out, 'agent of Hawkins.' He had read stories on the internet of Hawkins' high handed tactics. Was she trying to get his Sonic Microwave?

"I, too, am traveling to Key West. It looks like we will be on the same train for a while yet. Do you have business in the Conch Republic?"

"I work there on a boat called *Steel Balls.* I understand you are going to be a passenger on the ship? Don't look so surprised. The Hawkins empire reaches far and wide. I was traveling this way anyway and was informed of your route and chose to greet you, Dustin Horner. I wasn't asked to do so. Have I done something wrong? It isn't often I meet as nice a man as you. I hope we can continue to see each other and enjoy each others company." Dustin hated it, sometimes, when his brain was right. But, then, what could a Hollywood starlet type see in an introverted inventor who spends most of his time in a lab, who doesn't go to movies and who didn't really date all that much any more, now that he was looking elsewhere for happiness. For him a hot date was a piece of dried fruit warmed over a Bunsen burner.

"It is impossible for you to have done something wrong if both parties enjoyed the scenario. Would you care to hear my theories on play prediction in American football?" He cast his eyes towards the big screen TV with out turning his face from her. "I believe I am close to formulating an equation. A basic underlining equation." She smiled and sat down with him and looked attentive.

He pulled out his napkin to show her, but all the while his brain was shouting at him, demanding to be heard, that girls wear a ribbon around their neck to hide the little fold of skin that forms there if they had inherited the nymphomaniac gene.

"Oh, there you are. And you have found a friend. How pleasant!" Mary was smiling. Dustin wasn't fooled. Women were born to deceit and treachery. It was the mark of Eve. The mark of once having eaten of the forbidden fruit, instead of repenting, she had lured her mate into sinning also, so as not to be alone when banned from Eden.

"Mary! There you are, too. You were sleeping when I left. Let me introduce you." He stood up and made a courtly gesture towards his acquaintance. "I'm afraid I forgot your name," he lied. He looked at

Hawkins' agent, which is how he still thought of her, in askance. He took off his heavy glasses and polished them with his tie.

"How wonderful. My name is Mary also. I guess I will be Mary One on the ship, while you will be Mary Two. That is how we do it on board."

"She is crew on the *Steel Balls*, Mary. Isn't that extraordinary?" He looked at both women, face grinning on the outside. Inside he felt he was slipping into quicksand. There was little wonder why he never found love while dating. As powerful as his brain was, it didn't seem to be able to keep up with females on the prowl.

"How wonderful, indeed. I imagine that you will be just ahead of me at the cafeteria, being Mary One. You know, since we are guests aboard, and you are part of the crew, why don't you just call me Dustin's Mistress? How would that be, Mary One?"

"I think I will just leave you two love birds and get back to my cabin. I do have quite a lot of organizing to do. Nice to meet you both." She smiled a bit wanly and quickly left the car.

"Mary, would you like to hear about my new formula for play prediction in American football?" Dustin tried to smile. It was hard work, looking up, with Mary staring down at him, like a bug. "I believe I am, that is, I am close to a basic underlining equation." His voice spiraled downwards towards the end of the sentence.

Mary just stared at him with cold eyes and firmly sat down across from him and drummed her fingers on the small cocktail table.

Erhart decided he loved the Keys. He loved driving down over the many bridges spanning hundreds of jewel like islands and sand bars. When he arrived, he pursed his lips and decided he really truly loved Key West. It was so camp and historic at the same time. So many famous people had lived there through the years. The Hemingway and Audubon houses had been preserved from the ravages of time and hurricanes. He was well aware that David Porter had established the naval base there during his fight against pirates. More recently, Key West was the first American city to be fully reliant on desalination for its fresh water supply. As usual, Erhart knew all the facts, most of the rumors and some of the lies.

The town had a reputation for being kind towards gays, but Erhart didn't see many of them around, and he was looking. He was sure he would recognize a gay if he saw one. Stands to reason, doesn't it? He traveled from one famous bar to the next before he gave up his quest to discover hidden gay hideouts. Finally he made it down to the docks at sunset, a Key West ritual. Acrobats jostled with magicians seeking the approval and support of the crowd.

The crowd was huge. It seemed everyone in town was down at the docks in the hopes of seeing a green flash. Everyone was drinking, smoking, partying, laughing and having a great time. He worked his way to the front of the crowd, being small had its advantages as long as he wasn't stepped on. Finally he got in front but unfortunately his view was ruined. Between him and the setting sun was a monstrous, huge motor yacht. It was ghastly long and had far too many stories or decks or whatever one must call them. After a few minutes of feeling put out, it occurred to him to find out the ship's name. Could it be? He walked south along the boardwalk until he could see the stern.

There it was. It was the *Steel Balls.* This ship was to be his new home for a couple of weeks. Erhart couldn't believe his luck. If it was luck. What would the owner of such a huge ship want with him? He thought he would be traveling to Cocos Island on a tramp steamer of some kind, much more his style. Kind of bohemian, adventurous, rags to riches type of style. Maybe with an Errol Flynn type as Captain and a one legged First Mate.

Below his feet, down a ramp leading to a floating dock next to the water was a beautiful old wooden Chris Craft. The boat shone with gleaming varnish in the setting sun. The driver of the boat had just finished tying it to the dock and was admiring his work with quiet pride. He was the most beautiful young man Erhart had ever seen. Sparkling white teeth in a tanned face, tousled curly sun-kissed brown hair, muscles everywhere, bulging. It wasn't a man, it was a god slumming, come down from the summit of Mount Olympus. It was a Hollywood leading man. The young man turned and stared up at the crowd. On his shirt, above his heart, were the words: *Steel Balls.*

Erhart turned and ran from the dock. Ran all the way back to his hotel room. Up the stairs, through the door, slamming and locking it behind him, he threw himself on the bed and shoved his face into the pillow, his eyes squeezed tight.

The next morning he was ashamed of himself. What would the crew of the ship think of him? He was an important part of the expedition. Who else knew all of the details of the treasure of Cocos Island? Or more importantly, who else knew which tales were true and which were fairytales? They needed him. That is why they had sent him a personal letter, a real letter, not an e-mail. He imagined the Captain would be calling to him day and night, worriedly asking him important questions and waiting breathlessly for his answers. He had to get hold of himself. He didn't know what had come over him last night. It must have been all the driving. Yes. That was it. He was overly tired. He tidily packed his few bags and walked cheerfully down to the docks ready to begin his new adventure.

It was a different man by the floating dock today. An older man but with the same kind of shirt. Erhart wondered if he would be issued the same uniform. It was very natty. The dock was moving very slightly in a southerly swell that was working its way into the mouth of the harbor. He quickly checked his pockets for his seasick pills. It just wouldn't do to be sick on the first day, especially before even sailing.

"Good morning, Sir. What is your name?" The man was very polite and deferential. Erhart noticed that just below the words *Steel Balls*, in smaller letters and a different font was the man's name, Bill.

"Morning, Bill. Erhart Peterson. I am a member of the Cocos Expedition." Erhart stood as tall as he could as the man, Bill, ran his finger down a list.

"Yes, Sir. They have you in the Moroccan Cabin. Would you like to go aboard now, Sir? Or if you like, I will deliver your bags for you."

"I believe I will become acquainted with my cabin, now."

"Yes, Sir. Let me help you with your luggage."

The ship was even bigger up close. Huge was an inadequate word. The stern had lifted up somehow, like a cargo jet, and inside were jet skis, scuba tanks, windsurfers and inflatable boats with fishing gear. There was even a water skiing and parachute flying boat, inside the back of the *Steels Balls*! He wondered why the ship didn't sink with all those toys in the cracked open, hinged stern.

He went up the gangway to an officer at the top who asked him his name again, and if he was traveling alone or was to be accompanied. Erhart instantly thought of the beautiful young man he had first seen on the Chris Craft.

"My companion will report in shortly."

He was gratified to find his cabin had not a porthole but a window, a big window! He could stand inside his cabin and observe the world in perfect safety and comfort. He found a little bell that when rung sent a steward to his room asking what might be his pleasure.

"Chocolate ice cream with mint chips and walnuts sprinkled on top and crowned with a cherry." The steward rushed away and was back in seven minutes. Erhart timed him. His ice cream was perfect. It was exactly what he had ordered plus there was a plate of mint candy arranged artistically and on a separate platter, a split of champagne. The steward didn't hang around and wait for a tip as they so often do. He delivered his order and then disappeared as good servants are trained to do. Erhart thought he had never been so happy. He was in seventh heaven and never wanted to leave.

As he was finishing his snack, his wonderful delicious snack, an envelope was slipped under his door with a polite knock. Eagerly he tore open the note wanting more of this delightful paradise.

"Hawkins will be honored to entertain you at 6:35 this evening." It was only signed with an indecipherable symbol on the bottom. Erhart gulped. Where was he supposed to go? What was he supposed to wear? Was he and this Hawkins going to be alone? Erhart quickly sat down and held his head in his hands. This was a lot of pressure for someone who had only rudimentary social skills, who spent most of his life in front of a computer screen. Right now, he needed an assistant. A master at arms, a royal regent, a prince consort, someone who knew what the blazes was going on. He wished he really did have an companion like he told that officer. Suddenly he thought of the boat driver. Could he be so bold? Should he be? Before he lost courage, he rang the bell again. Within minutes, a small knock came at the door. He stood up straight from the bed and marched himself over to the door. Outside was the same steward that had brought him his ice cream.

"There is a young man that drives the shore boat. What is his name?" The steward looked at him for a split second, then politely answered,

"His name is Rogers, Sir. John Rogers."

"Would you please call him for me, I have to ask him some questions, important strategic questions."

"Right away, Sir."

It was so easy! This must be what it was like to be rich. To have such power! Rich or to be a famous con artist. This is what it must feel like to be a criminal! To be so sure of yourself, so confident, to have such inner fortitude, inner power! He wondered if he should have grown up on the wrong side of the law, but only for a second. He had stolen a bag of army men from a store when he was five. His parents found out and made him bring them back and to apologize. Was he ever sorry. He was so embarrassed, his face still reddened just at the thought. No, he wasn't a crook. He was a good old fashioned red blooded American. A knock came at the door.

Erhart opened it slowly. His hand trembled slightly. The movie star boy from the boat stood outside, hat in his hand.

"They said you wanted me, Sir?"

"Yes. I have a problem. Come in please." The boy, John Rogers, he reminded himself, came in but left the door wide open. Erhart handed him the letter from the mystery man, his employer, Hawkins. "John, I don't know where to go, how to dress, what this is all about, I don't know anything. Any light you could shed on my dilemma would be appreciated."

"Yes, Sir. Hawkins is the owner of the *Steel Balls*. He just joined us, yesterday, and none of us know very much about him. However, the Owner's Stateroom is aft of your quarters. Turn left outside your door, go all the way to the end of the hall and turn right. There is only one door. Usually, knock once and enter. As for clothes, what do you have?" John was properly trained for duty on a luxury yacht, and never let a suspicion of surprise or disbelief enter his face or eyes. But his brain! He was wondering about these new guests. There was so much scuttlebutt about a search for treasure. But these people didn't look like the usual treasure hunters that usually were bitten with the gold bug. They looked, well, normal. This one looked like any computer nerd from any city in the world. He even had a plastic protector in his shirt pocket for his pens. His

clothes were terrible. It looked like he shopped at Pennys. Or worse.

"None of your clothes are appropriate. However, not to worry. It may be that the new owner, Mr. Hawkins, is not interested in stylish attire. Best thing is to go with the jeans, this shirt," John held the button down white shirt between two fingers and at arms length. "No, that tie is heinous, just wear the jacket and please, if you have only the white socks, don't wear any at all."

"Thank you, John. You saved me from a social blunder. I'll let you know afterwards how it went." Erhart went to touch John's upper arm but at the last moment changed it into a handshake.

Robyn, as she called herself, took a photo of the small man boarding that beautiful, luscious, millionaire's boat anchored off the old sub base docks in Key West. In fact, she took many photos. More of the boat than of the man. That is what she did. Took photos, wrote stories, made money. Not necessarily in that order. Ostentatiously, she was a free lance journalist. In reality, in the dark of the night, her favorite time of day, she was a cat burglar.

She considered herself a modern day Robin Hood, she took from the rich and gave to the, well, the poor had welfare these days and the needy had a grand assortment of churches and really didn't need anymore, so, she gave to herself. Ok, so she was half of a Robin Hood. Just a Robyn. She started out life as a Margaret Chambers. She never liked the name. There were so many Margarets in the world. She wanted her own name. She didn't want to share. Not in something as important as an identity. Not when she was trying to establish her name as a photographer and journalist.

She got her start in photojournalism in college. She took photos of study halls and libraries just before exam week in the early morning, just as the buildings opened and sold the photos of the empty chairs and bare tables to the town papers with titles like, 'Students study hard for upcoming finals.' Newspapers loved that kind of stuff. She dropped out in her Junior year and traveled the country selling the same kind of photos to newspapers in every city that boasted a 'name' school. She didn't make much money but she had a lot of fun seeing the world, or at least, her part of it. Soon she branched out. She remembered going to class as a real drag, especially in massive lecture halls with a hundred other students, just to learn something inane. Useless information that the university required to graduate. They called it education, she called it organized babysitting. Now, on the outside, it occurred to her that if she could record the lectures, format them on to a DVD, she could sell the movie to an unending number of up and coming students who would rather study the subject in their own time and leisure than get up at seven in the morning to attend a boring class. She hired herself a student, supplied her with a inconspicuous digital camera and waited for a saleable disc.

The waiting got to her. She would have to wait for an entire term to obtain an finished product. That was when she found out that some professors pre-recorded their lectures just in case they were unavoidably out of town, then their students wouldn't lose an important day of school and fall behind. A quick look at the professor's offices told her that they had far too exotic locks for her to jimmy. They were used to the thought that students might try to break in and change their test scores and were thus, well protected. She walked around the campus, feeling a bit frustrated, and happened upon the audio-visual department. A freshman sat behind the desk in a work-study program. A program where he received a scholarship for working between classes. He had a pimple on his nose, was a little short and had a lisp but she smiled and poured on the charm. In five minutes he was putty in her hands. She didn't even have to sleep with him.

It turned out that they kept the masters of all the professor's recorded lectures, here in the audio-visual office. In a file cabinet. Unlocked. It was a simple matter of sending him out to get her a cup of coffee and she had several DVD lecture series in her purse, complete with quizzes, tests and final exams. Soon she was selling an entire year's of study in campus dorms and then on the internet. She was really raking in the dough went someone ratted on her.

Jail wasn't much fun. It wasn't fun at all. She did manage to get on to the warden's staff as a toady. There she translated the warden's chicken scratches into something resembling the rambling rationality he wished to communicate. And there, in jail, she returned to school. Not math and english and civics. She studied safe cracking, grand theft auto, drug dealing, assault, murder, and her own personal favorite, extortion.

It was amazing to her that people would pay money to hide the truth from their friends. If someone tried to get her to pay to hide the truth, to extort money from her, she wouldn't pay, if her friends didn't like the real her, then she would simply get a new set of friends. Simple. Realistic. Intelligent. If her old friends didn't like her or what she did, no peoblem, they weren't real friends after all.

She made money on the inside by changing the warden's behavior records while she was alone in the office. But more than money, she earned the goodwill of the high ranking cons. The ones that had their own society. The ones that were 'on vacation,' as they called it. The professional criminals. They asked her questions about her photography and encouraged her to continue studying the art. When she was released, they gave her the addresses of a number of 'safe houses' where she could stay. She would have to work to stay there, only a couple of hours a day, she would have to do what they said, but she could order out and the house would pay.

They had her take pictures of government officials through windows, at first, late at night. They always told her when and where. They never told her why. She could guess. The officials were being set up with prostitutes of both sexes in rooms with flimsy curtains. Then they had her entering houses. It was easy picking the locks now. She had been to school. She took her photos through partially open doors, through the jam, reflected in mirrors, sometimes she entered the room while they were in the throes of passion. She started taking a knickknack with her when she left. After a while, she started taking more valuable items. A crystal vase, DVD collections, money from the john's wallet. It was really a turn on. She got a fabulous adrenalin rush from sneaking into the houses. It put her right on the edge, every molecule of her body felt alive. Her hearing was more acute, she saw dust motes in the air between her eyes and her camera, she felt the air itself vibrate when she walked. It was a very addictive feeling. Soon, it seemed to her that when she was not breaking and entering, she wasn't really living. On off days, she robbed houses just for something to do and for the thrill of it. She stopped taking knickknacks. She just went for the money and jewels. Easy to fence. Almost untraceable. Almost. And always she took photos as she preformed her crimes. It was a stupid thing to do. She knew it. She was supplying potential evidence for the DA in the future, but she couldn't stop herself. It was who she was. She was a photographer.

The mob became more insistent about how she did her jobs. They emphasized her timing. Her entry and exits. One day she had to take photos of a murder. And she had to be in the room while it occurred. It was a young girl. She was throttled to death by a U.S. Senator while he was having sex with her. As the naked girl died, as she struggled against the ropes that tied her spread eagle, as her body fought for life, Robyn kept taking photos. She wondered if she should help out, hit the man over the head with a lamp or something. But still she just took photos. As the girl struggled, the Senator seemed to get more excited. Just before she died, when every muscle in the poor girl's body started to pulsate, including her vagina, the Senator finally got his rocks off. Robyn quickly exited the room and house, still wondering why she hadn't tried to save the girl. Was something fundamentally wrong with her?

Robyn didn't like it. She wanted to live her way, to do what she wanted, when she wanted, how she wanted. Obeying the man or obeying the mob, it was the same as far as she was concerned. So she just disappeared. It wasn't hard. She took busses at first, then hitched for a hundred miles. She didn't care where she was going. Finally, she caught a flight to Hawaii, another to Fiji and a last to Puerto Vallarta. She took a boat out to a little town called Yelapa. The village had no roads, cars, phones, banks, post office or cops. It did have a bar, a restaurant and a laundry, and the most beautiful waterfall she had ever swum under. She spent her days photographing birds and lizards, yachts and naked jet set types, tourists, donkeys and the waterfall. After six months, the hurricane season came to town with torrential rains and floods, so she left.

She wasn't afraid of the mob. She was determined to live her life her way and to hell with the consequences. She went back to taking unusual photos and selling them to the rags down in Southern California, far away from the mob's territory. She had a close call when she spotted torpedoes that she knew, watching the airport at Lindbergh Field. Finally she jumped a Greyhound with a fake ID and traveled all the way across the country to Key West. No wise guy who hoped to be made one day would ever walk down the street of a gay community. But still, she was, well not worried, maybe just a little concerned. It might be a good time for a long sea voyage. And here was a boat. A millionaire's boat. Perfect. Millionaires always had secrets. They had plenty of money to pay for embarrassing photos. And she so much liked to sneak into places. It would be a blast. It would be so much fun. If, if she could only get on the ship.

As the *Rose Marie* sailed through the heads of the harbor of Acapulco, Jill was sitting on the spreaders directing her father with an abundance of information about buoys, other boats, birds, boys on the beach and interesting looking clouds. Janet sat in the cockpit remembering their former visit to this romantic port just a few months ago. Life had seemed simple then.

They were so happy, life was so grand. They had survived an attack by a pirate and by desperados and lived to tell the tale. Life seemed so much sweeter after escaping death. Janet was the happiest of all. Jill was stuck with school work, Harv was doing his exercises to recover use of his hand. Janet had no problems, at least that is what she thought. She didn't know then that she had something inside of her. The last time she was here they anchored off the Yacht Club and she had noticed a group of people who practiced yoga early every morning under a banyan tree across from the club but she never found the time to meet them. Janet made herself a promise that this time she would join the group while she was in port. Maybe it would bring her some inner peace or, at least, ease the wrinkles between her eyes.

The next morning she was up early and rowed herself ashore while Jill and Harv were still sleeping. A few people were stretching against some park benches, others were staring at the colors painting the eastern horizon. One older man, balding, with a straggling white beard and bushy eyebrows, dressed in sweat pants, was checking names off on a clipboard.

"Excuse me, could I join your group?" Janet couldn't believe how bold she was being. Usually she let Harv handle new people and once the ice was broken, she slowly took over. The man turned and looked at her. He looked back at his clipboard and then did a double take, dropping the clipboard to his side.

His eyes stared into hers. It seemed as if he was going to take a step back, he wobbled for a second, and then made a baby step towards her, folding his arms, holding his clipboard in front of his chest.

"We always have room. But someone like yourself, why would you want to join us?" He looked deeply into her eyes. She faced him and didn't turn or hide her eyes.

"I don't know what you mean. I have practiced yoga in front of the TV, but that is about it. What do you mean, someone like me?" He looked surprised. He saw the genuine puzzlement in her eyes. He guessed at the goodness of her soul.

"Maybe, it hasn't developed. Maybe, if you are lucky, it never will. I have met several people similar to you, in my life, people of power." He stared closely at her for a moment and then leaned forward and smelled around her head and her torso. "Your aura is strange, it is white with wide streaks of red. Very worrisome. But your aura also smells of honey, which is good." He reached out and ran his hand down six inches from the front of her body. "Your aura feels rough, like a saw blade. That is not good." It seemed for a minute he was going to take a step back.

"Stay and do yoga with us, young one. It will do you good and won't hurt you. There is a battle going on inside of you which you might not even be aware of. It, essentially, is the battle of good against evil, ying against yang, self-enlightenment versus degradation. With luck you might never have to make the choice. Try to live your life as pure as you can. Avoid vexatious and evil people, avoid also churches and self serving people. Seek to make peace with your inner self. Don't condemn that which you don't understand, also don't glory in the power you might suddenly find inside of yourself." He looked again at her hands and her solar plexus. "Churches are a great danger to you. If they discover you, they will try to tear you apart. Stay away from them." He turned and faced his students.

"Now, we must get started. After we meditate, we will perform the Salutation to the Sun." He clapped his hands once. His students aligned themselves in orderly rows and sank down into a lotus position. An hour later the practice was over and the students dispersed. The old teacher called out softly to Janet.

"If you can, try to do good." He didn't know if she heard him or not. 'At least now her aura is more white that red,' he thought to himself. He felt he should do something more, but for the life of him he couldn't think of what he could do to help.

'A shove in the right direction now might avert a great disaster,' he considered. Then he thought about her saw-blade like aura and he pulled back inside of himself, suddenly afraid. 'That is a very, very dangerous woman.'

Back on the boat, Harv was making breakfast. As Janet climbed down the companionway, he handed her a cup of fresh brewed coffee. As she took the cup his fingers lingered for a split second. They shared a secret glance of mutual devotion. Janet was filled with a sensation of contentment, of belonging, of being where she was meant to be. It seemed that during the stress of the day, their nerve's electrical impulses strayed away from the ideal for them, when they touched, they reset their bodies into the right rhythm. She thought for a time that that is why she fell in love with Harv originally, he made her feel good. Just touching him made her feel right in her body. And she did the same for him, she was sure of that. She snuck up behind him as he was cooking and gave him a quick hug. He turned, smiled down at her and kissed her, a long lingering kiss. She sat down on the settee suddenly weak at the knees and watched her husband make soft boiled eggs. He was good at it. His hand had recovered to the point where he could easily twist the teaspoon inside the eggshell to scrape out every last piece of egg. He handed her a bowl. The aroma was heavenly.

She thought about what the Sensei had said, about the aroma of her aura. She had never heard of such a thing. She knew that auras, a field of energy that surrounded living things, could be seen by some people. But smelled and touched? That sounded really weird. She wasn't at all sure she believed in any of this mumbo jumbo stuff. She was half sure people just made it up to sell magazines and books.

"Honey, do you believe in ESP and all that occult stuff?" Harv looked up from his bowl and put a finger to the side of his head. Slowly he started to tap it against his temple.

"Ah, yes. As a matter of fact, I do. Yes, indeed. Why, Madam, I do believe you have secret powers of your own." He proceeded in his best W.C. Fields voice. "Yes, I believe you could develop those powers and become the talk of the town, belle of the ball, queen of the hen house. All you need is this little bottle of elixir. Yours for the measly price of forty nine dollars. For less than your grocery bill you could become famous; appear on Oprah, be interviewed by Diane Sawyer, meet the President. Yes, indeed. You might even become the president." He had his little finger raised high in the air as he ate his last bite of eggs with a twinkle in his eyes.

"Come on, this is important. I need to know. Do you think I have something inside of me, or not?" She had her hands on her hips and was giving him *that* stare.

"Hey, baby doll. I *know* you have something inside of you. I can feel it in there every time we make love!"

"Oh, you men. Why can't you ever be serious." She suddenly looked so sad that Harv walked over and put his arms around her.

"Janet, honey. Are you worried that you caught something from that pirate? That Larry? Are you? He did some amazing things. Like how he killed that evil woman without even touching her. It was like he tore her heart right out of its moorings from ten feet away. Or how he avoided all those bullets from that midget."

"I don't know. I hope not. I hate him. I really, really hate him." As she said the words, an image of him flashed in her brain, his black on black eyes, and a chill went down her back.

"But, honey, he never raised the near dead from the doorstep of the grave. He was always talking about killing men and seducing women. Far as I can tell, you are just trying to help people."

"Yeah, but, Harv, I get this feeling that whatever might or might not be inside of me is still growing. It is still a baby. It is gathering its strength for, for I don't know what. And that is what scares me. It really scares me, Harv."

He ran his fingers through her hair, slowly, sensuously rubbed her back all the way down to her bottom. There he gave her a quick squeeze and then kissed her gently, tenderly, their lips hardly touching. He brought his right hand back to her head and held the back of her neck as he lowered her to the settee. This time he kissed her more passionately. Harder, more demanding. He forced her lips apart with his tongue. He brought his left hand up from her hips, slowly, rubbing her skin as it traveled. When he reached her breast, his fingers encircled the base of it and tenderly closed, her nipple above his fingers. His hand pulsated in unison with his tongue, searching, seeking, passionately wanting.

His left hand left her breast and slowly traveled down to raise her skirt and push her panties to one side. Suddenly he was pushing at the heavenly gate between her legs. She raised her hips and spread her legs to help him. She was squirming on the settee with desire for him. She wanted him so. She needed him so. Her life was so topsy turvy. She needed him. She needed him in the worse way. Nothing else made any sense, life was too confusing. But this, this was so elemental, so basic, she threw herself into the love making with even more abandon.

He was on top of her now, he forcing himself inside of her, pounding himself into her and she was opening herself to him and trying to match his thrusts. He was pounding so hard, it might have hurt but she loved it, she wanted it. Her brain turned off and her body took over and all her body was saying was, "Yes, Yes, Yes!" As they approached climax she hooked her heels around his legs so she could pound back in unison with him. When they came, every hair on his body came erect, every molecule of her body joined together in the same song of joy, every pore in her skin opened to experience, to breathe the completeness of their lovemaking. The whites of her eyes shone, her pupils radiated joy, her skin became soft and silky, her hair, flexible and creamy. She was sixteen again as every line left her face, if only for a half an hour.

"Quick, Honey, take my picture! Right, now!" He took a lot of pictures. He used up all the memory on their digital camera. His eyes loving her as he snapped photo after photo. Afterwards they looked at the pictures together. She looked so young, so happy. So filled with happiness, and she seemed to have a glow around her. A white glow, a white pulsating glow with just the slightest tinge of pink. Just a little tiny bit of pink.

At least there weren't any fucking caves on the limestone and sand island called Key West. None that he had found, so far. Not that he wanted to go down into the earth. He hated caves. He wanted to get on that yacht and get as far from land as he could. Damn sure, there weren't any caves on a boat. He parked his car down by the docks in an alley where no cop was likely to see it.

He had a wild ride down from Colorado traveling by night, hiding out by day. It wasn't his fault. It wasn't. That cop had just got in his face one time too many. Then busting up his equipment! It was just too much to bear. He knew them cops were scientific cops. No way they wouldn't tie him to the crime, if you could call it that. Justice is more like it. That cop got his comeuppance, his justice. And the fucker was going to have trouble convincing St. Peter of anything else.

He hid during the day in woods off dirt roads, fixing his equipment that damn cop had broke. Had to go into towns sometimes to get parts. He usually parked in Wal-Mart parking lots. Big enough to hide in, plenty of exits if he started to attract any attention. Then he hoofed it to little electronic stores. The big stores, they wanted to know stuff, wanted ID's, wanted credit cards. Fuck them.

The boat was there in the harbor of Key West. Big. He watched for a while. Other people were walking down a little ramp and getting on a little boat which took them out to the big boat. Didn't seem to be a problem. A few cops around, riding bikes. That was a new one. Wouldn't catch any of those fat cops up in Colorado in the mining towns riding bikes. Where would they put their donuts? On the handle bars?

He grabbed his tools out of the trunk and walked down to the ramp. Couple of people took his picture and waited for him to do some act or something. Disneyworld had ruined these Floridians. They expected everyone to entertain them. One cop rode by and ignored him.

The boat driver was a young good looking kid. Should have been in show business. He helped him with his tools and then drove him out to the big boat. He went up a ramp there. At the top some guy in a white uniform was waiting for him.

"Good morning, Sir. Welcome aboard the *Steel Balls*. May I please have your name?" The guy was holding a clipboard like them drill instructors used in the Marines when he was a kid. Had a pencil all ready and everything.

"Yeah, I'm the Prospector. Don't have any other name. Forgot my old one once when after a big strike I drank straight for a week."

"Yes, I have you listed here, Sir. Welcome aboard. Mr. Prospector, you have been assigned suite number 12. The Diamond Room. Do you have a companion? It is a double."

"I sleep by meself. Always have. Had a roommate once but I strangled him for snoring too much. Since then, just haven't had a hankering for much company. That a problem?" The officer stared at him for a second. He ticked something on his clipboard.

"Not at all sir. I'll just reassign you a single room which will be far more to your liking. It is next to the galley so it will be easy to get a snack should you be so inclined. There, all set. You are in room 8, Sir. Bill! Bill! Show Mr. Prospector to room eight and help him with his luggage." Bill looked at the officer with a question on his lips but he was far too well trained to verbally say anything.

"Yes, Sir. Right this way, Mr. Prospector." They went through a door and down a couple flights of stairs and to the end of a hall. There were many staterooms all with numbers. Finally they came to number eight. Bill opened the door and held back to allow the guest to enter. There wasn't enough room inside for both men.

"There you are, Sir. All nice and cozy. The facilities are right down the hall." Bill pointed. "There they are, labeled Heads. That is what we call the facilities, shipboard. There aren't any separate rooms for men and women. We all share and share alike. The bed here in the cabin folds down when you are ready to sleep. As you can see, it is quite roomy when the berth is in the up position. Any questions, Sir?"

"Doesn't seem to be enough room for my tools. Where do I keep them? I have to have them around me so I can work on 'em."

"Not a problem, Sir. Just behind that curtain is a quite roomy closet that should fit almost all of your belongings. The rest, I am sure, will stow nicely in the drawer by the desk. There, Sir. All nicely on board. I'll leave you to sort out your luggage. Dinner starts at five sharp, although if I might be so bold, the food is a lot better down here in the crew's quarters. Up there you have to wear a tie and use the right fork and everything. Down here we just stuff it in our mouths before someone else gets their hands on it. Dinner down here starts at seven and continues till we run out of food."

"Sounds like I'll be eating with the likes of you, then. I ain't ever owned a tie."

"Good choice, Sir. Show up early and we usually have a few rousing bouts of gin rummy, or the like. Spur of the moment kind of thing if you know what I mean." With that Bill closed the door and scampered back up to the main deck with a grin on his face.

The Prospector knew it would happen. He had ended up in the closest thing this ship had to a cave. It was his fate in life. He guessed he better get used to it. They would be sending him to hell for all the bad he had done in his life. No doubt about that. And his hell would be him trapped in a cave that was falling on top of him. And that was God's truth.

He looked up at the ceiling nervously. It looked strong enough, but you could never tell. You just could never tell. He looked in his closet and found a broom. He grabbed it and gave the ceiling a few experimental pokes. Seemed strong enough.

He sorted out his tools. From long experience he disassembled a few crucial parts of each machine. They wouldn't work till he said they would work. That was just the way it always was and always would be.

After he had stowed his belongings, taken a shower in the surprisingly clean and spacious heads, he set out to explore the ship, this cave system he was in. Best to know the fastest way out in case of a cave in. Twenty feet down the hall he found the mess. He stuck his head in and was awarded with a couple of smiles and a dish of crepes suzette shoved in his direction. He grabbed one and nibbled at it as he continued down the hall. Food was Ok, he guessed, but you wouldn't want to have to live on it. No guts to it. All sugar and spice and air. No meat, no potatoes, no guts. He dumped the rest into a handy trash can as he passed it and turned into another door and was stunned into such a joy. A joy he had rarely experienced in his life.

He was in the engine room. The main engines were quiet. They were asleep. But over in the corner a smaller engine was purring like a cat. No, a cat made more noise. It was like an elemental force of nature. Having once heard it, he couldn't understand why that sound wasn't in every house, every store, every town, city, nation on earth. It seemed to him that it was the sound of the human race. Speech, the language, the writing that humans so prided themselves on was nothing to this, this harmony. Nothing to this joy of purpose. Nothing to this intention just waiting to be put in action.

The place was immaculate. He had marveled at the cleanliness of the upper decks as he walked up the ramp. The white sparkling paint, the gleaming varnish, the mirror like windows, were filthy compared to this, this, paradise. He still stood in the doorway, the hatch he remembered to call it, when a white haired man in blue jeans and a greasy tee shirt sidled up to him.

"Ain't no passengers allowed in my engine room, get out." He walked up closer and stared at him, eyeball to eyeball.

"I ain't no passenger."

"Bilge water. You sure ain't no crew. Where's your fancy shirt with your name on it all pretty like? You is a passenger. Get out of my engine room.

"Your generator has a main bearing that is getting ready to fail. I can hear it squeaking from here."

"Bilge water. That baby is running as sweet as a virgin. As it should be. Never been touched by any man 'cept me, and I always touched her proper like. Like a lady.

"Well, Ok. Thought I heard something but now I don't. Sorry, I just signed on the ship and no doubt my hearing is playing up."

"Where they got you, swabbing the windows?

"Don't rightly know. Put me right next to the galley down here so I don't rightly know. I thought it was going to be a free ride, but nothing ever came free to me my whole life. Why should this be any different? Looks like I'll be working for my passage."

"Ah, I understand. You be one of those new people, the ones going down for the gold on that island. Yeah, don't be surprised. We hear everything down here on the lower decks. Us'n know stuff before the captain hisself knows it, that's the bloody truth. I heard they was putting you types up in the fancy rooms. Must a run out of cabins. Well, no matter, you be having hell of a better ride down here. Lower you go in a ship, better the ride. Stands to reason. Less motion. Best place is right here next to the engines. They gives the best spot to the engines. Build the boat around them. And rightly so. She's just a hulk without them engines."

"So where will I be working? Who do I ask? This is the first ocean going boat I have ever been on. I don't know nothing."

"You'se knows enough to listen for a bearing even though you was wrong. You can work here with us'n. We might have to work hard but we have a lot of fun too, 'cay?"

He stuck his hand out and shook the engineer's paw. Both men tried for a bone crusher, but it was a tie. With a pair of smiles, they walked over to the galley for coffee and a big chunk of cherry pie.

The train didn't go as far as Key West. The Silver Meteor they had boarded in DC stopped at Miami and they were met there by a stretch limo. Dustin and the two Marys were whisked down the Keys in perfect comfort. Mary One, as he now thought of her, sat in front with the driver which greatly simplified things for Dustin. He never expected that having two women interested in him would be so much trouble. His Mary, Mary Two, was still being frosty with him. In desperation he searched the car. He quickly found the hidden bar and poured them both a shot of Funador. Small men shouldn't drink, at least not to excess. They don't have the body mass to absorb the alcohol. It wasn't long before Dustin was showing signs of inebriation. He heard himself start to slur his words and he was aghast. This wasn't him. What was happening to him? And it didn't seem to be helping with Mary either. The alcohol didn't seem to affect her and she was now looking somewhat superior, looking down at him. Sometimes his brain was quiet. It didn't offer any advice. He had to ask.

'What is wrong with this situation,' he thought. The answer, as always came in milliseconds.

'You are acting defensive and you have allowed a high level of alcohol to enter our blood stream.' His brain was right, as always. How un-intelligent of him to act defensive. You would think he would know better. He mused for a minute on how to proceed.

"Mary, find your pad and prepare to take dictation." He didn't look over at her. Instead he closed his eyes and concentrated on metabolizing the alcohol in his blood. It wasn't difficult to do. He had learned the trick as an undergraduate attending early morning lectures after all night orgies of drinking and sex. This was during one of his unsuccessful explorations into the roots of happiness. He slightly increased his abdominal breathing, flexed the muscles in the arms and thighs, and focused his eyes, while closed, as far distant as he could. He had learned by trial and error to avoid breathing too hard to avoid over oxidizing the blood entering his liver and unbalancing the ADh and NAD ratio.

Mary suddenly paled when Dustin spoke to her. What had she been doing? She was very lucky to be on this trip. If her boss wanted to talk or do anything to a stranger, that was his business. He was one of the smartest men in the world. Everyone in the department said so. Here she was, a lowly glorified lab tech, acting like a wife. How asinine of her. What had come over her? This was a chance of a lifetime.

"Don't blow it, Mary." She mumbled to herself, giving the tip of her tongue a quick nip, just to remind herself.

"Are you ready, Mary?" Mary looked over at him quickly. He was just sitting there with his eyes closed. She thought that he had been getting a bit smashed. He didn't look as if the drinks had affected him at all, right now.

"Yes, Sir. Ready." She had wanted to add, ready for you, but lacked the nerve.

"I wish to work on fitness reports. Inscribe. Joe McDonald." He felt quite a bit of nervousness from Mary and thought with satisfaction that, yes, he could detect emotions and thus perhaps thoughts from another person.

"Joe is an excellent employee. He is steady in the performance of his duties, he notices developing situations before they turn into problems and he always finishes his assignments on time. However, he does take excessively long breaks and thus does tend to be late for meetings and throws some of his work onto the backs of his fellow workers." Dustin opened his eyes to just a slit and closely observed Mary. Yes, his mind was right. She was getting more and more nervous and now she was definitely getting a bit pale.

"Joe McDonald is a good employee to have while the money is flowing from the endowment mother lode, but when times become more difficult, he will have to be let go." Definitely pale and now with a few lines between her eyes and at the corners of her mouth.

"Alice Rogers. Miss Rogers is a joy to have on board. She works hard and is always on time. She does first class work and needs little if any supervision. As soon as a opening develops, Miss Rogers would be an excellent person to promote."

Mary was pushing hard on her pad with her ball point pen. Alice was nominally under her level. While she didn't report to her, Alice seemed to realize that Mary was closer to Dr. Horner than she was and usually deferential to her.

Dustin droned on going through all the employees of the department, except for one. She hesitated to point this out. However the stress of not knowing finally got too much for her.

"Dr. Horner, how about me? Are you going to do a fitness report on me, Sir?" As Mary watched he opened his eyes and looked at her kindly. She again realized what a nice guy he was, even though he was her boss.

"I couldn't ask you to inscribe your own report, Mary. That would be neither proper or ethical." He closed his eyes again.

"But, Doctor, I have to know. What do you think of me. How do you view me as an employee, as a worker, as a, a, how do you see me as a person. Please tell me, please."

"Really, Mary. I understand your reasoning, however, I believe that would not be beneficial to our working relationship. But if you wish, I will consider your request for a few days and let you know then what my decision will be.

"Now, Mary. Since you brought up the subject, we have to consider our working relationship aboard the ship. There will be quite a lot of work to accomplish. I have no idea of the terrain or conditions of the island we will be forced to work in, but it is essential that you take complete field notes of every test and trial. Without field notes, we will not be able to defend the paper we will eventually write. Can I count on your total cooperation?"

"Oh, yes, Doctor! I will be at your side every minute of every day! I will always be ready to record."

"Remember, Mary, even if you rewrite your notes into a clean copy, you must keep your field notes in their original condition. Only the field notes have legal credibility."

"No problem, Doctor."

"I can tell you all about the terrain you will be working in, if you are interested." Mary One had turned around in the front seat and was looking at both of them with a smile that had components of a sneer in it. Without waiting for an answer, she continued.

"The island is honey combed with caves. If fact one story is that the ancient Incas knew of the island and used its many caves for a burial site for the high born. It seems that even back then, grave robbing was a national sport and they used the island as a secret graveyard.

"I know what you are going to say, that how could the Incas sail over so many hundreds of miles. But remember Thor Heyerdahl and his log raft, Kon Tiki. His theory was that the Incas made return trips to what is now French Polynesia. That amounts to over four thousand miles. Cocos Island is less than 700 miles from Peru, most of it following the mighty Humboldt current.

"Anyway, the island we are going to, Cocos Island, is on the Pacific Rim of Fire and is subject to many earthquakes. There is even an underwater volcano nearby. The terrain will be difficult. What flat land there is on the island is covered with the densest jungle imaginable. However, our crew on the boat will attempt to clear the areas for the scientists' instruments. Bear in mind, you are not the only scientist on the expedition."

"That will be very satisfactory." To himself, Dustin thought, other scientists? Maybe making friends with the crew and with Mary One would ensure that his desires and demands came first.

"Yes, I'm sure it will be. Which scientist gets helped first is another question. I am sure you have read your contract well and know that your
reimbursement is based on the amount of artifacts you manage to locate. And the more successful you are, the more help you might receive from the crew."

“I realize all of that. However, I must have a decent test for my sonic microwave. My needs must be met first. I believe I made that clear in previously correspondence.”

“You did request that, yes. We didn’t agree your needs would come before anyone else's.” Mary One sat back and looked very self satisfied. The two in the back seat were less content.

“Mary,” Dustin whispered, “I have a new plan. Why don’t you make friends with her.” He waggled his head towards the front seat.

“Me? It is you she likes, Boss. I think she hates me. You were the one getting the neck massage.” She looked at Dustin out of the corners of her eyes.

“Mary, that isn’t showing the team spirit. You do remember that you have a performance report coming up, don’t you. What would you like it to read? Always tries to help or tries to get others to do her work.” Mary Two looked cowed, she rubbed her hands together and shoved them between her blue jeaned thighs.

“Ok, Doctor. You win.” Her voice became smaller and smaller. “I will do anything I can to help. Of course I will. You have my fullest cooperation.”

Dustin reached over and patted Mary’s thighs in support. And then he left his left hand on her right leg, fingers angled down between them. He squeezed her leg a couple of times, but didn’t remove his hand. Mary closed her eyes and pretended she was somewhere else. Somewhere quiet and serene, and with no men. Her eyes were still closed when Mary One turned her head slightly and smirked at her. She ignored Dustin as a pink tongue darted from between her lips, formed a u shape, then disappeared. She turned slightly and gave Dustin a bored look and closed her eyes.

When the limo reached the west docks of Key West, Mary One jumped out of the car and hurried down to the shore boat. Dustin supervised the removal of his instruments and their transport down to the shore boat’s dock. Mary Two stared at the crowds on the sea wall for a few minutes and then shook herself as the shore boat returned and helped load their gear.

At the ship, crew took their equipment on board as Dustin and Mary Two climbed the gangway and met the officer at its head.

“Dr. Horner and assistant, I presume?” The officer had a slight smile on his face, whether from choice of words or in greeting, it was difficult to say.

“Yes, we are. And to whom am I speaking?” Dustin was picky about proper address in his classrooms and saw no reason to be less picky in the broader world.

"I am the First Officer, Charlie Ross." He put out his open hand and accepted Dustin's rather limp handshake. "Dr. Horner we have placed you in our best accommodation, the Kennedy Room, as we call it. Mr. James, here, will guide you there. Let me know if there is anything we can do for you."

The Kennedy Room was exceptional. It would have been the penthouse in any hotel in the world. The bed was a heart-shaped love nest with 800 count satin sheets, the dresser was a tonshu, a relic of pre-Perry Japan that a bride's brothers carried, filled with her possessions, into her new husband's house. The bathroom had gold faucets and a diaphanous silk shower curtain. Mary gave out a little shriek of delight and threw herself onto the bed throwing her arms and legs wide on the bed's wide expanse and then realized that there was only one bed in the room. She sat up suddenly.

"I thought there was going to be bunk beds or something. Didn't you say that, Dustin?"

"I did, Mary. I did. That's what I was told. It looks like we have been upgraded. I wonder who didn't make the boat, The President?" He ran his hand along the wood of the tonshu. "Mary, this tonshu dates from before the birth of Christ! This is the most amazing room I have ever been in." He looked away from Mary. "Too bad we will have to give it up."

"Give it up? Oh, yes, the bed. Yes, you are right. It is too bad. It is such an amazing room. Look at this lamp, I would swear that the base is a Grecian urn from the fourth century BC."

"Yes, it is a shame." Dustin looked at Mary out of the corners of his eyes. "Unless we could somehow share the bed? Draw a line down the middle of it. A great wall of China, or something."

"Do you think we could? We are after all mature, disciplined adults, fully capable of operating under every conceivable conditions. Doctor, I for one would be more that willing to give it a try."

"All right, lets entertain the proposition. Before we get settled, we better give it a try. Here, this will be my side of the bed. It is closer to the door, which is a man's proper side. That is your side. Let's see if there is enough room." They both lay on the bed, rather stiffly. Mary twisted
and turned, trying to get comfortable. She kicked off her shoes, but still fidgeted.

"This is silly, Dustin. Here we are in our street clothes. This is not a valid test. We should don our sleeping attire and pretend it is night. That will establish whether this arrangement will work out."

"You are right, Mary. You may have the bathroom to change in, while I will shift my clothes out here."

"Yes, Doctor, whatever you say." She grabbed her small overnight emergency bag and hurried into the bathroom. She quickly stripped down and took a quick shower spending more attention than usual on her armpits and between her legs. She dried herself off with an immense Turkish towel and was about to search for her little bottle of perfume an old boyfriend gave her for Christmas ten years ago when on a hunch she opened the medicine cabinet behind the mirror. The cabinet was loaded with every perfume made by man. She held herself back from screaming in delight as she liberally dabbed on a fortune's worth of Chanel No. 5 Reserve.

She looked at her farmer john pajamas and shook her head. This was the time for putting her best foot forward. Or her best something. She reached deeper into her bag and pulled out a baby doll negligee. As she slipped it over her head, her breathing became deeper and her pulse went up. Her cheeks reddened noticeably. She brushed her hair as fast as she could. She didn't want Dustin to be waiting. She sang to herself, quietly, as she brushed. Mrs. Horner. Mrs. Dustin Horner. Mary Horner, wife of the brilliant Dr. Horner of UCSD. The hell with that Mary One or what ever her name was. She knew she was after her Dustin. Well, if it was to be war, it was time to get fighting. Her eyes sparkled.

Dustin striped down to his BVDs. He usually slept naked. Like his hero, Thomas Edison. He put his thumbs into the waist and then stopped undecided. He liked Mary, true. But afterwards, he would have to work with her, too. What happened today might permanently change their relationship. But on the other hand, he always tried to recreate accurate conditions in any tests he preformed. If he slept naked, he should sleep naked now, or otherwise the test would be inadequate. He hated scientist who fudged their data. Who worked around corners trying to skew the results. With a look of determination he dropped his drawers and pulled back the covers of the bed. He just happened to glance over and see an image in a full length mirror across the room. Could that be him? That old man with the beer belly? What had happened to his muscles? He waved at himself just to be sure. Yes, it was him. As if there was any doubt. Suddenly he felt very foolish. What woman would want an old wreck like what he had turned into? He looked at his BVDs. A good scientist always wore protective clothing when undertaking unusual or dangerous experiments. With a sigh, he slipped his underwear back on.

It was a beautiful bed. The mattress was of goose down as were the pillows. He sank into the bed, the feathers supporting every part of his body independently. Every worry he had, escaped him in a burst of pure relaxation. He closed his eyes and let out a long sigh of enjoyment, only to open them a second later as the newly installed bathroom door opened and a vision of beauty entered his room.

Her bed clothes, if you could call them that, hid nothing. In fact, instead of hiding, they emphasized certain parts of her body that normally were hidden away. An aroma wafted through the air, carried by the slight breeze of the air-conditioning. Her blond hair glowed like it was made of thin strands of gold, her hands, she carried relaxed at her side in perfect self confidence. Her eyes sparkled with life and joy. Slowly she approached the bed and waited for him to fold back the covers for her.

She didn't lay down on the bed, she didn't jump in, she levitated in awesome grace and style and floated onto the mattress as if she was as light as a feather. He stared at her in disbelief.

"Mary?" His mouth stayed open on the last letter of the y sound and he forgot to close his lips. A slight drip of saliva threatened to drool down from a corner of his lips. "Mary? Is that you?" Mary magically rose to a sitting position without using her arms. She sat cross-legged facing him.

"Of course, it is, Dustin. What? You liked me better in denim jeans?" Her face rose in question but her eyes radiated joy and desire in equal amounts.

"I do, but I have never seen anyone, I have never seen you look so beautiful, so incredible, so desirable. It is amazing!" He ran his hand over his beer belly. "You are very beautiful," he mumbled a little more subdued.

"You just haven't seen the real me. I like to hide myself at work as who needs a pack of wolves following me around." Mary started to blush. She had never thought of herself as beautiful. Not really. She had always worked more on her studies than on her face. Sure, she went to the gym, but more out of a sense of commitment to her heart and circulatory system than of improving her body's shape. "Besides, I am employed to work, not to decorate the office." But, on the other hand, if Dustin thought she was beautiful, she wasn't going to dissuade him. All's fair in love and war. Especially war with that woman who dared to call her Mary Two. The nerve, the bloody nerve of that woman! If there were to be numbers, she should be One!

"Well, whatever, you are downright gorgeous. Really!" Mary's face turned a brighter shade of red and she pulled the sheet up to her chin.

"You are very handsome yourself, Doctor. Don't you know that the secretaries of the university run a poll every year and you have come in first three years running as the 'Best Man to Settle Down With?' Its true!"

“Yes, however I am afraid that I don’t have the body of some of the younger professors. It seems I have been spending too much time in the lab instead of in the gym. I really don’t think we have to erect a Great Wall of China in the middle of the bed. You are quite safe with me, young lady. Quite safe.” The last words were so sad that Mary reached out and touched his shoulder, just to commiserate with him. He didn’t react, but just lay there seemingly feeling sorry for himself.

Emboldened she scooted closer to him. He was a great boss, she thought. A really nice guy. He had always been kind to her. He always got her raises and never complained when she needed a day off. Poor old guy. He looked so sad. Kind of like a cat that had fallen in the river. Her hand started to rub his shoulder. She hadn’t directed it to do anything. Her hand seemed to have developed a mind of its own. Dustin didn’t react. He really was very sad.

“Roll over and I will rub your back.” Did she just say that out loud? It must have been her. There wasn’t anyone else in the room. She couldn’t believe how forward she was. Either way, Dustin rolled over and she was committed now. She started on his neck and worked her way out towards his shoulders. He was very tense. He had a massive knot just to the left of his spine in the thoracic region. As she massaged it she felt it relax, and as the tension left his neck, his whole body seemed to give a sigh of relaxation. A little thrill surged through her body. She had made a difference! Without thinking about it, she scooted over and spooned his back. As soon as she did it she was shocked at herself. How could she? How brazen! What a hussy! But she couldn’t pull back now. He would think she was repelled. That she didn’t like him. It wasn’t true. She did like him. He was a really nice guy. And he seemed so sad, right now.

After a few minutes, her top arm seemed to be falling asleep. She had to move it. It was so uncomfortable. Massaging was hard work. So she eased it over his body and rested her palm against his chest. She could feel his heart beat through her palm. She felt his top hand move over and rested on top of her hip. Of course, his arm must have been falling asleep also. With a shock, she realized that her palm was over Dustin’s nipple. Did men’s nipples react to warmth and pressure also? It seemed not, as Dustin didn’t seem upset at the presence of her hand. In fact, she felt his hand making little circles on her hip, his hand gliding easily on the silky material of her negligee. His fingers started to burn her skin. Or her skin was reacting to his fingers. It felt so good, so exciting! She felt a little rumble down in her nether regions and she was suddenly more aware of her breasts. They seemed fuller and more tingly somehow.

She held her breath a little and felt her hand head south over his belly. He did have a cute little belly. She couldn't believe how forward she was behaving, but it seemed right somehow. After all, the truth was that the human race would die out if women didn't keep things moving. Emboldened she continued the motion of her hand. It ran into something sooner than she thought. Something proud and ready for her. Her hand grasped it, adoringly, through his underwear and slowly stroked it. It got even larger. It was so big!

Slowly he rolled over and faced her. Gradually, he opened his eyes. They were the most beautiful color of blue. The iris had little sparkles of silver embedded between different colors from aqua to marine blue to almost black. She thought she could look into his eyes forever. She still held him in her hand. It was throbbing ever so slightly. She slipped her hand into his shorts and held him flesh against flesh. She felt her heart beat increase and her skin felt like it was alive and tingling. She felt the heat of him and the throbbing was much more intense.

His hand ran from her hip up towards her breast. She somehow knew just where his hand was heading before it got past her waist. Should she push him away? Stop his hand with a gentle little spank? But she would have to let go of him down there if she wanted to repel him. And she didn't. She just didn't. She liked the idea of him touching her, exploring her body. She knew that he might feel she was less than a lady if he allowed him to touch her, but just right now she just didn't care. She wanted him to touch her. She wanted to be his, his to do whatever he wanted. To take and to enjoy, to use and to make a baby.

A baby? She couldn't have a baby now. Her life was already too complicated. She didn't have time for half the things she wanted to accomplish in her life. A baby? No!

She had been taking her birth control pills regularly. That should be enough, she hoped. They weren't foolproof, though. She was just too busy to have a baby.

"Dustin, do you have protection?" Her face was as red as his tongue. She watched it as he opened his mouth and talked. It was a really cute tongue. Long and slender. When he said the 'th' sound it really stuck out of his mouth. He had finished talking. She looked at him in confusion. But it was okay. He was taking something out of his wallet. Ripping it open. He took off his underwear and was handing the open package to her. He wanted her to put it on him! How could she? What would he think?

He was talking again. She had no idea what he was saying but the sound of his words and the tone of his voice calmed her somehow. She pulled out this rubbery thing from the package and rose to her knees. His organ was standing straight upright now. Carefully she laid the rubber on top of him and smoothed the edges down over his length. She didn't want to hurt him. She glanced at his face. It wasn't hurting him. He was staring at her negligee, at her chest, at her legs, at her body.

His hands suddenly were all over her. Touching her, pulling at her clothes, he couldn't find the snap holding the back together so he took it in both hands and tore her negligee off of her. She was naked before him, totally naked. She put one arm over her breasts and raised one leg over the other to hide herself from his eyes, his now burning eyes. Suddenly she was very, very scared. What was going to happen to her? Who knew what he might do? His hands took her arms and pulled them apart and his hands pressed her wrists into the mattress on either side of her. Frightened, she squirmed trying to free herself as he lowered his head to one breast. He took her nipple into his mouth and was sucking at it. No, she didn't want a baby, especially a huge one like Dustin! But then, all of a sudden, it started to feel good. She relaxed slightly and when he forced a knee between her legs she hardly resisted.

He was kissing her on the lips now and it was heavenly. He had to love her, no one could kiss so well unless they were in love. Then he was pushing between her legs, pushing and thrusting, and suddenly he was inside of her! It hurt for a fraction of a second and then her head fell back as if her neck wasn't strong enough to hold it up. She felt her legs spread apart to make room for him and her now free arms held his back. Her breathing was coming faster now, she felt her fingernails scratching his back from his butt to his neck and she heard a low moaning. With a start she realized it was coming from her! She didn't care what he did now. He could do anything to her. Just don't let it stop. He was thrusting harder and harder into her and she felt her hips meeting each thrust with an equal or greater force.

She felt her heart racing, her fingernails dug deep into his back, her teeth found a muscle in his neck and bit deep into it, she felt her body thrusting against him with a force she didn't know she possessed, harder and harder and harder. She screamed. A low scream raising slowly, gaining strength and volume, her teeth released their hold on his neck and she fell back, his blood red on her teeth, her neck exposed to him and at his mercy, she screamed until there wasn't an atom of air left in her lungs.

After, she held him, as he held her, tightly entwined. She felt him fall asleep first and she wasn't far behind. It was a sleep of total relaxation, a rejuvenating sleep, as they slept together and shared each others breath.

Hawk and Mary One stood side by side in the Owner's Stateroom and watched the TV screen. As Dustin and Mary's cries of joy tinnily radiated from the speaker, Hawk reached out and turned off the sound.

"I believe you may proceed with the plan."

"Yes, Sir. Right away, Sir." She reached out a hand towards Hawk but he ignored her, watching instead the woman on the little screen. She stood for a moment in indecision.

"Now, damn it." Quickly she fled out the door.

Robyn couldn't decide how to get on board the *Steel Balls*. She thought about throwing herself at the good looking deck hand who drove the shore boat. Strip herself naked, drape herself all over him, put various parts of his body in her mouth and suck for all she was worth, to do whatever it took. Forget pride, just do it. But she didn't think it would work. She had watched as other people boarded the boat. They had to be vetted by an officer at the top of the gang plank. And it looked like he was a real stick in the mud. Shit.

She took out her binoculars that she had gotten cheap-just wait till the clerk turned his head-and scanned the ship yet again. They always seemed to be an officer on an upper deck, and he was always watching. A big ape like sailor was usually walking around directing ten or so sailors washing windows, renewing the already gleaming paintwork, scrubbing the waterline from a window washers derrick.

Derrick! She looked with greater care. Yes, it went up and down with controls on the little cage itself. If she could get on that and somehow find a place to hide. She wouldn't have to hide long, just a few days, just enough so it was too far for them to turn back and dump her thieving ass off the transom in Key West. A boat that size, there must be hundreds of places to hide. How would they know she was there?

She looked again at the anchor chain. It looked perfect, but unlike the derrick she would have to climb the chain herself. Again for the tenth time that day she hung her body from the hanger rack in an empty closet. Pull ups are difficult for girls to perform, partially because they hadn't been required to perform them from the third grade onwards and her silly D cups kept getting in the way. Sometimes she wondered why less endowed women wanted bigger boobs. Big breasts were a hassle, except for attracting men. She was determined to improve her pull-ups in just a couple of days. She had a head start. In prison, bored with nothing else to do, she lifted weights and played at pull ups. The way she figured it, someday she might have to climb up the outside of a apartment building, so she better be prepared.

The good part of using the anchor chain was that it was hidden from the bridge deck by the flare of the bow. Especially now, as she watched them put away the window cleaner's derrick at the end of the day. It looked like it was going to be the chain.

She separated her different clothes, her cameras, her money, her burglar tools and double bagged them in zip locks. Whatever she took would have to be pulled behind her as she swam and then pulled up to deck level by a cord after she somehow made the climb herself, and then hidden somewhere, she didn't know where, before she was discovered. If this was a mob operation, they would have all the schematics of the ship with all the good hidey-holes circled in red. But the last thing in the world she wanted to do was to get involved with those maniacs again. Whatever she did, she would have to do it all by herself. And it looked like they were getting ready to leave. Load after load of groceries had been going on board for the last day and a half. She decided, tonight was C day or rather night. Chain Night.

She looked at her watch. It was about time to change rooms. She had walked into a hotel with a good view of the ship at ten o'clock this morning, went to the top floor and found a room with a key in the lock. The previous occupants had left and had left the key for the maid. She took the key and placed the 'do not disturb sign' on the door knob. About a hour later a knock rattled the door. She pitched her voice as high as it would go,

"I'm not decent, come back later." They never came back. Maids would use any excuse to avoid cleaning a room, to leave it for the night crew to do. Soon though, the front desk would want to rent the room and wonder where the key was. She could lie again, but it was better to not even be there.

She went out on the balcony and gazed at the gap between her railing and the balcony next door. Looked OK. Maybe four feet. She had spent quite some time measuring her step length on flat ground. She found that if she took a giant step her reach was three feet, without jumping. All she had to do was take a step and jump one foot across to make it. She made a few practice jumps inside the room, and then resolutely went out and stood on the edge of the handrail of the balcony. It was a long way down to the ground. She tried not to look down. It was a long, long way down. She couldn't stay up there long. Someone would see her, think she was committing suicide and call the cops and trouble. She ignored the height, focused on the far balcony railing, took a big breath, a giant step with her left foot and made a little jump with her right, as if she were playing hop scotch on a playground. In the air, her heart made a little lurch, trying to help her across, no doubt.

She landed perfectly and immediately fell to the far balcony floor, gasping and panting for air. She berated herself. She had expended almost no energy, no reason to get so excited. She stood up and tried the sliding door and cursed. Some damn person had locked it. What? They thought someone would climb up here and steal their worthless sheets and towels? Bummer. She looked carefully around the property. No one seemed to be looking in her direction. She pulled out a roll of masking tape and applied five parallel rows of tape shoulder high three feet apart on the sliding door. She braced her feet, placed her hands against the tape and pushed her hands against the glass and lifted the heavy door up a half of an inch with the friction of her hands against the tape. When she felt the bottom rollers leave their track, she walked sideways, towards the other door, and felt the lock slip out of its catch. They used simple hook locks on these doors. You would think they would know better. She eased the door down onto the inside of the frame, made sure it wasn't going to fall and make an enormous sound, dashed inside, opened the door to the hall and quickly moved her few possessions into her new abode. Just in time, too. Not even an hour later she heard a bell boy open the room next door with a master key and grunt in displeasure on finding it un-serviced.

Robyn enjoyed a long shower and used all the towels. Boy, was some maid going to get in trouble! As a recompense for the maid, she left all her clothing that she wouldn't need for her next adventure. It might be used, but it was high quality stuff. She only took from the very best. And why not. It was the same penalty to shoplift at Saks, Fifth Avenue as it was to steal from the local Goodwill. She took out her binoculars and continued her surveillance of the *Steel Balls* now from a slightly different angle.

It was four PM and time to get out. It wouldn't be long before her new room was rented. The top floors were always rented out last, just in case some rich, high tipper suddenly appeared and wanted the entire floor or just a couple of suites. It didn't do to turn away the high and mighty who might have the ear of the owners. She walked right out the front doors, her head high and proud. It never did to sneak around. If you did everyone would think you were a sneak! If you acted like you owned the place, everyone would think you might, and leave you alone.

She found a nice restaurant and ordered the best on the menu. Lobster de Diablo, sweet rice sprinkled with real saffron, snap beans smothered in bacon and goat cheese. She didn't drink any alcohol. She would have to be at the top of her game tonight. The last thing she needed was a high that would make her think she was safe when she still wasn't. It wasn't the cops she worried about. Anytime someone was picked up by the police, the mafia learned about it within hours. For her, being arrested would lead to instantly being bailed out by the mob and then a very messy, painful, ugly death.

When she finished her meal, she headed for the Ladies leaving her purse on the table. It was empty, except for a beautifully penned thank you card. She picked up purses for a dollar a piece at the American Legion. She could have bought them from Goodwill, but she wanted to help out the troops. It was the least she could do. They were fighting to keep her lifestyle possible. Her criminal lifestyle.

People always wondered why the American justice system was light on crime. Or so they thought. The truth is, who was innocent? Let the man without sin cast the first stone as some innocent once said. Americans were bred to be an aggressive, pioneering race. People that didn't let a little thing like Indian ownership of land stop them from doing what they wished, taking what land they wanted. Who hasn't run a red light? Who didn't glance at another's exam paper, if you found a coin on the sidewalk
did you bring it to the police, or just pocket it? It wasn't yours. Finders keepers, losers weepers is a slogan for thieves. Who hasn't denied responsibility for an error at work? Who hasn't dreamed of slugging that big bully? Isn't thought just as evil as deed? The commandment is don't covet thy neighbor's wife. It isn't don't screw thy neighbor's wife. All Americans are half wild, the ones that get caught, the unsuccessful ones, are labeled criminals. She shook her head. This wasn't the right time to think about philosophy. It was the time for climbing chains.

She slipped into the water just after one in the morning and quietly breaststroked her way out to the ship. It was still lit up like a Christmas tree, but she couldn't see anyone walking around on deck. When she reached the chain, she didn't waste any time. She climbed up hand over hand, squeezing the chain between her thighs to rest. At the top, the chain went through a hole in the side of the hull which still soared above her. The hole was too small to crawl through and there was still four feet to the top of the hull which turned outwards above her. She reached up, her hand was not even close.

She slowly worked her way up the chain, balancing herself, until her body was above the hole and only her legs twisted around the chain were holding her. She squeezed her thighs as tight as she could. She imagined she had one of those mafia torpedoes between her legs and she was squishing the guts out of him. Thighs holding her in place, she reached up and out, backwards. She could hear her spine crack with the pressure and she knew she would have huge bruises where the chain links dug into her inner thighs' skin. Her fingertips just reached the cap rail, just barely curled over the top. The wood was so heavily varnished that it felt as slippery as glass. She took a big breath, let go with her legs and hung for a second by her finger tips. Slowly, very slowly she lifted herself up. She got her palms up and over the rail. She managed to get her head up to the rail when her strength started to abandon her and her tits were in the way again. Tears of frustration leaked down her cheeks. She was so close. Finally she reached out and chomped down on the wood rail with every tooth she had. Chomped hard. She felt her teeth penetrate the wood. She tasted the varnish flakes on her tongue as she bit even harder. She let go with one hand and curled it over the rail feeling for something, anything to hold on to. Her hand found a little bolt, a very small bolt, she grabbed hold of it desperately, as she seemed to feel her teeth start to pull out from her head. Quickly her other hand found something more substantial, a cleat or something, and she pulled herself over the rail.

She lay there for a moment, totally exhausted. She felt her mouth to make sure her teeth were still where they belonged. Her right hand was curled into a claw where it had grabbed the bolt and she couldn't open her fingers. Then she looked up at the bridge deck and felt how very exposed she was. She jumped to her feet and crawled over to the superstructure before she pulled up her line and her supplies. She looked around for a hiding place and for the first time she realized that she might have bitten off more than she could chew. The boat was lit with hundreds of lights, was painted pure white and there wasn't a dark corner to hide anywhere. She felt like a bug under a microscope. She was in a lot of trouble.

Honey, remember that sailor on the white ketch we met in Acapulco? The one with the eye patch? Remember? He said we were supposed to stay just a half a mile or closer to the shore while crossing the Tehuantepec. Don't you think we should be closer to shore?"

"I don't know, Janet. Look, there is the beach. We can see it. If the wind picks up, then we can move closer to shore. It isn't far. It won't take long. Can you see the beach?"

"Yes, but he said the wind was so fierce and so strong that if we were over a mile out we wouldn't be able to get back to the beach. That our engine was an auxiliary motor. That it couldn't drive the boat against such winds and seas. Can't we move just a little closer to the shore, please, honey? Please, Sir Honey? Please, you big sexy hunk?"

"Well, if you put it that way, okay, just a bit closer." He swung the wheel to port and watched as the binnacle compass card swung in the opposite direction. He eyed the shore. It wasn't far. Two or three miles, at the most. He glanced at the chart. He was right on course. He was taking a slight short cut across the top of the big bay. Yes, if you believed all the doom and gloom people he was taking a chance, but he was also saving an hour. The sooner he was across this bay the happier he and his crew would be. Or at least half of his crew.

"Seagull in sight, Sir Daddy, bearing over there on the starboard side about halfway up the middle, kind of. He is gaining on us, Captain. Should I blow him out of the water?"

"Blow away, sailor." Jill loaded her sling shot with another spit ball which when fired, traveled about five feet before it fell in disgrace to the deck. Lack of success had no effect on the enthusiasm of the younger member of his stalwart crew. "Enemy making maneuvers, Sir. Tricky, this one. Reloading." The deck was peppered with little pieces of paper. Harv just hoped that it wasn't Jill's algebra homework. Janet poked her head up the companionway.

"Look, Harv. Look at this cruising guide. It also says to keep within one mile of the land. Actually, it recommends to keep one foot on the beach, whatever that means. Don't you think we should be closer, Honey?"

"Alright, Babe, if it makes you feel better." Harv turned the wheel a tiny bit more towards the beach. He looked at his GPS. His Global Positioning Satellite System. He called it the Black Box. It used satellites in space to triangulate his position here on earth. These days, it had replaced the sextants of old time sailors, the ones from the last millennium. Every boat on the seven seas carried a GPS. Harv had two. The extra one Janet had bought for him, just in case, she had said.

The beach was now a little closer and he could see Janet relax slightly, but he could tell she was still apprehensive, not that she would ever admit it. She believed in keeping her inner fears to herself, except, it seemed, for the Tehuantepec. Not that he could blame her. In every port they anchored in the last year while they sailed south, sailors had told horror stories of this big bay. Especially those who never had been south of Acapulco. But Janet had handled their drivel with the calm tranquility that seemed to mark her personality in the last few months. He looked at her now as she handed him up some cheese and crackers.

"You know, Janet, you really are calmer these days. When we first got married you flew off the handle for the smallest things. Now it is like you are all grown up or something. Know what I am saying?"

From up above, on the spreaders, came a quiet whisper.

"Watch out for squalls."

"Listen, Buster, what exactly are you saying? You didn't like the way I was back then? I guess you can damn well make your own dinner. And if you don't get this boat closer to that damn shore, you will be finding your own berth tonight, because as sure as hell is hot, you won't be sleeping in mine!" Janet stormed down below. He could hear her opening and slamming drawers in the galley.

"Dad, when are you ever going to learn. Women don't really hear what you say. They hear the music behind your words. You told Mom that you liked the way she grew up, but what she heard was that she 'flew off the handle'. She didn't hear a thing after that. But, then, what can she expect, after all you are just a man."

"Now I have to put up with this crap from you too?"

"Dad, you just aren't paying attention. If you were in high school you would be sent to detention every day. Listen, do you want to know what you should have said to Mom?" Jill had climbed down from the mast and she stood in front of him, slingshot stuffed in the back pocket of her cutoff jeans. Her bare feet balanced her perfectly to the movement of the swells and waves. She eyed him for a minute, surveyed him from bow to stern as if seeing him for the first time. "Mom could have done better, you know. You know that she has been carrying you all these years, don't you?" Harv's brow started to furl. His eyes narrowed, his lips tightened, his nostrils flared, his hands tightened into fists. "What, Dad? You don't like them words? That is, more or less, exactly what you said to Mom, you know that, don't you?"

"It was not! It wasn't. I gave her a compliment. I did. I was being nice to her. I love your Mom. I do." The last words he shouted down the companionway.

"Oh, you silly daddy. You said Mom used to fly off the handle. Don't you know that us females want to fly off the handle every day of our lives? Don't you know how frustrating it is to be a female? The only way we can fight is to NOT fly off the handle, to be the peacemakers, to be calm and reasonable. To show our wisdom by making you men think it was your own idea, all along. To be a better, smarter and in many cases, stronger human, but always, to have to pretend to be a kind of lesser being?

"And then you said she had recently grown up! She was grown up at thirteen when she had her first menses and you were still playing with tree forts and watching cartoons. Really, Dad. You have to learn this stuff. Anyway, want to hear what you should have said?"

"God, yes."

"Janet, when I married you I thought you were the most fabulous woman in the world, but I was wrong. Yes, I was wrong. The woman you are today is better. You are better looking, smarter, wiser, sexier and damn, I hope you stop becoming so loveable or I am just going to spend the entire day staring at you, adoring you, enthralled, on my knees and at your feet.

"And that is what you should have said, big daddy." Jill shook herself a couple of times, ran her fingers through her curly hair, looked out to sea and pulled her slingshot out of her pocket. "Give those pirates a chance and they just sneak up on you." She fired another spitball at a passing bird. This wad just made it past the rail before it fell into the sea. "Damn birds. Take that, Buster." Jill glanced at her Dad, grinned with the corners of her mouth, flew to the mast and climbed back up to the spreaders.

The Prospector was exploring the ship, making sure he knew the easiest and fastest way to get out into the sky, just in case, when he ended up going through a last hatch and found himself on the main deck. He stared up at the sky for a long delicious minute. He always called the outside, the sky. What people called outside was just the same as inside. Houses were just caves, like cars and trains and them fancy aeroplanes. Might have windows in 'em but they was still caves, you still could get trapped in 'em. Not like the sky. When you stood under the stars, you knew that you was free of cave ins, forgotten turns, bad air and the chance of no light. Not like the sky. It was just his curse in life that he was condemned to live and work in caves when what he really loved was the sky. Couldn't do nothing about it. Jest the way it was.

He ambled along the deck, going forward, he thought they called it. The ship was cleaner than any place he had ever been in his entire life. There wasn't a sign of dirt anywhere. The anchor and chain were coming up, automatically, without any crew on deck! That Key West place was sliding aft. Up forward, back lit by the navigational lights, he noticed a crewmember, a woman. He almost turned around and went back to his cave when he cursed himself. Why should he turn back? He was out here exploring, checking out the exits, learning this new cave system. Doing important work. Damn woman, she should leave, not him.

"Good evening, Sir."

Damn woman didn't even have the decency to dry her hair after taking her half-hour shower like they all do. Damn water wasters. Then he noticed that her clothes were wet too. She wasn't dressed in the ship's uniform, instead she wore dark clothes and a pullover hood hiding her hair. Water from the clothes dribbled on the deck.

'What,' he thought, 'they take their showers with their clothes on, now?' He peered at her in the dim light. Half the time she was illuminated by the red port navigational light reflecting off a passing wave and half of the time the green starboard light flared over her. She looked a little scared. Well, he was used to that. For some reason he usually scared women and children. He didn't know why. Jest the way it was. She was pretty enough, though. Not Hollywood pretty, not glamorous, just nice looking. At her side, down by her feet, were stacked a couple of plastic bags, also soaking wet. He looked closely at her again. She was shivering, slightly. He could swear her lips were blue, tough to tell in the middle of the night with all them funny lights.

It slowly dawned on the Prospector that he was looking at a stowaway. A real stowaway! He had read of such things when he was a wee lad. Books like Treasure Island and the like. Now here he was, living his own adventure tale! He suddenly remembered what the Captain would usually do to stowaways, and it wasn't pretty. The Prospector slightly squinted his eyes. She didn't look like one of them cops that was always trying to bust his nut. As if they could. She looked like someone he could like. Except, of course, she was a woman, and most likely a claim jumper at that. Can't trust women. Stands to reason. Bible taught him that. That damn Eve sure ruined a nice claim Adam had on that Eden place. Tricked him she did. Talked him into eating that apple. Got both of 'em kicked out. Cost that Adam his claim. Nope, can't trust women.

On the other hand, he couldn't stand by and watch that Captain keelhaul this little creature. That wouldn't be right. He looked at the woman again. She looked even more nervous than before. Stood to reason, he was most likely glaring as he worked things out in his brain. Probably scared the stuffing out of the little thing.

"You look cold, Missy."

"I, I am. Very cold. I'm all wet, you see. That's why." She didn't say it sarcastic like or nothing. Jest matter of fact like.

"You got a place ta stay? Not that I am offering, you know. I ain't that kind. Might be able to find something."

"That would be wonderful, Sir. And if you might have just a crust of bread, no butter or anything. Just something that you were going to throw out anyway. I would be ever so grateful."

"Might at that. Just might." The Prospector thought for a few minutes. As usual his brow furled and his lips grimaced as if he was surveying a tunnel inside a mine, judging if it would hold up for a few more hours. He spent so much of his life alone, he had fallen out of touch with the human graces, being polite and all that crap. The girl started looking frightened again. "Alright. Grab your things and follow me." He already knew the least traveled tunnels down to his cabin. He had been in so many caves that he had developed the knack of creating a map in his mind and he could see himself traveling along the map like he was on some computer game screen or something.

The woman followed him obediently and at least she could walk quietly, not like some. He could hardly hear her footfalls and at least she didn't talk. Just as good. He had lost the talent to talk aimlessly, like most people liked to do. To talk just to hear a voice. Didn't do to talk in the caves. They might start talking back, then you might start listening, and then you would be in real trouble. Plenty of wilderness men never came back cuz they started listening to voices. Liked what them voices had to say better than what city folk talked about, he reckoned. So they jest stayed out in the wild.

He got to his cabin door and cracked it open, motioning her inside. He eased himself in after her and closed the door. She had squished herself over to one side of the door. There wasn't a lot of room in there with one person, sure wasn't any left over with two.

"It ain't much, but you are welcome to share. Don't take offense, now. But there is something I got to say. I don't take kindly to other people messing around with my things. Just leave my belongings alone. Can you do that?"

"Yes, Sir. And thank you. Is there somewhere I can, where is the, you know, the little girl's room?"

"Yeah, right down the hall. Might want to lock the door. Only got one room for men and women."

As soon as she was gone, the Prospector checked his luggage, making sure all his bags and cases were securely locked. He believed the woman when she said she wouldn't touch nothing, but no sense in taking chances. Especially not in a cave.

He looked at the bed. It wasn't very big. Where were they going to sleep? He thought about that officer by the gangplank when he first came on board. He had asked if he had an assistant coming with him. Maybe if he went back to him now and said that his assistant had suddenly arrived, he could get a bigger room. But what if they knew she was trying to sneak on board? Better to keep her under wraps. Safer for her. Maybe safer for him, if they found out he helped her. He couldn't remember anyone getting in trouble for helping a stowaway, but the damn cops had laws against everything. Hell, you couldn't even stand on a street corner and breathe the fresh air without committing a crime. Loitering they called it. Damn cops. Gestapo. That is all they were. Out to get innocent miners.

The woman looked better when she came back and knocked on the door. Washed up pretty good. Wasn't anyplace for two people to sit, so he gave her the stool and he crouched against the wall. His back flat against it and his rubber soles keeping him up with their friction against the deck. He didn't mind the position. He had been underground for so much of his life, crouching seemed as natural as standing.

"Thing is, ain't but one bed, ain't but one stool. Just the way it is. I figure we can share the bed long as you don't squirm all night long and you don't snore. Might have to sleep on your side. Have to see."

"Sounds all right to me, Sir. But just for tonight. I'll find other accommodations by tomorrow. What I would really like is, well, I don't know if you have one, but a map of the ship. That would really help."

"I ain't seen none. Ain't no trouble for me to draw you up one. I been looking around a bit. Where you going to stay, you leave here?" And then his blood ran dry. He had been looking around the small room as he talked, looking everywhere except at her, and he noticed an object in the corner of the walls and the ceiling to one side of the door. It was small and seemed to have a small piece of glass incorporated in it. It came to him in a flash that it had to be a camera.

"Just you keep looking at me, girl." He didn't change his expression or tone of voice. He remained as relaxed as before leaning against the wall, in full view of the camera. "It seems we are on TV. They got a camera, don't look around! The way you are now they can't see your face. Might think you are a member of the crew, coming to chat. Shoot the breeze." The woman had frozen. He wished she would be more relaxed. Little box like that, wouldn't think the optics would be any good, but these days with miniaturization and microchips and whatever else they thought up, couldn't tell how good it might be.

"Can it see me at all?" There wasn't any fear in her voice. The Prospector was impressed despite himself. Mostly he didn't cotton to women, 'cept, of course, fun and games when he came into Denver and he had a pile of dough in one pocket and a few nuggets in the other. This one, though, this one had sand. Sand with quite a bit of grit thrown in.

"Can't say. Best assume it can. Don't mean that anyone is watching. Might not even be on." He thought for a second. "Have to assume every other cabin has camera in it too. Likely they would have 'em on deck too, case of pirates or what not. Look like you picked the wrong ship to stowaway on, girl." She didn't look all that happy about it, on the other hand, she wasn't crying or nuttin. "Stay here, girl, don't move around. I'll scrounge whatever I can from that galley place. Then, I'll draw you that map."

E

Erhart paused outside the door of Mr. Hawkins stateroom. There was a large mirror down the hall. He backpedaled and stood in front of it. He thought he looked decent. He might have looked more than decent. It was hard to be sure. He did feel naked without his pens in his breast pocket, but John had refused to let him wear the pocket protector even though he had paid nineteen whole dollars for the shirt and he didn't want to ruin it. It was his favorite. He had bought it for a friend's wedding twelve years ago and he only wore it on special occasions. With a sigh, he raised his fist and tapped lightly at the door. Hawk had been watching the boy's hemming and hawing outside his door on the LCD screen on his spy wall as he now called it. He wondered briefly if he was turning into a pervert, a peeping tom. With a smile, he shook his head. If he was, so what? It was his fucking ship. He could do anything he damn well wanted on it. It was bought and paid for as were the people on it. They were his possessions. His. All his, to do with as he fucking wished.

A slight tapping came on the door. Hawk glanced at his screen. The boy had finally built up enough nerve. There was this button on his desk that opened the door remotely. God, he was really starting to love this boat. He could make some killer deals with the gear on it. His opponents on the Board would have their mouths' gaping open with these toys.

Kid's mouth was hanging open as he waved him in from across the room. He eyed the door as he sidled in. His eyes flitted around the room on the long way to his desk. Hawk had found another button under his desk that blanked his spy wall.

"You are Erhart Peterson."

"Yes, Sir." Hawk just looked at him. "I am, Sir."

"You are the expert on Cocos Island."

"Yes, Sir." He didn't want to say 'I am' again. He was a little spooked. Hawkins had penetrating eyes that blazed at him from under bushy eyebrows. Erhart didn't know what he was supposed to do. The great part about the modern era was you could think about what to say in a text message for as long as you wanted, thinking at your keyboard. It gave a

man time to come up with an intelligent answer. And you didn't have people staring at you from across huge desks.

"Tell me where the treasure is on Cocos Island." This was more to Erhart's liking. And a subject he was a expert on. He tried to ignore the eyes on the other side, eyeing instead various items on the desk.

"Which treasure are you speaking of, there are many." Hawkins blazed at him but Erhart wasn't worried now. This was a subject he knew inside and out. He looked around for a chair, picked a nice comfortable looking one, sat down and crossed his legs at he ankles. He shot his sleeves and pulled his collar tight around the back of his neck. Mr. Hawkins' face was getting red and his blue eyes were twin lasers.

"There have been many treasures buried on Cocos Island over the centuries. Without a doubt the Incas were the first, and the least documented, however you are referring to the modern day treasures, I am sure. The first pirate to use Cocos as a vault, and a vault it is, was a British officer named Bennett Grahame. He was a Lieutenant under Lord Nelson and his first command was in the vessel *H.M.S. Devonshire*. The Admiralty sent him to the Pacific to survey the coast between Cape Horn and Panama. There was little glory in such a task and he soon turned to piracy. You might say that a Brit attacking a Spaniard wasn't piracy, but at the time Spain and England were allied against France and Grahame was upsetting the apple cart." Erhart spoke without notes and effortlessly.

"Some of his crew didn't like the idea of going against their home country and threatened mutiny; if mutiny is the correct word on a vessel that is flying the jolly roger. Grahame had learned from locals of the existence of a island with no permanent inhabitants that had waterfalls that fell directly into the sea. This was important as, surprisingly, water was hard to come by in these latitudes and no inhabitants meant that he didn't have to worry about armed citizenry or militias. He dropped the dissenting crew members on the shore of Cocos promising them he would ask a whaler to pick them up. Instead he killed all of them while they explored the jungle, one by one with his service saber. He took an alias after this event: Benito Bonito. His remaining crew and the history books took it one step further and labeled him: Benito Bonito of the Bloody Sword. Treasure hunters still come upon the skeletons of his crew scattered where wild animals had left the remains.

"Bonito took a few smaller vessels to add to his crew and then attacked Acapulco by landing a few miles away and then sneaking to the rear of the town in the middle of the night to raid a treasure house filled with gold. This caused more trouble that he wished. Once his men carried the gold back to the ship, they seemed to think that if they had carried it all that way on their backs, then it was theirs by right. Soon the crew were gambling day and night. Fights broke out. Prostitutes brought sickness on board and Bonito had enough. He sailed back to Cocos and directed each man to bury his own share of gold on the island. Each man knew only his own site. Any gold left on board would be seized and it would belong to the Captain. Without the luster of bullion to drive them crazy, the crew returned to their piratical duties as best they could.

"Bonito fell upon a squadron of five Spanish ships. Three small men-o-war and two galleons, laden with gold and silver from Manila. In a running fight he managed to demast one of the galleons and the men-o-war fled with the other galleon which also held the daughter of the Governor of New Spain. The Spanish commander knew what would happen to him, his family, and any living relative if the girl was harmed. Bonito's *Devonshire* was extensively damaged during the battle and he switched ships. The *Devonshire* sank and he was left with the *Relampago*, which after it was repaired was a vastly superior vessel, especially after the weighty cargo was offloaded. Bonito returned to Cocos and buried twenty tons of gold in a tunnel 35 feet long. The silver he and his crew spent on wild orgies in little towns on the mainland where they threw silver coins by the thousands into the sea for little boys to dive after. Some say the practice started with him.

"He continued to reek havoc upon the ships of any nationality he happened upon, including British ships. Eventually the British Admiralty had to do something about what was becoming an embarrassment. Bonito's deeds were being reported daily in newspapers of the time and he was becoming a folk hero, much like Robin Hood. He stole from the rich and held wild fiestas in little towns on the coast which ended in wild pagan orgies. The Admiralty sent a ship to take care of the matter. However Bonito defeated the frigate. The Admiralty sent a squadron which penned Bonito in the Bay of Buena Ventura, sank his ship, took him in chains to England where he and his surviving crew were tried, convicted and hung. Reportedly, even under torture, neither he or his crew ever gave a lucid description of where they buried their various treasures other than the oft repeated words, "under the Bloody Sword, by my hat." None of Bonito's treasure has ever been recovered. There is absolutely no doubt he did bury his treasures on Cocos. Erhart coughed into his hand.

"Do you think, Sir, that I might have something to drink?" Hawkins' eyes had relaxed as Erhart narrated his tale and now he was leaning back in his chair, his face at rest and his fingers steepled together.

"Of course, help yourself, my boy." He waved his hand grandly towards the bar that took up one entire wall of his room. Erhart poured himself a shot of Jamaican rum, added a twist of lime and topped it off with coke with just a splash of Kaluha. He ignored the ice bucket. He considered ice in drinks a stupid way to get drunk. The ice delayed the absorption of the alcohol into the blood stream until you left the bar and sat in your car. Then the warmed up booze hit the brain all at once just as you turned on your ignition.

"Can I fix you a beverage, Sir."

"No, my boy, I'm fine. Come, I would like to hear more of your information. There was never a treasure map to any of Bonito's caches?"

"Treasure maps are a dime a dozen, Sir. And there are hundreds. Are there any real treasure maps to any treasures on Cocos? Absolutely. Have they ever helped in the recovery of any treasures? Absolutely not. But let me continue the modern history of Cocos chronologically.

"Another great buccaneer of the same general era of Bonito was Edward Davis. Davis was another pirate who preyed upon the Spanish on the Pacific coast of South America in his ship, the *Bachelor's Delight*. He was less successful than Bonito. However, it is fairly well documented that in 1684 he buried several chests of gold and jewels somewhere on Cocos. In 1702 he made an unsuccessful attack on Panama City. Pirates John Eaton and Charles Swan attacked from the Caribbean side while Davis and his crew attacked from the Pacific. The attack was mostly unsuccessful because Davis' crew happened upon a well defended warehouse that contained enormous amounts of silver and some gold. Davis and his men grabbed the booty and retired from the fight. The other pirates involved in the attack pledged revenge so Davis and his men buried the bulky silver somewhere on Cocos. The gold they kept for supplies and amusement. Reports vary on the amount of silver taken, as you never know how much might have been taken after the fact by the accountants and blamed on Davis, but the amounts reported averaged about 300,000 pounds of silver. Personally, I don't believe a crew of 120 pirates could carry that much on their backs. However, it was common practice to never list slaves in those days, as if they didn't really exist.

"As long as we are on the subject of pirates, Sir, we must travel back in time and, remember Sir Francis Drake whom the Spanish consider among the worse of the English pirates. When he arrived on the Pacific side of South America in 1578, the Spanish had never seen a hostile ship in the entire Pacific. Drake's ship, the *Golden Hind* was on the small size, 100 tons, but Drake's vast experience more than made up for the difference. He attacked Valparaiso, took two Manila Galleons, and by the time he reached the latitude of Cocos, the *Golden Hind* was well below her waterline, a dangerous situation in an area of light winds and unpredictable currents. He off loaded the bulky silver, the main part of his booty, some 26 tons of it and just kept the gold and jewels. Drake continued north as far as present day Vancouver before turning and heading west to round the world and return to England and a hero's welcome. Just the gold he carried back ran the English government for 14 years. No mention seemed to be made public about the silver, however it is well documented that Drake did bury it, either on Cocos or near Drake's Bay in present day Costa Rica, 300 miles to the east. Drake remained close mouthed about the exact location during his entire life. I did discover one account of an expedition sent by Queen Elisabeth to recover the silver, however, without Drake, then an old man, they couldn't find the silver, despite charts drawn by Drake. Historically, Drake's pirating was very important as the galleons had been intercepted coming from Asia, an area the Pope had awarded Portugal. This information was leaked by Queen Elisabeth forcing King Philip of Spain to invade Portugal and give England some much needed rest from Spanish harassment."

"Yes, this is all very interesting, but do you have any treasure maps? Any exact locations for the treasure?"

"Yes, Sir. I have many maps. However, so have many others who have gone before us. Over five hundred expeditions have been made to Cocos Island, none have found anything. Don't lose hope, though. Without a doubt that island should be sinking from the weight of booty that has been stashed there, that most definitely is on the island, and Cocos isn't that big, three miles wide by four miles long.

"I believe we have a good chance of finding the Treasure of Lima, the most famous of all the treasures in the world. Imagine, Sir! Finding the Virgin! A seven foot tall, solid gold statue of the Virgin Mother! Reportedly, just touching the statue's feet has cured all manner of diseases and afflictions, while it resided in Lima. But here, I have taken up a lot of your time.

"Here is a short book I have written about the treasure. Perhaps you might care to read it and then we can talk again and I can field your questions, and I will return to my files and collate my treasure maps, complete with my own personal comments on the likelihood of their accuracy."

Hawkins didn't say anything. He sat there and stared at his folded hands on his lap. His fingertip were touching and he seemed to be trying to see something within his steepled fingers. Erhart took a chance, but he felt it was a chance he had to take. He had to change his position from information giver, who could be disposed of as soon as he was milked dry, to an integral member of the expedition. He rose and walked to the bar and fixed himself another drink. He put a little extra shot of rum in this one. It tasted so good. He returned to the desk, laid his notes on the Lima Treasure on the corner of Hawkins' desk, tapped it with his forefinger once and then walked out of the cabin, carrying the crystal goblet.

Jim Banks was on deck when the *Steel Balls* rounded the west end of Cuba. He had directed the vessel within two miles of Cabo San Antonio. This was well within the territorial waters of Cuba but it kept him out of
the northbound Gulf Stream currents. The wind was coming down in a small northerner, common at this time of year and the last thing he needed was a viscous sea built up by a wind against sea condition. Like all super yacht captains, he dreaded getting salt water on deck. It was impossible for it not to get under the teak and to start rusting the steel. And that meant rust stains running down his topsides. That meant endless man hours to repaint and repair the boat. It was a lot easier to keep that salt water down in the sea where it belonged, where God meant it to be. Just in case, he had a man on the foredeck squirting the teak with reverse osmosis fresh water to keep any salt spray from building up. Fresh water wasn't a problem. The *Balls* could easily make 2,000 gallons of totally fresh water a day, every day, out of ambient salt water. Jim hated salt water. He dreamed of taking the *Balls* into the Great Lakes. No salt anywhere. What joy. What relaxation.

He only had another mile to go and he could head up towards Cabo Gracious a Dios, driving between the Caymans and the Honduran offshore islands of Roatan and Guanaja, and from there to run down to the Canal. An easy trip. He glanced at the reefs off Gracias a Dios on the chart. They peppered the sea for over a hundred miles out from the Mosquito Coast. They looked like a mine field. Reefs everywhere. He glanced up at the Navigation Board. He always had two GPS units running. Just as back up. They both were accurate to within a few feet. Gracias a Dios, Spanish for Thanks to God, was named by Columbus on his third voyage when he was heading north, tacking his way through the maze of reefs along the coast. Thanks to God that he could turn down wind in reef free waters. Jim shuddered, briefly, just for a split second at the thought of sailing through such waters without satellite navigation and in a clinker built ancient ship that could hardly get out of its own way.

Super Captains of super yachts were not supposed to shudder. They were supposed to be emotion free when gazing at certain death under their lee, always totally in control. Jim smiled slightly. Yeah, right. He glanced at the chart again. Just a few miles from Key West to the Canal, just over a thousand. 1099 nautical miles to be exact. Good to give the engines something to bite on. Engines in port rust from the inside out. At sea they rust from the outside in, if any damn salt somehow got into the engine room and wasn't caught by Piston, his

Chief Engineer. Funny name that, but the guy was a legend. Stories were still told about how he rebuilt a main bearing on a smaller vessel in the middle on a Cat 5 hurricane in fourteen hours, a job that would take a shipyard a week. Jim let Piston have as much freedom as he wished. Whatever he wanted he got, except for his walking papers.

They were coasting along at eighteen knots, watching out for flotsam drifting out from land that might scratch the boot stripe. Jim hated land, hated flotsam loaded rivers, hated Port Captains, hated pilots, hated cities, hated mountains. He hated just about everything except the *Steel Balls* and those on her. Like all super yacht captains, Jim hated owners most of all, however Jim knew which side of his bread was lathered with hundred dollar bills. Jim knew he was bought and paid for. He didn't let it bother him. It was worth it. The *Steel Balls* was his to love with all his heart. And he didn't mind all those Ben Franklins either.

Jim noticed one of the new guests wandering around the foredeck, keeping out of the spray from the hose. It looked like he was drawing something. Guests, what would they do next. Jim hated guests too, but he could get along with them. They almost always respected his rank as Captain and stopped any annoying behavior once they were told. He tried to think of a reason to tell the guest to get off his foredeck, but he couldn't think of one right off. When they rounded the cape and headed into the seas, then he would tell him. He planned to hug the coast a bit, to keep out of the west bound current, at least until the Isle of Pines, or as Castro renamed it, the Isle of Youth, where he sent his rowdier teenagers to 'educate' them. He didn't worry about the Cuban navy. The *Balls* had the legs to out run any of them. And anyway they were just a private vessel, which Castro always welcomed.

Jim looked out his forward bulletproof windows. The damn guest was leaning his piece of paper against the teak handrail and writing something. He turned without emotion, picked up a handset.

"A guest is scratching the varnish foreward." Within seconds a deckhand had the guest by the arm and was guiding him below. Most of all, Jim Banks hated anyone, anyone who scratched the varnish. Just that morning, the crew had found some damaged wood and varnish up forward. Had to be a guest. If he found out who it had been, there would be hell to pay.

A few minutes later the guest was knocking at his starboard side glass door. With a sigh, Jim walked over and let him in. He should have become an astronaut or something, far, far away from people. Just him and his ship sailing the far reaches of the universe. Peace and quiet at last.

"Excuse, me. They told me that I wasn't supposed to be on that part of the deck at sea. I just wanted to tell you that I am sorry for getting in the way where I wasn't supposed to be." He looked apologetic enough, Jim supposed. He nodded in the guy's general direction in response. It was never a good idea that guests thought that the bridge was an area of fun and games and he an actor, to be enjoyed whenever they wished.

"What I was doing was making myself a little map of the ship. It is a hobby of mine. I think a hobby is a good idea. It keeps any thoughts of sea sickness far away. I would hate to be sick. I would really hate to be sick on that beautiful teak deck of yours." He looked at Jim in expectation. Jim mostly ignored him. "Maybe if you could let me have some plans of the ship. Something I could learn from, that would keep me from wandering all over especially in places where I don't belong. And still keep the decks clean!" He ended in a high note of an argument well won and waited for his prize.

Jim went through his mind wondering if he had any plans of the ship that didn't include any of the secret additions. The elevator, the spy system and a few hidey holes were recently added. He was sure he could find some old plans that didn't include those.

"I might be able to find some discarded plans somewhere, Sir. What room are you in? I'll have them delivered to you."

"That would be great, really great! I am in room 8, down by the engine room. Thanks ever so much." As he exited from the bridge, Jim picked up a phone and rang Charlie Ross, his second in command. He heard the extension being picked up and a few mumbled words.

"Charlie, why do you have passengers billeted next to my engine room? Especially inquisitive type people, and guests at that? Surely we have enough suites? I want you to move every guest you have put down there into a proper room and then I want you to get up here and tell me why you put them there in the first place. Understood?" There were a few more mumbled words, a couple of 'but Skipper' and Jim Banks slammed down the phone. He had high hopes for Charlie but then something like this happened. He really needed someone he could rely on, especially on a long leg like this one; a few miles, sure, but lots of reefs along the way and Colon, one of the world's seven deadly cities at the end of the passage.

"I'll just have to stand double watches if need be," he mumbled to the radar. He rubbed his eyes. They were tired. But that didn't matter. If the *Balls* was in any kind of danger, if she might be disgraced by not being perfect to any passing eyes, if any of her all important crew were injured or sick, if anything at all was wrong with his *Steel Balls*, he wouldn't be able to sleep anyway. Might as well be up here fixing it.

Better than being in his cabin pretending to be sleeping. He heard the Owner's elevator operating behind him. And that was just the frosting on the cake. Now the owner was here to bug him. God!

"Captain, I wonder if we could have the privacy of the bridge for a few minutes?" Jim turned and looked at the owner in astonishment. He had that Mary under his arm half undressed. Owners. Damn. He should have been an astronaut.

"Sir, an officer must be on watch on the bridge every second while underway. Coast Guard regulations, Sir. Perhaps when we are at anchor?" The owner's face clouded over and squalls were breeding in the back of his eyes.

"I am more than capable of watching the bridge, Captain. I want my bridge now, I want it this instant. If you don't agree, find yourself another boat to play with. There are lots of Captains on the beach who would love your job. What is your choice?" Jim gulped. Hawkins was right. Many, many captains would jump to command a vessel like *Balls* and be paid in the high six figures to do it.

"Of course, Sir. I didn't realize you were qualified, Sir. I'll be up on the flying bridge should you need me Sir." The flying bridge had remote connections for the engine room, radios and radar. It was also higher up on the superstructure and exposed to the elements. The things he had to do as a captain. They didn't have flying bridges on space craft. It was too late to change now. He was wed to the sea.

It started with a low moan high in the rig. Harv looked up at the sky. It sounded almost like a distant jet liner. A plane might be just past the main, or hidden behind the jib. Soon a cloud started to form on the nearby beach. A cloud of sand and dirt. It swirled like a dervish on steroids, darting down the beach only to change directions in a millisecond and head back the other way. After a moment it headed out to sea and disappeared in a mist of water. The moan became throatier. Deeper, more powerful. A cloud of sand left the beach and raced, tore out towards the *Rose Marie*. Towards the little boat with all her sails set.

"Hey, Jill, come down from the mast. I don't like the look of this at all." Harv's voice had a sense of doom in it. Janet stuck her head out of the companionway where she had been in the galley looking through cruising guides.

"Jill, get down this instant. Now!" She jumped over the coaming and raced to the mast. "Right now!" Just as Jill reached her Mother's waiting arms the wind hit.

Hit is such an inadequate word, better would be, smashed, shattered, knocked down, invaded. The wind tore at her old worn out sails for a few seconds and then in an explosion, demolished them into a small collection of rags. It was just as well. The mast couldn't have taken much more. The boat was being held down with the mast parallel to the water by the now shrieking wind. Harv gazed in amazement for a second at the racing cloud coming towards his boat and then reached forward for his family.

"Get down below! Close all the hatches! Hurry! Really, really, hurry." Already the ocean was starting to pour into the open ports, gushing in with the force of a fire hose, fed by the boat being thrown down wind. The boat with her keel now near the surface of the water was being scudded away from the beach by the wind working on the surface of her hull. Her mast, thank goodness, was in the lee of the hull and almost in the water. Harv looked and felt impending doom in his blood and heart. If the mast went under water, the sea would use the mast as a fulcrum and turn the boat upside down, to turn her turtle until her mast would do a 360 and come up on the other side of the boat, if it came up at all. The
sea might tear the mast off the boat and send it down to Davy Jones' Locker where already reside the boats and bones of other careless sailors.

Somehow the mast stayed above the water as Janet managed to close all the hatches and ports and tie down the more immediately lethal missiles that were caroming around the cabin. Harv held the wheel down to port but it didn't do much good, being as how the rudder was barely under water. He jabbed the starter button for the engine and it started right up, thank God. He put her in gear and revved her up. Slowly, ever so slowly the *Rose Marie* responded. The propeller frothed at the surface of the water but found enough water in the increasing waves to do its job. She came up into the wind and as she came her mast lifted from the sea and stood almost straight again, held down still by the enormous wind. Harv pointed her due north, into the gale, hoping to get in closer to the land, hoping for calmer conditions. Less maelstrom conditions. The boat responded and made headway and Harv's heart which had been residing in his throat for the last few minutes returned to its moorings.

The companionway hatch slipped open and Janet stuck her head out, protected by the dodger. She looked around with fear growing in her eyes. Already the waves were ten feet tall and the *Rose Marie* was struggling to work her way through them. The water was white, white from the spume being thrown, ripped off of the top of the waves and snaked downwind, swirling, spinning, streaking and the water itself was thrown so hard, it felt like solid marbles as it hit. Janet looked at the GPS. She looked twice.

"Honey," she had to scream, just to hope to be heard, "we are still going south!" She pointed to the instrument with a shaking finger. Harv peered at the readout in amazement and forwarded the accelerator lever further. He had her up to 2000 revs now and his Yanmar engine red lined at 2400. They still weren't making progress, just losing distance slower. He pushed the lever all the way down. The engine was screaming, he could hear it above the roaring of the wind. It was shaking the entire boat as it forced the *Rose Marie* into the increasing seas. Janet stared at the GPS, willing it to show progress with every atom of her soul. Slowly it read 0.0 knots instead of negative numbers and then 0.5 knots to the north and there it stayed.

"Janet, work out how far we are from the shore!" He had to scream into her ear with cupped hands around his mouth just to be heard. Water was dripping from his hair, the hood of his foul weather jacket had been torn off and sent flying off to Antarctica. Janet nodded, wrote down their latitude and longitude on a scrap of paper and disappeared below to plot their position on their chart. She was soon back.

"Three miles off shore, Honey. We lost two miles in the knockdown. At this speed, it will take six hours before we can anchor." Harv just nodded and he gritted his teeth as he guided his boat through the waves as best he could. The waves were getting larger by the minute. Already they were topping ten feet and cresting. The tops of the waves flew off when they hit the boat, flew like guided missiles right at his face, it seemed. He quickly learned to duck behind the dodger when he saw a larger than normal wave. It was when one of these waves hit that he lost control of the boat.

When he ducked, his hand accidentally spun the wheel and the bow fell off from the wind. It was just a few degrees, but it was enough for the wind to grab hold of the bow and take control, powerfully. The wind was so strong that in seconds the bow was pointing south with the wind now aft. It was nice in a way, with none of this crashing into waves, comforting in a way. Harv, waited for a quasi lull, spun the wheel and forced the boat up towards the north, the beach, and certain protection. It was back to crash, bang, smash and spray. Down below, it was a circus. Janet had her hands filled with her loved possessions, trying to protect them, stuffing them into secure corners all over the boat. It was going to take weeks for her to put her boat back to rights after this. Her eyes were haunted. She could hear the sound of an approaching wave just before it hit the boat and sent the bow soaring into the sky. She tried to hold on as best as she could, it wasn't always enough. Twice she had been thrown across the cabin, hitting the opposite side with tremendous force. She thought she might have dislocated one shoulder, it ached so. A front tooth seemed to be very loose after she hit a locker with her face. When stuffing her music cd's away in the head, she glanced in a mirror. A stranger looked back. A desperate, half crazed woman with black and blue marks all over her body, and her eyes; in her eyes, a wild creature, bordering on insanity, peered out. She felt like sitting in a corner and howling for a second, just a second as the sound of another approaching huge wave filled the boat. Janet grabbed a combing and held on, shrinking down on her haunches so there was less far for her to be thrown. She started to cry, she started to cry with huge sobs, racking sobs. She let go of her combing and covered her face with her hands. Let the sea do as it wished. She was so tired, so very tired. The hell with it all. She just didn't care anymore. She just didn't care to fight anymore. She just didn't care.

She felt her body being picked up and thrown across the cabin. She just knew where she was heading, right towards the projecting edge of the table. She just knew she would hit it with her back. It was okay. Maybe it would only hurt for a second. Then it would be over. She wouldn't have to fight anymore, she would be dead. She felt a sob for her daughter, her poor helpless daughter, who would care for her now? Harv was outside, taking care of the boat. If her daughter died being thrown around, or was disfigured, she would never forgive herself, if she was still alive. Where was Jill? Where was her Jill? My God, where was her little baby? Jill!

She felt a strength pouring into her, soaring up into her body in the split second she flew through the air. Her body seemed to react by itself without direction from her brain. She felt her body spin in the air, her feet landing on the edge of the table in perfect balance. As the wave released the boat, she hopped down to the cabin sole and like a super woman had the cabin cleaned up in seconds, cleaned of any objects that would turn lethal when thrown across the cabin. She sped here and there, her eyes now rational and focused. If she had looked into a mirror now, she would have seen an alert, competent woman, but now even more, a stranger. She went forward, opening the door to the forward cabin and found her daughter in a gymnasium.

"Oh, Mom! This is so much fun! Come and join me!" Another wave came rushing in, the bow flew into the air and Jill was somersaulted to the other side of the boat landing on her vast collection of stuffed animals that lined the small cabin. "Whee, oh that was a good one.

Make that one happen again, Mom! That was so cool! This is like so much fun!" Janet looked in amazement for a second and then sank to her knees and started to laugh, and laugh, and laugh. The stranger in her eyes left her, and she joined her daughter on the forward berth, hugging each other, laughing, shrieking and giggling together as they were tossed this way and that, mother and daughter, one unit, once again.

It wasn't that much fun on deck. Harv was getting very tired. He really needed a cup of coffee, or anything hot right now. He wouldn't have believed that he could be so cold 16 degrees above the equator. The wind chill was turning the 80 degree weather to 40 degrees and he was freezing dressed as he was in shorts and a tee shirt. The waves seemed to have become higher and more vicious the closer he got to the coast. He guessed that it wasn't the distance from the coast that mattered, it was the length of time they had been out there. Time for the wind to work on the waves, to force them into higher and higher heights and to come at him from different directions. He hammered on the sliding hatch of the companionway again. There must be too much noise down there for them to hear him. He was sure they were hard at work trying to save the boat and all of their lives. Surely they must know what danger they were in.

The waves had become so steep that the boat couldn't rise to them in time, and she rammed through the waves, green water madly rushing over the deck. Harv eyed the hatches warily. If the water tore one of the hatches off, it would only be a matter of time before they sank. Maybe Janet was down there hanging on to a hatch, refusing to let it open, the fittings cutting into her skin, blood running down her arms. And here he was complaining because he was a little cold. Damn, he had married a firecracker! What a great girl!

With a start he realized that he had been day dreaming and the bow had fallen off. Again the wind caught it and forced the boat to head down wind. It took longer this time to work the Rose Marie back into the eye of the wind. He wondered if the wind was getting stronger or the boat was going slower. He looked over the side and tried to judge their speed. It was impossible. There wasn't any water. There was just spray, spume, and squall. The GPS was indicating that they were doing 0.4 knots, but that could be because he hadn't picked up speed again after falling off. He glanced at their knotmeter, but as usual in anything that wasn't a flat calm, the instrument refused to work. With a shock, he saw the GPS speed fall to 0.3 knots. He didn't think the wind was any stronger. He was sure they had enough fuel. He had topped off the tank when they left Huatulco just yesterday. Was it only yesterday? It seemed last year. They couldn't be running out of fuel. Suddenly his blood ran cold. Colder.

He had heard stories about Mexican dirty fuel. Stories about how the dirt hid in the corners of the tank until the vessel got into a storm, then it surged into the fuel and was sucked up into the motor. The Racor caught the dirt, of course, but the filter could only hold so much dirt until it was blocked. Just at the end, when the filter was almost full, the engine would go slower and slower. It would be one hell of a job changing the filter in the Racor in these conditions, but what choice did they have? Whatever he did it better be soon. It would be dark in an hour and a half. Not a good time to be out here in a full gale and an ailing motor. He hammered on the cabin top again. Janet, where was she?

He took a chance, he tied down the wheel, the brake wasn't strong enough to hold the wheel in such evil conditions, ran to the companionway and jumped down inside the boat. It was empty. No Janet, no Jill. His fear chilled blood seemed just a few degrees above zero. He felt the boat start to fall off again and he rushed out to the wheel, confused and desperate. Janet, his Janet, his Jill, they must have hit their heads, they might be dying! He figured the *Rose Marie* had to be within a mile of the coast, not that he could see it. They had to be close, the deck was filling with sand and dirt again. Surely that meant they had to be close. But what did that matter? If Janet and Jill were dying, he had to be with them. They were his life, not this boat. Where were they? He jumped down into the cabin again. He ran aft, no one. He ran forward, no one in the head. He opened the forepeak cabin.

"Daddy, I love this! Make it do those big jumps again, Daddy! This is the greatest trampoline ride ever!" Jill was airborne seeming in zero gravity, flying from side to side of the cabin. Janet was braced against the port side giggling.

"Hi, Honey! Is it time for me to steer? You have to try this. It really is a lot of fun! Jill, make room for your Dad!"

"Come on in, Sir Daddy. Welcome aboard our very own astronaut training ship. We are going to rent it out to NASA and make a mint! Daddy? Dad, what is wrong?" Harv struggled to mask his feelings. He wanted to rant and rave. He wanted to fly off the handle, whatever that meant; a witch falling off her broom stick? The hell if he would let them, later, throw this back in his face. He mastered his emotions.

"The boat is in great danger. I need someone on the wheel to steer as I repair the engine, and I really need a hot cup of coffee. And I need someone to navigate." Harv spun on his heel and rushed back on deck. The boat had fallen off the wind again and he laboriously coaxed her back on course. As soon as a chastised Janet plotted a position and took over at the wheel, Harv rushed below to find the proper tools and a spare filter. Only then did he shut down the motor and direct Janet to turn down wind and to try to keep the boat as level as she could. He thought a bit about carrying on, motoring as they were, but their speed was down to 0.2 knots and fading fast. Plus they were still a mile and a half to the shore. He had to change the filter. He had done it before, in a marina with a friend to watch over him and in absolutely flat water. It had still taken him a half of an hour. He hoped this time it would go faster. They would be blown miles away from the shore in just a half of an hour. He nodded, briefly, to the icon of St. Jude, the Patron Saint of sailors and hopelessly insane cases, just above his nav desk, and got to work.

Mary saw the message first. It had been shoved under the door. It wasn't that she had been looking for a message or anything. It was just why lab technicians were hired. To see things that were out of place, that were different, that didn't belong. They were the people who were very good at finding the differences between two pictures when they were three.

Personally, she was sky high, a personal high. She had always dreamed about bedding the boss, of holding him in her arms, of having him bend down and gently kiss her on the lips, and now it had happened, was happening. Who would have guessed that the boss would be this amazing love machine in the sack? True, he was a bit limited in the types of positions he choose, but Mary anticipated teaching him a few new tricks. She knew plenty, she had been reading Cosmo for years.

The message was inside a sealed envelope, quite a nice one, it read, 'Doctor Horner and guest.' She thought about opening it, it did say guest, but she remembered in time that curiosity had killed the cat or, more likely, got it kicked out of its lover's bed. She hugged herself as she floated over to the lavish bath where Dustin was shaving. He was such a nice guy. He shaved just before he made love to her, each and every time. They had made love so often last night she had lost track. She hoped he brought enough shaving cream! She walked up behind him, ran her hand around his cute little belly and fondled him, just for a second. She shouldn't let him get too used to it!

"We got a letter by special delivery, lover boy." She showed him the envelope over his shoulder in the mirror.

"Well, open it up and read it." She nodded her head and was filled with such joy. There weren't to be any secrets between them. She was such a lucky girl!

"Doctor Horner and guest are invited to cocktails at five in the Owner's Cabin. That's it. There is no signature. Shall I pen a reply?"

"There is no need. If he had signed it himself, yes. If not, no. Unless, of course, we weren't going to make it, but in this case, of course we will. That is, we will, if you can keep your hands off me for a few minutes."

"Me? You so and so! You are the one who is always feeling me up! A girl can't ever turn her back with you around, mister."

"Mary, you have it all wrong, I am only defending myself after you have raised the attack eminent flag. A guy has to be able to defend himself against women on the prowl. That only stands to reason."

"Okay, then, see if I touch you ever again." She pouted a bit and turned her back on him. Somehow though, she seemed to move slightly backwards and brushed against him. "That wasn't me! It was your damn male sex appeal that made my body move. You can't blame it on me. Really!"

"My sex appeal? Mine? You sexy thing, you." He just bent down and kissed her long and lingeringly on the lips. She slowly opened her lips and let him insert whatever he wished. She didn't mind the shaving cream that smeared all over her face. Not by any means, at all.

Later, much later, they dressed for the cocktail party. She wore her one expensive dress, a simple black number, recommended by Cosmo, that was a genuine, imitation Dior that she had found in her favorite dead aunt store. The store that relatives sell clothes to after the widow breathes her last. She had it dry cleaned twice before she wore it, just to be sure all germs, viruses and bad luck had been washed away. It fit her like a glove. To complement it, she wore a string of pearls close around her neck and a genuine imitation zircon on her ring finger of her right hand. She looked stunning, helped, no doubt, by the incredible happiness that bubbled out of her.

Dustin wore his regular old suit that he wore to all faculty functions. He saw no reason to make an extra effort. The owner, this Mr. Hawkins, the mystery man, was hiring his brain, not his wardrobe. He didn't want to seem ungrateful, the offer to fund his research completely for an entire year was a dream come true. But he also didn't want to mislead this Hawkins. He was just a university professor with an inventive mind. Nothing more, nothing less.

They stood obediently in front of Hawkins' door and knocked politely. The door seemed to open itself, and then close automatically after they entered the main room. A huge desk dwelt, there was no other word for it, on the far end of the room, and a man that looked a little like Santa Claus sat behind it. He stood up and walked around the desk as they neared.

"Welcome, welcome. It is so good to see you at last, Professor." He put his hand out to shake and Dustin felt his entire hand engulfed. It was a very strange feeling. As if he was a child again. "And who is this lovely lady? Lovely and looking very nice, indeed, in that fabulous dress." His hand reached out, ignored her stretched out hand, he ran his fingers over her hair, over the top of her head and then down to the back of her neck. Mary felt like he was her father, his hand was so big and he was so full of confidence. His presence seemed so powerful, like a Hollywood movie star or a major political figure. She felt irresistibly attracted to him and repelled at the same time. If he had kept his hand on her hair for one more second, she would have said something scathing. She was glad she hadn't had to. Private funding, for research in a university setting, was a mark of a professor who had finally, really, made it. "Have a seat. Relax, please. What would you like to drink? We do have a complete bar." He grandly gestured towards the wall to their left. There the young, incredibly beautiful boy from the shore boat stood with a linen cloth over an arm, ready to take their order. "Have anything you would like. John, I'll have a Harvey Wallbanger, tonight."

Mary had a glass of red wine which must have come from some secret vineyard as it was the most delicious wine she had ever tasted. Dustin ordered a single malt scotch that he always wanted to try but couldn't afford. John left a bowl of macadamia nuts on tables by each chair.

"Now, Dustin, if I may be so bold to call you that, tell me about the machine you have invented." Hawk sat down behind his massive desk and put an attentive look on his face as if to emphasize that a meeting had started.

"To tell you the truth, Mr. Hawkins, I am surprised someone hadn't invented it before. It works on fairly logical and pre-discovered scientific achievements, that I have just combined differently and with a bit of a twist. Basically, it is a combination of radar, sonar and a microwave oven.

"As you may already know, microwaves have several characteristics. One is they will not travel through even thin layers of metals or other very solid materials, and two, they travel through a very short path before extinguishing. These may seem to you poor characteristics for a metal detector, but with a bit of a twist, they aren't at all, if fact, they are an advantage.

"Most detectors work on a reflected image to discover a metal source, since microwaves will not reflect from a metal image, there is no return signal. However, that in itself is a piece of information. Microwaves do reflect, however weakly, from softer substrate, so we use this echolocation of a kind as a negative reading. Lack of a return signals a location." Dustin was relaxed in his chair, feet flat on the ground, his fingers folded together on his stomach. He was used to speaking, and to speaking to disinterested or even hostile crowds. The university life had sunk from the highs of the late '60's when the University of California system led the world in achievement and distinguished professors. Now students just wanted to learn their subject quickly, so as to become rich as fast as possible. Lecturing and especially testing about pure science created waves of disenchantment and interesting psychologically, resentment towards the professors.

"Microwaves also are very short waves, short but powerful. Because of the short distance they will travel, they have been ignored by all other inquiry. However, all metal detectors, detect for a very limited distance into the substrate, the ground. Other machines are limited because they leapfrog deeper into the ground because of their longer wave length which then don't have the power to send a return signal. Microwaves don't have the wave length to go deep into the ground, but they don't have to, we are just interested in as deep as we can dig after all. Microwaves also have the power to return a strong signal, or in this case, a lack of signal. There is that all understood?"

Hawk looked interested. He hid the fact that his mind was reeling a bit. But he was used to hiding his thoughts from others. 'Never let anyone know what you are thinking' was one of his two mantras, the other was 'Fuck asking, fuck begging, just grab the damn thing.'

"I assume that advanced electronics can map the 3D location of the non-reflected materials?"

"Yes, indeed. I am impressed, Sir, very impressed. It is rare to discover a mind that can digest new concepts so easily. Well done, Sir"

Hawk didn't say anything, but he glanced at the folder on his desk that he had been reading just before the Professor entered his cabin. It contained a copy of the complete manual for the Microwave Detector that Mary One had taken from the luggage of the Professor stored down in the hold.

"Does your machine require a great deal of skill to operate? I ask in complete ignorance. It would be useful that when we arrive on the site that we have your machine working as many hours a day that it will operate. I understand Professor, that you have been on such expeditions before, so you will understand that there is always a political side that wishes to increase the, how shall I say, the sweetener, that we were required to submit. As always, time is of the essence."

"I do understand completely, Sir. Both Mary and I are completely competent operators. The machine does require periodic maintenance and readjustment to be dependable, but I believe we can perform those after night has fallen. I fully expect that we can keep the machine operating during all daytime hours. Don't you think so, Mary?"

Mary had been watching the two men like a judge at a tennis match, her head twisting one way and then the other, following the conversation, yes, but also examining the two men. Dustin, she knew well, and perhaps loved. This Hawkins interested her somehow. He had the looks and the smell of money that would be enough to bed 99 percent of the world's women, but he also had a serpentine oiliness to him that tasted like dirty secrets buried deep. But he was interesting. Interesting enough to get to know better.

"I can keep working as long as you wish, Dust, I mean, Dr. Horner. I am an expert in both operation and maintenance of the machine." As well she should be, being as how she did all the work anyway, while Dustin sat behind his computer and liked to think he was directing her movements.

"Well, that is fine then. However, John here," he waved his hand in the general direction of the youth tending bar, "is very quick at new things. I would like the two of you to give him as much instruction as possible during the remainder of our voyage, just in the rare chance that one of the two of you might become ill. Is that agreeable? I do, of course, have no designs or interest in your machine, Professor, just in the success of our expedition." Dustin didn't want to share anything about his machine. But how could he refuse? He was going to be payed well for this trip. He looked at the young man. He looked innocent enough. He would believe anything that he or Mary told him.

"No problem at all, Mr. Hawkins, no problem at all." Hawkins smiled and stood up at his desk.

"Fine then. By the way, call me by my nickname, Hawk. You know, like the bird of prey."

Tugs didn't like the town of Colon, he didn't like it at all. It was a town based on crime. All of the workers, the pilots and line handlers for the Panama Canal, the shop workers, the gas pumpers, the checkers at the grocery stores, all of them lived in Panama City and commuted daily. No resident of Colon worked as a hired man. They preferred to steal, rob, con and kill instead. It was what they were good at. It is what their fathers, grandfathers and great-grandfathers had done. Ever since Spain mule-trained gold across the Isthmus, they had been born to steal. The success of the Panama Canal insured that there was a daily influx of new sheep to be shorn, arriving daily to keep their way of life going.

Joe liked Colon. It was like coming home. He understood the people around him even if they spoke that Spanish crap. He tried to teach the fuckers some English by yelling it at them. It didn't work. They didn't want to learn. But that didn't bother Joe. He didn't think the Don would look for them here in Colon. Back in the States, sure, but here, in one of the seven deadliest cities on the planet? He didn't think so. Joe liked the town because he didn't have to buy anything. He pointed his gun at anything he wanted and they gave it to him. He knew a price was coming. There was always a price. He would have to kill someone for somebody. It didn't bother him. He had killed a lot of people. He didn't mind killing, fact was, he kind of liked it. The drama, the fear, the feeling of self-importance he gained from the act. He never regretted any killing but one. He had killed his girl, not personally, but still in fact, when the cops forced her to turn States evidence. They slugged her and beat her till she agreed. She later died of her injuries. He didn't mind killing the cops who did that to her. He made them suffer. One lived for three days under torture. Screaming, bloody torture. Any humanity that ever lived in Joe's soul died that day along with his victims. Tugs hated Colon because the roads were so rotten he couldn't set up a decent car. The axle grinding pot holes would destroy any performance car in a few hours of driving. Of course the next day it would be missing, anyway. Tugs was having to walk to get somewhere. Walk, take a taxi, not that a man could really call it a taxi, pile of nutless bolts, maybe, or take a bus. Colon is where all the ancient school buses of the States end up. There were hundreds of them. Their drivers were all half mechanic and half artists. They were constantly fixing their vehicles at the end of each route and each bus was ornately airbrushed and decorated with tassels everywhere they could possibly be hung. To Tugs they were as old as ox carts and as slow. It was painful to go so slow.

Both men liked the Free Zone. It was like a candy store. Every company in the world that was worth its salt had an outlet in the Free Zone. It was *The* Free Zone. Free zones were world wide but the only one that came even close to Colon was Hong Kong. The place was guarded 24/7, but that could never stop men like Joe and Tugs. They even bought stuff. It was so cheap. Like 3 bucks a liter for the best scotch in the world. $1.75 for a 85 dollar bottle of Cognac. Course you were supposed to pay duty for it when you took it out of the Zone. Yeah, right. Tugs just waited till a couple of local girls with big boobs walked out. With the guards distracted with patting them down, he waltzed out. Joe just walked out. He eyed the guards with his meanest look. His 'are you ready to die' look. The cops studiously looked the other way. Everything you could ever think of was in the Free Zone. Reason was the place was loaded with warehouses. Companies stashed their product in Colon, tax free, import free, export free, totally free. Colon just charged rent on the land. Companies had ships coming and going to all corners of the world daily that they could send their goods to at a second's notice.

The biggest crooks in Colon were, as usual, the politicians. There was just too much money floating around. It wasn't long before Joe thought up a score. It could net them ten mil, easy. Not that he intended ever to give it to the Don. Fuck him. He and Tugs steal it, then damn, it belonged to them, pure and simple. Joe's idea was to kidnap one kid from each of the five top politicos. He'd tell them, the first guy that coughed up ten big ones, he'd get his rug-rat back. Tugs asked him what they would do with the other kids.

"Fuck if I know. Shit, give 'em to the zoo, whatever. Fuck 'em. Sell 'em to the slavers. They always need free labor out in the mines, the illegal uranium ones, that is. Diggers only last a few years at the most till they start to glow in the dark and pieces of them start to fall off."

"But, Joe, the others, they gonna be really mad at us. Really, really mad. Why not we ransom all of them back, Joe."

"That's the beauty of it, you dope. Big problem with kidnapping is they hem and haw about getting the money together and getting that stupid proof of life. By the time the whole thing is set, the cops are dug in and waiting to start World War V or whatever we are up to now. Competition. That's the American way. Yeah, man. We need our money right away and I mean, like pronto."

Tugs still wasn't sure about the other kids but he did like that he would be driving. Joe had found a Caddy for him to drive. He would be able to eat those streets in Colon with a vehicle like that. Bad part was they would have to ditch it after. Just too visible. Joe even found out which day the owner filled the tank. Why steal a car with an empty fuel tank? Kinda defeated the purpose. Tugs asked about the getaway, where they would go next.

"Fuck, any damn place we want, amigo. We should go buy a hotel somewheres and offer free rent to blond lookers with low IQ's. God, with enough money, we can live like fucking princes."

Tugs took the bus to Panama City. Place looked like Manhattan. Skyscrapers everywhere. He stole a motorcycle and drove it back to Colon and checked out the roads and cops. He was worried. There were only a few roads between Colon and the airport at Toucaman in

Panama City. It wouldn't take much to set up road blocks and they would have them in a trap. Joe just kept saying not to worry about it. He had it covered. Tugs somehow didn't believe him.

It was all going great until someone stole his motorcycle during the night. Tugs was supposed to meet Joe at the cruise ship dock, down by Colon 2000, so he pulled his Caddy out of the garage where they had stashed it and tooled through Colon for the meet.

At first it was just a feeling. Then a thought. Finally a certainly. He was being followed. He couldn't spot them, yet. Yet he knew they were there. He was used to the sensation. It could be the cops, the Don's men, hell, it could be the owner of the Caddy. Whoever it was they were good. No doubt they were waiting for him to contact Joe, then they would make their move. He called Joe on his cell phone, which were so cheap and plentiful in Panama.

"Joe, I'se got a tail. Don't know yet who'se dey are."

"Fucking shit, Tugs. Lose the bastards."

"Working on it. I'se going to tool round a bit, den I'll drive by da front of Dos Mil. Hang out there and try to spot dem, right? I'se in the Caddy."

"What the fuck you driving the Caddy for Tugs? No wonder the fuckers spotted you. Shit. This is all we need, fuck. Alright, alright, I'll be waiting."

There were a lot of bushes near the entrance to 2000. Joe set himself between two bushes and sat on a low wall with a newspaper held up to his face that he pretended to read. He really was pretending.

"Who the fuck could read this fucking Spanish, anyway?" He heard the Caddy before he spotted it. He kept his eyes on the paper, his head bent down. Tugs drove by. Finally they came, 300 yards back. Two men, black car, black clothes, no smiles. Torpedos. He called Tugs up.

"Tugs, you fucking idiot. A couple of torpedos are on your tail. They look like the fucking Don's men. The Mob anyway. Don't go down any dead ends. They don't look like they are happy little fucking killers." Joe knew he was going to have to kill them. Their orders would be, kill or capture. They were the same thing, except capture would be a infinitely more painful death. If he had a choice, he would just as soon be gunned down in a shoot out. He always laughed at how people tried so hard to avoid death. All the insurance scams, the hospital overcharges, the health food scams, the way Joe looked at it, you were going to die sooner or later. Everyone dies. Each of us will die, eventually. It was a hundred percent certainty. So you had a choice. Run and hide from death till it found you hiding on your back in a closet, or live your life to the fullest and say fuck to fate. Enjoy your life. It didn't matter if you ended up in Heaven or Hell, your memories were all that you would have. Make some good ones. He, for one, didn't want his last memory to be one of laying on a hospital bed, a shadow of his former self. A tired old husk that no one wanted. He wanted his last memory to be one of blazing glory, eyes full of fire and light, mind racing at full speed, outwitting, outplaying, outsmarting, outkilling anyone who dared to come up against him.

"Joe, dey gonna kill me. Ya gotta help me, Joe." Tugs had panic in his voice now, frightened and scared. It didn't matter if Tugs died in the street or on a bed. There was no iron core within him. Just a will that others twisted as they wished. Who knows what he will remember for eternity. How fast it all went by?

"Listen, they aren't going to kill you till you lead them to me. Head out towards Four Corners then come back along the canal. Don't fucking hurry. When you are within 5 minutes of Dos Mil, give me a call. I am going to set up a fucking ambush. Don't try to lose them. I want them to follow you into my trap. Tugs, do you fucking understand?"

Just down the street there was a blind corner by the yacht club. It didn't have any signals or one of those mirrors or anything. This was Colon where life is so cheap. The place was loaded with schools. Four grade schools within a couple blocks. Joe's evil mind turned over faster.

He found a house with a gated, barbwired yard within a few yards of the corner. He barged his way in, sapping the maid who came out to the gate. Lucky for them no one else was there. He found a crowbar and broke the lock on the back gate. Then he set up his guns. He loved guns. He loved the way they smelled, before and after, he loved the weight in his hand, the sight of his opponent bleeding in the dirt at his feet, he loved the fear his gun caused in others. Then that pussy Tugs called. They were a minute away. He picked up his Uzi to start the festivities.

Tugs came roaring down the street and drifted, rear wheels screaming, around the blind corner, the torpedos were close behind. Assholes. Think they would know better. He blew out their front tires with a full clip of the Uzi. The car spun out of control and ended in a ditch by a beach used for landfill. Joe didn't bother reloading a clip into his Uzi, he picked up his 16 gauge loaded with exploding solid shot. Custom solid shot. He had etched an x on each slug to make it explode on the slightest contact. He pumped three into the car, just to make sure. The thing was a living wave of fire, pieces of car and bodies flew into the air, landing all over the street, beach and bay.

Proper technique called for him to walk over and make sure of his kill by blowing apart each skull with his .45. He could tell from here that they were dead. He loaded his weapons back into the duffle and got out the backdoor before any heat arrived. He shouldn't have worried. The cops didn't get there for a half an hour. They were used to killing in Colon.

Elena stood on the bow of the small coastal supply boat, hugging herself in delight. Her boss, Lieutenant Dominic had given her a paid vacation, plus he paid for all of the supplies that she and Mercedes had wanted. She had been best friends with Mercedes since the third grade, so it seemed natural to pick her as a traveling companion. Mercedes was as lovely as could be, plus she was a practical girl, she could make a fire and toast tortillas over it as elegantly as if she was in a five star hotel with room service. Unlike herself. Elena would have burned herself over an open fire and ended up with ashes all over her face. But she didn't care. They were going to a practically deserted tropical isle! This was going to be so romantic and so much fun! Who cared if she had dirt on her cheeks? She could rough it. And dirt did wash right off, didn't it?

The two girls shared a small cabin on the supply boat. There were several other travelers, one a nice looking younger woman traveling alone and of course, the two rangers. They seemed as self reliant as always and sat on a cabin top as their expressionless eyes watched the vessel's crew load the last of the cargo for Cocos Island. Mercedes joined Elena on the bow and after a few minutes the other woman joined them.

"Hi! I'm Jackie!" She seemed friendly enough and her Spanish was passable.

"Hola. I'm Elena and this is Mercedes. Are you going to Isla Cocos also?" Elena knew that this boat only went to Cocos, but one had to work to keep lines of communication open, Especially in small isolated communities, like the only women on this boat. Maybe the only women on Cocos.

"Yes, I am! I am a researcher for an American University and I am working on my thesis for my Doctorate. My subject is diversity in isolated areas and how animals in different areas resemble each other's developments. Cocos Island is just a dream come true! It is so isolated and untouched. Everyone has done the Galapagos, the Line Islands, the Cloud communities of Papua New Guinea, but Cocos! Wow!"

"Where do you stay on the Island?"

"Well, I wanted to camp out, you know, to be totally connected with my subject, but that is forbidden, it seems. So I have to stay at the police barracks. Easier to keep an eye on me, I guess. Not that I am complaining, it took four years to get permission for this study. I am so stoked! Where are you girls staying?"

"At first, we were going to stay at the barracks, too, but the Commandant, he has given us his guest cottage over by the beach. We get to stay there till someone important needs it. Muy bueno, si? Plus the commandant said, his personal chef is going to make us our dinners! We have to fend for ourselves for the other meals."

"Not that we expect that to be a problem," chipped in Mercedes. "If two single girls can't get a luncheon date on an island full of men, we won't be trying very hard and you don't get a figure like this by eating breakfast."

"You are so lucky. I wish I could stay with you two. I don't suppose…" Jackie looked at them, fluttered her eyelashes and pouted her lips slightly.

"We can ask. But it isn't ours to offer. We only got in because Elena, here, works for the same department up in San Jose." Jackie's ears pricked up.

"Is it true that Cocos Island has more gold on it than Fort Knox?" Jackie lowered her eyelids halfway, turned one hip towards Elena, bent her neck slightly in her direction and grasped her arms behind her back. It was hard to say why the stance was so alluring. It had its affect on Elena, though.

"I'll try to get you to stay with us, if there is room. We haven't even seen the place yet. We haven't even left Punta Arenas yet. Look, we are still surrounded by containers, ships, docks and tugs. There will be time to worry about this later.

"And in the office, we don't worry about the pirate stories. We have enough trouble just keeping treasure seekers from destroying the Island. Know what I mean?" Jackie just shrugged and looked away.

Mercedes and Elena's cabin was small but serviceable. The bath was down the hall, however they had a handy sink in their cabin and the doors all had strong locks on them. Once the ship started to move the hot water, fed by the engine's cooling system, was more than hot enough. Elena took a sponge bath in the cabin before dinner. Mercedes tossed her long hair and locked herself in the shower room for an hour, then reappeared, even more gorgeous and self satisfied.

"It is going to take a lot more than a ship load of sailors to make me change my ways, I'll tell you that, Elena. If they have little peek holes in the shower room, then all they saw was a lot of suds and wet hair. But now I feel nice and clean after that dusty, dirty city. Really, Elena, it is going to be so great to live on a tropical isle, if only for a while. Are there any worthwhile hunks there? Anything to whet our appetite?"

"Everyone is game except those two rangers. Those men, they send shivers up my spine, and not nice shivers either. The rest, I have not met. They are not married except for the chef. He, they allowed to have the wife on the Isla, but now she has died. Very sad."

"Well, Elena, we are going to have the time of our lives. What did that American girl mean about gold on the island?"

"Mercedes, that is just stories. Stories to put children to bed at night. Never has there been gold found on the Isla. Never for hundreds of years. Don't worry about gold. Worry about getting invited for lunch! And getting a perfect tan! We are the two luckiest girls in the world!"

On deck, the rangers said nothing to each other. There was nothing to say. They both knew their mission. They both knew what the other was capable of. They both knew that variations would occur and that they would find a way to stay on track. Once one of the men stopped his isometric exercises just for a second and looked at the other out of the corner of his eye as a large case was loaded on board. Other than that, neither paid the slightest attention to anyone else on board. Neither did they go down below to their cabin while the vessel was being loaded.

Their cabin was bare. It contained no suitcases, duffle bags or valises. Nothing to be searched, definitely nothing to be found. Not even a toothbrush except one had a rug and a foreign book for some strange reason. Perhaps a gift from a loved one. They used their fingers to clean their teeth, the pinkie nail on their left hand was sharpened to be used as dental floss as well as other things. They did not sweat. They did not have body odor. If their clothes became dirty, a sharp oblique blow with the edge of a hand dispelled the dirt. They needed nothing the world had to offer, except, perhaps, a sense of purpose.

Jackie had a very small room just for herself. She had three large pieces of luggage, but she ignored most of it and piled it in a corner. Only her valise engaged her attention. Inside of it were an assortment of cameras, a pile of legal pads, an collection of pens and pencils and a Satellite phone. Jackie Sullivan was a freelance reporter. No one had ever done a exposé of Cocos Island. She was almost sure that the whole place was a con. That the stories of gold were just that, stories and that the biodiversity consisted of nothing except seagulls and clams. Costa Rica was raking in the dough in application fees. They charged a fee just to talk about getting an application, much less of actually getting one. She smelled a big story. If she could twist it enough, she could make a pile of cash on this one. Maybe enough to pay off her school loans, finally.

The seas had grown to incredible size in such a short time. It was only an hour since he had turned off the engine to change the fuel filter in the Racor. An hour of fumbling with oily parts in a boat rolling and pitching like a bronco. The seas were huge. More than their size, they seemed to climb up on each others' backs and once there, fall, collapse, somersault onto the small boat far below them. Somehow, someway the boat still swam. She darted this way and that, sometimes only at the last second, to avoid the worse the gale had to offer. The woman stood at the wheel, hair flying in front of her face, whipping at the corners of her eyes, eyes bright red from the flying salt, griping the wheel with an iron grasp and she was laughing in joy.

A force seemed to emanate like a glow from her, to surround her, to protect her from the storm. The thing inside of her was enjoying the situation, enjoying being in charge, showing what it could do. How it could make the woman drive the boat for hours at a time, never making a mistake. The thing gloried in itself; and as long as it stayed in charge, it grew in strength. It became more powerful and at the same time the woman became more used to it, to it directing her, using her, being her. And the boat was surviving.

Harv finally got the filter changed. It took an hour and when he took a position from the GPS he was astounded to find that the boat had drifted seven miles downwind. There was no hope now of turning back, not against these seas. He climbed out into the cockpit, out into the maelstrom, out to his wife.

"Thanks, Babe. Got it changed. Let's check it." He turned the motor on. It worked perfectly.

"Harv, it is too late to turn around. Look at these seas. We will destroy the boat fighting against it. On the other hand, we are being blown in the general direction we eventually want to go. Why not just ride the whirlwind? We are on the freeway, we just can't find the exit. Let's go for it! If we can edge over to the east when the waves let us, eventually we will get into the lee of Guatemala and El Salvador. What do you say, big man?"

Harv stared at his wife. Usually she always asked his opinion before stating her own thoughts verbally. Not that she was ever weak. Not his girl. As strong as they came. But now! Something was different. She seemed reinforced. He couldn't think of a better word. Her strengths were stronger, her weaknesses weaker, her eyes blazed with a power that was her, but more than her. Instead of worry and fear, her eyes radiated confidence and enjoyment. She was incredible.

He looked at the waves. They weren't. Waves that is. Liquid, moveable towering walls changing constantly, crashing, rebuilding, and always getting larger, meaner, more dangerous with each passing moment they got farther from the shore. They were very steep sided. When he thought he had the pattern figured out, waves from east and west came screaming across, 90 degrees to the main swell, tossing the poor *Rose Marie* in unexpected ways. He found himself grasping the boat as hard as he could while watching the ocean. He judged carefully. Janet was right. There was no going against these monsters. It was too late. Far too late.

Dusk came suddenly in the way of the tropics. No prolonged sunset down here. The sun streaked down to the horizon. With the night came the fear. It was bad enough when he could see the waves coming at him, when he could judge when and how to twist the boat to meet the waves' charge. When he could, he kept a look out for the huge logs common to this part of the world, floating time bombs, waiting to hole the bottom of a passing boat. Now, in the night, it was hope for the best, hope the builders of the boat knew what they were doing when they framed her. Now in the night they were in God's hands, and their boat was, oh, so small in the middle of the gale.

The first rogue wave hit just after ten. They could hear it coming before it hit. A sound, like the roaring of an avalanche, filled the cabin. The trusty *Rose Marie* tried to rise to it. She did her best. The wave was just too big. It broke over the boat, smothering her, burying her under tons of water. Just the spreaders high up on her masts were still above the sea. Soon the rogue was gone, off to terrorize Tonga or New Zealand, and the boat rose like a submarine, bow first, water bursting off her decks, her dodger had been ripped off. The man at the wheel lay crunched in the corner of the cockpit, wrapped in his tether and harness that tied him to his boat.

Janet was out in the cockpit in seconds and Jill helped her work the unconscious Harv down into the cabin. Jill took the helm and tried the best she could while her mother worked on Harv, giving him mouth to mouth. His heart was still beating but he wasn't breathing. She lay him over her knees, her knees in the pit of his stomach and pounded on his back. A flood of water spewed out of him and he inhaled deeply. Janet took his face between her two hands and kissed him tenderly.

"I love you, my Captain." Then she was gone and Jill came down to help Harv into a sitting position. She made him some coffee, spilling half of it but he drank it greedily. Both of them devoured a package of cookies, careful to leave some for the man on watch.

Outside it was starting to get nasty. Really nasty. The boat was now some thirty miles from the shore. The wind had beat the waves into huge
creatures normally seen only in nightmares. They climbed up on each other and then picked up the little boat and pretended it was a surfboard. They threw it down the face of the seas in any direction they wanted, sideways, backwards, whichever way chance and the devil choose. Harv crawled outside again. He didn't want to. The last time he had been out there he almost died. But if he didn't, he and his family certainly would. He yelled into Janet's ear.

"We have to tow warps." The two of them tied together all their old sheets, a stern line they kept in the hopes that one day they could tie it to a coconut tree in Tahiti, and an old anchor line. They tied one end to the sheet winch on the starboard side, led the line aft, outside everything, and ran it around to the port winch. Slowly they let the line out. At first the sea contemptuously threw it back onboard, but they kept trying. Finally they had enough out that it fluttered on top of the wave behind them just as it was starting to break. Messed it up just enough so the wave didn't curl over and break on top of them anymore, and the line held the boat's stern into the wave and wind so she surfed down the wave like a normal little sea boat. Harv wished he had some sails left to drive the boat. The remnants were flying from the foil and mast were helping a little. The stalwart crew were able to tie down the helm and the three of them went below to try to dry out and warm up. Once every ten minutes one of them stuck a head out to look around, to keep an eye on anything going wrong or any other boat so silly as to be in this same gale. There wasn't much they could see except at the top of a big wave, then, up there, miles of the sea's fury was exposed. At first Harv was frightened at the sight but as the stern line held, the bilge pump kept up with the water squirting through every hatch and port on the boat and the moon came up, he saw it with a new light. It was beautiful. Dramatic in a way Hollywood could only dream of, like a thousand Niagara waterfalls everywhere he looked, seemingly falling, crashing, clapping together at random. The more he looked, the more he saw some grandiose logic. He imagined himself as an ant looking at a freeway at rush hour and trying to make sense of it all. He felt the same. Once Janet came out with him to look around.

"You know, it really makes me feel small."

"Nonsense," Janet screamed back into his ear, "It makes me feel great that we can cross this huge ocean in our little boat during this storm. It makes me feel more powerful, not less." She wanted to say more but it was so hard to talk in the screaming, swirling, shrieking wind.

Down below they cuddled together on the salon floor, the quietest place on the boat; or rather, the least violent, least acrobatic, least bruise making place. By morning it was starting to ease off. They noticed the lack of the high notes of the wind first. Then the waves seemed to lose some of their violence and the boat wasn't being thrown around as much. By eight o'clock they had pulled in their warps, by noon they dragged down the remnants of ruined sails off the foils and broke out their light wind set, the only sails they had left. The crew was exhausted, at least Jill and Harv walked around like drenched cats. Janet seemed to have taken the storm in her stride, as if it was something she was used to doing on every day of her life. Either that or she had some inner source of energy.

"Mom, come and sit down. You are making me tired racing around like that. I'll help you clean the boat tomorrow. Please, Mom, you are giving me a headache." Jill pulled a half soaking pillow over her face. "Mom, stop," came a muffled voice.

"I'm not tired. And anyway, we will all feel better if our little home is all shipshape and dried out." Janet automatically dried some CD covers before placing them back in their rack even though they never got wet. Outside the rails were dressed with every sheet and blanket on the boat. Up the mast on the spinnaker halyard streamed pillowcases, dishtowels and throw rugs.

"Janet," came a voice from on deck, "we look like we are gypsies! We have all our wares for sale, all we lack is customers." Janet cheerfully climbed up the ladder to emerge in the glowing sunlight and cheerful little waves.

"Hey, Gringo. You like to see my wares, you big hunk? I got something you like. Si? You pay ze big dollar for what I got, you sexy man." Harv let out a wolf whistle and a muffled voice from down below cried out,

"I wish the two of you would grow up. You would think you are still in high school. I have a headache. Please be quiet." Harv made a big thing out of locking his lips closed with a key and then throwing it overboard. Janet was less kind.

"If someone had not spent the entire storm flying around in outer space in the forepeak, perhaps she would not have a headache now." A pillow came flying out of the companionway and a muffled cry erupted.

"Parents. Can't live with them, they send you to jail for mutiny if you push them overboard. It's a fixed game."

T

The stowaway was in the toilet, head, he guessed they called it, when the officer came. He was perfectly uniformed but he acted like he had his hat in his hand and was wearing torn clothes. Embarrassment reddened his face and tightened his tongue.

"I believe, Sir, that a mistake has occurred. This room is in the crew quarter group. As a valuable member of the expedition, you belong up in the guest accommodations. I am very sorry about the mix up, Sir. I do believe, however, that you will be pleased with your new quarters. May I help you transfer your dunnage, Sir?" The Prospector wasn't all that sure he wanted to move. He had become used to his room. But it was just common courtesy to look at this new place they had for him. Might be more room for the girl. The night had gone well. She only tossed and turned a little and she hadn't snored. They had agreed to sleep back to back. Both of them had been very modestly dressed. When he woke up, she had accidentally put her hand around him during the night. He let it stay. Little thing must be really tired to sleep next to an old fart like him.

"Well, I'll take a gander at this new place, if I like it, then we can come back for my stuff. Okay?"

"As you wish, Sir." The officer was sweating a little, despite the air conditioning. The Prospector followed the man up the spiral staircase, up to the fancy dudes suites, as his friend the engineer said. They stopped in front of a door with a small embossed sign, 'The Presidential Suite.' As the officer put the key in the lock he turned to the Prospector. "This is the best the ship has to offer, Sir. I, personally, would appreciate it if you took the greatest care of the furnishings, Sir," The Prospector bristled. He felt the hairs raise slightly on the back of his neck.

"What are you saying? I'm not good enough for you? For you and your room? By God, I am glad I didn't bring my effects with me. I'm not moving. And that's that."

"But, Sir. I mean, that is not what I meant, Sir. I apologize, Sir. I meant no offence. Would you like to at least look at the suite? After climbing up all this way? Please, Sir?" The Prospector stared at him. The guy was under a lot of pressure. Pressure from somewhere. Why would anyone care about him? He wasn't anyone special. He was just a good old boy from the hills, trying to get away from those holes in the ground. For a brief second, he wondered if he was being set up, if they knew about him killing that cop. Just for a second. His back track was clean. He made sure of that. He burnt his truck, especially the tires. His tools were right here with him. The one he used to bash in the cops head, he had rebuilt and thrown away the old casing. And anyway, he really thought that everyone would be glad that such an unhappy, idiotic man like that cop had been removed from the Earth's increasing burden of humanity. The Earth could only hold so many people. Might as well make them the nice people, or at least not sadistic weirdos.

The room was outstanding. It was built like a palace. A extra long king mattress lay in the middle of the room in a poster bed, complete with hanging curtains which hid the soon to be occupants behind a shimmer of translucent sheer silk. Two massive leather chairs stood guard over a chess set braced on a table which sported a well stocked bar beneath it. Mirrors hung on opposite walls reflecting each other into eternity, while on a far wall stood an incredible copy of the Mona Lisa, if it was a copy. The sliding glass windows opened onto a private balcony just below the main bridge. Two captain chairs were ready for would be captains or owners to pace their own deck. The bathroom was out of Cinderella. It was built of crystal. The sink and faucets were lead crystal, while the bath tub was a stainless frame inset with Waterford designed crystal portals. The mirror was within a crystal border and seemed ready to answer if questioned. The Prospector's mouth fell open. His eyes glazed over at such splendor.

"Okay. I'll take it. Yes, I'll be happy to move in. Me and my guest will move in at once."

"Oh, certainly Sir. I didn't know you had a guest, Sir." He seemed happy at the information as if having a friend placed him in a different level of humanity. "I don't recall you having a guest when you checked in, Sir."

"She came on board at the last second." The officer relaxed at the word, 'she'. He bowed himself out and the Prospector went to find his stowaway. As he went out the door he glanced at a camera up in the shadow of the bed from the corner of his eye. 'Damn,' he thought, 'the whole ship was bugged.'

At the door to the suite, Robyn had to blink three times, pinch herself twice and even then she was sure she was dreaming. She looked in wonder at her savior, at her passport to a new and wonderful life. Only thing she had to do now, was to get her greedy little hands on some of the loot that was obviously floating around here. This was the chance of a life time. And the way she figured it, it was time to pull out the stops. Let the engine red line, damn the torpedos, full speed ahead, don't shoot till you see the whites of their eyes, it was now or never, baby.

"That is one hell of a bed, and I don't mean any disrespect. Wow! I mean, my god, wow!"

"The only problem is, there is still only one bed. Could be I could sleep on the floor, slept on worse in my day, and that's the truth."

"Don't be silly. I think we should take a bath before we get into that bed. Here, let me help you with your clothes." She reached over and started unbuttoning his shirt.

"It ain't even lunch time, yet." He didn't stop her busy hands. "I ain't never been one fer sleeping in the middle of the day. Not when there is work to be done."

"The only work you have to do now is to wash my back, and I didn't really have sleeping in mind." She eased the open shirt off his shoulders, and started on his belt. It was a western belt and opened easily with a flick of her fingers.

"Whoa on there, little filly. Jest what exactly do you have in mind?" He put his hand on hers as she started to work on his fly.

"If you think for one second that I am going to sleep in a place like this and not get laid, you are sadly mistaken. This is the chance of a lifetime and I want it to be perfect. I owe you big time for taking me in, and you didn't even try to take advantage of me last night, even though I wouldn't have complained, you being so stud like and all, and anyway, I'm as horny as hell and I like you, so lets do it, together." She abandoned her attempts on his zipper, reached her hands up to his neck and molded herself to his body. Slowly, she raised her lips and kissed him, tenderly. He responded like she was his sister. Her eyes teared over slightly. "Is that all you've got for little old me?"

"I ain't as young as I used to be, you know. Parts of me have definitely reached their use-by date. Jest don't work like they used to, you know?"

"You let me worry about that, Stud." She punched him lightly on the arm. "Now help me take off this pesky bra. They always put the snap way in the back where a girl just can't get at it."

Obediently he reached around her. Somehow her blouse had seemed to have disappeared while they were kissing. He could see her point. Damn snap was hard to get off. Her turned her around so he could get a good look at it. Thing sure was a marvel of engineering. The girl bent over to help him get a good look, he guessed. Problem was her cute little butt pushed into his crotch area. That didn't aid in his concentration. Girl didn't know what she was doing to him. Finally, he figured it out. It was a reverse scissor fold. Damn smart using that. Somehow as soon as he released the snap, her bra just fell off and she turned and somehow his hands were full of her breasts. Nice set too. The nipples made his palms tingle as they grew harder and longer and as she arched her back. Her slacks seemed to fall off of her, like gravity had suddenly increased. Maybe it had. He felt all rubbery in the knees. Didn't seem to be able to stand up right.

"Not here, on the bed, Stud." He got his first good look at her naked body as she pulled him by the hand towards the bed. His breathing became more difficult. And his feet seemed to get all tied up as if he had forgotten how to walk. He reached out a hand and touched her right below her waist, right where her hips began to swell, she was so beautiful and he felt a stirring down between his legs that he hadn't felt for a while.

Last few years, when he went to town to sell his claims, he went to the whorehouse. He figured people had the wrong ideas about whorehouses. For a guy like him, who maybe had a little trouble getting it up, dating was out. Your average girl, she didn't know how a man's body worked, not like a whore did. Plus he didn't have a lot of time in town before he headed back to the hills. Seemed easier to use a whore, better, easier, purer in a way. Dating a girl just to get in her pants seemed dishonest, somehow. And a guy like him needed an understanding girl, they just don't make them that way anymore, if they ever did.

They should call whores, sex experts, that's what they should do. The word, whore, had so many negative emotional feelings. They all seemed to know that to ask a guy to perform on command was too much for most men. Well, when he was eighteen, sure, but now when he was on the wrong side of fifty? He had special needs, that's what it was. He was special. And he needed a special girl. And they just didn't make them anymore.

With a sweep of her hands, the Stowaway separated the hanging curtains and crawled up on the bed. On her hands and knees, facing away from him she drew back the bedspread and the sheet below it. He could see the mound of her sex between her legs. The hair was trimmed short so little was hidden. He reached out again and touched the side of her hip. Her flesh was so silky, so smooth. She seemed to radiate heat. The Stowaway looked back at him and smiled. He could have sworn she was purring like a very sexy pussy cat. She waggled her hips back and forth a few times and arched her back till her breasts were touching the bed and her sex rotated up from between her legs till he could see every detail, just for a second, then she spun around and had his zipper down in a flash.

"Take off those pants, lover and get in here. I'm getting cold all by myself." She burrowed under the bed sheet and lifted a corner for him to enter with her eyes half shut and a slight, satisfied smile on her face.

It didn't take him long to get naked. The satin sheets on the bed were incredible. He could move so easily. It was like his body was covered in oil, the slightest movement sent him soaring. It was effortless for him to run his hand up her spine as she lay on her back.

"I make it a habit of mine, never to bed a girl I don't know the name of. Sorry, jest the way it is. So if you don't mind?" He really didn't want to get her out of the mood, but a guy has to do what a guy has to do.

"Margaret. Margaret James. Call myself, Robyn. And what is yours?"

"Me? Don't use my name much. Mostly call meself the Prospector. That's what my bank calls me too. But for you? Name's Clarence. Don't right remember my last name. Think it was O'Brien. Been too many years. Never went to school so never got into the habit of writing it down. Anyway, Robyn, nice to meet you and all. You is the best thing that has ever happened to me in a long time."

"Likewise, Clarence. Now what do we have here down here?" Her hand traveled down between his legs. His member was still mostly sleeping. "Clarence, I really like the taste of a man. I really do. It turns me on so. Do you mind if I taste you?"

The Prospector nodded his head mutely as if he didn't trust his voice to speak. His eyes grew in size as the girl burrowed down further into the bed and he suddenly felt a warm, silky mouth around his organ. It was still small enough for her to take all of him into her mouth. The feeling was incredible. When she sucked, he felt himself being drawn down into her throat. She swallowed and her throat convulsed around him, in rising rings of rhythm. Then her hand grabbed his skin right by his body. Her fingers circled the loose flesh and squeezed his balls out and away from his member. He was surprised it didn't hurt. He was even more surprised when she started licking his balls through the tight, taut skin. It did something to him. It was a nice feeling and all, nothing special, but his manhood started to grow seemingly all by itself. And grow. Soon he was sure he was bigger than he had ever been in his entire life.

She returned to licking his member and then squirreled out from the sheets and sat on top of him. Slowly, ever so slowly, she inserted him into her inner regions. She was so warm and tight. Her body pulsed around him, starting at the base of his manhood and traveling towards the tip. The heat in her seemed to increase as she started to breath through her mouth, panting, her eyes thin slits, the pupils just peeking out were luminous with an inner glow radiating, unseeingly, outwards. She leaned forward and licked his nipples. He was surprised that they became erect. As she then nibbled on them he thought his organ was going to explode, it became so large. Robyn felt it too as her head fell back, her throat totally exposed, the flesh below her neck turned blood red as she screamed. Her hips were a blur as she rotated herself on his sex and as he came, and as his member grew and spurted, she came again, and again and again.

Afterwards they lay in each others arms. Her hand held his organ, protectively in her hand. He ran his fingers through her hair like he was petting a cat. Her other hand held him to her tightly as if she would never let him go. Tenderly, lightly, he kissed her and they lay there, lips almost touching, breathing each others scent, each others air, existing in each others spirit like life beforehand had just been prologue.

Erhart woke with a dream of John Rogers still haunting his mind. He had dreamt of standing on deck and seeing the naked young man swimming below in the sea. His body was so beautiful, every muscle developed to perfection, he was sure if Michelangelo was still alive, he would use John as a model for a new statue of David.

Erhart jumped from bed and stared at himself in the mirror. 'I am not gay,' he told his reflection. It was true. He loved the sight of a naked, beautiful woman just as much, or more, as John. 'I just love beauty.' He wondered for a second how John maintained such a perfection of shape. The answer was obvious. There must be a gym on board the ship. At breakfast in the nook overlooking the swimming pool, he asked his waitress for directions.

In between his order of Eggs Benedict, Blue Mountain coffee and his order of fruit salad which included kiwis, mangosteens, and red bananas, she passed him a map of the passenger parts of the ship. Two decks below his cabin, on the opposite side of the ship was the gym. Erhart promised himself he would explore after his morning nap. He awoke from his nap when he heard a slight knock at his stateroom door. He got up but by the time he opened the door, no one was there. He wondered briefly if he had been dreaming it all, then he noticed the envelope that had been stuck in between the door and the frame. He slit the flap, it was from the owner, Mr. Hawkins.

You are cordially invited
for dinner tonight
in the Owner's Stateroom
Promptly at eight.
Black Tie

It was unsigned, not that he didn't know what was going on. This meeting would decide if he was to be an important member of this expedition or just a hired hand to be disposed of as soon as possible after he was drained dry. He knew he was an indispensable part of the team, he had to make sure that the money man knew it also.

He hadn't packed a tux. He didn't even own a tux. He knew what to do, though. He wandered down to the gym and to his delight he found John. The boy truly had a beautiful body. He was stripped to the waist and was doing curls with what looked like an enormous amount of weight. It certainly made his arm muscles jump and knot. Erhart walked over to the boy. John nodded at him but continued his set. When he finished he lowered his weights into their sea going restraints and with a sigh turned to the passenger.

"Yes, Sir. What can I do for you?" John was the picture of politeness. He was very well trained.

"Sorry to bother you on your time off, John." Erhart got a little chill down his spine just saying the boy's name. "Our Master and Exalted Leader has asked me to dinner tonight and it is Black Tie. I didn't pack a tux. I don't know what to do. Can you help?" John smiled a little.
"Not to worry, Sir. No one expects you to wear a tux on board. It is kind of a joke. What it means is, you should dress a nicely as possible and for form's sake, wear an actual black tie, even if the rest of your outfit consists of blue jeans or a lava-lava."

"Oh. That is a relief, John. Thanks. You have saved me endless mental suffering. Is there anything I can do to help or...?" Erhart raised his eyebrows at the young man.

"Normally if you wish to give a tip, it is done on the last day of the voyage, Sir." Erhart had been thinking more of spotting the weights for the boy. Anything to stay longer in his presence. But he was too tongue-tied to ask. With nothing else to say, he nodded his thanks and left the gym as John went back to his exercises.

On the way back to his cabin he went out on deck and was surprised to find that the boat was entering a harbor. A huge breakwater stretched for miles on either side of the entrance. Inside the harbor hundreds of ships lay at anchor. He watched with interest as the *Steel Balls* found a clear spot, rounded up into the wind and lowered her anchor in a sudden rushing, crashing sound of chain running over steel. Ashore were miles of docks full of containers piled five stories high. Ships pulled into the docks, deposited a few containers and picked up a few more and then left the harbor. A few tugs raced around madly pushing here, pulling there, creating order out of chaos. He could hear harbor control talking on the radio up on the bridge. The voice was very well controlled. It instructed each ship, one at a time, where he should go and when he should do it. A few disobedient ships were told to obey or leave Panama and never to return. Pilot boats rushed everywhere at full speed delivering pilots to ships that were going through the Panama Canal. His ears picked up when he heard the words, '*Steel Balls.*'

His ship, he got a thrill thinking the words, 'his ship,' was instructed to remain at anchor until the morning when the pilot would board at 0800. The owner was requested to come ashore and complete official business.

Erhart mazed his way down to his cabin where he researched his choice of evening wear. It wasn't a big choice. He had a seersucker suit but threads seemed to be poking out everywhere. He had a nice pair of chinos and an aloha shirt, that seemed a bit too informal. His last choice was a pair of levis and a favorite button down white muslin shirt that was very comfortable. He choose the levis and the shirt on the principle that if he felt comfortable he would be relaxed. For a tie he wrapped a black ribbon around his neck in a fit of wildness.

At eight o'clock sharp he knocked at the door. It opened automatically to a meeting of Mr. Hawkins and Captain Jim Banks. Hawkins was yelling, standing behind his desk, huge fists on the marble, glaring at Banks.

"I don't run around doing errands. If I wanted to run around, why would I hire someone to do it for me, answer me that!" His eyes were glaring, his mouth was a thin slit of anger.

"I don't make the rules, Sir. The canal requires the transit fee in cash before they will schedule a transit. It has always been this way. If you argue, they will tell you to sail around the Horn. They have no competition. We have no choice."

"I gave you a check. Why isn't that good enough? Do they think that I am not good for it? Me? Owner of a ship like this?" He pounded his fists against the hard marble top of his desk.

"It is just what they do. I did inform you of this fact before we departed Key West as I am totally sure you remember. They will accept a letter of credit written on one of the five prime banks, that or cash in dollars. Nothing else accepted. Do you see all these boats anchored around us? They all are waiting for their owners to cough up the transit fee."

"Surely there must be some way to scam, that is, to convince them to give us the benefit of the doubt?"

"I don't know of one. Perhaps you would like to talk to them personally?" Hawk stared at his desk. This was a hell of a time to send his bodyguards out on a mission. They could obtain anything by just looking at someone. They radiated such potential violence.

Erhart stood frozen by the open door. He didn't know whether to retreat and risk giving offence for not being on time, or enter the cabin, making it even more obvious that he was overhearing what was certainly a private conversation. As he was hemming and hawing, Hawk looked up and saw him.

"You will have to excuse me, Captain. I have an important guest for dinner. I would like you to rack your brain during the night and we will talk again on this subject before breakfast." He ignored the Captain's outstretched hand and waved Erhart in and pointed to the table set in one corner. As Jim Banks shut the door behind him, Hawk sat down at the head of the table. John Rogers appeared out of nowhere and filled their wine glasses.

"Now Erhart, thank you for the treasure maps. I have a question. Some of them seem to be contradictory? Which ones show the true location of the treasure?"

"Why none of them, Mr. Hawkins, none of them."

"What?" His voice grew into a shout in the span of one word. "None of them? What fucking use are they or you, then?" Erhart remained composed. He had this conversation many times in his mind. He was comfortable with the subject.

"Let me put it this way, Sir. Would you write down the combination to a safe holding millions of dollars and give it away to a stranger you had just met in a pub? That is what happened to many of these maps. Some, of course, are fragments of imagination. Others are the real thing. But even the real ones don't state where the treasure is. Treasure maps are codes. They are meant to remind the pirate, who if the truth was told, drank far too much and always had the risk of being knocked on the side of his head by a cannon ball and having his brains addled. The map is a code to remind the hider where he hid his treasure. So, how do we get our hands on all that gold?" Erhart reached out and took a sip of wine. He patted his lips a couple times with the linen napkin.

"So, how for god's sake, damn it!"

"We study the pirate. Get to know him. Figure out how he thought. What he liked and disliked, who his loves were, what his favorite numbers were. These were not terribly sophisticated men, Mr. Hawkins, but they were sly and cunning. They lived in terribly overcrowded conditions for their entire lives and were used to keeping secrets. Most of the time when they gave away a map to their treasure, it was because they were bragging that no one could ever figure out the secret code imbedded in their map. They were bragging that they were smarter, trickier, and definitely more deceptive than anyone else.

"Remember, Sir, that the occupation of piracy was based on deception. Disguising their ship to get closer to their prey, flying all manners of false flags to deceive the enemy and deceiving their own crew as to their share of the booty."

"So how do I, rather, how do we get our hands on that gold?"

John chose that moment to bring out the first course, blackened pork chops, surrounded by deviled eggs and a rock melon and avocado salad dressed with an orange vinaigrette. However, to John's dismay, Erhart stopped orating and dug into the delicious food. It was cooked to perfection. When John had left the room, Hawk looked up from his food, took a gulp of wine. His eyes were hard, harder.

"How?"

"Easy to say, hard to do. I, or someone like me, a scholar of pirates, if you will, has to stand on the same spot as the pirate stood, knowing how he thought, how he planned, and figure out what exactly he did so many years ago. There is no other way.

"One warning, Sir. Past expeditions have suffered embarrassing defeats caused by gold fever. It is a disease that permeates into a person's brain and alters the logic sequences of a person's normal self preservation. Several expeditions have managed to sink their own boats in their rush to find treasure. Without a boat, life on Cocos Island is grim indeed. Every effort should be made to guide personal so that gold fever doesn't affect them. Some people will do anything for money.

"By the way, Sir. Am I to assume you are having financial difficulties? There was a promise of considerable funds being transferred to my account the moment I stepped on board your ship. Is this promise still valid?" Hawk's eyes became a little blacker.

"Of course it is, or was, that is. The funds have already been transferred. They are in your bank waiting for you upon your return. You are going to be a rich little computer geek, aren't you?" Erhart didn't reply. He thought of himself as a world expert, not as a computer geek. He did promise himself that as soon as he got close to a computer connected to the internet, he would access his account to check the balance.

Mary had left Dustin sleeping soundly in the cabin. She wasn't tired, in fact she was full of energy. She hated laying in bed waiting to sleep, trying to pretend to herself that she was tired, especially while listening to Dustin snore away. It really annoyed her. Life was too short to waste it pretending to do anything. And anyway, it was beautiful out on deck. Colon wasn't a big city, or a nice one, but its beauty was in the many ships surrounding the peninsula with all their lights on. In between them, smaller vessels rushed here and there, resupplying the ships, changing their crew, bringing pilots out to ships, the business of the Panama Canal never slept.

Sometimes she wished she smoked. This would be a perfect moment to lean against the wooden rail, strike a match and gaze moodily at the beauty around her, just like an actress would in a movie. She always thought she would have been a good actress. It gave her pleasure to play a part. To wear a mask, to hide her real self, hide it deep where no one could ever find it. To become a mysterious stranger that everyone was intrigued with. It would be so much fun. She remembered she had a pack of matches in a front pocket of her levis she used to light Bunsen burners. She pulled them out, lit the matches one by one and dropped them into the water far below. She squinted against the sulfuric smoke, pretending she was Katharine Hepburn in 'African Queen' pushing their boat through the leech infected swamps.

"You know, if the Captain saw you making sparks so close to his precious varnished rail, he would freak out." Mary spun around in surprise at another voice. There was Mary One leaning against the cabin housing, behind her, staring at her, her eyebrows arched.

"You surprised me. I thought I was all alone out here. And, anyway, I was careful to drop the matches overboard." She stood up a little straighter, squaring her shoulders, remembering that this was a possible enemy facing her, also remembering Dustin had asked her to get to know this woman better. Mary One smiled at her. "Now before you get started, I have to apologize for making a pass at your Dustin on the train. I didn't know he was yours. And anyway, the two of you really look good together." Mary Two relaxed a little. She never was one to carry on a grudge. "And this stupid Mary One and Mary Two thing. Let's stop it right now. My middle name is Naomi. I'll let everyone know that they should call me that. You are now the only Mary on the ship." Naomi stared out at the hundreds of ships at anchor. "This is a great time for a smoke. Can I borrow your matches, if you have any left?" She pulled out a pack of filter tips, pulled one out and lit up from a match Mary held in her cupped hands. "Care for one?" Naomi held out the pack.

Mostly, Mary hated the idea of smoking. She understood the value of smoking as a social tool and as an ancient medical remedy. The medical community had always recognized the danger of tobacco, a danger they embraced. It was felt in the 18th century that slight amounts of poison made a person a healthier being. It was a common practice to use an arsenic oil on hair, or add it to the paint on a child's crib. It was believed that the body, feeling threatened, would go into overdrive and protect itself from any invasion. But then they also believed that people became ill because the sickness sneaked into the body like the devil and made the body sick before it could notice. Mary wondered what Dustin believed. Was he more of a traditionalist or did he believe in the presently popular germ theory of disease. A reasonable theory but a theory nonetheless. Mary took the cigarette and lit up with a small defiant flip of her hair.

"Lean well over the side to tap the ashes off the tip. The Captain would have us keelhauled if we dirtied his ship," Naomi said with a giggle.

"Doesn't Mr. Hawkins care about his ship?" Mary puffed her cancer stick into a nice glow. She wondered if she was a secret arsonist as she stared at the living flame. Or if she was secretly suicidal. She knew that the nicotine and tar were only co-factors in lung cancer, requiring other chemicals to be present also, but why was she making it possible? With a flip of her finger she threw the half smoked cigarette overboard.

"He owns so much stuff. He expects others to care for his things for him. He couldn't be bothered to do it. He is a very strange man in a lot of ways." Suddenly, Naomi wondered if Hawk was up in his cabin watching the two of them, and listening to them. He had sent her down here to chat up Mary Two. To get on her good side. To be her friend. He wanted to be sure that if Dustin found any gold, he would be aware of it. Hawk felt all of the treasure discovered on Cocos Island belonged to him. He felt those old pirate captains had made a mistake sharing out the booty. The men only became wild, wilder, with lucre in their pockets.

Naomi finished her smoke and threw the butt overboard. She thought that if Hawk was watching he might as well get a good show. She looked closely at Mary. She was actually a beautiful woman. However, she used absolutely no makeup to emphasize her good points, to make her face a personal statement instead of yet another sample of one out of 7 billion faces. She wasn't even wearing any lipstick. She moved a little closer to Mary who turned to meet her in defense. Mary still didn't trust her. She still had her eyes squinted, like Joan Crawford.

"Mary, lick your lips." It was a command and Mary had spent most of her adult life obeying parents, bosses, boyfriends, policemen, and politicians. She licked her lips, her tongue flashing in and out like an animal.

Naomi quickly slipped a slim hand around the back of Mary's neck, moved closer and kissed her full on the lips. It was a gentle kiss and yet demanding. Naomi was a good kisser. She knew how to harvest power within herself by holding her breath for a couple of seconds, building up the carbon dioxide within her lungs and then slowly, ever so slowly release it into Mary's mouth and nose. Naomi ignored the rest of her body, aware only of her lips. And Mary's lips. Mary was so surprised that she didn't pull away instantly. That was her downfall. The feeling was so different, so gentle, so kind, so non demanding, she was entranced. The two women broke the kiss after a long 3 seconds. Mary gasped after, needing oxygen and to rid herself of excess carbon dioxide.

"What? I mean, why? Mary One, I mean, Naomi, why did you do that?" Mary put her fingers to her lips to wipe away the moisture. Her lips felt all tingly. If she had a mirror she would have been able to see that they were slightly blue.

"Did you enjoy it? Sorry if I took you unawares. You looked so kissable and I like you so much, I am afraid I might have taken a liberty. Can you ever forgive me?" Naomi's hand finally left Mary's neck and traveled down Mary's shoulder and side. The thumb just drifting past the muscles below her armpit.

"I have never done such a thing. Naomi, I am sorry to have to tell you, but I am not a lesbian." She stepped back a pace to be out of range of Naomi's wandering hand. "I am really in love with Dustin, with Dr. Horner, I mean. I am not interested in anyone else of either sex." Naomi smiled.

"I don't want to marry you, cutie. I do get tired of men and their heavy handed ways, doing what they want without a thought for the girl. It is demeaning, it really is. Haven't you ever been with a woman, Mary? A woman who wants and desires you for your beauty?"

"I am not beautiful. I never have been." Mary fussed with her hair. Why had she gasped so, after the kiss? She must have really needed it. Was she missing out by not trying it with a woman? Cosmo always said that it was better to regret the things you did than the things you didn't do.

"Mary, such nonsense. You are a very beautiful woman. All you need is a little touch here or there. If you changed your hair, just a bit, maybe like this." Naomi stepped forward a step and ran her fingers through Mary's hair, smoothing, petting, probing. "You could be so beautiful. You just need a sister to help out, to confide in, to be your friend. We girls really need a good friend to talk things over. Living in a man's world is so tough sometimes. It really, truly is." Naomi slightly, gently rubbed the back of Mary's neck. "Would you like me to be your friend?" Mary tried to step back, away from Naomi, but the rail of the ship was hard against the small of her back..

"Yes, I guess I could use a good friend. Yes, Naomi, I would love to be your friend, but just that. A friend with no, repeat, no, benefits, Okay?"

"Sure, Babe. I'm sorry if I scared you. It wasn't my intention. You just looked so lovely standing there by the rail, like a movie star, you know? Kind of like Nicole Kidman. I just got carried away by the moment. Sorry. I'll never let it happen again." Naomi smiled kindly at Mary. She really loved being a predator, it turned her on so much. Maybe that is why she and Hawk got along, two peas from the same pod. Two birds of prey soaring high in the sky. Maybe she should call herself, Falcon? Falcons were the fastest birds in the sky, weren't they?

Tugs didn't like the plan at all. He didn't like kidnapping, he didn't like stealing or killing, he didn't like any criminal activity, he just liked driving fast cars. And the worse part was, this time, he was only going to drive a few miles. It was a bad plan. Good plans included him racing cops across continents. He still didn't like the idea of grabbing five kids and ransoming just one. It seemed like waste to him. He was sure they were good kids. Kids usually were. He had grown up in foster homes across the States. He knew all about kids and growing up.

Both his parents had been sent to prison and none of his relatives had wanted him. The State took control and assigned him wherever they wanted. He had no choice in the matter. He was treated as an indentured servant in most homes, just smacked around in others. He hated crime as a child, crime had taken his parents away from him. As a teenager, he decided to hate the cops. They were the ones who really took his parents away. Crime? Crime he discovered was everywhere. Politicians behaved criminally all the time and received healthy pensions instead of doing time. Rich dudes were ripping people off right and left. Sure, they mostly did it legally, but not justly. They lived in big mansions and everyone respected them. They were all criminals but the cops didn't touch them. They went for the poor, the dispossessed, the hungry, the mentally damaged; they went for the easy prey. If they wanted to stop crime, they should start at the top.

The rich and connected were the ones keeping the poor and damaged at the bottom of the heap. It was all a set up. They had framed his parents. They had foreclosed on their house, seized their bank accounts, taken his bicycle, thrown them out on the street and called it justice. Justice for whom? When his parents had returned to their own house to get clothes and blankets, they were arrested for breaking and entering and given five years in jail by the judge after he learned they were living on the street. His parents had tried to explain. It didn't matter. The judge had made up his mind before he listened to the evidence. Their lawyer told them they were lucky to get off so easy. Some judges hated anyone who slept under bridges.

Tugs wasn't a violent man. He wasn't like Joe. He was just a wheelman. Joe, now, he was a criminal, born and bred. He had killed both his parents with a knife at thirteen after being grounded for a day. He robbed his first bank at fourteen, was a made man at fifteen and was spending life in prison at eighteen. He had broken out after killing three guards and had never been recaptured. If a cop pulled over the car he was in, Joe shot him down without a thought as the cop walked over to his car. Sometimes, Tugs thought Joe was truly insane.

And now he wanted to kidnap all those kids, right out of school. How mean, how cruel. If there was justice in the world, kids should really be kidnapped right along with their mothers so they could have someone to tell them it was going to be okay. No one should have their parents taken away or be taken away from their parents. But what could Tugs do against a torpedo like Joe? He was just a driver. Joe's driver.

Joe had found a kid on the street who had just been flunked out of one of the schools in Colon. Joe offered him what the kid thought was big money and he had his Judas. The plan was to fake a fire drill, only Tugs knew that Joe wouldn't fake it. A real fire would add that much more confusion to the scene, give them more time to skedaddle the hell out of there. Colon was covered in containers, some stacked as high as a five story building. The plan was to stash them in any one of five containers, or if Joe had his way he wouldn't pick one till the last second. They would grab them up on the side of the road by the school with the time honored lie:

"Your parents sent me to pick you up. They don't want you to be late for the party. You did know about the party, didn't you? Oops. Maybe I wasn't supposed to tell you. It's a surprise. Don't tell your parents, okay? It'll be our secret." It worked everytime. It had the right amount of humor mixed with fear. Lies always had to be a mix of humor and fear if they were to be believed. Tugs didn't know why. He had been told many lies in his life. He was experienced in being told lies. He wasn't much good at telling them, but hearing them? He had lots of experience.

Kid-Day arrived and Joe was stoked at the idea of a multiple kidnapping. As Tugs drove them down to the Kentucky Fried for breakfast, Joe was blathering away about how this was the first five way kidnapping he had ever heard of, they were making history.

"They are going to tell stories about us for hundreds of years! Yeah, we are going to be like famous! Fucking famous. You got this thing full of gas? Like as famous as Babe Ruth, as Ali, as fucking Robin Hood. Yeah, like Robin Hood, 'cept we ain't giving nothing to the poor. Fuck the poor." Tugs tuned Joe out. He could go on for hours like that. There was a nice turn up ahead. He could really take that turn nicely if all these stupid taxis weren't in the way. But that was Colon. Hundreds of old buses, thousands of old taxis, all running around a city that was old before those pilgrims stole Manhattan. Before our honored forefathers committed theft. Guy couldn't get up a decent head of steam, what with all the traffic. Not many pedestrians. Colon was not a town to walk around in. Dangerous, it was. He didn't know why the kids were allowed to walk home. Most be some Latino thing.

Tugs slowed down as they approached the first school. The fink sitting between them pointed excitedly at one girl standing by a tree, talking to a school friend, watching as kids ran from the building. Tugs stopped the Caddy right in front of them and Joe did his thing. First he tried his little speech. Girl couldn't understand English. What did they teach these kids, anyway? But Joe could really move, Tugs had to give him that. He tended to think of Joe as all mouth, the way he never shut up, but when money was on the table, the guy could give pointers to wide receivers. It was not but two seconds and he had the girl in the car and Tugs took off. The rat was helping Joe put duct tape over the girl's mouth, around her hands and feet. He was really excited. The fink was putting tape all over her face when Joe suddenly sat up.

"Stop the car, Tugs. This ain't the right one." Joe turned to the Judas and hit him across the face with the back of his hand. "Fucker, who is this?" The girl had managed to pull some tape off her mouth after Joe had let her go and was blabbering hundred miles a second in some kind of Spanish.

"Pardon, Senor. It is the wrong one. Next I pick the right one, Si?" Joe could understand a few of the words the girl was saying now that she had slowed down a trifle. Something about how she wouldn't let the rat copy off of her test paper on the test that was the last straw for the school board. With a cry of disgust and an oath, Joe threw both of them out of the car on the side of some road.

"God damn it. My plan is all screwed up. Fuck it to hell. Shit. I feel like killing something. Anything. I am so pissed. We still got to ditch the car, damn it. It is going to be red hot as soon as those kids talk. Go to Four Corners, Tugs. We'll ditch it there." Tugs was already heading that way and he pulled into the parking lot just minutes later.

They dropped the Caddy and causally walked away. Tugs even stopped for a minute to stare at a cloud. They went into a fast food restaurant with big glass windows where they could keep an eye on the car to see if they had been followed. Stupid to grab another car if the cops were watching. They would just follow them again and pick 'em up whenever they wanted. Like Joe was always saying, successful crime relied on clean breaks.

An argument was going on at one of the big tables. The Spanish was fast and furious with little hope for comprehension by a couple of gringos. When the waitress delivered their meal Joe turned on his manners and asked the girl what the big discussion was all about.

"Oh, it is nada, Senor. The big one there, he says he listen to one of the crew off that big yacht in the harbor? He was saying that they were going to the Isla Cocos to hunt for the treasure the pirates hid there. The others, they said no one ever found any treasure there, ever, you know?" A gleam radiated out of Joe's eyes.

"How much did the pirates hide there?"

"Oh, mucho, Senor. Muy mucho. It is so much it could pay off the monies the whole third world owe the Americans. Many, many millions, most in gold, you know?"

"And where is this island?"

"Ah, Senor. Manual, he sat next to me in the geography class? I write the note and pass it to Manual. And he write to me. Muy bonito, mucho amore, si, but I did not learn the maps and charts. Wait. I ask." She shouted out to the other table across the room. Various answers came back along with a variety of wolf whistles. "They say that it belongs to Costa Rica and is west of Punta Mala. This is a muy nasty point of land with bad winds." As the girl walked away, Joe turned to Tugs.

"Ok, that is how we make our wad. We go out to this island, knock a few heads together, get some answers, and grab the loot."

"But, Joe, nobody's ever found dis treasure. That's what da girl said. We don't know nothing bout pirate treasure."

"Don't have to. We get out there ahead of this yacht, let them find the treasure, and we grab it."

No one had paid the slightest interest in the Caddy, so after an hour Joe and Tugs went out to scout for another car.

"That one," growled Joe, that white pretty one with the fins and all that chrome and shit."

"Joe, dats a Caddy, too. Cops are going to be looking for a caddy. We got ta get a Toyota or something. Sumthing black and old with still a few horse dat ain't tired yet. Like dat one." He pointed out a Mazda with the rotary engine, an Rx-7, an oldie but goodie.

"What the fuck? You want me to ride in a slant eye car? Fuck that, you dimwit."

"You try it Joe, I promise you gonna like it. Thing moves on out and corners like a Ferrari." Tugs had his lock puller out and within seconds was sliding it through the felt liner of the top of the driver side window. The puller slipped down between the window casing and the door and presto, Tugs through the magic of a misspent childhood, had the car open. He popped the hood and had the alarm disconnected after only a few bars of siren opera. Inside of an hour and a half they were driving down the streets of metropolitan Panama City. Joe had been griping the entire ride. Finally Tugs had enough.

"I don't like dis new plan neither. Where am I gonna drive on a island? Ain't gonna be any streets, no cars, nothing."

"How you gonna live, I don't give you something on account? You gonna end up a bum eating out a garbage cans. Don't bust anymore brain cells, Tugs. You ain't got enough to spare. You let me do the thinking, alright? And fuck your driving, you do what I say and you will be swimming in gravy."

"You'se sound like dat snake in dat Adam's and Eve place. The one dat told her ta eat dat apple? Snake was always saying, don't think, I tell you what to do. God keeping the good stuff just for him. He won't mind, you eat just one. God should have put barb wire around dat tree, he don't want anyone ta eat it. He made dat Adam and Eve. They go wrong, why he cry. He the one dat made 'em. Anyway, now you say listen to you. Sure, I get sent to da pen, you gonna do my time?

Hawk didn't think of himself as a pervert. He didn't surf the internet for porn or buy dirty magazines. He could get as many women as he wanted and the ones he took, for the most part, wanted more. There were always the whiners, of course. The ones who thought they had been used and abused just so he could be amused. Fuck them. There would always be whiners. It was the way of the world. He knew there were a lot of perverts in the world, but he never thought of himself as one.

He had discovered that his little spy camera machine could record images to tape. So he could watch them over and over again. He was surprised at the thrill it gave him to watch someone he knew, some woman he knew, change her stripes when she lay between the sheets. Become like a wild animal, wanting, taking, using. Kind of like him. Briefly, he wondered if that meant he had female traits? With a shake of his Santa Claus head, he laughed. It meant other men were sissies, they weren't men enough to keep up with their woman. Well, he was. Damn, yes, he was. He would like to take each of the women he had watched on his spy machine and teach them what it would be like to be with a real man. One at a time or all together, he didn't care. But the gold came first. First the gold, then let the fun and games start.

He looked out the window. His ship was moving into the first lock of the Panama Canal. Steel cables were led to his bow and stern from huge locomotives that pulled his ship into the lock and secured the *Steel Balls* in the center as water poured in raising his ship up 30 feet in only a few minutes. Soon the locomotives pulled his ship into the next lock easing and taking in wire rope as needed.

It turned out he had to cough up the dough for the Canal. It really irritated him. He damn well better find that gold on the island. He hated to spend his money and get nothing in return. He wanted that gold. He was going to get all that gold. Anyone that stood up in his way was going to be very surprised. Very surprised and very dead.

John was setting his table for lunch. The Prospector was coming with his guest for a meal and a meeting with the Man. John promised himself that he would keep his ears wide open. He had heard so much already, it just whetted his appetite for more. His father worked as a hardware clerk while his mother was a checker at a grocery store. He had grown up on the wrong side of the tracks much to the dismay of his mother. She had tried to drill the behaviors necessary to be admitted into polite society into John as he grew up and she had mostly succeeded. But still there was the hunger for wealth that permeates through a poor man's soul like mud through a door sill during a flood.

He was lucky to get this job. He knew he was hired solely for his good looks. He didn't care. Anything to get up in the world. Life was easy for him on the ship. The other crew complained. Aboard ship it was eight hours on, eight hours off and working in between. The rest of the crew tried to protect their off time, John, he had worked hard his entire life, whether mowing lawns, delivering groceries on his bike, walking dogs or digging ditches. He liked living aboard. He liked eating three squares of delicious meals. However, he still wanted more. Much more. If only he got the chance. He knew no one would give anything to him. He had learned aboard this boat. He had learned that you took what you wanted. It was the only way. It made him feel kind of bad. The preacher back home always taught about the Golden Rule. Do unto others as you would like them to do unto you. No one on this boat seemed to have ever heard of such a rule.

The Prospector knocked on the door promptly at six. He had shaved for the occasion and wore a button down western shirt and levis, his best clothes. He even shined his boots. His guest was spectacular. She wore an A line cocktail dress created out of Thai silk that shimmered as she moved. A single black pearl the size of a robin's

egg resided within a gossamer thin gold cage worn around her neck and suspended to lay just
between the rise of her breasts. Around her slim left ankle she wore a platinum slave bracelet that jingled as she moved. Her shoes seemed to not exist save as a hint of crystal and light. Hawk rose from behind his desk as they entered. He came out to meet them in the middle of the room. He gave the Prospector his normal bear hug of a hand shake, just to put him in a defensive mood. The girl he half raped, at least with his eyes.

He ran his fingers up from her neck, following her skull, within her hair, massaging as he went as he greeted her with his other hand. He had watched her video far more that any of the others. He felt he knew her already. He kind of felt he was her lover. He knew he wanted her in his bed. Captain Banks told him that she must have snuck aboard as there was no record of her entering via the gang plank. Hawk didn't care. Her being a stowaway and an adventuress just whetted his appetite far more than a normal, secretary type could. The *Steel Balls* had been working its magic on him and he sure could use a bad girl about now, to screw, to use, to fuck within a inch of her life. This one, she was so hot, she would last a long time till he could discard her, a broken toy, broken by the valor of his sexual expertise. He felt a presence to his right. The Prospector was glaring at him. At him!

"You are hurting the girl. Let her go." His words were simple. The tone they were stated with was not. It reverberated with threat. The salty, coppery taste of danger emanated from him. Hawk felt like laughing off this old man, giving him a push with, say, one finger, knocking him sprawling. But he stopped himself. He needed this old man. He was Hawk's secret weapon.

He had asked far and wide for someone with a natural affinity to gold, someone who could find it with a natural instinct, an ESP. This man's name kept coming up. This guy without a name, just called, The Prospector. A guy who could succeed where scientists hadn't, who didn't need treasure maps. Who felt the presence of gold. This guy was *the* treasure, and he didn't even know it. All previous attempts on Cocos were loaded with playboys, would be adventurers and bored socialites. Not his expeditions. He brought a scientist, a historian, and a genuine gold magnet. How could he lose?

As he slowly let go of the girl, he stared at the Prospector straight in the eye. Most men would look away, smile to try to disarm the situation, or back up to prepare to run. Not this Prospector. He stood his ground and reached down, without looking and lifted the cigar box on Hawk's desk. Slowly the guy picked a good one and took his time sniping off the end, rolling it in a glass of brandy that Hawk had been drinking and lit it up. All while never leaving Hawk's eyes for more than a second. Hawk had to hand it to the guy. Not many men had the balls to stand eye ball to eye ball to a man like him. His face might look like Santa Claus, but not his eyes. They didn't seem to bother this guy. After a few minutes of puffing, the Prospector crushed the burning end of his barely touched ten dollar black-market Cuban stogie into an ash tray and looked back, straight into Hawk's eyes. Really looked deep into them, reading the variety of colors in their irises, the quality of the spirit residing within.

"So, Hawkins, are we going to eat, or what?" Hawk mutely pointed to the impeccably dressed table and the threesome sat down, Hawk at the head of the table, next to the windows, the glare hiding his facial expressions. It was a gorgeous meal. First came an appetizer of Cajun glazed mushrooms, followed by a brown rice jambalaya and trout almandine. The threesome dug in. The Prospector was much more subdued, watching the others carefully to be sure to use the correct fork. The food was delicious and no one spoke much to the dismay of John as he brought remove after remove. He was the main conduit of gossip for the crew. He enjoyed being the center of attention for something other than his looks. Plus in the back of his mind, if he got a share of any pirate gold, he could buy a house for his parents, clear them of any debt. A place
they could call their own as they entered their last third of their lives. He sent money to them every month but it never seemed to be enough As he brought out the dessert they had finally started to talk.

"How exactly do you find gold? Is it some kind of ESP?"

"That is one of them tough questions. Best answer is, how can't you find the gold? It be laying right there mostly in broad daylight. Just covered a bit. Why can't you see it?"

"I guess because I don't know what to look for. Do you look for the yellow glint of gold?" Hawk was keeping his face very neutral and it seemed he barely noticed when Mary One entered the room and sat down quietly at the table. The Prospector looked in askance at the woman. "I'm sorry. Let me introduce my associate. Mary, sorry, it's Naomi now isn't it? Prospector, meet Naomi, Naomi meet the gorgeous female and vice versa. Now about the gold?" Naomi looked at the Stowaway with raised eyebrows.

"Actually, it is Robyn with a y." Naomi smiled back at her.

The Prospector reached out a well lined hand and just held Naomi's hand, he didn't attempt to shake it. He just held her fingers between his thumb and his fingers. It seemed that he would have kissed her hand if he were closer. As he released her hand, he turned to Robyn.

"Damn, this boat is just loaded with women." And he leaned over and kissed Robyn square on the lips. He made it a long lingering kiss. As they broke, he continued to gaze at her, worshiping her and then turned back to his host. "Gold. Do you know that the world's oceans contain 10 billion tons of pure gold? Problem is, it is in such low concentrations that recovery is far more expensive than the gold is worth. Point is, there is a lot of gold on this old world, people just ain't used to looking for it. Now us'n, we don't have that problem. The gold is found, them pirates just hid it. Shouldn't be a problem. It's only a little island. How hard can it be? Only question, how come it ain't been found already? Are you sure it hasn't?"

"Totally sure. At least the more spectacular objects. Especially the Virgin. It is something that would be talked about. It could never be secret, once seen."

"They could have melted her down, kept the ice, sold the gold in ingots." The Prospector didn't think so. He knew the allure of gold objects. They had the ability to take over people's personalities, to turn them from adventurers to protectors, from seekers to hoarders. Hawk looked as if a dirty word had been uttered at a state dinner.

"Please, don't say such things. Let's be positive." Hawk looked almost discouraged. Naomi felt her heart twist. She did care for him. She did.

"I have a feeling about this. And I am sure Robyn would agree with me. Call it a female's intuition. I believe we are going to find the greatest treasure the world has ever made. I believe we are going to find the Treasure of Cocos Island. I believe that soon, the Virgin herself is going to stand there in the corner." Naomi spoke so convincingly that all at the table turned to look at the far corner. The Prospector raised his glass first, held high in salute.

"To the Queen of Cocos Island, born of the Incas, lost these many years. Welcome back!"

Everyone at the table raised their glasses in unison with cries of welcome and greeting and devotion and greed.

The *Rose Marie* looked more like a cruising boat now. All the wet gear had been dried and the interior aired out and put back into order. The winds were lighter now as she ghosted along, doing well with her light sails. The northerly winds wafted out the scent of land, of coconut and swamp, of burning cane fields and volcanos venting white, cloud like sulfur vapor out of the top of their peaks. The land was romantic at least from a distance. Occasionally, just beyond the beach, car horns indicated the complications of civilization.

"Will one of you tell me again why we can't sail over to that beach right there and anchor and row ashore so I can bury my waterlogged little toes in some nice hot sun and eat a hot dog?" Jill had crammed herself into a corner of the cockpit and was practicing pouting. Janet was at the helm, keeping a look out and making sure the autopilot was doing it's job.

"Honey, there is no anchorage by that beach. Look at this swell." She pointed at the 5 foot smooth waves passing the boat, coming from the south. "These little waves are going to turn into huge breakers when they reach soundings next to that beach. To anchor we need protection from the wind and waves. Your little footies are just going to have to wait.

"Why don't you paint your nails?" Jill stared at her mother in astonishment.

"Mother! Really! Like in Hollywood? Like on a date?" Jill was going to make a sarcastic comment, but suddenly the idea appealed to her. She dove below and was soon back with half the contents of her mother's make up kit. "Do you have to sand your nails first, like varnish?" To make it stick?" Her eyes were sparkling in excitement. "This is going to be so much fun!"

"Let's do it together. I'll go first and you can follow. The first thing to remember is you won't be able to use your toes while the polish is drying, so try to get everything under control before you start. Okay, then. I always start with my littlest piggy first, as it is the least important."

"Mother, my little toe is very important. I use it to pick my nose when my classmates are learning yoga!"

As the two girls busied themselves practicing their feminine skills, Harv studied his charts. He wasn't a very happy man. It seemed to him, these days, that he wasn't the man he used to be. In years gone by, he succeeded in most everything he tried, but lately he believed he had to be rescued by others after he got himself in trouble. And he didn't like it. He wanted to be the hero in his own play. After all, it was his life, why couldn't he be the star? At least in his own mind? He figured it was because he had so many reversals lately, but on the other hand, here he was sailing along the coast of Central America. It seemed to him that everytime he ran into a younger man, he ended up with the shorter end of the stick. He wondered if he was loosing his muscle mass that he had developed so industriously when he was younger. Was he turning into a 50 plus weakling? With a narrowing of his eyes, he dropped to the cabin sole and forced himself to do 10 quick push-ups. The last one was really tough and left him gasping. He stayed on the floor, panting. It was true then. He was indeed turning into an old man, a weakling. He rolled over on his back and did 20 sit-ups. It was a good thing he was laying down. A guy couldn't fall down and embarrass himself if he was already flat on his back. After a few minutes of feeling sorry for himself he rolled onto his side and preformed a few leg lifts. Maybe he wasn't that old. Age was all in the mind, wasn't it? Did his arms hurt this much as a kid during PE?

"Mom! Dad's having a heart attack!" The back of Jill's hand was covering her mouth and one eye as she stood in the companionway. "Mom, hurry!"

"Honey, darling, are you alright?" Janet leaned over Harv and counted his pulse with a hand on his wrist. She felt his forehead with her other hand. His skin was all clammy. "Jill, quickly, get me that book, 'Where There Is No Doctor'." She leaned down and tenderly kissed Harv. "Stay with me big guy."

"Janet, I am fine. I was just doing a few exercises. That is all. Trying to stay in shape. Just getting my breath now. Just taking a little breather." His breath came out in a whisper. Harv tried to sit up. His face turned pale, paler.

"Baby, just stay still. Don't move. Here, have a little water. You know how you like to drink water. Just a little sip for me, honey."

Harv lay there, getting his breath back and wondered again why he was getting old while his wife seemed to be getting younger every day. Younger and more competent. It just wasn't fair. People were supposed to get old together. He was getting old all by himself. Where was the justice in that? It just wasn't fair.

"Mom?" Jill was outside standing watch. "Hey, Mom? There is this ruffled water, kinda, and it is turning all white, like a squall, you know? Only kinda bigger. Can you come and look?" Harv grabbed Janet's shirt with his left hand.

"I was afraid of this. It is a Papagayo. Get all the rag off of her. Quickly!" Harv let go of her shirt. What a stupid time to be doing exercises.

Up on deck, Jill and Janet rolled in the jib in a flash and dropped the main in a pile on the cabin, then turned to the mizzen. The squall was getting closer. They furled the mizzen on it's boom and then turned to lash the larger mainsail as the wind hit them. It didn't hit all at once, it just seemed like it did. From a beautiful ten knot northerly, with puffy clouds and a warm sun, it turned, in a matter of seconds, into a cold, miserable 30 knot east-northeasterly, and the wind was building. With the main furled, the *Rose Marie* heeled over sideways to the wind, lying a hull. Harv pulled himself up through the hatch and looked out at the developing gale. He looked up at the flying clouds.

"Why me, Lord? Wasn't a Tehuantepec enough? Do we have to experience every storm you have ever invented?" The Lord didn't reply to Harv's upturned face. Instead the wind started to blow even harder, and the seas started to build. He reached over and started the motor. He let out a sigh as the trusty Yanmar kicked into life. He maneuvered himself across the cockpit and sat behind the wheel and with a half angry jerk engaged the forward gear. Slowly the boat headed north, north towards the beach strewn coast of El Salvador.

Harv had to head a little west to make any progress. He didn't complain to an unlistening god. He was just happy to be making progress. He could keep the boat up to 5 knots by dodging the bigger waves, not that they were huge like the last gale. The coast was only a few miles away. But that was what it was, just a coast. No bays, no harbors, a few roadsteads and a couple of mangrove estuaries. The estuaries would be good in this wind, if he could get past the breaking sandbars protecting their entrances, especially since in this wind the seas would build up into giants, great for surfers, not so good for cruising boats approaching soundings.

"Dad! You should be lying down or something shouldn't you? I mean, really, me and Mom can handle all this sailing stuff. You should be resting, getting your strength back." Jill had her fists on her hips and was smiling at him, taking away the sting of her words. "After all, now that you are old and all, you have to take care of yourself!" Harv smiled at his little girl, his strength returning.

"Up yours, Kitten." Jill's mouth fell open, half into a perfect 'O' and half of her lips, just the corners, turned into curls of a smile.

"Mom, Dad is feeling better," she shouted out, her normal volume as a teenager. Janet looked back into the cockpit and smiled at her husband. His eyes were lively. His joy of life had returned. She could see the man she had married again. A laughing fellow rover who could drag her out of her melancholy whenever she fell into a pit of despair. A man whose optimism countered her natural caution. A man whose friendliness joined with her inbred shyness to create a perfect social couple.

He smiled back at her as she stood on the foredeck, hands at her sides, feet spread, rolling and pitching with the boat, as one with the boat, not bothering to even hold on to the handy staysail stay a couple feet from her. A woman of the sea. A woman powerful in her own competence. A woman whose inner beauty ignited the air around her and those she met. A sexual creature who refused to admit it. She preferred to think of herself as chaste, except in the throes of passion when her desires took over her personality. She was a woman who could take on the world with just a smile as her only defense. A smile that is, plus that which dwelt within her.

Cocos Island didn't have much of a dock. Not that it needed one. The water was shallow enough for wading next to the beach but it quickly fell off to water too deep to stand. Not that Elena would want to. There were signs posted repeatedly on the beach in different languages.

Dangerous Marine Animals. No Swimming Allowed.

If that wasn't enough, as the boat was approaching they saw a commotion in the water. Something had died and hundreds of sharks were thrashing around, biting, killing, eating. She had always heard that sharks were silent when they attacked. These weren't. She could hear their jaws snapping as they fought for every last morsel of remaining meat.

Elena felt shivers yoyo up and down her spine at the sight. Once the boat tied up to the end of the dock, she rushed to the beach to take off her shoes and to sink her toes into the warm, toasty sand. The bay was so beautiful. A line of coconut trees leaned over the beach offering a welcome shade. A little line of waves lapped onto the shore. The jungle leapt up the jumble of rocks and caves, across mountains and waterfalls, through rotting vegetation and bursting life that dared call itself an island rather than chaos. As she slipped her toes into the water, cooling them with pleasure enjoying the contrast from the hot sand. She saw a grey shape zigzagging along the shore. When it was just abreast of her it seemed to hesitate, then turned suddenly. Without warning a monster leapt out of the water, leapt onto the beach, mouth gaping wide open, eyes staring at her, eyes as black as death, then, just as the evil, rotting, filthy teeth were about to close about her upper chest, she was jerked backwards, falling onto the sand, away from the huge shark.

Mercedes held her wrapped protectively in her arms where they had fallen after Mercedes had pulled her to safety. "Elena, I have an idea. Maybe we shouldn't walk so close to the water." Elena just nodded mutely as the shark thrashed its way back into the water and disappeared after a baleful stare at the two girls.

"I think maybe you are right, Chica." Still, Elena held onto Mercedes long after the monster was gone. Finally, Elena gave her friend a quick kiss on the corner of the mouth. "Gracias, Merc."

"Nada, Amiga, it was nothing." The girls wandered over to the dock. There was a boat of scuba divers getting ready to take off for an adventure. Elena wanted to rush over and tell them not to go into the water. Mercedes held her back.

"I think they know what they are doing, Chica. Look, they are careful not to get close to the side of the boat. Come, let's find our guest cottage."

There were signs haphazardly posted here and there. Elena kept looking for one that had a big black X on it, X for here lies the treasure. Eventually following little trails they discovered the manager's house, and just beyond a trail to a rambling beach cottage. As they approached, an ancient oriental man exited from the cottage. He had a long pigtail down the middle of his back, wore black slippers with white socks and loose fitting clothes.

"Hello, Missies. You the girls Dominic sent? That Dominic, he likes to have beauty around him, yes? I am Ben Atcham Chang, I cook. Just call me Ben. Everyone does. I show you around the cottage." It was a derelict looking building. The front door wasn't locked. It didn't even have a lock. Not that there was much to steal. Two bedrooms branched off of a central living area. The bedrooms were small. So small, Ben just opened the doors and gestured for them to look in. The main room had a double burner camp stove with an old hose that led to a propane bottle outside. A makeshift sink that drained into a garden outside was next to a table with three legs. The empty space where the fourth leg should have been was nailed to the wall and two of the other legs looked like they were in dire need of splints. A filthy couch completed the cottage's furnishings.

"I see why there isn't a lock on the door. There isn't anything here worth stealing." Elena looked a bit dismayed. "How bad are the barracks?"

"Nonsense. This is perfect. We'll take it. Thank you, Ben." Mercedes bowed slightly with one hand enclosed within the other, held next to her solar plexus. Ben looked pleased. Elena's mouth fell open and she shook her head, violently. As Ben left, Mercedes looked at Elena's face, white from dismay. "Elena, snap out of it. We can clean this mess up. This is a trick. They want us to stay at the barracks where they can ogle us to their hearts' content. Let's not let them. Come, grab the other end of this couch. This thing belongs outside. Maybe we should burn it? Should we have a party tonight and burn it for illumination? Oh, Elena, this is going to be so much fun!"

H

Hawk lay in the huge bed in his Owner's Cabin and watched as Naomi walked out of the shower. She hurriedly dried her hair with a few furtive glances at him. She could tell he wasn't in a good mood by the scowl that hung over him, threatening lightning. She started to pull on a pair of pajamas when his growl stopped her. Obediently she climbed into his bed naked and a little nervous about what might happen this time.

"How is our little plan working out?" He spoke a question but she knew it was a threat. A threat that if she hadn't worked hard, she would be punished. She also knew better than to lie to him. Naomi quickly sneaked a look at his face. He wasn't going to be happy. She took a big breath and tightened up her body in case he hit her, again.

"There are a few challenges, Sir. The foremost is the Prospector. He keeps all of his tools in his cabin which limits the time I can examine them. However, to the best of my knowledge, they seem to be fakes. At least, I can't get them to work. There are no manuals or start up sheets in his gear. He could carry everything around in his head but he doesn't seem to be one of the brightest stars in the sky.

"Whenever I ask him how he finds gold, he replies with a question of his own circling around the idea that my eyes are closed or I would see gold surrounding me. I don't know how we can proceed until we see him in action. Logically, we have to consider the thought that he might be a fake."

"I have it on the highest authority that he is genuine. The very highest. A very, very rich and cunning man has made quite a bundle off this man's gold sense. I believe he is the real deal, I certainly hope that he is."

"Yes, Sir. We will have to wait then. Should I continue to try to discover how to operate his 'tools'?"

"By all means. It is of the utmost importance that we can rely on our own people if a general mutiny occurs, for whatever reason." Hawk looked pensive for a brief second, if it was at all possible for such a man to look anything but totally self-confident. He had the Captain sabotage the telex, internet and phone services. Sooner or later, however, these people would discover that he had not paid any monies into their accounts. For a while he could always rely on the old, 'the check is in the mail' line. The longer he could keep his search team ignorant, the better for him. His biggest fear was if one of his 'passengers' owned a satellite phone, they would discover his deception before he found any gold, any gold at all.

The thought angered him. He wanted that gold, he needed the gold, and he damn well better get it. He picked up a priceless Ming dynasty vase and threw it against the bulkhead. The vase created a satisfactory crash but not enough to assuage his anger. He glanced at the girl. At his able assistant in his plan. He was happy to see fear in her eyes. Fear of him, of what he might do, of how he might hurt her. She was behaving and performing well. He wouldn't hurt her badly, this time. She was a good girl. Still, he could see her legs shaking ever so slightly. Shaking in fear. In fear of him. The sight of her fear caused him to go wild.

With a curse he leapt across the bed and tore her legs open. Kneeling between them he picked her up high off the bed by the hips and rammed himself into her. She wasn't ready for him, but that was how he liked it. It made her feel tighter. With a snarl on his face, he pounded her body against him, like a toy. Her spine was arched back painfully, her head barely touched the bed, her widely flung arms lightly oscillated on either side of her, her legs achingly tried to curl around him, to slow him down, to control him. Hawk paid no attention. His eyes closed as he increased the pace, her body now a blur as his huge hands pounded her hips against his. Finally, thankfully, he screamed inarticulately, primally, gutturally, and with the last of his seed pumped into her, he tossed her from him, like a used condom, and walked over to his spy system and toggled the screen through the various cabins on board, looking, looking, looking for who knew what.

Naomi closed the bathroom door of the owner's cabin, switched on the light and turned to look at herself in the mirror. 'Why do I let him treat me in such a way?' she thought, a single tear appeared in the corner of her left eye. 'I have such bad luck with men.' Slowly she reached behind her neck and undid the pink ribbon tied there. She let it drop to the floor and stared at the tiny fold of skin just below where a man's adam's apple would have been.

"Is it true what they say? Does this really mean what they say? She pinched the fold of skin as hard as she could between her forefinger knuckle and her thumb and her knees bent with the intense sensation that traveled up and down her body. Her other hand fingered her right nipple and teased it till it ached. Then she pinched it too. Her eyes rolled back in her head and she had to quickly grab the sink before she fell from a loss of balance.

"Am I really a nymphomaniac?" She had first discovered herself when still a young girl. A very young girl of six. In the first grade, her teacher had accused her of lack of concentration and attention. She was too kind to report that she had found her in the toilet, naked, rubbing herself over and over again. They had always passed her, no matter what her marks. She was so pretty. They felt that while she may not be an Einstein, she wouldn't have to be. She would be a very satisfactory wife. It didn't work out that way though. It didn't work out with Brad. He was such a nice man, just a boy really. It was a beautiful wedding. He liked to bring her flowers before he took her. But then, after only one time, he fell asleep. By then she had an assortment of vibrators to finish herself off. Sometimes, as he slept, she could suck him till he grew again and then sitting atop him, please herself over and over again. The problem was he only liked doing it on Friday nights. She liked doing it twenty or thirty times a day. He divorced her when he came home unexpectedly and found her in his bed with three men and a woman.

"It just wasn't meant to be, I guess." She married Henry. They eloped in Vegas. He was a big man, big in a lot of ways, and he liked doing it, too. They did it in elevators, while driving on the freeway, in the bathroom of high flying jets, in the back of busses late at night. What they didn't do was make love in bed. Henry was an exhibitionist of the first order. He only wanted to do it if there was a chance of getting caught. It was fun for a while. She left him after six weeks after she got a vaginal infection from a dirty toilet.

"Maybe I'm not the marrying kind." A madam had found her looking for men in a bar and was the first one Naomi had met who knew what the tiny little fold of skin on her throat meant. She worked for the whore-house as a prostitute, then left after almost a year, mostly because no one ever brought her any flowers. She traveled around on the money she had saved, seeing the country, looking for something. Anything. Sometimes she was so lonely. Sometimes she even felt like offing herself. Life was so hard. Then she met Hawk on the ferry going out to Martha's Vineyard.

"Hawk." For the first time a man truly pleased her. At first it was wonderful. He could keep going hour after hour, day after day. After a while he became more and more abusive. It turned out he was a sadist of the first order. He loved using his big hands to explore every one of her orifices. If she did the slightest thing wrong, he hurt her, sometimes badly. But she got used to it. She didn't really mind him pinning clothes pegs on her vaginal lips or the electrical shocks most everywhere, or the wax from a living candle dripped onto her softest tissues. Her nipples hurt after he pierced them with little silver rings. Whatever. At least she was getting off. Once he even brought her a flower. Not that a flower could make up for the days he hit her. He was a violent man. He hit everything around him when he was angry. It wasn't personal. But it sure felt like it. Sometimes she fantasized about killing him. She would tie him down while he was sleeping and cut off his hands first. Then force his big thumbs down his throat and up his ass, see how he liked it. Sadist.

"It's not forever," she told her reflection in the mirror. "Soon as I get my hands of some of that gold, I am so out of here." She didn't know why she couldn't be satisfied with doing it once or twice a week like other girls. It was a shame really. She could have been so happy. Thing was, she had a big sexual appetite. That's all. It was just like overeating only different. So what was the big deal? People were so weird. Why did they look at her so strange if she even mentioned the nymphomaniac word? When she was rich, she could pay men to do her whenever she wanted, and if they didn't last long enough? No tip, Hah! Just as soon as she got that gold.

Book II

So where is the gold?

Who is more foolish?
The child afraid of the dark or the man afraid of the light?
The Koran

It is the child who seeks to undo what he has done.
It is the man who seeks to finish what he has started.

Elena and Mercedes were not having a good time at all. They had hoped this would be such a great vacation, but it was turning into a disaster. The day after they arrived, Mercedes had declared a beach day at breakfast. The girls gathered their towels, sun crèmes, books and iPods and happily traipsed down the steps from their cottage on a tall hill to a small, isolated, private looking cove.

The beach was soon buzzing with tiny sand flies which sought out every inch of unprotected skin. Scratching madly, Elena led the retreat back up the hill and to safety. There they discovered a couple of hammocks rigged in the sun between a pair of lime trees. There was enough wind to keep any bugs at bay. Happily they mounted the netting with sighs of relief. Later that afternoon while taking showers, they realized that disaster had snuck up on them again. The hammocks had curled their bodies over so they both had big white lines under their breasts.

"I can't go back to work like this! I will look horrid!" Mercedes looked at Elena in amazement.

"Chica, no one is going to see your body at your work, unless you intend to go topless?" Mercedes was having a ball, she always did; no matter what life threw at her, she turned it into a lark. She met life with a smile and open arms.

"I will know these horrid, terribly ugly white lines are here. I won't be able to hold my head up. We can't use those hammocks ever, ever again." Mercedes looked at her questioning, but then shrugged her slender shoulders with a gentle smile.

"We'll figure out something tomorrow, don't worry, Chica. We will find the perfect place to take the sun."

That night during a wonderful spaghetti dinner, Ben supplied a possible answer. The meal was served on the veranda of a sparkling clean cottage. Ben had even managed to sneak a couple of clean beds out of the barracks with Mercedes' help.

"What girls should do is go on roof. This house, she collect the water on roof. Have little wall all round. Go up ladder in closet. Ben show later." Mercedes smiled sweetly at Ben, rewarding him. He wiggled in pleasure.

"Ben, I didn't know spaghetti was a oriental dish, I thought it was Italian. You must have traveled widely." Ben put his fists on his puny hips and swung his pigtail this way and that.

"Show what girl know. Noodles invented during Ming Dynasty. Many forget, half of people on earth live either side of Himalayan mountains. People there, they have to invent many foods to feed children. Italians come, like noodle, take home and put tomato on it. Then say invent spaghetti." Ben continued on angrily in a smattering of incomprehensible Chinese.

The next morning after breakfast, the girls prepared themselves for a new adventure. Beach towels, bug spray, iPods, hats to protect peeling noses, two broken beach chairs and even a pitcher of limeade Mercedes made from the limes on the trees they found yesterday were gathered together. The ladder in the closet folded down easily just as Ben had showed them. On the roof, a little retreat was revealed. The ladder exited out of a little conning tower, slightly lower than the surrounding walls of the sides. They had a fabulous view of Chatham Bay far below them and the surrounding beaches and valleys. The girls quickly had their gear set up and lay down with sighs of relief. It was so nice in the tropical sun, especially after cold San Jose.

"Elena, lets go topless! No one will know, we won't have any tan lines and it will be fun!" With a scared look Elena followed Mercedes' lead with a shiver of excitement radiating from the pit of her stomach. Costa Rican girls are descended from the upper class of Castilian noblemen who came to the new world to make their fortunes. Today, almost sixty percent of Costa Ricans have pale, white, easily burnt, Spanish skins and Spanish egos that fear making a social blunder.

"We better be careful not to get sunburnt, Elena. Let's keep an eye on each other, just to be cautious."

"Mercedes! Look out! That bird is going to eat your nipples thinking they are berries!" Mercedes shook an elegant fist at the fast disappearing bird.

"You better run away, you peeping tom!" Jokes and laughter filled the roof and sky as the girls finally found the holiday they had been looking for. Far below them on the base of the dock, unseen by the reclining girls, the two rangers stared at the shark filled waters.

Crossing the border between Panama and Costa Rica was no problem for Joe and Tugs. Crossing borders illegally was part of a major skill set practiced by criminals. They each had three or four passports, each laden with five hundred counterfeit American dollar bills paper clipped inside on the last page. It was a talent to pick the proper immigration official to bribe. Too many criminals picked a younger man, thinking they would share a distrust of the Man. Joe never did that. He didn't trust younger men or women. They tended to be too ambitious for him. He liked older women. Women were more practical than men. Older women had seen too many others promoted over their heads. They appreciated a good bribe. It was only right that they could get something out of the system after years of service. It did help that Joe had criminal written all over his face. There was no chance he could be a plant, set to trap them by internal affairs. His eyes, his glaring, glowing, intense eyes could never inhabit the head of a school educated cop.

In Punta Arenas, Joe and Tugs found the supply boat just returning to its pier from the run to Cocos Island. A gun in the Captain's gut and a thousand dollars shoved into his hand soon convinced the Captain to turn the boat around and to take them out to the island. Thirty-six hours later, they arrived. Just before disembarking, Joe found the Captain in his cabin, hit him over the head with his pistol, took his grand back and left the guy on the floor, bleeding and dazed. Joe didn't care that the money was counterfeit anyway. He just liked to hit and take, to scare and kill. It was who he was. A natural born torpedo.

Joe and Tugs got off the supply boat and walked down the pier without a backwards glance. No one was there to meet them. No one expected the boat or them. Tugs looked in dismay at the jungle. He was a city boy. There wasn't even a street here much less a freeway.

The best Cocos had to offer was a rutted dirt track wandering into the jungle. Suddenly Tugs missed Panama City, Colon, even Cartagena. What was he doing here? What could he do here except supply mosquitos with blood?

Joe loved Cocos at first glance. This was the kind of place he had always dreamed of. A wild west place where a halfway decent gunman could set himself up as top dog, kill the rooster and rule the hen house. Frighten the shit out of the men, take any woman he wanted, whenever he wanted. And there was the gold. Joe loved gold. He loved money, yes, but gold couldn't be counterfeited. Maybe if the islanders gave him enough gold, he wouldn't do anything to them. Maybe, but then, maybe not. More than gold, Joe liked people to fear him. He loved it when they sprawled at his feet, begging. Begging for life, for property, for their loved ones. It really was too bad for them. Joe hated beggars, too. There was little he didn't hate. And now there wasn't anyone to stop him from doing whatever he fucking wanted to do. Whatever sick thought entered his brain. Whatever weird fantasy occurred to him. There wasn't anyone to stop him. Fuck it all, he was going to have a ball!

The *Rose Marie*'s forward progress slowly decreased. The Papagayo wind was a full gale now. Not like the last gale, this one showed all the signs of becoming a long lasting, fortnight long storm. Harv sneered at the wind tearing the tops off the waves around the boat. He listened to his engine stutter a little while going over an extra big wave. He didn't have another filter for the Racor.

"Janet? Janet, babe, this wind is in our favor. Why are we fighting it? Let's ride the storm! Let's go for it! What do you say, Babe?" Janet stared from just inside the companionway, speechless for just a second. She had trouble taking a full breath. Her man was out there, the wind tore at his hair, his eyelids were slits protecting his vision from the salt, his lips snarled with a piratical 'the hell with the circumstances' look as he judged the next wave, decided just how to maneuver over it. She almost fell to the deck as her knees were suddenly weak. Her man, the man she fell in love with, the man from her honeymoon, her man, he was back! She stared up at him standing watch by the wheel. Adventure and daring were poring out of his eyes.

It was all Janet could do to nod her head in agreement. Her heart was singing so loudly, her soul was so elated, she was so happy, it was all she could do to stop herself from bursting out into the cockpit, tearing that man's clothes off, and giving him the ride of his life, right there in the middle of the tempest, screwing him as the storm tore at their hair, tangling, intertwining as they lay.

"Mom, why are you crying? Dad is alright. Listen, he is starting to sing his stupid sea chanties again. Oh, no, he is getting really loud. Mom, where is my cotton wool?"

Suddenly, Janet spun around her boat, making sure everything was ready for the gale. Luckily, most of her stuff was still packed away from the Tehuantepec. Some things she unpacked and then repacked again just to be sure and to hide from herself the incredible happiness she felt. Her *man*, he was back! Oh, sweet Mary, thank you, thank you ever so much! She had to hide such happiness. If anyone knew, any imp, any devil, any genii, she feared they would take her happiness away out of pure jealously. She glanced in a mirror. She hoped no one would see her eyes; her eyes so full of happiness and contentment.

The storm never quite reached the full gale force of 48 knots. In the afternoons the wind seemed to be stronger, while during the wee hours of the night, Harv could stand in the cockpit without holding on to anything. He let the Hydrovane, the wind-powered self-steering equipment, direct the boat downwind. He wasn't too worried about where they were going. He knew they were paralleling the coast, a few hundred miles out. He didn't care. He was having an adventure. The *Rose Marie* was showing what she could do as she surfed down the big off-shore waves. There were no islands or land or reefs ahead. Nothing but blue water.

He and Janet would hug for a few minutes between watch changes, as one woke up and the other went to sleep. Their hugs were so intense, so filled with contentment on her part, excitement on his, that in a way, they were better than sex ever could ever be. A better emotional connection than a mere coupling, even as they touched, they felt sparks arc between them. He felt himself storing energy within. The next time they made love; the next time would be so intense, he knew he would scream as he came. She felt herself soften between her legs and her breasts swell as they kissed. If he only knew how much she wanted him. But some things were best unsaid. Wouldn't do to give him the idea that she couldn't live without him. As they stared for a second into each other's eyes on the steps of the companionway, even the thing within her was quiet for once.

She felt herself as she once was, a new bride setting out on a grand adventure, full of hope and intention with eyes shining. She could, for a moment, ignore this new being that the thing was turning her into. This new woman who could ignore the problems of life; the aging, the graying, the forgetting were not for her. She found she could forget about food, do without sleep, work 24 hours a day, without noticing.

When she looked in the mirror, her face seemed to renew itself daily. It was if she was growing younger. She got into the habit of not looking as she brushed her hair. It was a bit unsettling. If it could do this to her face, what else was happening in there? Inside her body? Sometimes at night, she could feel her face change. She could feel the lines on her face, around her mouth, slowly disappear. What did it want from her? Was there going to be a price to pay? A terrible, painful price?

The wind drove the boat on and on, south and east, paralleling the far away coast, across the ocean, towards the only land anywhere in the area, the small island of Cocos.

Dustin stood on the foredeck of the *Steel Balls* as she approached Cocos Island. It didn't seem like a big enough island to hold all of the gold that was rumored to be buried there. He held up his hand and held the island between his thumb and forefinger. He tried to calculate the distance between the ship and the island knowing only that the island was four miles wide and his fingers three inches across and his fingers 28 inches from his eyes. In a few seconds his brain came up with an answer of 6.43 miles distant. He promised himself that he would check with the Captain to make sure of the ship's navigational equipment's accuracy.

The island was a riot of green piled on green all under a variety of white to dark clouds which were either raining, about to rain or having emptied themselves were being blow out to sea. The greenery descended all the way to the shore and was broken in places by only a very thin line of black volcanic sand with a few splashes of white coral beaches. The ship turned and made for the north end of the island. Mary stood at his right side, she turned slightly towards him, her left leg was pulled back a little, which angled her hips towards his.

"Looks like we are heading for Chatham Bay. Do you think that is where the treasures are buried, Honey?" She glanced at Dustin with a smile just flirting with the corners of her lips. He snaked an arm around her waist and then stopped himself.

What was he doing? Why was he behaving like a teenager? If he didn't watch out, at the end of this expedition, he would have to either fire Mary or wed her. He knew this. He knew it. His brain knew it. Why, then, was he acting like a teenager? Mary seemed to have a way to communicate directly to his childlike id, to his basic instincts. He would have thought his massive super ego would have better control over his actions.

"I don't know, Mary." He removed his arm to point to the island. "It isn't our job to decide where the first testing should take place, and no doubt there are formalities to be performed." Mary turned even more directly at him, the apex of her hips only inches from his body. "After a few tests, no doubt we will be asked for our input on further test sights, don't you think?" Mary arched an eyebrow. Her man was becoming different. Dustin never asked. He dictated, ordered; sure that his brain would reach the correct conclusion many nanoseconds before anyone else. He told, he directed, he commanded. He never asked.

"You are so smart, Dustin. You are really an amazing man." While she spoke she slowly and intently brought her left hand down the length of his back, a few inches behind his spine. She smiled when he slightly shivered. At the end of this downward stroke, her hand slowly closed just behind one cheek of his buttocks, again never touching.

"Not at all. It is nothing to do with me. I just trained my brain from an early age to think clearly and distinctly." He suddenly bent at the waist slightly, jutting his bum backwards a few inches. He stood up again, quickly. "A few waves out here. It's hard to stay balanced. Maybe reflections of waves from the island." He rubbed the right cheek of his butt.

Mary just smiled. She loved being able to influence Dustin Horner. Doctor Dustin Horner. Mary Horner, wife of the world renown scientist. She smiled within herself again and then shivered with pleasure and excitement. Life was so good. It would be so good to be a famous woman. Mrs. Dustin Horner. The Mrs. Dustin Horner.

Hawk stood by the forward window of his cabin. He stared at the island like an enemy. He had invested a lot of money on this venture, more importantly, he had invested a lot of his time. He had to find the treasure. He just had to. He was mortgaged to the hilt. Without a fresh influx of capital, his teetering empire was going to fall and he would burn in the ashes. He changed his focal length and glared at his reflection in the window.

"I will find the treasure. I fucking will." Naomi stood next to him, a step behind, as she had learned was expected of her. She gently placed a comforting hand on his arm.

"I'm sure you will, my darling." He turned and looked at her, struggling for a second to remember her name, who she was. His eyes flared with anger.

"Who the fuck asked you? What the fuck are you doing here? Doesn't the galley need cleaning? Go swab a deck or something. Get the fuck out of my sight."

She ran. She thought about slamming the door behind her as she left. But she didn't. Naomi leaned against a bulkhead outside his door. She knew he verbally abused her because he was so worried about the success of his expedition. She knew that she should be angry, that she should leave him for such an outburst. But she couldn't. Where else would she go? Besides, there was a matter of all that gold. If she could only get her hands on it, he would come crawling to her on his knees. She would smoke cigarettes and drop the ashes in *his* belly button. She would shove unmentionables up his you-know-what, and he would just have to take it. She just had to get her little mitts on all of that lovely gold. Her happiness, her life depended on it.

She opened his cabin door slowly, peaking inside. He was still staring at the window. He was her ticket. She had to stay on his good side. At least, for now. Slipping inside, she quietly closed the door behind her and stripped off her clothes. She walked over to his bed and lay tummy down with her legs spread, which she knew turned him on. She reached behind and spanked herself on her bottom. It made a loud smack. He turned from his window and looked at her.

"What are you doing to yourself?" She raised a hand a spanked herself again, hard, then peaked at him over her shoulder.

"Don't you know that spanking a girl makes her twat tighten? Want to have a virgin? Come on over here and give me a good spanking, Hawk." He stood rock still for a second and then tore off his clothes as he trod quickly to the bed. His huge hands made a resounding clap as he spanked her over and over again. Her behind was soon cherry red. Her eyes filled with tears from the pain but she hid her face from him. Not that she had to. He was so weird, her tears would probably turn him on. He had to shove hard to get inside of her. She could feel every vibration of his cock and when he came, she was so tight, his spasms jolted through her entire body. She lay there crying, afterwards, as he showered off, and she whispered into her pillow.

"Fuck, the things a girl has to do to get ahead in this world."

The two rangers shrank back into the jungle of Cocos Island. They disappeared within seconds of entering the dense vegetation. Neither seemed surprised to see the supply boat return. Neither gave the impression of being able to be surprised at anything. The ex-Seal leaned comfortably against a moss covered tree. He didn't seem to mind when a trail of ants took him to be a short cut to the ground and walked down from his neck to his foot, part of the path passing inside his shirt. The ex-Taliban wasn't as comfortable in the jungle. He didn't mind scorpions or snakes, bats or wasps, but this overwhelming jungle full of bugs was a lot to take on. He spread his prayer rug and knelt towards Mecca after a quick look at his compass. He tried to ignore a hairy, intensely poisonous caterpillar crawling across his rug as he prayed to Allah for the endurance to outlast this test.

Two players got off the supply boat. On board, a crewman crawled to the side of the boat and let the lines go, while another wearily engaged the engine for the long passage back to Punta Arenas. As the boat headed off shore another took its place. It was huge. It was a millionaire's toy. The ex-Seal's eyes narrowed. This would be the treasure hunters he had been warned to expect by the guy in San Jose. His eyes glinted slightly as he spotted a bikini clad girl on the foredeck. The ex-Taliban rose from his rug, shook the bugs from it and stared with disinterested eyes at the yacht. 'So,' he thought, 'it is about to start.' He nodded ever so slightly. Sooner the better, then he could get off this hell of an island and return to a nice clean desert.

The players on the dock turned and watched the yacht come to anchor a couple of football fields distant from the shore. The big one seemed elated at the sight of the women as they crowded the rail for a first look at their home for the next couple of weeks. A couple of them waved at Joe and Tugs. Joe just sneered. Tugs waved back.

A soon as the anchor was down, a highly varnished shore boat splashed in the water from its davits. A couple of men climbed down into the boat and it drove towards the dock, piloted by an extraordinarily attractive young man. For the first time the ex-Taliban seemed interested. He watched the boat intently. The players on the dock turned as an old rusted out land rover bounced down the dirt trail from deeper in the jungle. An older man climbed out and straightened his uniform. He walked up to Joe.

"Who are you and what do you want? This is a reserve. There is no admittance without special permission from San Jose." Joe just jabbed a thumb over his shoulder towards the approaching shore boat.

"You want to talk with him. We are just a security team, the owner doesn't take kindly to aggressive people. Now, if you don't mind, spread your legs and raise your arms. We have to frisk you."

"What? The hell you say. This is my island. Stand here. Don't move till I talk with your boss. This is an outrage. I have received no notice of a vessel asking permission to anchor. It can't be allowed. It can't. Outrage, I say. San Jose will hear about this. I am warning you." His voice faded as the official strutted towards the end of the dock where the shore boat was landing. Joe grabbed Tugs by the arm and pulled him towards the dirt road.

"That is our cue to get lost, Tugs. See? Didn't I tell you we were going to fall into a bucket of milk and honey?" He seemed to feel his words were not effective enough. "A bucket filled to the top with pieces of eight. And they are going to be all for us, me hearty. All for us."

"Me hearty? What? You'se a pirate now? 'Sides, I don't see no gold, nowheres. No decent road, no hotel, no bar, no nothing. This is a stinking island, Joe. Another one of your crazy ideas." Joe just smiled at him and dragged him up the road. They were soon hidden within a tunnel of green riot.

Without a glance between the two men, the ex-Seal stood up and brushed off a few of the hundreds of ants covering him and noiselessly tailed Joe and Tugs, slipping through the green jungle maze as if it didn't exist.

Hawk stood on the dock and waited for the Commandant to come to him. He lifted his nose and smelled the odor of the rotting of tropical plants on a island that had over 200 inches of rain a year. He wondered if the Prospector really could smell gold. He better be able to.

"Who are you? Why are you on my island? Get off. Get off now." Hawk blinked his eyes and turned to look at this little man waving his arms in front of him.

Back at the base of the dock, the driver of the land rover opened his door with the sound of tortured rusty metal and pulled out a Thomson sub-machine gun which he casually pointed towards Hawk and the ship behind him. Hawk heard a metallic sound as the man ratcheted a round into the chamber and grinned evilly at the *Steel Balls* and the women aboard. Hawk smiled as the driver's face suddenly turned blood red as his right eye and nose exploded from behind in total silence. It was nice to have his bodyguards back, Hawk thought.

"Didn't you hear me? Answer me, you idiotic gringo. Answer me or I will have you shot!" The man fumbled with his side arm, yanking in his fury. Hawk held up a palm, aimed at the jungle and then calmly tore the pistol out of the Commandant's hand as it finally cleared the holster.

"I heard you, little man." Hawk engulfed the man's head with his huge hand and forced him to his knees and forced his head back. "The question should be, are you listening to me?" The man seemed to be in shock from the ease with which this Santa Claus character had manhandled him.

"This is my island. I am in charge. I want..." His voice faded out as Hawk cocked the pistol and shoved it under the joint of the man's right jaw. He looked up, hoping for mercy. All he saw was total indifference. Hawk pocketed the pistol, stretched the Commandant's neck, enclosed the man's neck with his left hand and squeezed his fingers closed. The man grabbed Hawk by the arm, trying to stop this terrible, vise like pressure. This huge hand was shutting down all blood flowing to this brain, all air trying to inflate his lungs, even the spittle he normally would have swallowed, dribbled out of the corner of his mouth. His eyes pleaded for mercy. His mouth opened as if for one more, one last plea as his eyes glazed over and he sagged in Hawk's hand.

Hawk wasn't even paying attention. He was gazing around the island looking for a good staging place for his scientist's equipment as the man died in his grasp. He knew he was lucky that the supply boat had just left. It was that much longer before a relief party could be organized. But still, he had to hurry. Who knew how long it would take to find the treasure. He looked down at the now dead husk of a man hanging from his hand. He let the body go and with a flip of his foot, pushed it over the side of the dock. Almost instantly, a swelling pulse of water approached the body. Then it was gone in a furry of white water that quickly turned blood red. Hawk turned to John who was still in the shore boat, looking like he might throw up as he stared at the sea at the base of the dock.

"Get the scientists organized. Find out where they want their equipment set up. Quickly. It is time to go to work." John tore his eyes from the sea. He stared for a second, uncomprehendingly at Hawk, at his hands, at his face, and then nodded slightly, eyes still in shock and drove the boat back to the *Steel Balls*.

The sun was blazing hot on the roof top but the wind cooled the girls down as did a few passing showers. At first Elena shrieked as raindrops fell on her and ran down the ladder to hide in the house. Soon, however, she followed Mercedes' lead and ignored the rain. They got wet, sure, but it didn't matter. The sun soon dried them and it was good for their complexions. It felt good to air dry. It left their skins feeling ever so clean. And lifting their faces to the passing showers, allowing the rain to pour down on them, unabated; to accept the drops rapping gently against their bodies and faces, left them rinsed clean of worry and fear and tension. It was a release. Not having to worry was so nice, it made life so easy. Elena realized she didn't have to fear life.

The world beating against her, wasn't going to do any harm. Her body was built to resist the ravages of nature. She didn't have to worry, didn't have to run and hide. She could welcome the world, head held high, and laugh at the wonder of it all. She found that after she let the rain beat against her face, all the tiny lines around her eyes and mouth disappeared like magic. It felt so good to totally relax. To not worry about being hurt, about being yelled at, about being punished, sent to the corner, being spanked. All the baggage she brought with her from childhood disappeared, as it was washed away in the rain. It left her feeling so pure, so good, so happy.

Now, instead of scrunching up her face in fear, she smiled at the falling rain and shrieked in joy along with Mercedes as they tried to catch rain drops on their tongues with their eyes slit open, seeing thousands of droplets falling down on top of them from high in the sky.

After the rain was over, they thought they heard an anchor chain being lowered down by the bay. Neither girl was interested enough to stand up and to look at what was going on. It was just too comfortable lying there, letting the sun warm their rain chilled bodies. An hour later, they ran out of limeade and Mercedes got up to climb down the ladder to make more.

"Elena, that dive boat you were interested in is coming back. And it looks like they still have all their divers with all their arms and legs! Maybe they have a secret anti-shark amulet they wear next to their skin! And there is a big, humungous yacht in the bay."

"Let me see." Elena rushed to the side of the roof. It was true. There were still six divers on board the small panga. Elena shivered at just the thought of being in the water with such sharks. "Mercedes, I would die before I could go in the water with those man eaters. I would."

"It depends on the man, Elena. I've known a few men I wouldn't mind eating, even if I had to share!"

"Oh, Chica, for you everything is a joke."

"Not everything, Elena. But close."

On the dock, they saw a man talking to the dive boat people as they climbed out onto the dock. Several shook his hand and then accompanied him to board a beautifully varnished motor boat and all the divers went out to the yacht.

"We should try to get an invitation to have lunch on that boat, Mercedes. That will give us something to do, something to aim for, do you think? Maybe if we dress up, dress to kill, you know? Dress so well that no man could take his eyes off of us, much less say no to the slightest request we might let drop. Mercedes, let's do it." Mercedes smiled delightfully at her friend's enthusiasm. It was great to see her excited about something.

As the girls climbed down the stairs, they noticed two men climbing up the hill on the old road heading for the barracks. They didn't look like nice men. One was dressed in a polyester shirt and the other just looked plain. Either way, they decided they didn't look like men they would welcome into their boudoir. The plain man was dragging behind the other, while the fancy dresser turned every few meters to yell at his companion. They didn't look like a happy couple. Soon the girls lost track of them as they hiked through the jungle, going past their knoll and up the small path leading higher up the mountain.

Hawk brought the divers into the dining room and directed John to bring them anything they wanted. Most opted for ice cream. Hawk sat down next to the Skipper/dive master of the boat.

"How do you survive diving around all these aggressive sharks. I would think they would tear you to pieces."

"Not at all. The sharks are very aggressive by the pier. I really don't know why. Maybe years ago people threw edible garbage or dead animals into the water there, but certainly not within the memory of any particular shark. In any case, we dive out by the pinnacles, volcanic rock spires that jut straight up thousands of feet from the ocean floor. Even then, we do Special Forces entries. Normally, diving from a boat, everyone jumps in the water, stays on the surface, checks their gear, finds their buddies, you know, their dive partners, and as a group descend to the dive site. We can't do that here in Cocos. Sharks are always interested in anything on the surface. No one knows why." Hawk forced his face to look interested.

"What is a Special Forces entry?"

"That is when we do a jump roll off the boat and continue swimming down to at least 70 feet before meeting up. Down there, the sharks are much less aggressive. If fact, one of the reason we like the Pinnacle dive site is the current carries our bubbles away. The sharks don't like bubbles so without current we can't get close to them."

"You try to get close to them? Don't they eat you?"

"The whole idea is to get close. Cocos Island is the foremost site in the world to dive with Hammerheads. Divers won't come this far to see little dim shapes in the distance. Of course, we get close. In fact we touch them." Hawk couldn't help himself. His eyes widened into twin spheres of astonishment.

"You touch them? From a shark cage, of course."

"No. Out in the clear. A cage is too confining. Besides, if one of those babies really wanted to eat you, a flimsy little cage with aluminum bars isn't going to stop them. No, we wedge ourselves in between rocks next to cleaning stations and just sit back and enjoy the show."

"What are cleaning stations? Cleaning what?"

"Cleaning stations are the habitats of small fish, often less than a quarter inch long, most often wrasse, that live by eating the parasites off of larger fish. In a good station there will be many thousands of these fish. The sharks, especially the Hammerheads, congregate at these stations and one at a time go in and turn off their hunting instincts. It is like they fall asleep, much as if they were in a coma. The sharks just lay there, as the tiny fish clean their skin and even between their teeth, the wrasse swim in and out of the shark's mouth looking for left over morsels. A brave diver, one with nerve, can swim right up to a 12 foot shark and run his hand over the shark's sandpaper like skin. I have actually put my hand inside a hammerhead's mouth, ran my hand over his teeth while he was being cleaned."

"My God." Involuntarily, Hawk glanced at the man's hands as if to count his fingers. They were all there.

"Course, it isn't just sharks. Huge schools of manta rays swim by routinely and stop to get cleaned, whale sharks are a common occurrence, whitetip sharks, pilot whales, sailfish, giant groupers and many other species in the thousands, they all enjoy cleaning stations."

"I don't understand how you can take people like those out among such predators. They look like average people; people you would never guess would free dive amidst sharks."

"Cocos is the center of a number of ocean currents, all of which bring nutrients to its shores which support an amazing number of fish. The sharks are all well fed. The only real question is why they are so aggressive by the pier. Of course a further problem when diving is sharks often attack when full. Aggressor animals will attack anything which doesn't fit the norm. Anything out of the ordinary. That includes divers. Scuba divers don't look like fish. Just as wolves will attack a lame or sick deer, sharks will attack a weird looking animal like a diver."

"Amazing, just amazing. Out of curiosity, have you ever investigated the stories of buried treasure on Cocos?" Hawk asked keeping his voice bored, as if he was just making conversation.

"Oh, sure. You're talking about the Treasure of Lima? With the Virgin? Yeah, that is a mystery, all right. But people have looked everywhere for it. Jacques Cousteau dove on some mysterious humps in Chatham Bay when he was here in the *Calypso*. Problem was, they used an old fashioned underwater pulse induction detector, the best they had back in those days, but anyway they found nothing.

"Stories abound here abouts. One 'treasure map' had a treasure buried in a underwater cave over in Water Bay. The cave is there, the treasure isn't. Nice cave though. Big lobsters." The Captain held his hands four feet apart.

"What are these mounds that Cousteau was interested in? Treasure ships?" Hawk cursed himself. He had to play it very cool.

"I don't think treasure ships ever came to Cocos. They were mostly headed into Panama or into Mexico via Manzanillo and Acapulco. What you got here were pirate ships. This was a great spot for them to re-water as often they weren't sure of their reception on the mainland.

"Cousteau investigated these mounds about over there." He pointed to a spot about a hundred yards away. "From the surface they look interesting. Problem is that as soon as you start to clear the rumble, the water clarity goes to hell and the sharks move in. They always do, you know, they love weird and strange sounds. It is very dangerous to work with sharks in reduced visibility. No one knows what the mounds are. Cousteau checked for gold and iron. Gold for the glory and iron for cannons. Museums love cannons. He found neither."

"So, no one has ever determined what is in the mounds?"

"Not all of them. Franklin Roosevelt came through here with his uncle's Great White Fleet, you know, Teddy. He fired his big guns at some of the caves but found nothing. He dragged his ship's anchors through some of the mounds but discovered nothing but coral, mud and organic matter. What formed the mounds is a mystery. My best guess is we are in a volcanic area. Maybe a mini eruption or something?"

"Well, I would like to find out. If Roosevelt started it, another American should finish it. May I hire you to lead a dive to investigate the mounds? I will gladly pay you 100,000 dollars."

"A hundred thou..., you have to be joking."

"On the contrary. I am dead serious. And I will give you half to help get you started, the other half on completion. We have instruments on board which just have to be lowered to the sea bed. No digging is required unless, of course, we find something of, something of historical importance. Easy money, yes, but I have a lot of it and don't mind spreading it around. Can I write you a check right now?"

"For that kind of money, sure! When can you get your instruments ready? How many divers do you have and how qualified are they?"

"Why don't we meet here, this evening, and discuss our plans after dinner. How say you?"

"I say, you just hired yourself a dive master!"

Up the mountain Joe and Tugs climbed following decreasingly obvious trails. They passed the barracks, keeping in the shadows. Tugs wanted to stop and steal some food. Joe just handed him a melted candy bar. The jungle became less humid as they passed 500 feet of altitude. And still the island soared above them.

"Joe. Where's we going, Joe? Ain't nuthing up here's anyway. Ain't no gold, no road, no houses, nuttin. Ain't even a trail, no more. Where we going, Joe?" Joe didn't look back at his lagging driver.

"Best way of finding stuff is from above. You wanta kill someone, get higher than them and shoot down. People disguise stuff from the street, not from the mountain. Not from roofs. Not from skyscrapers." Tugs tried to catch up.

"Yeah, but Joe, ain't nuttin but jungle here. Can't see down, can't see up, can't see nuthing but green leaves and shit." As soon as Tugs sped up, Joe increased his pace.

"Wait for it. Get high enough and the jungle will die out. Then we will be able to see the whole island. Then we will be able to see the gold, the place they hid the gold and the people trying to find the gold. Do you think they will look up? Naw, they'll be too busy bellyaching about the jungle."

"But, Joe. What are we going to eat? When are we going to eat?" Joe ignored him and kept climbing. Every once in a while he lost his way and had to back track. He didn't know who had made this trail but they had disguised it well. And he knew someone else liked to look down on people. Look down on them, spit on their heads, then shoot them down from above and take all their gold.

"Just like a fucking eagle," he murmured to himself, "Just like an eagle screaming as he kills, diving from above."

The ex-Seal had no trouble keeping up with the pair. The fat one was so slow and noisy, he could have followed them with his eyes closed. He didn't trust the black haired wiry one. That one threw in back tracks when the trail was perfectly obvious, at least to his eyes. He could have killed either one or both at any time, in less than a second but that wasn't his instructions. He was to follow anyone who left the camp, the shore or the barracks. He was especially to follow anyone who acted like they knew what they were doing, where they were going. Especially, especially if they headed deep into the island. These ones were. He was allowed to kill them after they had dug the gold out of the ground, not before. His boss, he wasn't one for doing work if others would do it for him. And do it for free.

He was glad they were getting higher. He had been stung several times by poisonous insects, once by a snake. He ignored the insects, and killed and skinned the snake for dinner. He had been exposed to thousands of poisons during his career, he was totally immune to almost all of them.

Whenever he passed a termite nest, he thrust his open hand deep into the side. There he closed his fist and pulled out thousands of termites. He blew away the mud nest particles and ate the termites with obvious relish. It wasn't often he got termites this spicy. Lots of warriors in the mix, full of acid that they produced to spit into the eyes of intruders. Once in a while, one got some acid in his face before he ate them. Refreshing. Like aftershave, but stronger. Kept one alert.

He found a great variety of fruit on the island. He was told that the island had never been settled. He doubted it. Such a variety of fruit rarely grew on its own. It normally was imported from other islands. By people. He had been keeping a good watch. There was zero evidence of people except for the track the pair were following. People must have come and then left or died out.

Most of what he ate would have been ignored by a civilized man. He was well trained. He was more at home in the jungle than he was in a city. He didn't like cities. Too many people to keep track of. Any one of which could have evil designs on his person. It was enough to send a man over the edge. He didn't like stopping at traffic lights or walking with people behind him on sidewalks. It made him nervous knowing they were there, not knowing who they were or what they had in their hands. Movie theaters were the worse. Perfect place for a napalm bomb. Take the whole place out. He ended up spending all his time in hotel rooms watching old movies which made him feel even more isolated. Better to be in the jungle. Little wonder so many Vietnam vets couldn't readjust to the world after a few tours over there. A least in the jungle, you knew where you stood. Everyone and everything wanted you dead. Often even your own commander would be happier without you. They considered you a loose cannon. In the jungle, kill anything and everything that stood up. Shoot first, then move. Move and find a new target. Kill and kill and then kill some more. Fuck peace.

J

Jackie was having a blast, considering everything. Her day didn't start well. When she first arrived at the barracks the commandant read her the riot act. He made her sit in a short chair while he loomed over her, pacing back and forth, sticking his fat belly in her face, shouting at her, telling her all the things she couldn't do. She made a note to herself to remember what he said so that she could break every one of his commandments. Foremost in his list was she could not ever leave the settlement. And never ever go up the mountain.

She wanted to ask him 'What settlement?' There was the barracks, a cookhouse, a latrine, the dock and the Commandant's house. She felt like taking his picture as his belly jiggled as he paced, just to show him how ridiculous he looked. Somehow she restrained herself. 'How to win friends and influence people did not include making blood enemies,' she reminded herself. When he finally ran out of steam, she perked up.

"Where are my friends, Elena and Mercedes staying?" That was a mistake. Now his face turned red and he sputtered as he yelled. Some of his spit landed on her face. She got the gist. Thou shalt not ever leave the settlement. Finally, luckily, he got a call on his walkie-talkie. He and his driver jumped in a rusted out land rover and left in a shower of dust.

She found her bunk and footlocker. She locked her stuff up. She quickly scoured her barracks for hiding places. If they found out she was a member of the press, the commandant would have a coronary. She took great care in hiding her cameras and her satellite phone which she used to send in her articles, hopefully she would need it to up-load articles on Cocos Island, if she could uncover anything newsworthy.

"Maybe I should tell him who I am while rolling with my mini-cam," she murmured. She could sell the film to medical schools. 'How to recognize a Coronary.' Once she hid her gear as best she could, she went out on a recognizance. Her youthful hunger led her first to the cookhouse. The cook wasn't there but she did snitch some apples out of the fridge after sampling that night's fish stew. At least she hoped it was fish. Then she found a locked door at one end of the barracks. Pay dirt was just on the other side of the door but it had a Japanese padlock on the door. A type of lock she had never even heard of before. It had no keyhole, no number rings, no dial, but there was no doubt it was a padlock.

"Fuck a duck." She thought about searching for a hacksaw, but knew better. If the 'powers that be' knew their secrets were compromised, they would destroy them. Then she wouldn't ever be able to confirm her story during an investigation. "Oh, poop!" She stamped her foot in frustration.

If she couldn't do anything else, she thought, she might as well leave the settlement and climb the mountain! After all, it was just right there, jungle and all. She was in the mood to break the rules. All she needed was a trail.

The trail was easy, the bugs weren't. They were everywhere. They flew around her head, bit her ankles, crawled up her shirt and burrowed under her bra till they found tender skin and then they bit. It was terrible. She ran back to her room and sprayed herself head to toe with insect repellent, a reporter's best friend. Armed with a miniature camera hidden in her hair brooch, she went out to see what she could find that was controversial. So far she hadn't seen one endangered species, not that she was completely up on what a species was, but it stood to reason that it would be beautiful and photogenic. Or if it wasn't, there wouldn't be any human interest in it. No interest, no story. That was the first thing she learned in reporter school. Same thing as if a tree fell in the woods and no one was there to see it, did it make a noise? If a story had no human interest, did it ever really happen? Or if it did, who cared?

The trail went straight up the mountain which was fun till the going got tough. After she broke a second nail, she told herself that endangered species would naturally be closer to cook sheds. Preferably ones with cold beer. Going down the trail was a lot easier than going up. At the cook house she didn't find cold beer or the cook. The stew was boiling over. She lower the heat.

"Shit." She scoured the jungle around the barracks looking for other trails. Nada. It occurred to her to wonder where all the troops were. Here was an entire barracks, but no police. There was a story. 'Cops eaten by endangered species. Species dies.' She looked in the other lockers by the bunks. They were all empty save one. She thought that policemen would at least leave gum wrappers or something laying around. There wasn't a sign. It was if they had never existed or had been removed from the island or were eaten by endangered species. 'Mother Nature strikes back. Endangered species eats only soldiers. War called off for lack of combatants.' She giggled, she should have been a headline writer.

Lacking any other plan, Jackie returned to the trail and headed down hill. Maybe the supply boat was still there? She tried to remember how often it came to the island. Even when she shook her head, stamped her foot and crossed her eyes, she couldn't remember. She finally came to the beach. There was a huge yacht there! A yacht, no doubt with cold beer and dozens of endangered species in the freezer pretending they were T-bones! With a yip of joy she burst out of the jungle and waved her hands energetically. She was getting ready to shout when something hit her across the back of her head and the beach rushed up to smash her in the face.

When she came to, she found herself tied against a tree, her arms were stretched behind her and lashed on the far side of the tree. A rope lashed her neck tightly against the rough bark and her legs were tied at the ankles and knees. A wooden stake was hammered between them and into the ground. A hard faced Arab slept across from her. She started to yell, to scream. Maybe someone on that yacht would hear her. She couldn't. Something was shoved into her mouth. She looked down her face but couldn't tell what it was. Her mouth was extended open, that was all she knew. She tried to spit whatever it was, out. No good, it was stuck in there. Tears leaked out of the corners of her eyes. Tears of frustration, she told herself. Seasoned reporters, don't cry. They never cry, no matter how sad the story, they had seen it all. Still the tears poured down her cheeks.

The Arab opened his eyes. He didn't wake up. One second he was asleep, the next he was eyeing her alertly from head to toe. He stood up, without effort, without struggle. He was lounging against a tree, and then he was fully erect, like gravity had momentarily stopped working. He walked over to Jackie and pulled something out of her mouth. He whispered in her ear.

"Who you?" Jackie opened her mouth to scream and the thing was shoved back into her mouth. It grated against her teeth. A corner of her lip was caught between her teeth and the gag. She blinked back her tears.

"You scream, you die." The Arab pulled a long, wickedly curved knife out of his robe-like clothes and sliced the front of her dress down the front, including her bra. He flicked the point of his dagger against her nipples. "Scream, I cut." He poked the tip into one of her breasts as if to emphasize the words. He pulled the thing out of her mouth again. She gulped.

"I am a scientist here to study species development on this island and to compare them to similarities of development on other islands. This is my first, maybe my second day on the island. I can't remember. Please don't hurt me. I am no threat to you." The Arab reached down and squeezed her right breast and bounced it a little on the palm of his hand. "Please don't. Don't hurt me, please."

He ignored her words. He cut her clothes completely off, one by one. He ignored the area between her legs and seemed more interested in her thighs. He prodded them and pinched the skin between his fingers.

"What do you want with me?" He gazed at her; he look at her like an animal, like a thing.

"Food. We are not allowed pork. But there is no rule about humans and I am told that they taste almost the same. This part," he poked her breast with a dirty finger, "this tastes very good fried up, like crackling. This part," he poked her thighs with his knife, "very good as stew." Jackie fainted as he shoved the thing back into her mouth. The Arab smiled at her unconscious naked body.

He loved to scare people. It gave meaning to his life. Terror was his favorite game. When he first saw this one he thought she was a young boy, her hips were so thin. When she turned, he was so disappointed. Women were for cooking, cleaning and bearing children. They weren't for sex. They weren't for enjoyment. At birth the head of the worm between a girl's thighs was cut off, cut off to be sure she couldn't ever enjoy sex. The Koran was very specific about that. Women were never for enjoyment. Boys, they were not forbidden. They could be touched. Too bad about this one. This woman. She was forbidden. Unless she fought against him. Then she would be allowed. But, of course, she wouldn't. Oh, well. Every life had many trials.

The Prophet said terror was very effective against women. They scared so easily. And in the Great Satan, women controlled the men. American men were such sissies. He had seen them on the television. The woman told the men what to do, and the men obeyed. Obeyed women! And they walked in front of the man! They were the way to control America. Once the women were afraid, they would tell the men to give in, to not fight. And they would obey. Terror was so effective. It was a great game. He might as well keep in practice.

Maybe he would be allowed to die terrorizing the Great Satan one day soon. He could terrorize the world and they would fall at his feet in fear. That would make his life worth living. May Allah make it so. In the meantime he had to practice for the great day. He kicked the naked woman in the ribs to see if she was awake yet. Stupid, worthless woman. There was nothing else to do on this forsaken, insect ridden, pathetically wet island. Besides, maybe he really would run out of food.

Hawk pounded on the *Steel Balls'* dining room table with one of his huge hands. He wasn't used to people talking after he stood up to speak. Their impoliteness riled him up. How dare they talk when he wanted to! He pounded again, the table groaned under his blows.

"If I can get your attention. People! I know you are all excited about being at our destination, but we do have a job to do, a job for which you have all been paid considerable sums of money. I'm sure I don't have to remind you that there are still performance grants to be awarded for those who assist the most in the goals of the expedition. That is what we are here for today, to decide who receives the additional 100,000 dollar grant. Who wants to earn it?" A sea of raised hands confirmed that he had their undivided attention. "Who has a question." The sea of hands were now waving furiously. "Dr. Horner, I believe you were first."

"I'm sure I speak for us all when I ask what we have to do to earn this totally astounding amount of money!" Cheers and nodding heads confirmed his question.

"Simple enough. It has come to my attention via a diving professional that a pirate ship filled with treasure may well lie under our keel. No doubt it will be filled with metal for you to experiment with your metal detector, Doctor. We will need divers to assist Dr. Horner in maneuvering his machine. Who wants to help? Who wants to share in the bonus?" A voice came out of the back of the now deathly quiet room.

"Dive in the water with those sharks? Those man-eaters?" Everyone had seen the voraciousness of the hammerheads, bull sharks and white-tips by now. Captain Banks was almost sure he had spotted a white pointer.

"Come now. I do not wish to send any of you to an early death. I have hired a professional who has been diving these waters daily for three years. He assures me that with a little training there is no risk. It certainly won't assist the goals of the expedition if sharks start eating off the important associates upon which our success depends. Now who would like to attend the first of the orientation lessons taught by our own dive master? Here, lets hear a few words from him." Hawk pointed to Sam sitting in the back of the room and started to applaud. Sam smiled, got to his feet as all eyes turned towards him and as he walked up to the front of the room. He either was a natural speaker, or he had given this talk so many times that he was well practiced.

"All sharks are dangerous, even little two foot sand sharks. Equally, all dogs are dangerous, even a little Pekinese. Yet, people walk up and pet dogs every day and walk away with all their fingers intact. We know that any dog will attack under enough provocation. Why don't we fear dogs the way we fear sharks?

"Sharks like dogs can sense fear. If a dog senses you are afraid of him, the chance that he will attack is multiplied many, many times. It is the same for sharks. Unfortunately, we have all been exposed to Hollywood's horror movies featuring a variety of sharks, but mostly White Pointers, the so called Great White Shark. And we have thus been taught to fear all sharks. Needlessly. I can teach you how to dive with sharks safely. Notice I say, dive. Snorkeling on the surface in a shark intensive area like Cocos Island is very dangerous in certain locations. We are going to spend as close to zero time on the surface as humanly possible. Your jobs will be simple. I have talked to Dr. Horner. You simply need to arrange his equipment in a prearranged sequence of positions. That is it. Shouldn't take more than thirty minutes. Your training will take much more time than that.

"Now, if anyone who has previously received scuba training would please raise your hands? I should add that my own divers are not allowed to join this expedition purely for insurance reasons. Mr. Hawkins has kindly allowed them to stay aboard the ship for the duration." He smiled at his divers. They had given up on ice cream and had discovered sirloins and baked potatos. "Now, a show of hands?" Everyone looked around to see if anyone would raise their hand. Finally Erhart raised his right hand up to the level of his ear.

"Excellent." Hawk boomed. "What are you going to do with a whole 100,000 dollars? Do you want the money now?" Hawk pretended to do a problem on his calculator. "My God. That comes out to more than $3,000 a minute and more than $50 a second. That is a lot of money even by my standards!" Hawk flipped up his fingers as the seconds ticked by on his watch. "50, 100, 150, 200, 250 dollars." John from the back of the room raised his hand.

"Can ship crew volunteer, Sir?"

"Certainly, you may, John. As well as any other crew. Expedition members do have first choice, however." Hawk tried to remember under what conditions crew had been hired. Would he be better off if a shark ate a crew member or two? It was such a hassle bringing a ship this size on a treasure hunt, but he was well aware that finding the treasure wasn't the most difficult problem. The trick was in keeping it from the government's grasping hands. Every government. He had to have a ship with legs, a ship that could disappear at sea and reappear at the port of his choosing anywhere in the world. Right now he was favoring Goa on the west coast of India. Bombay, or whatever they called it now, was too obvious. Goa was only a couple hundred miles south. It was a small port where he could easily bribe the authorities. People in India didn't believe in banks. They turned their savings into gold and wore it around their person. A perfect place to melt gold down and sell it piecemeal. Maybe it would be better to keep the crew intact, if he could. A waving hand brought him back to the present.

"Mr. Hawkins, I would like to volunteer." It was his ship's own stowaway. He struggled for a minute for her name.

"Glad to have you, Margaret. No wait, sorry, of course, Robyn. I'm sorry, I meet so many people." Robyn paled at the mention of her true name. How did he know? The spy camera, of course. But that meant he was watching while they, while they made love. She felt dirty all of a sudden. Like she was a whore and he a john. She shook it off. Money was money. And a 100,000 dollars was definitely money. She felt the Prospector whispering in her ear. Hawk thought he was trying to talk her out of it.

"What is it, Prospector? Why don't you share your thoughts with all of us?" Hawk's voice had a definite snarl in it.

"I don't mean to be cutting in or nothing. Just whispering. Sorry." He didn't look sorry. But then he never did.

"No, we are all interested. What did you say?" Hawk's voice was demanding. There wasn't any politeness at all in his words.

"If you really want to know, I just said that there wasn't any gold under the water hereabouts. That's all." Hawk's fist hit the table again. This time the table broke under his blow. It split right down the middle. Hawk never noticed.

"Authorities as renown as Jacques Cousteau believe there are treasure ships sunk in this bay. Who are you to contradict them?" The Prospector looked up at the overhead and ignored Hawkins.

"Irregardless, anyone else who would like to volunteer, show up on the stern at six o'clock tomorrow morning." The meeting broke up with excited conversations breaking out all over the room.

The waves had gone down with the wind. The *Rose Marie* had out run the Papagayo winds and was now wallowing in the leftover sloppy seas while drifting south and east. There wasn't much wind, not that it was bothering her stalwart crew, at least not the younger crew member.

"Yep, I always did say the best place on the whole boat to do school work is sitting on the spreaders. Get more oxygen up here. Makes the brain work better. You guys should try it. Are you listening to me down there?" She received no reply. "Hey, you two better not be eating the last of the cookies! I already dibbed my share." There was no answer. With a flare of youthful anger filling her eyes, Jill half climbed and half slid down a halyard, landed lightly on the deck on the toes of her bare feet and dashed down below. The salon was empty save for a packet of cookies on the table, an empty wrapper of a packet of cookies. Just as Jill was starting to stamp her foot and think of some grown-up swear words, the door to the forward cabin burst open, her parents jumped out, and started singing Happy Birthday at the top of their voices.

At least her father was. Her mother's beautiful alto was drowned out by Harv's tone deaf voice. In their hands were two packages wrapped in old newspapers, Mexican, if Jill's eyes didn't deceiver her. Plus a plate with the entire contents of the last packet of cookies on it.

"Birthday? Is it my birthday already? I thought that was next week. Are you sure? I've have got to start keeping a diary so I can remember the day's date."

"Congratulations, my sweetheart. You are now thirteen and officially a teenager!"

"God help us all, Pumpkin!" Her father smiled and passed her the first more or less wrapped package. The newspaper was water damaged but luckily the duct tape it was secured with, was as strong as always. Quickly she tore apart the package to reveal her very own battery powered, waterproof GPS unit.

"Now you don't have to keep climbing down from your mast to make sure we are still on course. You can tell from up there! And see? It has a nifty lanyard so you won't drop it on top of the boat or in the sea!"

"This one is from me, Honey." Her mother watched carefully as Jill opened the package to disclose a make up kit including a variety of finger nail polishes.

"Wow! Green and purple and pink and orange! Mom, can I make each toe a different color?" Janet smiled tenderly and ran a smoothing hand over her daughter's hair.

"Try to express the real you, Honey." Jill grinned wickedly.

"So if I'm in a bad mood, watch out. Too bad I don't have a black color!" Her mother's hand on her hair felt really good. Jill felt something like love emanating from her Mother, something that almost made her shake from head to toe, it felt so great.

"Don't stop that Mom. It feels so wonderful. Like your hand is alive or something, well, I know your hand is alive, your whole body is alive, like. But your hand feels different, you know? So nice."

Janet pulled her hand away and her face paled. Her eyes widened in shock. Her mouth fell open slightly and lines reappeared around her lips.

"Hey, I didn't mean for you to stop! It's my birthday! You have to keep going. Its like a rule or something. Plus I really liked it!" Janet sat down and put her face in her hands. For a moment it seemed she was weeping. Harv sat beside her and put an arm around her hunched over shoulders.

"Jill, leave your Mom alone for just a minute. She is sad about..., she is so happy you are growing up. Let's eat some of your cookies." Janet buried her face into Harv's chest, her brain in turmoil.

'I can't even touch my daughter without this, this thing taking over; without worrying that it might infect my daughter. Oh, God. What am I going to do? I can't live like this. Always worrying , always wondering what will happen next.

'Thank God, that Harv seems to be immune to whatever it is inside of me. Oh, why did that stupid pirate, that Larry, have to give it to me. Maybe he thought it was a gift. Idiot. Some gift. It is driving me crazy. It is making me into someone else. Why? Now that everything is going so good, why? Please, Mary, mother of God, take this thing from me. Take this from me and let me live my life like I am supposed to. Please, oh, please. Take this from me.' Janet nipped at her lip in frustration.

Harv held Janet to him. She seemed to be sobbing. Sobbing and shaking, trembling, vibrating. Her skin became warmer, almost hot. Slowly she stopped crying. She was biting her lower lip. Hard. She lifted her head away from Harv and gazed, clear eyed, at her daughter.

"Now then, Jill. Are you all caught up on your homework? If not, today is the first day of the rest of your life. It's up to you what you make of it."

Complaints of having to do homework on birthdays filled the cabin as the boat slowly drifted south.

The Prospector held Robyn in his arms as they leaned against the starboard rail watching the moon pass over the mountains of Cocos Island. Faint calls of wild tropical birds were echoing off cliffs and between vine encrusted trees. A light misty rain was falling and for a few minutes a moonbow arced over the trees.

"I have never seen such a beautiful thing. Its just like a rainbow only fainter. How perfectly wonderful. It has to be a good luck sign, doesn't it , Clarence?" The Prospector's eyes squinted at hearing his proper name.

"You can call me Stud, you can call me Prospector, but please, don't call me by that name. I'm sorry I ever told you." Robyn blinked.

"Are you sorry that we met and made love?"

"No, that part I liked. Still do. Got to realize though, I'm a private person. Used to the wide open spaces of the Rockies. Couldn't go down into those holes if'n it wasn't for the wildness of the mountains."

"Sorry, Stud. You sex god, you. Think we could do it out here? Don't see anyone looking." She looked forward and aft and cuddled up closer to her man, if that was remotely possible. She hoped he would become her man, that this wasn't just a shipboard romance. Plus, she really liked him. He didn't ask questions.

"Damn Hawkins is probably looking at us with his little, junior scientist, spy set right now. We could go ashore? Do a little treasure hunting of our own by moon glow, what do you say?" Robyn's eyes widened at the thought and the moonlight reflected off her eyes just for a second, prisming the faint light into a symphony of colors.

"Oh, yes! Please, let's do it!" She stood on her toes and kissed her Stud on the chin. "But how are we going to get ashore?" The Prospector pointed at the varnished shore boat, tied up alongside.

"It wouldn't be stealing. We would just be borrowing it for a few hours, and anyway, we are expedition members, right?"

"Right! We most certainly are!"

The boat was tied up with simple bowlines and it was just a matter of seconds to untie her and jump aboard. Laughing, they half fell and half leaped into the forward seat and looked around for the start button. All they found was an ignition switch, without a key. Still laughing they scoured the boat looking for the key while the boat was carried out to sea by the current. Once in a while they felt something give the hull of the boat a bump. The Prospector started to get worried. He found a radio but it didn't work without the ignition being switched to accessory. There were no anchor or paddles on the boat, he thought about paddling with their hands until looking over the side he saw a multitude of sharks lit up by phosphorescent algae, leaving torpedo looking trails.

Robyn wondered how far she dared go. If he got too much information too quickly, would she loose him, scare him away? But she didn't want to
to be eaten alive by sharks either, or to drift out to sea never to be found again.

"Here, Stud, let me take a look at that switch." She lay down on the front seat on her back and stuck her head and arms under the dash. She felt her skirt ride up over her hips and her blouse ride up showing a great deal of her midriff. She was glad that she wore undies today. She didn't always. She felt him lightly rubbing the inside of her left knee. She ignored him. Men. They had such one track minds, it was amazing they ever managed to organize a war. That must be why they didn't want females in the military. They figured the soldiers would return to their one track, mindless behavior of going gaga in front of any woman within a hundred yards.

"There, that will do it." She pinched two wires together, knowing the voltage would go through a solenoid, not through her body. The engine roared into life. She wiggled herself back into a sitting position and found the Prospector gazing at her with one eyebrow raised.

"Hell, I had three brothers. What did you think?" She bravely met his eyes without blinking.

"I was jest thinking it was a good thing you was properly dressed, or we wouldn't of had to go to that island to play around." He lowered his eyebrow and smiled wickedly at her. With a grin she slipped behind the wheel, engaged the transmission, hit the throttle and laughed as the acceleration blew her hair straight back. She drove the highly varnished boat straight at the dock, throwing the boat into reverse and swerving the wheel yards from the dock. The boat sidled gently alongside where they threw lines on cleats and walked down the dock hand in hand.

Ashore the jungle came right down to the beach. A rutted dirt road, more of a trail, ran from the dock up into the green maze of the mountain. The Prospector looked around in interest. It would be very difficult to find anything in this jungle. If someone lost a 747 in these trees, it would be practically impossible to find it. It was one hell of a jungle. As he was gazing at the mountain, at his girl under his arm, it started to rain, yet again. Weather forecasting was easy on Cocos. Either it was raining, getting ready to rain or had momentarily stopped raining.

Together they walked along the beach, hugging the trees, trying to keep out of the weather. Every once in a while, a huge leaf full of water reached its balance point and tipped over, sending a waterfall of freezing rain onto their heads. At first, Robyn tried to hide under the Prospector, but after she was totally soaked, she tore away from him and ripped off her blouse. She wasn't wearing a bra, not that she needed one with her arms reaching up to the heavens, hands open, welcoming the rain, dancing and laughing, twirling around her Stud. The cold water puckered her nipples till they stood out inches from her breasts. The Prospector grabbed her around her tapered waist and lifted her up into the sky and sucked on her nipples, pulling them into his mouth. She ran her fingers through his hair, then tightened her hands into fists, his hair intertwined between her fingers, she pulled his hair, hard, hurting him. She loved her body inside his mouth. She loved feeling his passion, the heat of him. She smelt the rain steaming off their warm bodies. She felt so hot, so sexy, so ready. Her nipples felt so good, warmed after the cold rain. Suddenly she wanted him so badly. She had to have him right now. Her whole body wanted, needed him. She wanted him to take her. To force her. To take her for his own pleasure.

"Bite them, lover. Make me groan. Make me scream. Take me, use me, screw me." He lowered her and tore off his clothes, and then hers. He turned her around and knelt her down in the wet sand of the beach and took her from behind. She arched her back till her hips were high in the air and her nipples were buried in the sand. She reached between her legs and grabbed his balls. She pulled him into her faster and faster till their bodies were a blur. She came seconds before him. She raised her head as high as she could, high into the driving rain and screamed, mouth open, eyes glazed. He, in turn, groaned from the bottom of his lungs and breathlessly his mind tried to inhale while his gonads were forcing him to groan out what air he had managed to inhale, while his body spasmed uncontrollably over and over again.

Finally, sanity returned and he disentangled their bodies. He had to pry her fingers off of his balls as she tried to keep him inside of her for as long as she could. He gathered their clothes, picked up her still spasming, vibrating, nearly comatose body, cradled her in his arms, and slowly walked up the trail. The rain cocooned them as he took her deeper into the jungle of pirate lair of Cocos Island.

Mary lay in bed staring at Dustin. She was sure he was pretending to sleep. They had argued before retiring. Well, she had argued. Dustin didn't argue. He logically, methodically stated his views and then shut up. His mouth shut up but not his eyes. Mary could tell that his eyes were giving her a failing grade as she tried, vainly, to get him to change his mind. She new she might be losing him by continuing her tirade but she was right. She knew she was right. He was going to be eaten alive by sharks.

Dustin volunteered after the meeting was over last night. He insisted that this young dive master knew what he was doing, that it was his invention, he couldn't ask someone else to risk their life when he was the one to profit if the experiment was a success and that, anyway, he had received straight A's in dive school. Mary didn't insist. She screamed, she pleaded, she cried. Nothing seemed to work. Her Dustin was determined to get himself eaten alive by giant sharks. She didn't know if she could watch him do it. Dustin insisted that she had to run the machine as he repositioned the sensor on the ocean floor. She was the only one who knew how. Yes, John had learned a little, but not enough, Dustin insisted. She had to be there when he swam down into the shark swarming sea.

She started to wonder if she really wanted to be The Mrs. Dustin Horner if he was going to be insisting about everything. What? He was going to insist about the color of her dresses or the design of the flatware? Maybe it was better to live in sin. Who really needed marriage? Her eyes were sad when she thought that. She loved Dustin so much, she always had. He was just such a great guy. Most of the time. But not when he was being so stubborn. If she had a baby with him, she hoped it wouldn't be a brat. She put her face inches away from his and stared at him, right at his closed eyes. It didn't work. He was still pretending to be sleeping. She blew softly in his ear. Then not so softly. He could really be stubborn when he wanted to be. Finally, she reached down between his legs and tickled. Nothing. Flaccid. Stupid man! Why wasn't he paying attention to her? She looked at the clock. An hour till it was time to get up. With a fluff she rolled over and pretended to sleep. If he wanted some morning fun and games, he was just out of luck. What did he expect? Love only when he wanted it? What about her? What about her needs? Men. Can't live with 'em and they get so fussy when you put 'em out of their misery.

Erhart struggled with his BC. He reminded himself to call it a buoyancy compensator. He knew it attached to the tank a certain way. The regulator of his second stage always had to be on the same side of his body, so if he lost it while underwater, it would be easier to find. He knew his weight belt went on last, so it could be dropped easily if he got in trouble. At least that was a little weight he didn't have to worry about yet. He felt so bulky. Sam, the dive master, insisted that everyone wore a full wetsuit. He said that exposed skin was a lure for sharks and the bodies' odor was transferred to the sea that much easier without a suit. He said black wetsuits, a neutral color underwater, were better than bare skin. Sam's wetsuit was multicolored, one leg was blue the other green, one arm black with red stripes while the other was blue with yellow stripes. He wore different color gloves and even his fins were of different colors. It was difficult to look at him as a whole. The eyes seemed to lose focus amidst all the different hues. Erhart wondered if he should wear different colors too, but none were offered. Sam came over and helped him with the rest of his gear.

"How many dives have you logged since you were qualified, Erhart?" It was just a question, Erhart told himself. He wasn't being judged. He didn't have to be afraid.

"Actually, this will be my first dive. I got busy after I qualified with other projects, you know how it goes." Sam just looked at him with blank eyes.

"Ok, listen. You have to stay right next to me. Don't stray. Don't take your eyes off of me. Whatever you do, don't panic. Do you have any questions?"

"I have never done a, what did you call it? A special forces entry?" Erhart tried not to look embarrassed. He had volunteered for this dive. He should be treated like a hero, not a chump.

"Easy. Just jump head first off the boat and try to tuck your chin into your belly button. You will land in the water on your tank which will break your fall, the Teams sometimes jump off of destroyers safely, so don't worry. It won't hurt. Your induced turn will continue under water and when the bubbles clear, you will find yourself head down. Keep swimming straight down. Sharks don't like bubbles so they won't immediately investigate your entry spot. If they approach after that, push your purge button on your regulator to scare them away. Got it?" Sam didn't add that White Pointers seemed to find bubbles extremely interesting. "We are going to dive first on a pinnacle with a feeding station so you can get used to being in the water with large sharks. The thing to remember is the sharks will be more interested in their place in line to get cleaned than breakfast. The last thing they will do is swim away from the station to see what you are. So don't panic. All sharks react aggressively towards panic. Stay with me, swim down to the bottom, remain calm and collected at all times. Swim with just your feet. Keep arm motions to a minimum. Wearing a black wetsuit and using arm motions make you look like a seal to a shark. And sharks love to eat seals. Swimming steadily and quietly will make you look like a slightly demented weird kind of fish to a shark. Most predator fish will immediately attack anything strange. Sharks won't. They always investigate first. If a shark gets too close, don't panic, point him out to me and I will take care of him. One last thing, never lock eyes with a shark. If you do, like a tiger or lion, he will attack instantly. Got it?" Erhart nodded mutely. What had he volunteered for? Sam went off to help Dustin with his gear. His third volunteer, Robyn, didn't show up this morning, nor could she be found in her room. Sam shrugged his shoulders. Two out of three wasn't bad. John, the crew member volunteer, had talked with his Captain who had refused him permission to join the dive.

When both of his divers were comfortable in their gear, he started the seventy horse on his panga, and drove out of the protected waters of Chatham Bay. He drove the skiff just north and west out of the bay to a dive site named 'Dirty Rock.' He grabbed a mooring just off a small guano covered islet and they prepared to make their entry.

"This dive is a vertical to 100 feet. Being so deep, and using air instead of nitrox, our bottom time will be limited. What I want you to get comfortable with, is making an entry off the boat and checking your gear either on the way down or preferably on the bottom. Dustin, are you comfortable with this?"

"Not a problem, I understand the theory perfectly." Sam looked at him questioning, but Dustin refused to meet his eyes and busied himself with checking his gear yet again.

"There will be a lot of sharks on this dive, mostly white tips, bull sharks and maybe a few hammerheads along with huge schools of manta rays and the odd whale shark. Don't get involved with the mantas or the whale sharks. I can guarantee that hundreds of sharks will be watching your every move. Stay with me. Once on the bottom you will have a few minutes to look around.

"Now for the ascent, the three of us will link arms, facing outwards and release a column of air which we will ride up. The sharks will have managed to get a good look at us by this time and will have built up enough courage to come and take a look. We want to discourage this. The bubbles will help. Any questions so far?" Dustin raised his hand.

"Why do sharks dislike bubbles?" Sam smiled and nodded his head.

"Good question. It is because sperm whales dive deep under sharks and use bubbles to corral them into a tight group. Then one at a time they charge through the sharks snapping up as many as they can eat. Sharks actually have very good memories, some believe they are genetically instilled. Anything else?" Both men shook their heads. "Ok, then, line up sitting on the rail, today we will do a back roll as this boat is so small and neither of you are used to more advanced entries. All set? One, two, three, go."

The water was crystal clear, unfortunately. Unfortunately because the men could see hundreds of sharks patrolling below them, swimming back and forth, looking, hunting, seeking. Sam was swimming quickly, straight down at the sharks. Erhart and Dustin hurried to catch up. Erhart had a little trouble clearing his ears, but remembered from his class that it was easier to equalize the pressure between his outer eardrum and the inner ear by descending feet first. It worked, his ears cleared, but he also fell behind Sam and Dustin. He raced to return to his little human school and just managed to join up when they went thru the first layer of sharks.

Erhart couldn't believe his eyes. They were huge animals. The smallest was twice his length and thrice his girth. They were beautiful in a way. The slightest motion of their tails sent them speeding through the surrounding seas. The school suddenly divided and a school of gigantic manta rays, each over twenty feet in width soared through the sharks in formation. One shark got too close to one of the rays. With a single languid flick of a wing, the manta sent the shark tumbling head over tail. His former pack members quickly turned on the shark and within seconds nothing was left but a reddish tint to the water. Soon the divers were on the bottom.

Sam pointed out crevices between rocks for them to hide in. Dustin's eyes were wide open. He couldn't believe how easily the mantas and sharks propelled themselves. Why did submarines have to struggle so hard to do the same? He thought that maybe it had something to do with size? What an invention if he could formulate an equation! Off to one side, a cleaning station was in full operation. Dustin blinked his eyes repeatedly when Sam swam thru crevices over to the station, rose up and ran his hand along the shark's side. The shark ignored him. Around the station other sharks sat or swam slowly, waiting their turn. He swam back to his divers smiling through his mask at their shocked eyes.

Other sharks seemed to sense that the humans were hiding in the rocks and crisscrossed above them, carefully keeping away from the bubbles rising from their regulators. All too soon Sam signaled them to get ready for the ascent. Dustin and Erhart stared at the multitude of sharks above them and looked at Sam questioningly. Sam raised his air pressure gauge and tapped it while looking at them. If they didn't go now they would run out of air and die on the bottom of the sea, a hundred feet down, their dead bodies would be eaten finally by the predators of the deep. Go now and live, maybe, or stay and die for sure. Sam didn't seem concerned.

The three men linked arms, back to back and swam upwards. Sam released the valve on a pony tank he wore around the small of his back. It released a torrent of air. He urged the men upwards and manually popped their BCs. The men rode the stream of continuing bubbles up, careful to go slower than their bubbles, right past the sharks, the rays and at the last moment, a huge, solitary, black and white, polka dot, whale shark that looked, underwater, almost as long as the *Steel Balls.* On the surface, Erhart tore off his mask, hung on to the boat and laughed in joy. Suddenly he felt himself pulled up and into the boat. Sam stood above him. His eyes were filled with anger.

"I thought I told you that the surface was the most dangerous part of the whole dive? Never, never, never hang out on the surface!" Erhart wilted under Sam's angry glare.

"Sorry, it won't happen again." It didn't take long for his spirits to revive. "Wasn't that just the most fantastic dive ever? Wow!" Dustin grinned in reply. Sam didn't.

"Again, the surface is incredibly dangerous. With your head above water, you can't see below you. You are defenseless. Go in quick, get out quicker. Got it?" The two men nodded seriously. "Now we will change tanks and go for another dive, a more serious dive, ready?"

"Again? We are going to swim with the sharks again?" Erhart's eyes were huge saucers. "I kind of thought we were finished for the day." Sam shrugged.

"It's a beautiful day, good visibility, the sharks aren't that hungry. Why not?" Dustin thought about asking about the pack eating up the shark that the manta hit, but decided that he had insufficient information to formulate an interesting question. "Erhart let go the mooring line." As the boat motored back towards Chatham Bay, Sam continued.

"We are going to dive Manuelita Island. The west side mind you. Normally we would dive the east side which is only 50 feet with turtles and reef fish, but I know you haven't got your fill of sharks yet so we are going to the west side." Dustin and Erhart looked at each other and gulped.

"The west side is 120 feet deep and is inhabited by hammerheads, big hammerheads, as you will see, and not much else. It is the hammerhead's street, their block, their territory. This will be your graduation. After this you might be ready to dive Chatham Bay. These sharks will be aggressive. They are man eaters and might like to prove it. Most likely, they will indeed, try to prove it. To stop them we have to do the same thing we did before. Make sure as we ascend that you keep your arms and fins within the column of bubbles. On the surface, get the fuck in the boat, alright? Don't even spit out your regulator first. Got it?" Dustin and Erhart nodded in frightened agreement. Dustin half raised his left hand.

"This will be safe, won't it?" His voice had emotional timbers of fear within it that Mary would never have recognized. Sam nodded.

"If you do as instructed, it is safe. If you don't, well, listen, just do it right, OK? Stay with me. No lagging behind. Lag behind and you will die. Horribly. Simple as that." Erhart thought about mentioning his problem with clearing his ears on the last dive, but didn't, not wanting to sound whiney next to someone as obviously brave as Sam.

"Alright, then. I'm giving each of you an extra five pounds of lead. Don't put it on your belt. Put it in your BC's pocket. This will help you descend quicker. On the bottom, we will drop the five pounds before the ascent. Got it?" The men nodded their heads. "Every few months we send a man down with a line to collect all the extra weight. If you see the extra weights down there, don't collect them thinking you are helping. You won't be helping, you will be dead."

"Lastly. Never, never look a shark in the eyes. Got it?" Dustin and Erhart nodded again. "Alright, check your gear and sit on the side of the boat. It's a roll entry again. Meet up on the bottom in 120 feet of water. Again there are rocks to hide between. Get in between them quick. Don't come out from the rocks until you are instructed. Got it?"

Again the water was crystal. Easily 100-150 foot visibility. Not that Dustin noticed. His eyes were glued onto the sharks below him, on either side of him and as he descended, above him. They were all hammerheads and were swimming back and forth much more energetically than the white-tips on the last dive. They seemed to resent the men's presence in their water. Dustin noticed that Erhart was having trouble keeping up again. He seemed to be turning around and descending feet first for some stupid reason. Dustin grabbed hold of one of Erhart's arms and pulled him along. It didn't take much force, Erhart wasn't much bigger than a large child. Dustin did look back once and saw Erhart's face screwed up into an acute expression of pain. He failed to notice a thin trail of blood leaking out of Erhart's left ear.

The hammerheads eased out of their way as they descended through them. Not willingly. Some of the larger 18 foot sharks didn't move until they were just feet from them. Finally they were on the bottom. For some reason all of the sharks in the area were congregated just above them, zigzagging back and forth, moving in jerky, erratic motions. Sam looked at them in wonder. He was used to aggressive hammerheads, but this was something else again. The sharks above him were definitely on the prowl. Something was wounded nearby, somewhere, bleeding. Sam decided to wait for a few extra minutes in the hope that the sharks would find their prey and leave them alone. He checked his air gauge. He had just enough for a few more minutes. He turned to check his diver's air gauges and was shocked to see a thin but steady stream of blood pouring out of Erhart's left ear. His heart shrank within his chest. Christ, what next?

Sam always carried a bang stick, in pieces, on his weight belt. He never carried it assembled in his hand as it was far too easy to hit a fellow diver with it, blowing a hole in him. It was really frowned upon, in his circle, when you blew a hole in one of your divers. Tough to get divers to sign up for future dives after that. As he reassembled the bang stick, he checked to see how many extra shells he had. He felt like hitting his head with his fist when he realized he had left them on the panga to make room for the extra lead weight. He searched his other pockets. He found one extra shell and that was it. He checked his dive computer, it was time to go.

He signaled to Erhart to jamb a finger in his ear. Erhart looked at him strangely but obeyed. As one the trio dropped the extra weight, popped their BCs and headed for the surface through an almost solid wall of sharks above them. Sam opened his pony bottle and sent a column of air soaring above them then just jabbed his bangstick out of the air wall, not even aiming. He didn't have to, it was solid sharks out there. The shotgun shell hit something and the pressure wave of sharks rushing to attack pushed the trio this way and that. Sam reloaded the stick with his last shell just as his pony tank ran out of air. He looked at it in amazement. He must have used more air than he thought on the last dive. The curtain of air disappeared. They were visible to the shark packs around them. The sharks who had missed out on the last meal were royally pissed off. As soon as they saw the humans they hunched their backs and flared their gill slits. Sam knew attack was eminent. He quickly stabbed a look at Erhart's air gauge. He still had 1500 pounds of air left. He was so small he had hardly used any air. Quickly Sam pushed the purge on Erhart's octopus, his spare regulator, and released a torrent of air. At the same time he jabbed his bangstick out of the new column of air, blindly. Again he found a target. They were within 50 feet of the surface.

They kicked their fins for all they were worth. They all forgot about not going faster than their bubbles, going faster than their bubbles meant that the nitrogen in their blood couldn't release fast enough and would be caught in their joints. The gas molecules would expand as the water pressure eased as they rose, giving them the bends, so named as their bodies would be bent grotesquely and in astonishing, agonizing pain; for life. For the rest of whatever life they might be able to bear. Erhart's air lasted till they reached the surface. Quickly they threw themselves in the boat. Sam started the motor and pulling a knife, cut the mooring line. He redlined the throttle, throwing Dustin and Erhart, who were giving each other high fives, onto the deck. They looked at him in astonishment.

"The bends. We have about fifteen minutes before they hit. We have to get back down before then, we have to. My God, please God, we have to! Change the tanks." The fear on Sam's face which hadn't showed emotion while looking at hundreds of man-eaters was enough to throw the two men into high speed. Sam raced the boat around Manuelita Island, around to the east side. He cut the throttle and threw a spare anchor and line over the side. "Water, get in the water. Get down to 50 feet, the depth we were when we got bent, get down, NOW!"

Erhart looked at Dustin. They had just left the ocean seconds ago. Did they really want to go back? They didn't have a choice after Sam tackled them and sent all three wind milling into the water in a huge attention getting splash.

This was a different ocean, a different world. Little fish swam this way and that. Turtles gazed at them in wonder. Coral fans gently waved in the light currents. They rushed down to the bottom and drifted on the bottom in 50 feet. Sam carefully examined his dive computer. It computed the amount of air his blood had absorbed during the first two dives. He cursed himself. He should never have tried a deeper dive after a hundred footer. Slowly he watched the numbers decrease. It was OK. They hadn't suffered any damage. He checked Erhart's ear. It seemed to have stopped bleeding. Sam closed his eyes and said a silent prayer to St. Jude, the patron saint of hopeless cases and bent divers. Dustin looked around happily. This was what he called diving. It was beautiful. Hard to believe that just on the other side of this island were hundreds of man-eaters. His hands shook when he remembered what Sam had said. That last dive was easy compared to diving in Chatham Bay. He wondered if he had the nerve to dive again, especially somewhere worse. Maybe much worse.

Joe and Tugs had spent the night in the jungle and Tugs looked like it. His face was covered in the bites of hundreds of mosquitos. For some reason, Joe was untouched. 'Professional courtesy,' Tugs thought sourly. 'One blood sucker for another.' Joe insisted they continue climbing up the now invisible trail.

"There ain't no trail. There ain't no path. Can't see down. Can't see up. What the hell we doing here? I need a cup of coffee. I need a doughnut. And I really need some air-conditioning." Joe looked at Tugs in amusement.

"They really went to town on you last night, didn't they. Fuck, every bug on the island must a bit you. You should see yourself." He thought that bugs wouldn't bite Tugs, the way he smelled. Didn't he ever bathe?

"I'm turning back. I'm going back to that barracks we saw and steal myself some coffee. Then I'm going out to that fancy yacht and get myself some decent breakfast. Stay here if you want. I don't care." Joe smiled at Tugs. It wasn't a nice smile. A gun appeared seemingly magically in his hand.

"You got a choice to make, kid. Going up the mountain or dying right here. You turn back, you take one step back, I'm going to shoot you right through the heart." Tugs looked at the gun and then at Joe's face. He wasn't joking. Tugs had seen him kill too many people not to know the look. Joe could kill so easily and so quickly. And he never missed. There wasn't any choice to be made.

"So where is this stupid trail?" Joe kept his gun in his hand and motioned Tugs ahead of him.

"Find one." Tugs forced himself into several impassable copses of tree supported vines, making no headway, until by chance he found a little trail. As he walked along it seemed to get better. Flatter, smoother, soon even the roots were gone leaving nothing but sand. Joe trailed behind, wondering how sand got up so high, so many feet above the ocean, when Tugs disappeared. One minute he was there, the next he was gone. Joe stood stock still, his gun rotating back and forth. He couldn't hear anything. Not a sound from Tugs which wasn't normal. Even standing still that man made enough noise for a regiment. It was one of the reasons Joe liked him. He was a great bush beater. Especially when following trails where no trails had any right to exist.

Joe waited for an hour. Waiting in an ambush was as normal for Joe as waiting through TV commercials was for the rest of us. There wasn't a sound out there. Not a bird call, not even insects in the bush. Whatever got Tugs was still out there. He finally sidled off the trail carefully. He worked his way ten feet to one side, looking, sensing for a ambush. He saw where the trail leveled out onto a sand floor. He saw Tugs' footprints on the sand. He followed them with his eyes and saw where they suddenly disappeared. Not a sign of struggle, no ropes from above, no disturbed sand below. Joe backed further into the jungle and carefully, slowly moved around the piece of sand path where Tugs disappeared in wider and wider circles. Whoever did this would have left some sign. Joe wasn't an expert in the jungle, but he was an expert in his fellow man.

He knew men were flawed. They always made mistakes. Sometimes very little ones, but mistakes all the same. He just had to find the errors. To follow them down. To find the source. That would lead to the gold or someone who knew where the gold was. Joe bet on it. Maybe he might even find Tugs again. He might even be alive. Joe wasn't worried either way.

E

Elena and Mercedes had breakfast on their roof. Last night they had moved some folding beach recliners and a couple of tables up the stairs. It was a close fit but they managed with a lot of laughing as they helped each other. Ben had come to check on them and had admired how they had moved in.

"Girls know how have good time. Is good. Girls stay up here. Safer. Strange things happen now on island. Don't know what. Me, I bring extra food to house. Girls stay here? No go out?" They agreed and thanked him. After he left, Elena turned to her best friend.

"I would be perfectly happy to spend my whole vacation right here. This is so delightful. Only thing that would make it better would be if we had a couple of good looking men to wait on us, you know? Obey our slightest wishes?"

"Ah, Chica, men, they just mess things up. They would try to divide us, to take us into separate rooms. What is the fun in that? Best friends should share everything, don't you think?"

"Si, Mercedes. You are right. Men. They are nothing but trouble. I am off men. I hate men!" 'Except,' she thought, 'except for Dominic. I have to thank him properly for this awesome vacation!' She shivered at the thought of all the things she would do to thank him. When she was finished, he would be so drained, his wife wouldn't get any for weeks!

Mercedes smiled at her friend and reached behind herself to release her bra as she leaned back on her chaise lounge. She arched her back to stretch out her breasts from the confines of clothes. She peeked between long eyelashes at Elena for a second, then hooked her thumbs under her bikini bottom and in one smooth, practiced motion slid them down her legs and off her feet.

"Chica. Look." She had one knee raised up and her back arched. She watched as Elena turned and stared.

"Mercedes! What are you doing? What if someone sees? Who knows what they might do. Put them back on, Mercedes. Quickly." Mercedes slipped one foot off the recliner and opened her legs slightly. Her other foot she raised up to place one beautiful heel on the arm rest. Mercedes was clean shaven.

"Try it, Chica. It is so releasing. No one can see us up here. This way we can get fresh air everywhere! I love it so much. In a city, there is never a chance. There are always eyes. Here we are alone. You might never get a chance again, Chica. This might be the last chance you get for the rest of your life!"

Elena stared at Mercedes. She was so beautiful. So elemental. Like a force of nature. She could believe that she once was one of those beautiful naked Greek gods she learned about in school, and had been returned to earth to guide Earthlings back to a more natural way of life.

Elena, like many of her social class, was educated by the nuns in Catholic schools. The nuns were very strict. Any disobedience was punished immediately and cruelly. The students soon learned to do it the nun's way. Modesty and politeness were the two lessons that were drilled into them each and every day. To take off the top of her bikini was a walk on the wild side for Elena. To sunbathe nude, that had to be a mortal sin that would be punished by unspeakable horrors in hell. At the same time, Mercedes was the older sister that she had never had, a sister to show her the way through the world. Except, of course, that Mercedes and she were born only days apart. It just seemed like Mercedes was older, more mature.

Mercedes had her head down on the chair now with her eyes closed. Elena let her eyes travel the length of her body and immediately felt dirty. She shouldn't be looking at a woman's body, a nude woman's body, especially. She shouldn't, but she couldn't stop herself. Mercedes was so beautiful. Her body was perfect. Her skin was flawless and every curve was poetry in motion. Elena watched as she breathed, as she turned her head this way and that as clouds drifted overhead, momentarily blocking the sun. Mercedes was a god sent down to guide mortals. She was so beautiful. Elena looked down at her own body. She had a little fat around her belly. Cursed fat! She had a couple of hairs on her upper lip that she continually had to pull. She looked at her red toe nails that she worked so hard on. She peeked at Mercedes. She didn't have a speck of paint. Of course, she didn't have to. She had the body of a goddess. Mercedes turned her head and opened her eyes looking straight at her without having to focus, as if she knew exactly where she was.

"Take off the bikini, sister. If only for a minute. Just for the experience. Then put it back on, if you wish. God gave us these bodies. He made Adam and Eve nude. The way he wanted them to be. It was when they fell from grace that they wore clothes. Sunbathing nude brings us closer to God." Elena stared at Mercedes for a split second and then striped her bikini bottoms off and then lay down like a victim about to be sacrificed. She looked up at the sky half expecting a bolt of lightning to come searing down at any second. Nothing happened. The clouds continued drifting across the sky. A brief shower cooled them off, the sun returned a minute later to warm and dry them.

At first Elena kept her arms close to her sides and her legs tight together. After a quarter of an hour she relaxed a little. It was very comfortable to sunbath without clothes. The wind blew where wind had never touched before. It was exciting in a way. Daring, radical, modern. The nuns would have her bent over the desk and would be whipping her bare bottom if they knew. But Mercedes was right. There was no one here. No one could see. It was paradise. She smiled up at the sun, with her eyes closed and spread her legs slightly apart. This was her chance to get a truly perfect tan.

Robyn awoke at the first glint of light on the eastern horizon. She lay on a cot, her head on The Prospector's arm. His other arm was around her stomach, keeping her from falling from the cot in her sleep. He was gently snoring. They were inside some kind of building. It looked like a boarding school dormitory or a barracks. There was no one else in the room.

As she moved around, looking about the room, she pushed her butt against her Stud. He was certainly Studdly this morning. Stud like and ready to go. She thought about staying in bed for fun and games as soon as he woke up. Or, doing it right now, as he slept. Pleasing herself on him as he slept. She shivered, thinking she was so wicked. If he did wake up during, then what a nice way to waken. But her curiosity was stronger, so she carefully disentangled herself from him and found her clothes on the neighboring bunk. Quickly she dressed, her eyes sparkling. She was on a treasure island! Their might be gold anywhere!

She checked out the room. It was filled with 20 bunks. Each had a standing grey locker or a foot locker at the foot of the bed. It didn't take long to discover that they were all vacant except two. The first was boring. The obligatory photos, clothes, driving gloves. No gold. Well, it wouldn't be that easy! The second contained a few clothes, a book on biology, one of those plastic cards showing the mammals of Costa Rica, another with birds. That was it. Where was everybody?

At the end of the room was a locked door. As she approached it her heart soared! It was locked with a Japanese magnetic lock! There had to be something valuable in there. That damn lock cost five grand. It could only be opened with a individual magnetic ring worn on the right hand. At least that is what the brochure said. She knew better. She spotted a loud speaker. She managed to rip it off the wall by getting her fingers under the flange. Outside she found a log and wailed away, busting up the plastic cover. Inside she removed the remains of the black felt speaker and twisted off the magnetic ring on the end. It was heavy she noted happily. Speakers have very powerful magnets. Strong enough to slide tumblers.

Back at the locked door she held the lock in one hand, pulling the body of the lock firmly but gently. With her other hand she brought the magnet closer and closer to the lock. She felt one tumbler click and she immediately pulled the magnet away. She brought the magnet closer on the other side, again a tumbler slid. Her right hand pulling the body of the lock kept the tumblers from sliding back in. It had taken her weeks to get the right pressure to pull the lock while in the clink, but then she had nothing else to do; neither did the cons who taught her. Within ten minutes and 360 degrees of magnetic force the lock slid open in her hand. A cough from behind her froze her heart. She spun around.

"Able to hot wire ignitions in seconds, able to open the most advanced locks on the market, makes love like a courtesan, who exactly are you, Robyn or Margaret or whatever your name is today?" Robyn turned and looked at him in sadness.

"You aren't going to be one of those men who are challenged by a talented woman, are you? Would you ask the same question if I was a man?" The Prospector thought about that while looking up and down at her. At the lock in her hand and the clothes that barely covered her luscious body.

"You are right. I would have just said that you would be a good man to have by my side on a stormy night while in a dark alley." Robyn smiled beautifully, rewarding him for telling the truth.

"See?" She debated whether to tell him the truth or not. It was always difficult to guess which way a man would jump when faced with reality; fangs and blood all showing. The Prospector was a hell of a man, great in bed, not so hot on getting started. Sometimes he acted like he didn't know what to say. Like most men his age, he needed a little encouragement to get it up, but once he was primed, watch out. The tiger showed his stripes!

"Let's just say that I had an unusual education, you know, what with my four brothers and all."

"Yesterday it was three brothers." Robyn looked at him straight in the eye and never missed a beat.

"I usually don't count Billie who went to prison. He wasn't around most of the time. He was the one to show me this trick." She tossed him the lock underhanded.

"You know, this lock is supposed to be unpickable. What did Willie get sent up for?" Robyn smirked at him, just like a man, so predictable.

"Billie. He never did say. Not that I asked. I was more concerned with making the cheerleading squad in those days." She turned and looked at the door. "Think there is a pile of gold on the other side of that door?"

"There isn't." She turned back and looked at him.

"Now it is my turn to ask you who you really are Clarence or Stud or The Prospector or whatever pseudonym you are using today. Who exactly are you and can you really smell gold? Don't look so shocked.

Everyone on the ship gossips about you. Hawkins thinks you are his ace in the hole." It was The Prospector's turn to smile at her.

"So are we going to open the door or what?" Robyn didn't need any more encouragement. She turned, grabbed the handle with both hands and pulled. It was a heavy door. It opened slowly. The early morning light dimly lit the interior. It was vacant. The floor was reinforced cement, the walls and ceiling were heavy steel. The room could have contained a small nuclear blast. There was no place to hide anything. No secret doors. There was nothing in the room. The Prospector raised an eyebrow and smiled again.

"Now why go to all the expense of building such a room and buying such a lock, if you had nothing to put in it?" He walked around in the small walk in safe looking closely at everything. It seemed to Robyn that he was sniffing at the walls and floors.

The Arab was getting tired of eating bugs. He had to when the ex-Seal was with him. The Seal expected him to eat them and like it. He kept giving him the tastiest morsels. Or at least the most gut filled ones. It was all the Arab could do, not to throw them up after forcing them down. He still had some dried figs that he rationed out to himself. Two a day. He was eating his morning fig when the girl started to thrash about. He knew she had been awake for sometime now and was just pretending to be asleep. Just like his second wife. Always play acting. Women.

"I am very hungry and thirsty. Could I have something, too?" Her eyes were pleading at him. More acting. Women were all the same, no matter what their nationality. They all shared the Crime of Eve. It was Eve who had tricked Adam into sinning, by her deceit. Tricked him into eating from the tree of knowledge by lying. Thus spoke Allah, through Mohammad, his prophet. He unrolled his prayer rug and began his morning ritual. He prayed five times a day as did all good Muslims. He always checked his compass to be sure he faced Mecca, the most holy of cities. Within Mecca lies the Ka'bah built by Abraham as the House of God. It was in Mecca that Mohammad was born just yards from the cube like Ka'bah and the cube
has been the center of Islam ever since Mohammad's death. The Arab thought on these matters as he prayed. When he finished he rose, shook his prayer rug till it was clean and then turned to his captive.

She had a pleasing form, for a woman. He could tell by the way she twisted and turned, that she was trying to seduce him. He said a quick prayer to Allah and after felt clean and pure inside again. She was asking for food and water again. Just like a woman, always asking for something instead of waiting for Allah to provide. Had she no faith? She should be readying her soul for the journey to the afterlife where she would have to face Abraham and Jesus and all the other prophets. Human desires are really such a small matter when you considered the long eons of eternity.

"Please, please, kind sir. I am so thirsty. Please may I have some water?" He walked over and stood over her. Carefully he worked up a wad of saliva, released it and watched as it landed on the woman's lips. Some went in through her slightly open mouth. The woman spat it out. She made loud noises of disgust.

"How could you? That was so gross. You, you savage!" He fell back for a second in surprise and then hardened his heart.

"I give you water from my own lips and you spit it out? Truly, you are a jinni, or maybe even Eve reincarnated. If you are truly Eve, then you will die a most horrible death as you so justly deserve." He turned his back to her and said to himself in wonder, "She spat out water from my own lips."

Captain Jim Banks had moved the *Steel Balls* closer to the island until she was anchored directly above one of the strange humps of sand on the bottom of the harbor. Hawk was bouncing back and forth, stalking the deck forward and aft, smiling with an ravenous looking glare. Morning had shown his shore boat tied up to the dock. A quick muster at breakfast had shown Robyn and The Prospector were missing. Hawk was furious. Everyone tried to keep out of his way. Naomi brought him a cup of coffee and he practically bit off her head for getting in his way. Charlie had launched one of their jet skis and towed the shore boat back to the *Balls*.

The crew had rigged a platform on the side of the boat a couple of feet above sea level. They had the scuba gear all rigged up, ready to go, and lots of line ready to haul up whatever might be found. Lots of helping hands packed around the side of the boat. They watched the Dive Master, Sam, check the dive gear for the tenth time, but mostly they stared at Dustin as he pulled on his wetsuit on deck. Erhart was donning his gear also. Sam looked over at his third diver.

"Erhart, you can't go. You are a danger to yourself and to us if your ear starts to bleed again. Plus you stand a good chance of damaging your hearing permanently. You can't come." Erhart looked for a second like he might cry. He turned to Hawk as he bounced by, going aft.

"Sir, can't I make the dive? Please, sir? I am fine, really." Hawk looked down at Sam who was shaking his head negatively.

"Give these two a chance, if they can't do the job, maybe I'll send you down. Can't be fairer than that." Erhart thought about going down all by himself. His guts started to quiver. His knees started to knock.

"Yes, Sir," was all he could say.

Sam lowered down three sets of twin 80's with their valves barely cracked. They released torrents of air and should last for an hour at least, he hoped. He tried to do the math in his head. An 80 contained 80 cubic feet of air. They were diving to a depth of 55 feet. He bogged down there as he watched a larger than normal shark swim by. He had never dove Chatham Bay. He was familiar and accustomed to sharks, but the sharks in this bay seemed to be their own species, their behavior was so different. Finally everything was ready, there was no excuse for not getting on with it.

"Check your gear twice, Dustin, then check mine and I'll check yours. We will try to descend together and in any case, we will meet up on the bottom. There aren't any rocks on the bottom to hide between. Best thing to do is get on the bottom, do our work, then get back on the boat. Any questions?" Dustin shook his head. He was as white as a fish bone washed up on the beach and left to dry. He felt he had to be the one to do this. It was his invention. He felt if someone else did it and was killed, it was practically murder. Mary was very upset that he was determined to dive. However, there were somethings that a man had to do, if he was to be a man. At least in his own eyes. But still, he feared.

"We are going to do a Special Forces entry. That will get us down faster. Are you ready?" Dustin nodded. Dustin held the sensor in his arms. John stood by ready to pay out the umbilical cord as he descended. No excuse to delay any longer. Sooner in sooner out. Early bird gets the worm. His mind didn't understand that one. Didn't the early bird get the early worm? Shouldn't the worm have stayed in bed? His mind was babbling. He told it to stop. It did with a grump. He turned his head to look at Sam full in the eyes.

"Ready."

"One, two, three, go." Both men did a flip in the air and landed on their tanks and were lost to view amidst the bubbling waters.

Dustin was having a harder time swimming while carrying the sensor with its dragging cable. Sam had offered to carry it. But it was Dustin's responsibility. He carried it in his arms like a baby. He felt safe inside the column of bubbles. Since he couldn't see the sharks, he could pretend to himself that they weren't there. It was like a ride in Disneyland, kind of. Except he knew that the illusion of safety was just that, an illusion. Soon they were on the bottom and by random he picked out a spot on the side of the mound and pressed a waterproof magnetic switch on the sensor's side. Sam swam above him, on guard with his full armament of ten bang sticks and five poles.

Soon a red light flashed signaling that data had been uploaded and Dustin swam 90 degrees around the mound to the next sensing spot. For some reason the bubbles were less dense here. He sited the sensor, turned it on and then faded back into the bubbles. He knew it should take approximately 93.5 seconds to complete its program, so after 95 seconds by his watch, Dustin swam to the edge of the bubbles and retrieved his sensor. Two more to go. He was starting to relax. This was easy. Why had he been so worried? He swam on to the next site.

On the *Steel Balls*, everyone was watching the water. The air from the tanks flowed up out of the water and burst in bubbles of froth. On the outside of the column of air the sharks circled endlessly getting more and more frustrated. Perhaps they could sense the vibrations of the sensor or smelled the divers. It didn't matter. What did matter was the sharks were getting very angry. When Dustin changed locations for the sensor, the sharks really got mad. Instead of orderly circles around the column of air, now they changed directions, moved up and down, ran into each other, pushed each other out of the way. The entire pack of sharks was getting very irate, maybe angry enough to dare to enter the area of air bubbles.

To Mary, it looked like a solid ring of sharks swirling around and around, faster and faster, and her Dustin was in the middle of them all. A shout came from high up on the bridge. It was Jim Banks pointing out to sea. She could hear him shouting something, it was hard to make out the words. She thought she heard the word 'point.' Sure, she could see him pointing. So what? She continued monitoring the instruments. They were getting some good returns here. She was running a continual save to copy the data to an external hard drive just as a safety measure. She heard yells and screams. She looked up to see Captain Banks next to her, leaning over the combing of the ship shouting down at the dive platform.

"Get them up. White Pointer!" He was pointing just a hundred yards away now. She tried to remember. She knew what white pointer referred to. It was a shark. It was the real name of a Great White Shark. She jumped up from her station and rushed to the side of the boat. All the other sharks in the area were moving out. All the hundreds of hammerheads, white-tips, bull sharks and tigers were running away. John, down on the diving platform was yanking the signal line, the line attached to Sam to signal a warning. There was no return signal.

With a flash, Erhart, still in his wetsuit, had his scuba gear on his back, his weight belt on, another in his hand and jumped in the water while
pulling his fins on. Almost all the other sharks had left the area. The Great White was at the bow of the ship. Mary had her hand in her mouth and her eyes were wide open in shock. The size of the great white was immense. She had thought the hammerheads were big. They were like toys compared to this shark. It's tail was bigger than the shore boat. She could make out the details now, the beady eyes, the horizontally blunt nose. Other sharks were streamlined to make it easier to swim through the water while making sharp turns. Not the Great White. It was so powerful, it bashed its way to wherever it wanted to go. Anything that got in its way, got thrashed, destroyed, or devoured.

Erhart was swimming straight down for the bottom. The extra weight belt in his hand was helping to speed up his descent. He didn't seem to have a problem clearing his ear. The air seemed to go right through the eardrum. Salt water was poring into his throat from his busted eardrum via his Eustachian tube. He hoped he hadn't completely destroyed his hearing. On the bottom he went straight to the twin 80s' and closed their valves. He had remembered that Sam had told him that Great Whites were attracted to bubbles. Bubbles scarred other sharks. Great Whites feared nothing. It was strange down there without the bubble column making such a racket. Sam turned towards the tanks when the noise stopped. He was surprised to see Erhart. Before he could move, Erhart pointed over Sam's shoulder at the Great White. Sam turned, froze, and then slowly sank towards the bottom like a sinking piece of flotsam. Erhart got Dustin's attention. The three of them headed for the bottom. Sam stared at the White Pointer. 'No', he told himself, 'it's not a White Pointer. This close, in the water next to him, its a Great White Shark. No other name came close. No other name could communicate the size, the power, the physical dominance of this animal.'

There were no rocks to hide between on the bottom, just the mound and a few straggly strands of kelp. The Great White swam towards them barely moving his tail, his eyes always moving, his huge head turning this way and that. He opened his jaws once, as if yawning, displaying three sets of huge triangular teeth. Great Whites grew new sets of teeth continually. Every year the outer set, or what was left of the outer set fell out and the next set took its place. Some biologists felt that the shark's famous bad temper was generated by always teething every day of its entire life.

Sam tried to breath slowly and evenly. He looked over at Erhart. He was hyperventilating. Bubbles were flowing out of his regulator like visible bursts of fear. Sam signaled to him to slow his breathing and to close his eyes. It didn't really matter how close the shark got. If he wanted to eat you, there was nothing on Earth or heaven that could save you. Dustin was lying prone on the bottom, a few weeds pulled over his body. Sam noticed with approval that one of them was fire coral. It must have been burning Dustin's hand, but it would discourage the shark from investigating closer. Sam sat there and tried to be one with the sea, a piece of coral, a strand of sea weed, part of the mound. He wasn't an animal. He just was. He had always been there, always would be there. He tried to peek at his air gauge without moving. He had looked at it five minutes ago and it had showed 1250 psi. Enough for another 15 minutes, easy, at this depth, if he could control his breathing.

The Great White was feet away from him. It passed between him and the watery sun shining so far away on the surface. Sam ignored the surface. That way led to death. Great Whites loved to kill seals while the herd swam on the surface. They would eat a few, if they happened to be hungry, but they loved to kill them. They wouldn't stop killing until they had killed them all. They were the only other animal on Earth that killed for the pleasure of killing. Like man, the Great White could fall into a blood lust state and just kill and kill and kill. All other sharks ate what they killed. Great Whites continued to kill long after they were full. He felt the water from the great tail push him aside. He didn't resist the force. He allowed the pressure wave throw him any way it wanted. He looked down at the bang sticks still in his hand. They would only enrage such a huge animal. He peaked over at Erhart and was pleased that he had his finger in his ear, just in case and was breathing lightly and was relaxed on the bottom.

It looked like the Great White was going to leave to go and terrorize another part of the sea when it turned and headed back towards them. Something was drawing him back. Sam looked around as much as he could with out moving his head or his facemask. Over by Dustin he could see the sensor light signaling that it was starting another sensor run. Sam knew that a line of sensory imput cells on the sides of sharks was very sensitive to electrical impulses. The cells ran the length of its body, forming a lateral line, and was actually a very advanced sonar system, especially in a shark as long as a Great White. The lateral line was so long it could pick up even small variations in the magnetic fields that surround all living things. Dustin's metal detector was releasing so much electricity it must look like King Kong on the Empire State Building to the shark as the electrons magnetized the iron in the sea water. As long as that machine was on, the shark wouldn't ever leave the area. The sensor was nine feet away, from Sam, the Great White was fifteen. Any movement on his part was certain death. Again Sam pretended to be inert, again he was thrown around as the shark glided past. By bad luck the shark's tail snagged the sensor's umbilical cord leading up to the *Balls*. The sensor was pulled off the mound and trailed after the shark like a flea chasing a Great Dane. Sam closed his eyes in relief. That solved one problem. Maybe it would go away now.

Tugs awoke hanging from a tree. He had a beautiful view. The ocean went out for miles and all the island was laid out at his feet. Looking down he noticed that he was naked, swinging in the wind, his hands were tied above his head and they were in turn tied to a large branch of a tree. He wasn't cold which surprised him. He would have thought he would have been freezing. The wind was strong enough. He was high enough. Right at the top of the island. Swinging in the wind.

He tried to remember how he got here. He was finding a trail for Joe. A sandy one. A nice sandy trail. He was walking down the trail and he fell, fell down a hole in the trail. There wasn't a hole there before. It must have been some kind of trap. He was knocked unconscious by something and when he came to, he was here, swinging in the wind.

It was kind of nice, in a way, in the wind. He wasn't hungry. Finally no bugs were biting him. The wind kept them away, he guessed. He wasn't uncomfortable. Surprisingly. He did feel a tickling along his scalp and down his spine. Not too bad though. Just a little. Could be annoying if he thought about it. The view was nice. Big yacht down in bay. He could see houses. He saw a couple of girls sunbathing on the roof of one.

The tickling was down between the cheeks of his ass now. How weird. Maybe sweat. He wasn't hot. Why sweat? Weird. Now it was going down each leg. On the inside. Tickling. Now tickling going down arms. He wanted to itch the tickling but he was still hanging by his arms.

Something was yanking on his head. Something was going down his forehead. Blocking his vision. Getting hard to see. Looked like hair. Looked like a person's hair. A hand came into his vision. It pulled at the hair. Yanked. The hair came down and covered his eyes. He felt something pulling along his spine. Strange sound. Like ripping. His back and head started to get cold. Weird. Rest of him was warm. Two hands were digging in the crack of his ass. More ripping sound. Hands down his legs, arms. Ripping. Getting hard to focus, to think. Weird. Pulling at his face. At his eyes. Tickling around his eyes. Suddenly he could see again. Hair was gone from his forehead.

Something white with streaks of red was bulged out below his nose. No, his nose was gone. Weird. Just a bone, cartilage, sticking out. White thing was gone. He looked down his body. There it was. Down by his waist. He pushed out his lips. Funny. He couldn't see them. Getting tired. Time to sleep. So tired. Tickling down by his cock now. More ripping.

No noise now. No tickling. Whole body was cold. Very cold. Freezing. Tired. Cold. Cold. So cold. Might as well sleep. Sleep.

John felt the cable that led to the sensor yank out of his hands. Extra wire was piled in a coil on the dive platform. It acted like something alive, ripping out and up at an incredible speed. When the coil was gone it tore itself out of the back on the monitor up on the *Steel Balls* and disappeared into the sea with a snake like hiss. Mary sat by the monitor and watched as it went blank. Everyone stared at the water where the last bit of the cable disappeared, except Jim Banks.

"John, stop pulling that signal cord. I think they know as well as we do what has happened. He noted with approval that the torrent of bubbles had stopped. The air in those tanks might save their lives. Unless they were dead already. He tried to look down to the bottom of the sea. The water was still too stirred up by the bubbles to see anything. There was no sign of life down there. Jim turned to his second in command.

"Charlie, break out the weaponry. That shark choose the wrong boat to pick on. Arm the crew, small arms, only. Station them all around the rails." Charlie Ross nodded and turned to obey. "And Charlie, pass the word. Please don't shoot my divers when they come up."

"Yes, sir." Charlie went down deep in the boat. He closed his eyes to think just for a second. He had only been into the armory twice before. It was in a smuggling hold. Not that they were smuggling guns. Major yachts had no need of the pittance of a few thousand dollars, arms dealing brought in. However, whenever they cleared into foreign countries, the authorities always seized all weaponry on board saying that the would return the guns and ammo when the vessel left. Usually, they actually did. Jim Banks felt that, it was while they were in local waters that they had most need of weapons. At sea, the *Balls* was so fast, nothing save an American warship could catch her. Jim had secretly installed a four by ten foot locker under the elevator while it was being installed. The door was tricky. It was like one of those Chinese puzzles. You had to slide this to the port, that to the starboard, push that, then pull the other thing, all at once. No chance it could ever be found by accident.

Once the door was open, Charlie pulled out all five of the magnum pistols, three of the double barreled shot guns loaded with depleted uranium solid shot that had been crisscrossed into dumdums. He eyed the bazooka. It would be too unwieldy against a shark, plus the exhaust would stain the paintwork. Finally he pulled out a dozen concussion grenades. He eyed the Stinger missiles regretfully. Too bad the damn shark wasn't metallic. He closed up the locker, careful not to leave any fingerprints. He stopped at the engine room on the way up.

"Hey, Piston! Want to shoot up a huge Great White Shark?" He didn't have to ask twice. The Chief Engineer and his two mates poured out of the hatch following Charlie up to the deck, with shouts of excitement. Charlie looked in at Sam's divers. They were watching movies on the big screen, drinking beer and eating popcorn. He closed the door quietly.

On deck all was quiet. There were still a few bubbles coming up from the dive site. Hopefully that meant the divers were still alive. There was no sign of the Great White. Charlie noticed that the other sharks hadn't returned to the area. That could only mean that the big one was still down there. Lurking. Waiting. Stalking.

Sam watched the Great White as it made a wide circle around them. It didn't seem to realize that it was dragging a ten pound sensor and a hundred feet of umbilical cord. The cord was tangled now between its caudal and pectoral fins. It didn't come back to the mound on the next circle. Looking for other sharks, Sam guessed. If the shark was going to continue to swim in circles, he was going to go for the surface the next time the shark turned its head away. He hoped it would be enough. He knew how very fast Great Whites were. They could accelerated from zero to twenty knots in a second and a half. He looked around him. The water clarity had improved dramatically. Far, far in the distance, he could maybe see a few hammerheads swimming back and forth waiting till it was safe to come back for a snack. On the next circuit, just as Sam was planning to go for it, the shark turned suddenly and came back to the mound. The men remained still. They were used to playing possum by now. He hoped Erhart's ear wouldn't bleed again. If the Great White got a whiff of blood, who knew what would happen.

The shark came up to the edge of the mound and muzzled it with his nose. There was no other word. The Great White lost its aggressiveness and acted as if the mound was a lover. It fanned the sand with its pectoral fin on the side of its body. Little particles of sand flew up into the water, swirling here and there. The shark lowered itself down until its eye was right next to the mound. It watched the mound for a few seconds and then swirled sand onto the mound. With a flash of its huge tail, it was gone in a split second. Sam signaled to Dustin and Erhart with a raised thumb, the sign to go for the surface. They didn't need any prodding. Sam couldn't help himself. He had to see what the Great White had been doing.

The shark seemed to be gone. Sam watched carefully. He did a quick spin to make sure the hammerheads weren't heading back yet. The coast was clear. He dashed over to the side of the mound and flicked his hand back and forth, washing the sand away. His mouth opened so far his regulator dropped out. Shark eggs lay under the sand. He grabbed one and sped for the surface. He found his regulator and shoved it into his mouth all the while shouting to himself, 'No Way! Great Whites bear their young live. They are a meter long when the mother gave birth with fully developed bodies and the babies start killing other fish with in minutes of birth. Then his mind screamed at him. A new species! A goddamn new species! He would be famous. Get on the cover of Time Magazine. Not just any new species. A new species of Great White! A White that lay eggs. And he had an egg! The egg alone would be worth millions to Scripps or Woods Hole. His eyes widen in pleasure. Up above he saw Dustin and Erhart climb up on the dive platform. He was next. He raised his hand up and touched the platform. He felt a pressure wave behind him. He turned his head and accidentally looked directly into the Great White's eyes. It was only feet from him. There was such intelligence in the eyes, such composure, such certainty. Sam froze as if hypnotized.

He didn't feel it when his legs were chopped off. He just noticed that he wasn't going up anymore. He popped his BC to help and looked down. He couldn't see. The water was all red. He couldn't see the Great White turn and come back towards him, one of Sam's swim fins sticking out of the side of its mouth. At the last second as the shark raced at him he finally could see. He made out a huge, jaw, lined with sets of gigantic triangular teeth. The jaw was wider than he was tall, than he used to be tall. The shark seemed to gently grab him around the waist, the remains of his legs fell to the bottom of the sea. His shoulders and head were thrown upwards. The shark raced back, and gently nudged the egg from one hand slowly drifting towards the bottom of the sea, and carefully balanced it on one fin as she carried it back to the nest.

The ex-Seal was watching the man with one eye open. He decided the guy was a halfway deadly man. Far deadlier than he looked. Which is why he had only one eye open. The human subconscious retained a genetic terror of two eyes watching, waiting, stalking. The mind might not sense the eyes amidst the foliage of the jungle, but the subconscious certainly could. People knew that they only used 10% of their brains and wondered what was going on in the other 90%. That was the area of the subconscious' genetic memory, memory passed on through untold generations' of DNA. The memory that warned of two eyes glaring in the dark belonging to a saber toothed tiger waiting at the entrance to the cave or the twin eyes of a raptor eyeing their babies in their cribs lying next to their parents in the fields or groups of vaguely human eyes staring out of the forest getting ready for an attack on the village. The subconscious never forgot. That is why the ex-Seal only had one eye open. The subconscious didn't think one eye was a threat, so it ignored it.

The guy had some how managed to start a fire. It was about time. The Seal was getting tired of following this guy. He actually seemed to be lost after his partner disappeared. He wandered in circles, around and around the mountain. Whatever he was looking for, he didn't find. He had a fair amount of woodcraft. He made little noise going through the woods. He seemed to recognize fruit and veggies and only picked and ate them off the trail and left minimal sign. He cleaned his gun three times a day, and did it quickly, only after he checked his perimeter very carefully. The fact that he didn't notice the ex-Seal couldn't be taken away from him. The ex-Seal made Rambo look like a sissy.

The guy seemed to give up on whatever he was searching for. He stood up, stomped out the fire, creating a lot of smoke and followed the trail heading down the mountain. He walked carefully. He held his gun in his right hand and on his left was a set of brass knuckles. He whistled as he walked. He pretended not to have a care in the world. He was suddenly making a lot of noise. To the ex-Seal's eye, he was expecting trouble every step. It came soon enough. It was a different sandy patch. One minute the guy was there, walking along, every sense alert, the next he was gone. The Seal opened both eyes in surprise, it was so quick. He heard muffled gun shots from somewhere. Three, four, then all was quiet. The guy hadn't managed to empty his clip.

The Seal didn't move a muscle for an hour. He didn't even move his eye. His one open eye. He knew that the eye's peripheral vision was superior than its frontal vision when it came to detecting sneaky motion. Another holdover from long ago days, and nights. Nothing moved out there that wasn't supposed to. There were no other gun shots. No one came around to check on the pit trap. It was a hell of a good one. He couldn't spot it from here, thirty feet away, and he sure as hell wasn't going any closer until he knew who was setting it. However, aggressive locals weren't in his job description. He had been told to follow the people on the boat who walked around on the island, plus any locals who were digging holes, and if nothing else, stand guard on the boat and the person of his employer. He wondered if sneaky trap makers qualified as locals. He looked again at the sandy patch and told himself that his duty lay elsewhere. To take on these trap makers would take a bigger team. A much bigger team.

He was on retainer, in the service of Hawkins. Had been for three years. He worked only for cash, only in advance. Nothing against Hawkins. His arrangements were the same no matter who he worked for. Good people or bad, he didn't care. He certainly had killed a lot of people back when he worked for Uncle Sam, people who looked like fine upstanding tax payers. He was told they were bad. He didn't ask questions. He tracked, he stalked, he killed, and he didn't ask questions. He always was in demand. He could pick and choose who he worked for. As long as he never asked questions.

After night fell, he worked his way off the mountain top and headed down, back to the beach; to see if anyone else was moving around, down there. These two, if they were still alive, weren't going anywhere that didn't include a pine box. Anyone who could build a beautifully designed pit trap like the two that got the men, weren't about to let anyone get away.

Robyn and The Prospector walked down the dirt path to the dock. Their shore boat was back against the side of the *Steel Balls* and everyone was staring down into the water on the side of the boat. The red water on the side of the boat. They walked out to the end of the dock. No one paid them the least bit of attention. There were two divers on dive platform by the boat and they were being helped up onto the ship. Mary was sitting by some instruments crying. Hawk was pacing back and forth with a ferocious grin on his face. The crew were all armed and lined the side of the ship. Several were pointing guns down into the water. Nothing was to be seen down there.

Suddenly the ship took a lurch to starboard. It was as if something had rammed the ship on the port side. Several crew rushed over and fired guns into the water. One threw a grenade into the water which shook the ship again. People were running back and forth on the deck, looking over the side. After a few minutes, all was quiet and the crew were giving each other high fives. Robyn saw Hawk look in their direction. He stared at them for a couple of seconds and then purposely looked away and went to talk to Dustin. Robyn looked at the Prospector who shrugged his shoulders. He turned and walked back up the dirt path. He thought about his instruments on the *Steel Balls*. He didn't need them. They just made his life easier. While walking back up the trail, he stopped every few feet and smelled the air. He seemed very happy to be walking around on a deserted island. Robyn on the other hand wanted to know where her next meal was going to come from. It had been hours since they had eaten.

"Stud? I'm really getting hungry. Any chance of finding anything to eat in this jungle? Sometimes I think I have a tape worm or something. I just lose all my energy if I don't get regular meals."

"We had some of that fish stew up at the cookhouse not but three or four hours ago."

"I know, Honey. Could we go and see if there is still some left? Besides, with some chow in me, who knows what might happen?"

It took the ex-Seal exactly three seconds to find the Arab's hiding spot. He stared at the naked girl. He thought he had seen her on the supply boat. Hard to be sure with her naked. He tried to eliminate her body in his mind. Yes, he had seen that face. Not that it mattered. The Arab nodded in his direction and went back to staring at the yacht through binoculars. They were shooting guns out there at something. The Seal took a look. Everyone was running around with their heads cut off. No one was in command. Amateurs. But what else can one expect with rich boys? Spoiled rich boys. An older man stood on the end of the dock with a woman. There was something about him. The Seal couldn't put his finger on it. He didn't recognize him, but there was something familiar. Maybe on some distant battlefield. He turned and looked at his fellow bodyguard. He was about to ask him if he recognized the man on the dock. Not that any Arab would know. They always thought about themselves first. Themselves, their religion, and their enemies. The rest of the world didn't exist for them.

"What is the girl for?" The Arab ignored him. He went over to the girl, pulled a knife and slit her bonds, careful to always keep the girl between him and the Arab. There was a cut piece of hardwood in her mouth. He pulled it out, grabbed her by the back of her neck and raised the woman to her feet. He pushed her towards the dirt trail to the beach, keeping his eyes on the Arab.

"Go. Don't come back." Jackie looked at him thankfully for a second and then rushed through the bushes, a few thorns cutting at her upper thighs. She turned at the trail leading to the dock, looked down at her naked form, hesitated, and then turned towards the barracks and fresh clothes. Half way there she stopped and listened. She was sure several people were following her. She rushed faster. She just couldn't stand up for herself and fight if she had to, if she was naked. She just couldn't.

Elena was sure she heard gunfire down by the bay. She stood up and looked over the side of the roof. People were acting like clowns in a circus running this way and that down on that big motor yacht. One threw a rock into the water which exploded throwing water up in the air like a World War II movie. From her altitude she could see deep into the water. Something large was circling around the yacht. Every once in a while it would go deep and swim under the ship to look at something there. Then it would go back to circling. The people on the boat had stopped running around and were celebrating something. Maybe they were having a party.

"Mercedes! They are having a party down at that yacht! Let's get dressed up and go get invited! We both have killer tans. Let's go show them off!" Mercedes, stretched her beautiful naked body and turned over.

"Are they serving liquor, Chica?"

"Mercedes? Who wants to drink? It might ruin my complexion. I just want to do something. I mean we have been here, in this little house, for days and days. Maybe I am getting the, how do you say, the cabin fever. Let's go have some fun!" Mercedes barely lifted an eyelash, just enough to stare at Elena.

"I thought you wanted to spend your whole vacation up on this roof? Yes?"

"That was before they were having a party. I could wear my blue dress, the one with the pearl buttons and the back that goes all the way down past my waist. I guess high heels are out, since we have to walk on sand to get to the dock. Wait! There is an old truck down by the dock. It was there yesterday, too. I wonder if we could find the owner and he could drive us around the island. That would be exciting. Don't you think?"

Mercedes closed her eyelashes again and listened to her friend as she babbled on and on. She was so content here. What a great vacation. Soon she would have to return to the mainland and all the problems she had left there. So many problems. But she didn't want to think about them now. She just wanted to lay on the roof and relax. Elena was good for her. She was so superficial. It was a tonic for her soul not to have to think deeply. To get swallowed up in Elena's endless talk of parties and men. Not necessarily in that order. She felt the sun warm her belly and her mouth smiled while her eyes drooped in worry.

Dad, watch this one!" Jill stood on the cabin top. With a shout of joy, she ran to the side of the boat and somersaulted, landing in an impressive splash. Her father was applauding from the water while she was still in the air.

"Way to go, Jill. Your splash went eight feet into the air, at least. That had to be a ten in the Olympics!" Jill blew water out of her nose and looked at him in pleasure.

"Think that one was good, let me get out and I'll show you a thirteen!" She swam back to the boat and climbed up the boarding ladder on the becalmed *Rose Marie.* Janet stood in the cockpit and eyed her daughter calmly.

"Jill, fair is fair, it is my turn to swim and your turn to play safety. Remember, if the wind starts to draw the boat away from us, start the engine and back into the wind. We will swim to you, don't come to us. OK?"

"Mother, I got it the first time. I am a big girl now. A teenager! Don't worry. Go have some fun with your lover." Janet was already leaping over the side when she heard Jill's last words. She turned in the air and looked at Jill in dismay, disbelief, and interest. In the water she swam over to Harv.

"You will never believe what your daughter just said to me. I thought her teenage years would kick in gradually. It doesn't seem to work that way."

"Don't sweat it. If you react, she wins! She is just experimenting how to be a quasi-adult. And anyway, whatever she said, tomorrow she will think up something worse! Isn't it fun to be a parent?" Janet splashed him in the face with water.

“Ahoy, you two in the water. I can see a puff of wind approaching. Do you wish to be towed like fish bait, or are you going to come aboard like proper little sailors?” Harv leisurely swam over to a line trailing from the *Rose Marie's* stern and pulled himself to the ladder. Janet ignored the line and swam over to the boat with a beautiful Australian Crawl. She slipped one hand over the toe rail of the boat, raised an tendon striped heel over the rail and easily pulled herself up and onto the boat. On board, Harv stared at her.

“Since when did you become Miss Expert Swimmer?” Janet blushed and then glared at Harv.

“This is me. This is what you have got as a wife. Don't like it? Too bad, but listen, Bozo, stop with the snide comments.” As soon as she spoke, as soon as the words exited her mouth, Janet looked at Harv in disbelief, her eyes widened in sudden fear, she covered her face in her hands and raced below. They could hear her down there sobbing in the forward cabin. Crying as if she had just lost her soul.

Joe lay on the floor of some sort of cave. He pretended to be dead. When he fell though the trap door, he was expecting it. He had hoped for it. He had put enough sign out, smoke, talking, he had even whistled. Whoever had taken Tugs was the top dog on this island, and the only way he knew to take over the island was to knock the existing top dog off his throne, by plugging him right in the middle of his eyes. So when he fell through the trap, he had put his brass knuckled hand up over his head to protect it. Sure enough, something came flying threw the air and hit him hard, right on the knuckles. He fell to the floor after a drop of twelve feet, pulled his revolver and fired a shot into each quarter of the fairly large cave and fell to the floor to try to avoid ricochets. Then he quietly moved away and hid in the shadow of a corner.

The light was coming from several holes in the ceiling. After a while his eyes adjusted and he could make out a few details. He couldn't see anyone anywhere, neither could he make out the trapdoor he come in through. He peered around. Didn't look like there was a door out either. The room was lined with blocks of rock. It didn't look like they were cemented together but he couldn't find any cracks between the blocks. He slowly rose to his feet, keeping an eye out for head hitting obstacles and crept slowly around the perimeter of his cave. Not a door to be found. Stood to reason. Anyone who could craft such a well disguised trapdoor, would make an equally well crafted access door. It would be easy to hide with all the blocks of stone in here. No one seemed to be interested in him at all. He decided that he might as well make some noise, stir things up and see what happens.

"Fuck if I am going to sit here and starve." He banged on the stone blocks all around his cage, listening for hollow spots. His fist got sore after awhile so he used the butt of his pistol. He wondered if they knew he was using a Berretta, which had a nine shell clip. If they thought he would be out after six shots, they had another think coming. When his banging on the walls produced no results, he started shouting.

"All right you mother fuckers, I'm right here! I'd love to see the color of your blood! Come on out. Let's see what you got. One on one or bring your whole army, I don't care. Let's get it on!" After he started to get hoarse from shouting, his cage was still as silent as tomb. He finally fell asleep as the overhead lighting dimmed with dusk.

Something awoke him. It was day. He thought he saw Tugs standing at the other end of the cave. He rubbed his eyes. He still saw Tugs. Overjoyed he leaped to his feet and followed as Tugs slowly backed up, his finger to his lips.

"Tugs, Tugs. Where are we going?" he whispered. Tugs put two fingers to his lips and kept backing. Joe carefully slid through the door.

The door was made of solid rock. No wonder he couldn't get any echoes from it. Outside the door the lighting was better. There was something odd about Tugs. He couldn't put his finger on it. It was the same old ugly Tugs. He would recognize that face anywhere. Same clothes he was wearing before. Could it be something about the eyes? He had it. Tugs wasn't talking endlessly, yacking away, like normal.

"Maybe you learned something down here about making noise," he whispered. Tugs kept backing away. Joe tried to catch up, to grab him by the arm, to look into his eyes, somehow though, as fast as he went, Tugs equaled his speed. He sure had become more coordinated down here. They were going down a long hall, without doors, lined with cut blocks of rock. Assumingly without doors, he reminded himself. Finally Tugs backed into the sun on a ledge on the side of the mountain. He slipped to one side and was out of view. Joe hurried not wanting to loose his guide. As he rushed into the sun, he was momentarily blinded by broad daylight, people on either side grabbed him, he was lifted into the air and carried to a carved rock block. They laid him on top of it, a small rock projection under his back thrust his chest upwards.

"Tugs, Tugs, help me!" He struggled as he yelled but it did no good. Whoever held him were well muscled and used to holding people on this table. No one was paying any attention to his pistol. If he could just get a hand free, then he would show them some fireworks. Finally Tugs came into view and he relaxed just a bit.

"Hey, Buddy. Tell these people to let me go. Must be a mix up here." He tried to see his captors but they were crouched down below the rock, pulling his arms and legs downwards. Tugs was scratching himself on the back of his head and then suddenly his face collapsed. Tugs pulled down his hair and his face came off with the hair. Someone else was under his face. Joe relaxed for a second. That explained it. He was having one hell of a nightmare. He watched with interest as some guy pulled all of Tugs skin off and then donned some kind of weird mask. He was going to have to remember this later. Maybe he should start writing down his dreams. Someone tore open his shirt and the Tugs/masked guy, stood next to him and raised a wickedly sharp stone knife. He thrust it down putting his whole body into it and pulled something out of his chest. There wasn't any pain. A blow, sure, but that was it. He had to stop watching science fiction movies, he would be wasted tomorrow. The chest thing in the masked guy's hand was beating, squirting blood everywhere. As his vision started to fade, he wondered if he could make a movie based on his dream, make millions. Millions. Be top dog in Hollywood.

The Great White hit the starboard side this time. Hit it hard. Hit it like a Mack truck slamming into a brick wall. The whole ship vibrated with the power of the blow. Jim Banks looked over the side. He half expected to see a dead shark with a bashed in head. But the water was clear, there was no shark to be seen. Hawkins raced over to the side of the main deck.

"Will someone please kill that stupid animal for me? I'll give a hundred thousand to the person or persons who will kill that monster." People rushed over the rails. Several grenades were thrown over the side. People were firing off guns at seagulls, at fish in the water.

"Stop it. Stop all firing! Someone is going to get killed." Jim Banks was livid. "That shark is no danger to a vessel of this size. Everyone relax. If you want to shoot at the shark, fine. Nominate one person a side and take turns. And stop throwing those grenades, you are going to knock out my sonars." Hawk looked up at his Captain in irritation. It was his boat, wasn't it? He corralled Charlie and grabbed him by the upper arm.

"Don't you have any stronger weapons on this ship? Please tell me, yes." Charlie looked at Hawk in hesitation then turned to look at Jim Banks up on the bridge. Hawk grabbed his neck with his massive right hand. "Don't you dare look away from me. This is my vessel. Don't you want to be Captain of her one day? I can make you her Captain, today. I can fire Banks. Got it? Now, where are the weapons? Tell me now."

Charlie gulped. He would love to be Captain and Hawk was the owner. Charlie knew he could pick any qualified man to be the ship's Captain that he wished, however the lessons of the sea are driven deep and the foremost of those lessons is, always obey your Captain.

"He is my Captain, Sir. I have to obey." Hawk looked like he was about to have a stroke.

"Banks! Get down here, NOW!" Hawk roared at the top of his voice. Even the Piston and John who were fighting for the possession of a shotgun, turned to listen. It only took thirty seconds for Jim Banks to slide down the ladders and to stand proud and determined in front of his owner.

"Banks, I want to be taken to the armory. I want this shark killed. It killed my dive master, it will kill more when we go down again. I want it dead." Banks was dressed in his uniform, four gold stripes on his shoulders and scrambled eggs on his hat. He looked at Hawkins like he was an alien from some subhuman planet.

"We won't have to wait for the shark to kill people if the crew get a hold of serious weapons. They will kill each other, firing at anything that moves. What weapons they have are already dangerous enough. This ship's hull is built of half inch steel. That shark, whatever kind it is, can't even make a dent. We are in no danger. Besides, I refuse to allow further diving expeditions from this vessel. The crew and passengers are my responsibility. The White Pointer down there is but one of many sharks. Further more, the mound you were investigating has no metal in it."

"What are you talking about? Explain yourself!" Jim Banks put his hands to his mouth to channel his voice and shouted out for Mary and Dustin. Soon, they arrived from the instruments that they were studying by the dive platform.

"Tell Hawkins about the mound." Mary spoke up first.

"We didn't complete our study, however it seems that there are no metals at all in the mound. We only discovered organic materials. The further scans we had scheduled were for orienting any metals to determine their exact positions. Therefore, I believe we can eliminate this mound from further inquiry." Hawk looked dismayed.

"But there are other mounds? We have to investigate the other mounds?"

"It is unlikely that they will produce any different results. On sonar they appear to be identical." Dustin spoke up.

"The Great White shark is a very real menace. I can not condone any further studies while that shark is in the area. It has already killed one man. I for one refuse to dive while it is in the area."

"Exactly, we have to kill that damn shark. Captain, we need stronger weapons. I want to be taken to the armory right now. Immediately!"

"Mr. Hawkins. As the Captain of this vessel I refuse to allow more diving in the area and I refuse to allow unqualified crew to handle seriously dangerous weapons. Weapons that might endanger the safety of the ship. If you want to use such weapons, we will have to institute a training program first."

"Mr. Banks, you are relieved of your position as Captain. Vacate the Captain's cabin immediately. You may berth below by engineering. Charlie Ross, you are now Captain. This is your ship to run. Your first job is to show me the Armory." Charlie looked over at Jim, half in apology, have in embarrassment.

"Yes, Sir. Right this way." It took only a minute for Charlie to open the secret locker this time. When the door finally opened, Hawk was on his knees reading the labels on various crates.

He took one look at the Stinger Missile and knew that was the weapon for him. The rifles and the pistols were fine, but he wanted something big and powerful. He knew deep inside of himself that it was because he was a little afraid of the Great White. Not that it mattered.

'Won't matter a smidgeon after I blow that fucking shark to smithereens,' he told himself. There was a brief set of directions in the cover of the case. The writing was very small. Hawk ignored them. Charlie Ross looked on in concern.

"Sir, first of all, the Stinger seeks metallic targets, second it is a lot harder to operate a Stinger than it looks like on the nightly news. Would you like a brief operator's lesson?" Hawk turned to him, his eyes full of scorn and just a little bit of fear.

"If I need your help, I'll ask. In the mean time, drive the ship where I tell you to and keep out of my way." Hawk struggled with the case and finally tore the stinger out of it, re-assembled it, and took the elevator up to the bridge. There he had a good view of the surrounding waters. Off in the distance, he could see Dustin's sensor being towed along by the Great White. It was slowly coming towards the ship.

'Seeks metal. Hah. What do I pay these idiots for,' he asked himself. The shark was approaching the starboard side. Hawk got himself set up, braced against the rail, figured out how to engage the eyepiece and flipped the safety off the trigger guard. He followed Dustin's sensor with the telescopic sighting eyepiece willing the shark to surface. In the corner of his eye he saw Jim Banks throw a sea bag into the shore boat and he and John climbed down into it. Hawk ignored them. Time enough for deserters after he had dwelt with this shark. For a second he thought about turning and blowing up the tender and Jim Banks with his missile but with a smile he continued to track the sensor.

The shark was coming up to the surface. He thought he could see the dorsal fin in the water. The Stinger was wailing, signaling that it wanted confirmation of a target. Hawk ignored the sound. The shark was a hundred feet away and he pressed the trigger. The Stinger was programmed not to explode within 300 feet of its launch so it burst out of its launch tube with a pillar of fire erupting behind it and raced out to 300 feet to arm and then screeched around in a U turn aiming for the closest metal, Dustin's sensor. Just as Hawk fired, the shark sunk under the *Steel Balls*, sinking to swim by the mound. A second before the Stinger reached the sensor, it disappeared under the water.

The missile normally would have fail-safed having lost its target but Hawk had failed to select the target and to wait for tone. As a result, the Stinger seeked the next biggest piece of steel it could find. It wasn't difficult. There was a huge wall of it right in front of it. The missile struck the *Steel Balls* at the waterline just at the engineering area. The explosion was immense. The missile managed to penetrate the hull of the ship before it exploded, igniting the reserve gasoline tanks kept for the shore boat, water-skis and the like. The flames engulfed the ship within seconds. Luckily almost everyone was on deck and most were thrown up and outwards by the blast. The life rafts were automatically launched also and inflated as soon as they hit the water.

The Great White was disorientated by the blast. It started swimming in circles upside down, snapping it jaws, almost blind from the bubbles and debris in the water. Its lateral line relayed the information that there were multiple prey kicking and splashing on the surface. The shark knew it should eat but was so confused by the explosion it couldn't pick between swimmers. Instead it raced in circles on the surface, bumping against all the flotsam, human and not.

The *Steel Balls* took fifteen minutes to sink. The explosion had broken the ship in two. The last Hawkins saw of his ship was a camera, part of his security system, spinning this way and that, on the top of the ship's mast.

Elena and Mercedes jolted upright at the sound of the Stinger launching. They got to their feet just in time to see the missile destroy the *Steel Balls*. They saw people thrown into the air, somersaulting into the ocean, arms flailing, legs kicking. The girls stood by the side of their roof, hands to their mouths, eyes wide open, in shock. Elena put a hand out and touched Mercedes to balance herself. For a minute, it seemed her whole world was turning upside down. The rock that was Mercedes steadied her. In the water a few less harmed crew members managed to crawl onto the life rafts that had been blown into the water and automatically inflated. The shore boat was preparing to dock at the pier when the Stinger hit. John started to bring the boat around as people splashed into the water, the beautiful varnish of the tender was pelted by pieces of wood and steel and flesh.

The girls didn't know that sharks were irresistibly attracted to explosions, Hammerheads especially. The Hammerheads had always remained in the area, just out of the Great White's way, circling, waiting. Now they moved in. They sensed the massive shark was still in the area, but they also sensed that it was wounded, easy prey. Their caution evaporated. Adrenalin long held in check, saved for fleeing from the Great White, surged into their blood streams and the pack turned and raced towards the remains of the *Steel Balls* as one, like a flock of vultures. They ignored the people helplessly flailing in the water. They raced each other towards the Great White. Together they attacked. Hammerheads bit and tore, gulped mouthfuls down with a toss of their odd shaped heads then forced themselves back into the pack surrounding the slowly struggling animal for another bite. The Great White tried to defend itself, snapping its great jaws, killing a hammerhead here and there. There were just too many of them. At the end, with the last of its strength, the huge shark sped as fast as it could straight away from the strange looking mound lying next to the remains of a once magnificent yacht; swam fast as it could, drawing the Hammerheads away from the mound. Soon the great white was nothing but some pink water and a few scraps drifting towards the bottom, fought over by remoras and pilot fish. Crazed by the taste of blood, the pack of sharks turned to search for other prey in the water. They didn't have to look far.

Mercedes tenderly snaked her fingers into Elena's long black hair and gently turned her head away from the carnage and buried it into her breast. She forced herself to watch the end of many of the crew as they were torn into bite size chunks by the pack. Tears fell from her eyes as their last cries thinly carried up to her hill. At the end, when the last survivors were picked up by the little motor boat and brought to shore, she turned her head away and her legs giving way sunk onto her chaise lounge. She stroked Elena's head, easing her fears, talking gently to her, bringing her slowly back from the terror of her memories; all the while trying to conquer her own as she tried to stop the flood of tears pouring from her eyes. The people from the ship had behaved so bravely. One pushing a fellow crew member up onto the little tender even as sharks tore into him from below. The only exception was a Santa Claus looking character. A thin girl on the boat reached down to give him a hand. He grabbed her hand and yanked her into the water to give the approaching pack something else to eat as he pulled himself into the tender.

"Mercedes. Oh, Mercedes, we have to go and help. They need our help. We have to do something." Mercedes looked down at her gentle little friend. She did have a good heart.

"Yes, little one. We have to help." They climbed off of the roof and were looking through cabinets for bandaging material, when Ben timidly knocked on the front door.

"Missy? Missies? It is Ben here, Missies." Elena rushed to let him in and to cry on his shoulder.

"Missies. Very important Missies stay in house. Bad things happen now. This happen before, long time ago. Very bad things. Very bad for Missies, if they know you are here. Must stay inside, Missies. Here, I bring food." He reached outside the door and dragged in a cardboard box of cans and vegetables.

"Missies must promise Ben. Missies must stay in house. Promise. Please, promise." Ben looked so terrified that Elena stopped seeking comfort and looked at him straight in the eyes her hands on his upper arms.

"The boat, Ben, the boat blew up. We have to help the people. We have to."

"Girls never get to beach. Bad people everywhere. Must stay."

"Ok, Ben, we will stay. You must stay here too." The cook looked away for a second.

"No can. I live in cave. Cave very far away. Girls stay in house. Promise."

Again Elena and Mercedes promised, and Ben slipped away into the forest, avoiding the thin path. As he disappeared, Mercedes thought he seemed very at home in the jungle for a cook. He must have been on island for a long time she finally decided.

John and Jim Banks had rescued everyone still alive and ferried them ashore. Piston was barely alive, but not for long. He had lost both legs above the knees and the shock was killing him, plus Hammerheads have particularly dirty mouths. The serrated edges of their teeth held particles of their past meals where the food rotted and grew bacteria. A bite from them invariably led to gangrene. Jim Banks walked up and down the beach, keeping away from the water, checking off his diminished crew. His past crew. Charlie Ross, while uninjured, had pulled the mutilated body of one of the stewardess out of the water and was slowly losing his sanity. Her head and face were untouched and flawless. Below, were one bare breast and a few ribs. All else was gone. He sat on the beach, hugging his knees to his chest, and cried endlessly. Tears ran down his face unabated. Hawk, who seemed unharmed, unbothered, pointedly ignored Charlie, who was across from him. Finally, Hawk stood up and got in Jim Banks way as he checked his crew.

"Look, I was wrong. Captain Banks, I should never have relieved you of your office. You are hereby honorably reinstated as Captain." Jim looked at him like an insect.

"Captain of what?" Hawk turned and stared at the empty bay save for the once beautiful tender to the *Steel Balls.* It wasn't beautiful anymore. It had been rammed countless times by sharks while rescuing the crew. Now it was a sinking hulk. Erhart looked at both men, who were getting ready to square off for a fist fight.

"Historically, a Captain retains his authority after a ship is sunk or destroyed. There are countless historical examples of this. A Captain is both Master of his ship and Commander of his men. Equally, if a Captain is disabled," he looked briefly at Charlie Ross, "a new Captain is always elected or designated, usually from among the most capable men available." Erhart had become an immediate hero for diving in to rescue Dustin and Sam from the Great White. He was happy he did. Before he had a ruptured ear drum that was incredibly painful. After his emergency dive, his eardrum was totally destroyed and the pain was considerably less. Especially now that they were far, far away from civilization and hospitalization. Besides, hearing was definitely overrated. Especially for men. Erhart looked pointedly at Jim Banks.

"When is the next supply boat due in, Captain?" Jim rubbed a hand over his forehead and pinched his nose next to the corner of his eyes.

"Alright. Listen up, people. It has been suggested that I should be your new Captain. I'm putting it up to a vote. Raise your hand if you want me to be your Captain." Three or four people looked up and slowly hoisted their hands. "All who would prefer a different person as Captain, raise your hand." Most of the crew continued to stare at their memories of the dead and dying, and took little interest. No one raised their hands. Hawk beamed.

"There, that's good. Now it is all legal." He looked around the island and slapped his hands together. "Now, it is time to find that gold! Erhart!"

"I'm right here, no need to shout." In the past, Hawk would have reacted violently to such veiled insolence. But now, in these new circumstances, he let it pass. Not that he would forget. He would mark it in his black book when he had the chance. He padded his pocket. Yes, he still had it. All ready to fill with names. All was good. He could still succeed.

"Do you have those Treasure Maps?"

"I gave them to you in your cabin, as I'm sure you remember. I had copies but they and all my notes went down with the ship." Erhart looked out at the now placid but vacant bay. "Which you sank." Hawk ignored the last comment.

"Can you remember any of the locations of the treasure?"

"Of course, I have an excellent memory. Especially for maps. Would you like to hear of a treasure near here? One that I think might possibly be real? The description, that is." A frown covered Erhart's mouth.

"Yes!" The word was uttered as Hawk inhaled, accenting his surprise, wonder and hope. People sitting on the beach started to look up and show a little life.

"Alright. This is accredited to Keating, one of the mutineers of the *Mary Deare*, some say the ringleader." He swept flat an area of sand and drew a map as he spoke, as he recited from memory.

"We have buried at a depth of four feet in red earth: Altar trimmings of cloth of gold with baldachin, moonstones, and chalices containing 1,244 stones; one chest weighing 120 pounds with bar gold, 624 topaz, carnelian and emeralds, and twelve diamonds; one chest weighing 160 pounds with gold coins, 860 rubies and nineteen diamonds; one chest with 4,000 gold doubloons of Spain marked 8 and 5,000 gold crowns of Mexico; one chest with 124 swords, 64 dirks and 120 belts; 8 caskets of cedar and silver with 3,840 cut stones and 4,265 uncut stones.

"Also, 28 feet to the north-east at a depth of eight feet in yellow sand: 7 chests with 22 gold and silver candelabra and 164 rubies.

"Twelve armspans west at a depth of 12 feet in red earth: the seven foot Virgin of gold with the child Jesus, her crown and pectoral of 780 pounds, rolled in her gold chasuble, embedded with 1,684 jewels. Three of these are four inch emeralds on the pectoral and six are six inch topaz on the crown. The seven crosses are of diamonds." The crowd of the beach had stopped breathing as the list of riches was listed. A few looked around for yellow sand and red earth. The terror of the sea started to leave the crew. Hawk never blinked.

"Do you consider this description as real or one of the many fakes?" Erhart was amused. Hawkins had been paying attention on the boat.

"Some of both. The bad part was the repeated numbers: 12 arm span and 12 feet; six, 6 inch topaz. Liars and drunks like to use similar numbers. However, it was buried somewhere by this bay. It should be easy enough to find yellow sand and red earth on a black sand beach. Don't you think so?" He was talking to himself. Everyone who could was walking up and down the beach looking for red earth and yellow sand.

"I found some! I found some red earth! I found it!"

"I found some, too! Yellow sand. My God, we are rich!"

"Don't we have any shovels?"

"The hell with shovels! I've got two hands!" Erhart sank to the sand and watched the circus around him with amusement. Hawk started to dig but seeing Erhart thought better of it.

"The treasure isn't here is it." Hawk looked as crest fallen as his personality would allow.

"It could be. You never know. However, pirates were tricky enough not to bury their booty just anywhere. Look." He pointed to John and Jim Banks digging a huge hole just above the high water mark.

"Pirates would never bury something where the shifting sands might reveal it to any passer-by. They knew the oceans well. Any spot they picked, would have been unique. Buried on the beach? Not likely." Hawk was regaining his equilibrium.

"Then where the fuck is it?" His brows were lowering over his eyes and his lips scribed a thin line. The frown remained on Erhart's face.

"Where are they, Mr. Hawkins, where are they. No one has ever been able to re-create a complete list of treasures buried on this one little island. There have been so many treasures buried here, you would think that any good spot would naturally have a treasure already buried there by default, wouldn't you?" Erhart was having a good time. He had played such episodes in his daydreams. And now his dreams were coming to life. He smiled wanly at Hawk and then leaned back against a cushion from the tender propped up in the sand, and smiled gently as he closed his eyes.

Jackie found her spare clothes where she had stowed them, untouched. With a sudden grimace, she grabbed a towel, a bar of soap and then entered the shower room after a quick peek to make sure it was empty.

The water felt so good. The hot tap released a lukewarm stream at best, not that Jackie cared. It was so good to get clean. That Arab was the filth of the earth. The way he treated her. The way he looked at her, like she was some kind of animal, some beast put on earth to service men. She scrubbed between her legs extra hard in her anger. It was when she had turned off the water and was toweling off that she heard the voices again. They were coming from the bunk room of the barracks.

"So you big hunk, I imagine you have designs on my little pristine body, don't you? Was it your plan to get me here all alone, just so no one could here me scream?"

"Depends if you are screaming in terror or joy."

"Oh, sure. Get all cutesy. Got news for you, big boy. With women it is always both. Terror that you might hurt her and joy that you didn't. Terror that she really likes you and that she isn't as free as a bird anymore, and joy that she found a life partner and she is held captive by her love. Terror for fear that you can't make her come and then she'll scream in joy that you did." Jackie couldn't help overhearing, even though they weren't speaking loudly. She wrapped her towel around herself, tucked it in carefully to be sure it wouldn't fall at an inappropriate moment and walked out into the barracks.

"Eek. I didn't know anyone was here." He was an older man, but trim and nice looking if you ignored his graying hair. The woman was in great shape, almost like she was a high wire trapeze artist or something. Shorter than he but not by much. They were hugging when she came out and on seeing her the woman hugged her man even tighter.

"Hello. My name is Prospector and this is Robyn. I don't believe you were on the yacht. Are you staying here?" His voice was well modulated and his eyes found hers and focused on her, without staring. She felt a little stirring in her tummy she hadn't felt for a few years.

"Hi. I'm Jackie. I came on the supply boat. I'm a biologist here to do a study on species development. Not that I have had a lot of time for my study, what with being held captive by a terrorist."

"Terrorist? Here? In the back of beyond?"

"Yes. Some kind of Arab. He hit me over the head, tied me up and cut my clothes off me. He might have done worse but another terrorist, a bigger one, came and released me. That is about it. I haven't had a chance to do any exploring, any species research, that is."

"If you are a local, tell us, where are all the people?" Jackie ran her eyes over the empty bunks.

"I just arrived myself. I really don't know. There should be a security force here to keep the island safe from gold diggers, you know, people who might destroy the island while looking for pirate gold."

"There is pirate treasure on this island?" Robyn some how managed to instill disbelief in her voice. Jackie nodded.

"That is the story. However, it is probably just a story. As far as I know, no one has ever found any treasure here." Robyn opened her eyes as wide as she could.

"Have you searched? Do you know where this treasure is buried?"

"No, I don't. Actually, I'm more interested in finding something to eat. Are you two hungry?" Robyn energetically nodded her head.

"Absolutely starved! I could eat a horse, I could eat your terrorist if you catch him for me!"

The Arab sized up the ex-Seal, not for the first time. Allah had created a massive killing machine in him. In vain. The man did as he as he wished instead of obeying Allah's commands. He killed for mere money, not for the glory of Islam. The Arab had, at first, tried to convert the man. He hadn't been interested. The Arab prayed for Allah to bring the Seal enlightenment. It hadn't happened. The Seal wasn't interested in religion. It was a shame. A terrible shame. He would have to kill the Seal now. He might guess, might report the Arab's existence, his mission. It was his job to get hired by the rich and mighty, and then accept, or if necessary take, all their money and return it to his spiritual leaders in the mountains of Afghanistan. This Hawkins was his third mission. This one was very sly with his money. But now, things were opening up. He was out in the open where he might have to call for funds. And when he did, the Arab would be there. The only fear he had was the Seal.

That unfortunate man had released his captive without even asking his permission. He had her tied up in a proper position for supplication. She had, no doubt been finding her peace with Allah before she would meet him face to face. But the Seal had ignored him and released her. The Seal would never see the inside of Paradise!

The safest thing to do, the best thing to do, would be to kill him here in the jungle where these nefarious bugs would depose of his body. Either that or let the sharks of the ocean devour his body as was only proper for a man who had killed so many. It was Allah's will that he be Allah's instrument in the death of the Seal. He could see that clearly now. It had to be done. It was the will of Allah that it be done. By the beard of the Prophet, it would be done. And if it be done, better it be done before another sun had set.

The Seal had followed the girl up the trail, as usually as quiet as death itself. Keeping inside the jungle, he moved like a hulking lion who had just received wings. The Arab followed at a distance, stopping and hiding, only to let two people from the beach pass him by. The place was becoming a thoroughfare. By the time the people had passed, he had lost the Seal. Quickly he went to ground. He could now be the hunted. Quietly he moved ninety degrees away from his last position. And then forty-five degrees and then ten degrees. He could never equal the Seal in woodcraft, but with Allah's guidance, his bullet would find a lethal place to lodge. Slowly his path brought him to the long house they called the barracks. He hid and waited. He was sure the Seal was somewhere near him also waiting, patiently waiting like a killer whale keeping an eye on a walrus till it hungered again.

He would wait also, and then he would strike. He would strike like a cobra. Without warning. Not like that sissy American snake, that rattlesnake, that warned before it struck. The Arab had been born in the house of a Nizari Isma'ilites, the group of Arabs who had practiced assassination since the eleventh century to attain its political aims. As a young man he had entered the secret Gardens of Paradise of his master, where his every wish was fulfilled, where the scent of hashish filled the air, where the women saints bowed before him and serviced him, hoping for his child, wanting nothing but to please him in every way possible. As it is written, for the Children of Allah, for the pursuers of Jihad, nothing is forbidden. He had drunk of the juice of the grape, he'd eaten swine, he had enjoyed women! He couldn't wait to die and to experience such delights forever!

The next morning, refreshed by a day and night of incredible pleasure, he went out on a mission, to kill an enemy of his house, knowing ahead of time, in great detail, if he fell, if he was killed, exactly how he would spend eternity, in Paradise. He knew that all his past sins would be forgiven by Allah if he fell in Jihad. That he would see the real Paradise, not a recruiting tool of his master. He knew that the purpose of a candle is not to illuminate itself. He was a sword of the Prophets!

The Arab shook his head. Now was not the time for reminiscing. His enemy was out there, possibly looking for him, hunting him. With a lurch, he turned and quickly looked all around him. Then cursed himself for the sudden movement. A single mistake was lethal when dealing with a man like the Seal. He looked again at the barracks, nothing was happening. Behind him, he heard something, something like a leaf falling. He turned and shook as the huge bulk of the Seal blocked out what little sun managed to seep through the jungle.

"Brother. Why did you leave the Hawkins?" The Seal's mouth was asking the question, his eyes contained nothing but contempt. Contempt for him, for a child of Allah!

"I go as I am commanded." The flames of hatred for the high and mighty replaced the fear in his heart.

"The Hawkins told you to come?" Again there was no question mark in his eyes. Nothing but that terrible, evil contempt, contempt of him, the Chosen of God. The righteousness of Allah flared in his breast. The power of Mohammad burned fiercely in his veins, but the craftiness of Bin Laden stayed his hand and waited for his moment.

"Yes. He instructed me to follow the two." The Seal nodded and then he disappeared into the jungle as if he was but a dream. The Arab felt himself in horror. He had wet himself in terror. Like a baby. His nostrils flared as his lips snarled. His hand found the haft of his holy knife, the blade of the Jihad, the weapon of Mohammad.

"Soon," he whispered to himself, "soon I will soak the earth with his blood and spit in his guts. Soon, he will die by my hand. Soon Allah shall be victorious. None can stop me. None dare!" He slashed at a tree with his knife and glared in victory. Still he looked over his shoulder in fear of the Seal.

The *Rose Marie* was drifting slowly south, pushed by ever lighter winds. In the old days of wooden ships and iron men, the masts soared over the ships, just for situations such as these. They could set their royals up hundreds of feet above the water where the wind still lived and thus make progress. Down by the water, down by the *Rose Marie* whose stubby mast reached only to forty-five feet, there was little wind and what there was came and went in cat's paws.

"Dad! When are we going to get there? I didn't know there was so much water on this planet. I need some land. I need a tree to climb. I need to run my little legs. I need an island, and I need it now. Do you want me to get cabin fever?"

"Is it mutiny that I hear in your voice? Do you know why it took Moses forty years to cross 200 miles of mostly flat desert? Mutiny, that's why. Every time his men complained he took them on a detour until they learned their lesson and obeyed their Captain's every command. Now, were you saying something?"

"That is five miles a year or, wait, my calculator is right here, seventy-two feet a day, or six feet an hour! That is like falling down once an hour and calling it progress!"

"See, that is mutiny if I ever heard it! Now, you aren't going to mutiny are you? Of course you aren't. You know we get there when we get there, right?"

"Yes, Sir, Sir Daddy. You are the Big Kahuna, the best of the best, the leader of the pack. All us little, insignificant women can do is huddle at your feet and adore you in your magnificence! Sir Wonderful Daddy who falls down once an hour."

"Why can't they stay cute and cuddly forever? This growing up is for the birds."

"That's why they call us women, 'birds'. Cuz we grow up and fly wherever we want, even to islands over the horizon, that have trees to climb! Sir Daddy."

"Janet! Will you teach your daughter some manners?" Harv's wife poked her head out of the companionway.

"Are you telling me you are having trouble dealing with a thirteen year old? Whatever are you going to do when she is fourteen? Or fifteen? When she starts to bring boys home?" Harv covered his eyes with his palm.

"Maybe I'll be able to talk to the boys without getting sassed!" Jill and Janet passed a secret smile.

"Okay, Sir Daddy, I'll have to start bringing boys home right away."

"No wonder, Moses stayed forty years in the desert. He was waiting for his daughters to grow up, until they had children of their own! Insanity is hereditary, you know. You catch it from your kids!" Janet laughed and then looked at Harv seriously.

"We are getting a little low on supplies. How far are we from this Cocos Island you keep promising to take us to? Unless, of course, you are expecting manna from heaven, Sir Captain, the Captain who can Never be Disobeyed!"

"Now I know why men single-hand their boats! Fewer women!"

"We're sorry, Sir Daffy, I mean, Sir Daddy. When do we get to the island?" Harv put his one palm over his eyes and one over his heart.

"You two will be sorry when you don't have me to pick on anymore. As soon as we land, I am going for a long walk! And we will get there sometime the day after tomorrow, if this non-breeze keeps up!"

"Why couldn't you just tell us that at the beginning, Honey?"

"What? And deprive you of all your creative bantering? How is your daughter going to defend herself against horny male teenagers if she hasn't practiced her banter?" Daughter and Mother looked at each other and together raised their eyes to heaven and said,

"Men!"

Dustin got tired of digging in the earth after a minute and a half. He was surprised it took him that long to come to his senses. A beach was a terrible place to bury a treasure. One piece of beach looks much like another, important landmarks like trees or rocks might get blown down or covered with sand, the tides and currents might change and scour the sand away, revealing the treasure. He turned to Mary and Naomi who were digging like dogs, throwing sand out between their legs in their eagerness to find gold.

"We have been had. It isn't here." He turned to Erhart sitting on the sand ten feet away.

"The treasure isn't here, is it?" Erhart stretched with both hands over his head.

"It could have been buried here. But you are right. The likelihood of experienced pirates like the ones who frequented Cocos Island, burying their treasures in beach sand or next to the beach, would approach zero."

"Then why in God's name did you even mention it?" Everyone else stopped digging and stared at Erhart. He leaned back against his cushion and enjoyed the limelight.

"A rabble is no way to find a treasure. Digging here and there is ridiculous. You are just as likely to be piling dirt on top of the treasure as unburying it. Proper excavation requires planning and obedience. If we are going to find this treasure, it will only be because we were smarter and more disciplined than the more than 500 expeditions that have proceeded us." He grabbed hold of his knees and pulled himself erect. "Perhaps the best way to proceed now is to separate into two groups, the people who would like to dig in a well mannered, professional manner and the others who would like to dig pell-mell, anywhere they wish. What do you think, Captain Banks?" Erhart was having a blast. He had daydreamed about how he might influence a mob-like group of treasure hunters since he was a child. He didn't know then if he would ever get to utilize his dreams. But now here he was, on Cocos Island, the queen of the treasure islands! On Cocos Island when all around him were reeling from disaster after disaster and only he retained a level head. And when the treasure was found, no one could ever say it wasn't because of the efforts of a little man called Erhart.

"I think Erhart has a point. He seems to have a firm grasp on the situation. Let's follow his suggestion. All those in favor of organized treasure hunting, stand over here by that tree." Banks pointed at a half blown down coconut tree still slightly smoking from the *Steel Balls'* explosion. As a group everyone gathered by the tree. Only Hawk hesitated for a second, until he also followed the group with a look on his face like he had eaten something disgusting. "All right, then. Erhart, you have the floor." Erhart smiled at the crowd. They didn't smile back. They felt that they had been manipulated like children. They still resented the loss of all of their belongings, the death of friends, the uncertainty of the future. Anyone who stood up as a leader was frowned upon.

"So, who would like to hear about a more likely location of the hiding place of the Virgin?" A growl of consent arose from a slightly less unruly crowd. "This clue will require scouting parties. Captain Banks, will you select personnel for three parties." Banks stood next to Erhart.

"Alright, any who are for scouting stand over here. Any who would like to look for food and set up camp, stand over there. Plus, we need a burial detail for Piston, who as you may or may not have noticed, has died." As one, everyone moved to the scouting party area. No one even bothered with a glance at the engineer. Erhart could see that gold fever was taking hold on the survivors.

"Ok, everyone is looking for gold. Divide yourselves into three more or less equal parties." There was quite a bit of shoving and tugging but in the end Dustin and Mary were one group, Hawk and Naomi another and John and Charlie Ross the third. "OK, that leaves Erhart and myself to set up a camp and bury the engineer. Erhart you have the floor." Erhart brushed off some imaginary sand from his pants. Hawk barged in front of him before he got started.

"In the interest of keeping our scouting parties' minds on the job, I think couples should be separated." Banks nodded in agreement.

"OK. Dustin, you go with Naomi; Hawk, go with Mary; Erhart, why don't you go with John?" Everyone looked at each other, some with pleasure and excitement, others with fear and worry. Erhart spoke up.

"As much as I hate to disagree, my ear is still too painful to be active. Charlie will have to go with John." He smiled regretfully at John. He would have loved to go with John. To have an adventure with John. Maybe later. Maybe when the time was right. When his star was in ascendancy. "Now are you ready for the clues?" Everyone suddenly crowded around.

"Here is the exact wording of the treasure map. Again this map is attested to Keating, who seemed to delight in crafting maps. This one I think, may be more accurate."

"Starting from a bay on the northeast side of the island, follow the coast line of the bay until you find a small creek which at high water flows inland. Step out seventy paces, west by south, until against the skyline you will spot a gap in the hills. From any other point this gap is invisible. Turn north and walk 120 paces to another stream, until you spot a rock with a smooth face, rising sheer like a cliff. In the cliff, at the height of a man's shoulder, above the ground, you will see a hole large enough to insert a thumb. Thrust in an iron bar and twist it around the cavity, and behind you, away from the cliff, a you will find a door that opens on the treasure of the Virgin of Lima." Erhart stopped talking. He glanced quickly at Charlie Ross and Jim Banks. They were memorizing his directions. He barely smiled, slightly sarcastically.

"Alright, I see where Erhart is going here. There are three bays on Cocos; Water, just to the far west of us, Chatham, where we are, and Weston, in between the two. Another, Yglesias Bay lies far to the south east but I think we can ignore that one for now as we have no way to get there and anyway it is on the Southeast side of the island, anyway." Jim Banks ran his fingers through his thinning hair. "Let's divide this way. Dustin and Naomi, you are the weakest of the groups. Start on the end of Chatham and scout its entire length. Hawk and Mary, you two take on Weston Bay. You will have to work through some bush, but it doesn't look bad from here. John, you and Charlie Ross are the strongest group. You will have to find a way through to Water Bay.

"I'll draw a map here in the sand. Here we are now, thus. Next door is Weston, shaped like this, and lastly, Water, lying thusly.

"If you find a thumb hole in a cliff, report back here. In the meantime, Erhart and I will try to find an iron bar, set up camp and bury Piston. In any case, everyone should be back here before sunset. Find likely creeks. High water is in three hours from now. Any questions?" There weren't any questions. All Erhart saw was six backs of rushing treasure hunters.

Ben, the cook, had lived on Cocos Island for over fifteen years. His was the second longest recorded stay. Mostly people came to Cocos, looked for treasure or plants or animals, and left. Only a German named August Gissler had stayed longer. He landed on Cocos in 1889 with an old map that was reportedly been drawn by Benito Bonito. He never did find the treasure. He did find one piece of eight on the trail leading up the mountain. He also found a rock carved with a 'K' and an arrow pointing to a hollow tree under which there was an iron cable attached to a hook.

Eventually Gissler gave up treasure hunting, but loved the island so much, that he set up a plantation and a trading business with the whalers. In 1909, twenty years later, in bad health, broke and insane, he left Cocos never to return.

Ben didn't like to look for treasure. He didn't know what he would do with it if he found it. His life was here on Cocos Island. In Asia he was a wanted man. Interpol had warrants out for his arrest. Not that he had ever done anything wrong. Unless you call blowing up a few government buildings in Hong Kong, wrong. Ben thought that the less government, the better. Especially governments that assassinated his father, for no good reason and without proof. He had jumped onboard a fishing boat out of Macao and when it momentarily stopped at Cocos Island for water, he had slipped over the side and swam ashore. He didn't know to this day what saved him from the sharks. It could be that he worked at cleaning the bilges on the fishing boat, a job normally reserved for stowaways, and smelled so bad, that the sharks didn't recognize him as anything edible.

Eventually he got a job raking the bug infested seaweed from beaches and was paid two meals a day. From there he became a fry cook, and then, years later, the Manager's personal chef. He had ordered a wife from Cambodia with all the money he had saved. He was happy with her. They didn't share a common language, but that didn't seem to matter. She had died last year from a shark attack. She had been five feet from the water and thought herself safe. A huge shark jumped out, grabbed her and pulled her slight frame back into the sea. Ben had been heart broken for months. He was older now. He was past the time for sex. A good bowel movement was of more interest to him. But he did miss the company. The two girls up on the hill were enough company for him now. If they lasted. The bad times were coming again. He had heard stories. Twice before many people had died. Some from the sharks, some went missing, some killed each other. Bad times. Always when the new moon blocked the sun, always when Cocos was in the path of a total eclipse of the sun. Always when treasure seekers were on the island.

He hoped the two girls wouldn't be among the dead. They were nice girls. And he liked to watch them from his secret cave high in the mountains. There he could look down at their beautiful bodies and remember his little Cambodian wife. He liked the tall one, the one that liked to be naked. She was very beautiful. If they had to die, he hoped she would be last. Her body was perfect. It would be a shame to have her beauty destroyed. A shame.

Jackie, Robyn and the Prospector followed the dirt path outside of the barracks to the cook shed. No one was inside. It looked like a tornado had hit it. Tables were topsy turvy, all the pots and pans were scattered over the floor. Sharp shards of shattered china plates were sticking out of the walls and the ceiling. The freezer and refrigerator doors were wide open displaying white emptiness. The Prospector shuffled through the mess, pulling up larger objects to look under them. His first glance was proven right, all the knives were missing. The wood blocks where the knives normally lived were empty and they weren't anywhere else. Robyn stamped her foot against the tiled floor.

"There isn't a morsel of food in all this mess. What a rip off. I want to know who took the food. I'm very hungry! It is simply not fair." Jackie gave up looking in empty cupboards.

"Yeah. If this is someone's idea of a joke, I want them to know that it isn't funny. It's sick, that's what it is." She had her hair brooch in her hands and was fiddling with it. Her eyes gleamed in the dusty light that ricocheted through smeared windows.

The Prospector didn't say anything. After looking around, he went back outside and circled the cook shed. There were tracks everywhere except for one direction. There the dirt looked almost like it had been swept. He wandered in that direction, veering back and forth almost like a hunting dog seeking a scent. His wanderings led him to the edge of the forest where the swept area disappeared into the dense jungle. Robyn and Jackie soon joined him as he stared at the trees. One area of the edge of the vine infested, interwoven, impassable jungle seemed more dead than its surroundings. The Prospector grabbed a handful of branches in his hand and pulled. He almost fell backwards as an entire twenty foot section of bush pulled out as easily as if it had been on a hinge, revealing a continuation of the dirt path. With glances at each other, the trio followed the path into the rainforest.

Robyn saw the house first. It sat in the middle of the clearing like a jewel in a setting of tarnished silver. The ground was planted in grass which had gone to seed, the tawniness of the stalks emphasized the crystal of the multitude of windows shining from the house. A back door swung this way and that, breaking the mood of sanctity the house seemed to generate. The Prospector and Jackie knocked on the front door. Robyn circled the house and walked in the back door without a qualm. She searched the house for inhabitants before opening the front door for the politely waiting other two.

"No one is here. Haven't been at least for a couple of days. There is another trail by the back door. Want to check it out?" The Prospector looked straight into her eyes for a couple of seconds, and then nodded. The trail led to another cookhouse. For a minute they thought they were saved, but no, this one was trashed too. There wasn't an ounce of food anywhere to be found, nor were there any knives. There weren't any other trails.

The Arab followed as quietly as he could. He didn't have the Seal's skills. What he did have was an intense desire to re-acquire his captive. His captive that had already prayed in the required position for hours and hours. Killing her would erase all of his sins. Allah would cleanse him of the Earth's filth, of its hypocrisy, of its lies and treachery. All which the earth made him commit. Killing her would insure he entered into Paradise. Too bad she had to die. But it was a small price for her to pay to save such a magnificent soul as his.

He followed her down the trail, past the cleverly made camouflaged screen, keeping well back, waiting for his chance. Past the house, it must be the Commandant's house, the one who the Hawkins had fed to the sharks. Terrible way to die. To die being eaten by the swine of the sea. Animals that would eat anything. The Commandant would never see Paradise. Many were dying on this island. Many would not see another sunrise. Next the girl. If the others had to die as well, that was just karma. Too bad they hadn't prayed first. But the girl, she had to die. It was written. And after all, she was just a woman. No one would care. Why would they? The world was full of women. Might as well put one to good use.

The threesome were scouting around the house now, looking for another blind. The man seemed to be smelling the air. They couldn't find one. If there was one, it was too well hidden. To the Arab, it seemed the first blind was so obvious it was like a shining arrow pointing the way someone wanted them to follow. It was the only answer. But why did they want the three to come here? Or, did they seek him? Knowing that he was following? Was it a trick of the Seal? He tried to settle the fear in his belly and to look around carefully for traps of any kind. If it was the Seal, it would be ingenious. The Americans had learned much in their defeat by the hands of the Vietnamese.

There! The man had found another trail! A small crawl thru opening covered by dead branches. The ground was not swept before it this time. Wait. Something was wrong. It was not a trail. The three were just staring at it. The man was backing up, pulling the women with him. His captive was struggling, fighting to be free from the man's grasp.

"There. It is so. Truthfully, she has no obedience. She is the spawn of Eve," he said to himself. She finally broke free and rushed into the small tunnel and reached for something. It happened faster than thought. A sharpened stake fired from high in the trees, swept down in an accelerating arc and skewered the woman in the back, through her heart, pinning her to the ground like a butterfly on a piece of cardboard.

'It is good, then that she had time to repent while his captive. Allah obviously wanted her. No doubt to send to hell to enrage the devils below into higher fits of passion and anger.' He nodded self satisfied but sad that his knife hadn't preformed the deed. shrunk deeper into the woods, looking even more alertly for snares and traps.

Naomi and Dustin walked to the East end of the beach, which wasn't far. The jungle spread downhill following decaying cliffs and touching the high tide mark in places with green tendrils. Bushes and trees over hung the sand along the shore creating a humid, insect ridden shade. Naomi touched Dustin's arm, gently.

"How are we going to find this creek? A creek that flows inland? Can there be such a thing?" Dustin smiled down at her.

"A creek that flows inland at high tide, which, if my calculations are correct will occur in two hours and forty minutes. I believe the best usage of our time is to survey the beach, mark possible creeks with sticks in the sand, and then wait for high tide to show us which creek is the correct one."

"I can't believe any of these creeks could flow inland with all this rain. It has to flow out, doesn't it?" Dustin looked up at the peaks of the island. Clouds seemed to be permanently anchored there, dropping rain and then easing off as another water laden cloud took its place. He wondered briefly if the top of the largest peak was above the cloud level. He told his brain to stop wandering and to start surveying.

"If the creek's entrance was part of a lagoon, at high tide it might flow into it, replenishing water lost from evaporation."

It was tough to spot the creeks. There were many run off spots along the beach. At each one they crawled under the looming bushes

and trees to follow the bed to see if it was a creek or not. Most were dry, well, relatively dry. The endless rain had broken through the sand barrier which had been thrown up by the waves of far distant storms. The giant
seas those storms created had continued across the oceans until they finally crashed against something. In this case, Cocos Island.

Their first real creek was only a quarter mile from the pier. The water had cut through the sand and was flowing out into the ocean. Naomi picked up a stick from along the shore and stuck it vertically into the sand to mark the creek.

"Should we explore this creek now, Dustin?" Her eyes were shining. She had read of pirates and buried treasure as a young girl. The yearning for the adventurous life of those days must have lay dormant deep within her only to burst out into flowering glory on exploring this beach. "We might find the treasure!" Inside her larcenous heart she was already thinking of ways to get the lion's share.

"We must complete our survey before the high tide. Who knows how many streams might flow inland at high water? The day after tomorrow
is a new moon. But according to the tide charts, today is when the tide will be highest." There were only two streams that to Dustin looked like they were likely candidates. Naomi marked both with sticks.

"Dustin, we know which streams might be the right ones. We have lots of time. Let's explore both. The other teams will be forever getting back. What if we can find the secret door!" Naomi looked so excited, so flushed with excitement, that her beauty increased, dramatically. The area below her throat and above her breasts turned red with increased blood flow. She bent her head to one side and then turned her body away so she looked at Dustin from the corners of her eyes and just below her eyebrows. Dustin, for some reason, was so turned on he found himself incapable of denying her anything.

"Of course, my Lady. Whatever you want." Naomi stared at him in amazement. She hadn't thought of him as one who might use endearments. She rushed into his arms and kissed him on the lips before he knew what she was doing, and then she jumped away before he might either complain or get interested, more interested.

She felt eyes on the beach. Eyes that might be watching. She eyed Dustin, evaluating him.

"I want to explore those two creeks. Come, my Knight."

When The Prospector had pulled the dead fall bush away from the hidden trail, he smelled gold. Just a little, a couple ounces. Enough for a small nugget. As the bush pulled clear he saw it, a gold coin. It was laying there just at the foot of a small tree. There was no dirt, or leaves, or branches on it. It was like it had been dropped there just a few minutes ago. His soul yelled to him. 'Trap!' It looked like a trap. The gold was the bait in a trap. Slowly he backed up, pulling the two girls with him. His eyes swiveled all around him. More than likely, they, whoever they were, were watching them. It did seem like he could feel someone watching. Suddenly, Jackie broke free from his grasp. She dashed into the trap and reached out for the coin. Her hand broke a thin, almost invisible piece of thread. A wooden stake spun down from high in the tree and pierced her back with an audible thump, sped right through her heart and exited her chest via her left breast. Robyn covered her eyes and mouth with her hands and moaned. The Prospector continued to work backwards.

"We have to save her! She might still be alive! We can give her CPR or something." She yanked at the Prospector's arm. "We have to try." He held her with both hands.

"Whoever set that trap just sweetened it with fresh bait. They want us to get close to her. Maybe to pull at her legs, to lift the stake. If we do, we will be dead. Besides," he said, rubbing Robyn's neck, "She is already dead. It was quick, which is more than can be said for us if we don't keep a look out. Someone is watching us. Stay with me. Don't dawdle. Be ready for anything."

Mary was intensely worried about abandoning Dustin to the hands and lips of that, that, Naomi. She was so worried about him, but the chance to have Hawk alone, to be able to speak to him without interruption. To be able to promote herself and, of course, Dustin, into his consideration. Whether they found the treasure or not, she had a bonafide millionaire almost within her grasp. It wouldn't take much to make him a lifetime supporter. On the other hand, Dustin didn't really understand the power that a woman like Naomi could command against a man. Dustin thought he and his little brain were all powerful. He didn't realize the primal force that a siren like Naomi could utilize. She could twist him around her little finger so easily. He wouldn't even know what was going on. Maybe he could resist for a little while till she got back. Maybe. She hoped he could.

Hawk was frowning at her again. It seemed his job was to walk along the beach and point at likely creeks. It was her job to crawl on her belly under bushes and vines and thorns to see if it was a real creek or just a depression in the sand.

"This might be a good one, Hawk. It is a creek and the sand along the beach is lower here than what we have seen so far. Maybe the sea could flow inland in this one. Should we explore it?" Hawk thought about sneering at her but he liked the look of her, butt up, looking under bushes. He remembered the cries she made while making love on the *Steel Balls*. He had replayed the tape of Dustin and her making love many times. So far this treasure hunt had been boring. Who wanted to be bitten by insects while crawling through the bush? On the other hand, he had something more interesting right here. The others would find the treasure. That's what he paid them for, wasn't it? Or at least, promised to pay them.

"Yeah, it does look good. You're right. Let's explore it!" He let the girl go first, to bash the way through the prickers. He giggled at the thought of the thorns stripping her clothes off leaving her naked. When she stopped to work her way through a tricky bit of bush, he slapped her gently on the butt.

"Hey, keep your hands to yourself." She bit her lip in consternation. "Listen, Hawk. Let's work as a team, here. Time for you to take the lead." He smiled as she turned around to confront him.

"In case you have forgotten, you still are on my payroll. Let's keep that in mind as we give orders, shall we?" Mary instantly became filled with remorse.

"Sorry, Sir. It won't happen again." He glared at her.

"It better not. Now to show you are sorry, take off your clothes." She thought for an instant that he was joking. One look at his face showed that he wasn't. She shook her head as she backed up a step.

"Mr. Hawkins, we have a treasure to find. Why don't we celebrate after we have found it? Wouldn't that be great?"

"If you don't have your clothes off in five seconds, both you and Dustin will never see a dime from me. Cooperate, and you, personally will receive an additional ten thousand." Mary knew how much Dustin counted on getting financial support for his research. It would destroy his hopes if he didn't get it. Slowly she started to remove her blouse, trying to think of something to do or say. Hawk didn't feel like waiting. He grabbed her pants at the waist, breaking the button of her Levis. He twisted her onto her stomach and pulled the pants down to her ankles. With one huge hand he yanked at her briefs. The skimpy material ripped easily.

With one arm he held her torso down, with the other he explored her between her legs. As he forced one of his giant thumbs into her, she screamed in pain. He smiled evilly, forced a knee between her legs and undid his buckle and dropped his pants. Something was wrong. He was not aroused. His organ lay there ignoring the treat before him. He took it in his hand and wiggled it, trying to wake it up. Nothing. He sat back on his heels and stared at it. This had never happened before. This had definitely never happened on the *Steel Balls*. The girl was crying now, her butt still up in the air. He loved it when they cried. It really turned him on. He shook his meat again. Nothing. With a curse, he buckled up and worked back through the bush to the beach. Mary lay there for a moment in tears, then she pulled her pants up, secured them with a bobby pin and followed the stream further into the jungle, her tears mixing with yet another rain shower.

Charlie wasn't much help bashing though the bush. John helped him along for a while. Eventually, Charlie sat down under a tree, put his head in his hands and sobbed like there would be no tomorrow. John stood watching him for a few minutes. He wondered why he ever considered this man his superior. With a snort, he carried on towards Water Bay. He wondered how the Prospector could smell gold. Every tenth step he stopped for a second and smelled around him. It had to be a story for children and gullible millionaires. The bugs were bad, but as long as he didn't stop for more than a few seconds, they just flew around his head. Nevertheless, he was happy to finally break out of the bush and onto a black sand beach. A black sand beach with traces of yellow sand here and there.

The first creek he found was running inland. His eyes shone in exhilaration as he followed the creek inland. What was it again? Seventy paces southwest or something? Look for a gap in the hills? The jungle was so intense he didn't understand how he was to spot a hill much less a gap. He should have asked Charlie for his compass before he left him. Southwest? He followed the creek for seventy paces. Or as best he could judge seventy paces when he was curled over going under trees or climbing over log jams. At the end it was still jungle. This was getting him nowhere. He backtracked down the creek to the beach and returned to Charlie who had cried himself to sleep.

"Charlie! Wake up! I have found it! Wake up, man!" Slowly Charlie returned to consciousness, regretfully.

"John. Hi, John, I was having the most wonderful dream. We were anchored off St. Barts and all the stewardess were swimming naked.

The water was so lovely. Jim was Captain again. They dragged me in to swim with them. It wasn't like, I mean, here, the boat didn't blow up, I mean," Charlie started crying again.

"Charlie, listen! I found the creek! Come help. You and me, we can get the gold! You can buy yourself a hundred stewardesses! Come on, you have to help me!" John's excitement seemed to get through Charlie's tears. He looked up as his brain started to function again.

"The treasure?"

"Yes! The treasure! Let's go get it!" Charlie pulled himself to this feet and followed John through the jungle to the beach where John proudly showed off his creek.

"Look the water is flowing inland! Now we have to go seventy paces southwest!"

"Not southwest. West by south." Charlie pulled his compass out of his pocket. "Southwest is there, following the stream bed. West by south is further west, almost paralleling the beach." Charlie started to get excited. "Listen, we can walk seventy paces here on the beach and then walk inland for, let me see. Yes, inland for ten paces on a course of south by east. It should work. Let's do it!" If John was excited before, it was nothing to what he was feeling now. No wonder previous expeditions never found the treasure. They didn't understand the compass like sailors did! They were going to find it. They were going to find the Virgin of Lima, the most sought after pirate treasure of all time!

They each paced out seventy paces independently hoping that the difference wouldn't be too great. It wasn't. They ended up five feet apart. They divided the difference and headed inland. The jungle was just as thick here as it was by the creek. Again, they had to climb under and over trees, roots and fallen logs. Ten feet in from the shore the jungle seemed

to clear slightly. At ten paces, twenty five feet, they stopped and stared at the jungle all around them.

"Not to worry," he told Charlie's crestfallen face, "I'll look for a gap. John searched in all directions. He could see a few hills, but no gaps. Dejectedly the duo worked their way back to the beach. Charlie stared at his compass with a question on his face.

"We aren't in the right place." John kicked at some sand.

"You can say that twice."

"No, I mean the directions are wrong for this bay. Listen, I wrote down the directions that Erhart gave us. Find a creek flowing inland." Charlie pointed at the creek down the beach. "Walk west by south until you spot a gap in the hills." He pointed west by south. "Turn north and walk 120 paces to another creek." Charlie looked at his compass and pointed north. John looked at his finger. He was pointing out to sea.

"Excuse my English, but fuck! Either the treasure is underwater, or you are right. This is the wrong bay. But which bay is the right one?" Charlie flattened out a section of sand and drew a map of Cocos Island from memory.

"OK, here is the island. We are here in Water Bay." He pointed to a bay on the northwest side of the island. Here is Chatham Bay where we anchored." He started to cry again as memories rushed back in. John threw a rock out to sea.

"Where is the treasure then?" Charlie looked back at this map.

"Well, that Erhart said that the pirates were tricky drawing their treasure maps. Suppose that they lied saying the bay was on the northwest side of the island. In each of these bays, the directions given would be wrong. I should have spotted this right off. However, lets say that the fourth bay, this bay down here to the southeast of the island is the right bay. We could go seventy paces west by south and then 120 paces to the north without ending up in the ocean. That is more likely where the treasure is. That would be an easy trick. Change northwest bay for southeast bay. Easy to remember. Completely throws treasure hunters off." John nodded in agreement.

"But how do we get there? My shore boat is history. It won't make it a hundred yards in any kind of sea."

"We can hoof it overland. There has to be some kind of trail. We just have to find it. Or else we will just have to make our own. Anyway, what else are we going to do with our time. Sit here and cry?"

Naomi and Dustin hadn't gotten far into the jungle when they ran into an impassable vine woven barrier. Without a machete there wasn't any way through. Dustin stood staring at the wall in frustration. He stamped his foot once. Then he felt two arms curl around him and a feminine body push itself against his back.

"You know, Dustin, ever since that day on the train, I have had the hots for you. You are so masculine. You turn me on so." She didn't add that she couldn't get the memory of the video of him and Mary out of her brain. He had turned that Mary Two on, so hard. She had never seen any woman turned on so much. Maybe if she really got off like that, she wouldn't need it twenty times a day. She let her right hand head south. He certainly had a decent package down there.

"Honey. Would you do me the great honor of making love to me? I know you like Mary, but it is just this once. Please, Dustin. I will never speak of this to anyone. I'm not that kind of girl. Please, Honey, please." Not waiting for his answer, she sank to her knees while spiraling around his body, ending up in front of him, and she unbuttoned his pants. He was already half aroused. As soon as she took him into her mouth and inhaled him into the back of her throat, he definitely was aroused. He was so long that she swore he was tickling her tonsils. Before he could come she had her clothes off and was rubbing herself against his manhood.

"Take me, Dustin. Take me anyway you like. I just want you. I want you inside of me. Do me, Honey. Do it to me." She lifted herself up on her tiptoes and rubbed the head of his member against her softer tissues and then slipped it between her legs, below her sex. She lifted her mouth up to his and bit his lip as she lifted one leg and curled it around his back. She inhaled sharply as he pushed it into her. She threw back her head, tightening the muscles of her throat which then tightened her belly muscles. As her throat tightened she felt her vagina squeeze him. She could feel every vibration of him, every thrust. He was very ready, very close. As she felt him swell for the final blast she opened her mouth as wide as she could and threw her head back even further. He gasped at the tightness of her, thrust a few times more and then came in waves of incredible pleasure. The muscles of his back and buttocks convulsed over and over again. His cock took over his body and forced him to pound into her, his mind was lost to sensation as he pumped his seed into her. Her flesh softened around her vagina, absorbing his increasingly violent thrusts. Her muscles inside of her vibrated in concentric circles, pulling him deeper and deeper into herself. Deep inside she felt the head of his penis double in size trapping him until his work was done, his seed spent. His swelling caused her to convulse and convulse and convulse. She screamed through her wide open mouth. A deep releasing scream. A scream of contentment, of success, of achievement, of joy, of heaven attained.

He felt very relaxed as he lay there off the ground. He felt an insect climbing over his foot but he ignored it. To move would be to end the experience. He had never had a woman like Naomi. So forward, so giving. He gazed down at her, at her throat. The black ribbon had been dislodged. The little fold of skin under it was a rosy color and seemed to be pulsing.

He felt her moving now. Her head moved down to his crotch and she pulled him into her mouth. 'My god,' he thought, 'she is cleaning me up with her mouth!' She sucked him in and out and then deep into her, stretching his now limp cock to its full length. He felt her inhale him into her trachea and squeeze him as she held her breath. His cock felt like it was in a vise, but a nice one. Slowly, surprisingly, he started to grow again. He heard her purring as he grew. Soon her head was going up and down like a piston, then in a flash she spun, she was on top of him and he was inside of her. He gazed up at her. Her body was very trim. She must exercise everyday he thought. She reached down, grabbed his hands and placed them over her breasts. She whispered to him.

"The more you get turned on, squeeze my boobs harder, and pinch my nipples. Let me feel your passion." It didn't take long. Her hips were rotating like a machine and gaining speed. He felt the area at the base of his cock hurt a little, like it was being torn, but he ignored it. Everything else felt so good. He squeezed her breasts and she increased her speed and threw her head back. The little fold was cheery red now. He pinched her nipples and she screamed as she came. He felt his cock being sucked up into her, like a vacuum cleaner. He came suddenly, hard. He tried to squeeze her breasts but lacked the ability. Every ounce of his strength was pulsing through his cock and into her. After they lay in each others arms again. He felt completely drained while she seemed full of energy. Again her head traveled south to take him into her mouth. He tried to shove her away.

"Stop honey. I can't take anymore." He tried to push her head away from him. Her teeth sank into the flesh of his cock and he heard her growl. At least it sounded like a growl. Maybe she was trying to say something. "Honey, Naomi, stop. I am all used up. I can't go again." She ignored him. Again he felt himself sucked deep into her throat and he was horrified to feel himself respond. She moved and suddenly her legs were over his head and her sex was in his face. Her legs opened wider and his nose was forced into her vagina. He tried to push her away. Again her teeth closed around his cock. She was growling again. Her fist squeezed the base of his balls. She twisted them around and around till the tightening base skin squeezed his balls until he thought they would burst from his scrotum. It really hurt. His head arched back in pain and away from her cunt. She quickly found his throat and rubbed herself against his Adam's apple. He soon found it hard to breathe so he tucked his chin down, protecting his throat. He was afraid that she was going to bite his cock off. He quickly took his hands off her hips, stopped trying to push her away. She was pleasing herself, rubbing against his nose again when suddenly her sex was over his mouth.

"Suck me, lick me, please me." It was hard to understand her with his cock in her mouth. He tried to lick her, whenever he stopped to swallow, the teeth bit down again. It felt like the head of his cock was being bitten in two. Finally, she came. Liquid flowed out of her in spurts. It burst all over his face, drenching him. She fell back exhausted. Quickly he pulled away from her momentarily inert body, gathered his clothes and rushed through the bush back to the beach. He could hear her crying out his name.

"Dustin, come back. I love you, I need you. Please, Dustin, come back to me. I need you." He quickly dressed and walked back to the pier, his eyes haunted.

The Arab slowly rose above the bushes to eye the dead body of his captive. It was unchanged. No one had touched it. The two had left and gone back down the trails towards the barracks. His eyes were angry as they glared between leaves covering his head. He was well camouflaged. He moved ever so slowly towards the woman, checking every inch for any trip wires. Ahead of him he stabbed with his knife, feeling for any pressure plates, any mines, any snares. The snare that got the woman was a very good one. He still couldn't see the trigger. No doubt he would as soon as he got closer. From five feet away he spotted the gold coin that the woman had reached for, the bait in the trap. It appeared untouched.

The woman was his. She was his captive. He resented that Allah had not granted him the kill. He liked to kill an infidel at least once a month in case he had committed some minor infraction against Allah. His soul would be cleansed clean by the spilled blood of the woman. He wanted to be sure he was clean in case he died. He wanted to be sure he could enter the gates of paradise. He wondered for a second if she was a person of the book. A Christian or a Jew? Both religions were recognized by Mohammad. They were required to pay a monthly fee to Islam to be allowed to exist. If they didn't pay, they were allowed to be killed. They could be killed. He doubted if she had ever even bowed in a mosque. Infidel! Her blood should have been his!

Her body was his by right. She had been his captive. He should have the honor of debasing her. Of cutting off her hair, of slitting her belly open and letting her guts mix with the dirt of the earth. He should be able to braid her hair to give to his first wife. Thus blessed she might be able to sit outside the gates of paradise to gaze with love at her honored husband within, thusly attaining the highest honor a woman could strive for in the eons of eternity. He moved closer. The body was his by right. A plant grew faster than he moved.

He reached out and touched her leg with a stick. Nothing happened. He moved closer and poked her in the ribs. Nothing moved. Maybe it was just a simple trap, a snare for the unwary. He touched the coin with his stick. The birds of the forest continued to sing. Slowly he rose to his feet and looked down carefully at his captive. He couldn't see any tripwires anywhere. He reached down to her body and lifted the stake away from it. His would be the final victory. As the body cleared the stake, the wood fell to the ground and four stakes, from four directions flung upwards to impale him in the guts and the chest. This was the work of the Seal. The Vietnamese had taught the Americans so much about snares and traps. Fuck, him.

"Curse you, Allah! I was supposed to win! The Seal was to be mine!" His eyes opened wide as he realized what he had done. He had soiled his soul. He had cursed his god as he died. He would never see the inside of Paradise now. Tears filled his eyes as his blood flowed into the dirt of the earth and the insects burrowed into his body, eating and defecating in the temple of his soul. In horror he saw a wild pig carefully creep out of the jungle and start to gnaw on his leg. With his last breath he lifted his head to the sky, to the rain and clouds.

"Forgive me, Mohammad, forgive me Allah. It was just a moment of weakness." He wished he had a infidel nearby to kill to cleanse his soul, but it was too late, far too late. An insect burrowed into his dying right eye and ate its way into his brain.

Just when are we going to get there, Sir Dudley, I mean, Daddy?" Jill didn't have the strength to sit up on her spreaders. It was too hot. The sky was pure blue with not a gnat's breath of wind. "Why don't you turn on your motor? At least then we might pretend we have wind." Janet was stripped down to her bikini bottoms and was holding an umbrella over her head.

"We don't have the diesel, Sweetheart. We used up too much fighting the storms up north. Now we have just enough to get to the mainland of Costa Rica, maybe." Janet looked around at the horizon. Still no sign of wind. Jill eyed her mother's umbrella jealously.

"Well, this is one fine way to organize a cruise, that is all I have to say. Who wants to go to this Coco Island anyway. I need a McDonalds, I need a Big Mac and fries. I need a tree to climb. This sailing is for the birds. I give up trying to be a good little girl. I have half a mind to turn into a brat starting now!" Her mother gave her a stern look.

"And who was it that washed her hair and left the water running for a whole fifteen minutes? The pressure water? Who was it that used up a month's worth of fresh water in minutes?" Janet put her hand to her eyes and gave a sigh. "Now we have to go to Cocos Island to get water. We only have enough for another two days. Thanks to you, Sweetheart, our good little girl." The last words came out sarcastically.

"It wasn't my fault! The faucet got stuck, my watch was broken, the suds got in my eye, the boat lurched, I tried to stick my thumb in the dike but it didn't work. I'm the good guy here!" Her mother just looked at her as if she was a slug, and not a nice one at that. "Mom? Aren't you on my side?" Her mother just turned her back.

"Go talk to your father. He might understand." Jill peaked down below where Harv was trying to get some sleep before his night watch started.

"Sir Daddy?"

"What happened to Sir Dudley?" He never raised the arm that was covering his eyes. He lay on a beach towel that was hopefully catching at least some of the sweat poring off his body.

"Oh, Daddy, I was just joking. I didn't mean it. It was the hormones, Daddy. Those hormones made me say it. Those hormones that are turning me into a woman!" The last was said triumphantly, as if she had scored a winning point at the end of a long game. Her father grunted and rolled over.

"Teenagers! Since we brought you into this world, we should be able to take you out, permanently." Jill slumped on the cockpit seat and pouted. She stared out at the endless sea, the placid, flat, momentarily benign sea.

'I wish we could have some excitement around here,' she thought to herself.

The treasure hunters returned to the camp by ones and twos. Naomi was the last in. She kept her head down and refused to even look in Dustin's direction. Jim Banks and Erhart had worked hard to make a livable camp. Just before the shore boat sank forever they managed to remove the bimini from her cockpit. It was propped up in the sand casting shade on lifejackets that had floated ashore from the wreck of the *Steel Balls*, torn and serrated lifejackets, destroyed by the exploratory teeth of inquisitive sharks. They had built a lean-to out of lashed together sticks and coconut fronds. Somehow they had started a fire. As John and Charlie entered the camp, they stood right above

Erhart who was attempting to sew together a mosquito screen out of extra clothing. He wasn't succeeding.

"Your directions to the location of the treasure are bogus. Why did you send us on a wild goose chase, again?" Erhart stood up to his full height, a full foot and a half below John, and brushed sand off his legs. He looked around the small group.

"Did anyone find a creek that flowed upstream?" Charlie stood up from where he had been resting. He seemed to be all cried out.

"We, John and I, found the creek, followed the directions. They lead us back to the beach and out into this damned, shark infested ocean." He had his fists on his hips now. "Here I will show you. Everyone check this out." He knelt down and drew a map in the sand.

"It all went well till we had to turn north. North brought us back to the ocean, well out into the sea. If your directions are right, these are the wrong bays. Either that or this Keating was just spinning fairy tales." Erhart didn't seem upset.

"Did you find the gap in the hills?"

"No, we couldn't see anything, the jungle was too thick."

"Did you climb a tree to check the horizon?" The explorers stared at him. Climb a tree? "In the old days, the ships were made of wood and the men of iron. Now we have steel boats and glass men who shatter at the first sign of adversity. The sailors back then climbed their masts like monkeys. The first thing they would have done in the jungle would be to climb a tree to get their bearings. I would have thought that would have been obvious. You are right that the magnetic course would have taken you back to the sea. However, volcanic islands are famous for magnetic variations. Often the iron in the ground, in the centuries old lava flows would throw a compass as much as thirty degrees off true." He walked around in a little circle. "I would have thought that would be obvious to one of your profession, Charlie." Charlie looked thunderstruck.

"Yes, but, well I." Tears returned to his eyes once again and he lay down on a torn life jacket. Dustin was hitting his foot against a rock on the beach.

'I should have thought of that," he told himself. 'Where are you brain when I need you most?' His brain replied instantly as always. 'I always respond to properly formatted questions.' Dustin was sure he heard a air of superiority in its voice. 'Fine for you, you weren't just raped.' He was sure he heard his brain giggle. 'I found the experience enlightening.' Dustin looked down at his hands. Was he going crazy? Was he over the edge? Was he developing a split personality? Women always talked about how being raped destroyed their personality, they became different. Was the same thing happening to him? He looked over at Naomi on the opposite side of the camp. He felt an instant feeling of hatred, of wanting to perform serious violence upon her body, and then almost as fast a passionate desire for her. God! He was going crazy!

Hawk hadn't said anything since he had returned to the camp. He sat by himself and stared at the last resting place of his ship, *Steel Balls,* and threw rocks into the sea. Mary sat on the other side of the camp from him and played with the bobby pin holding up her jeans. Once in a while she stared at Dustin with an expression resembling guilt.

John looked at Charlie. He was crying again. He shouldn't have trusted him in nautical matters. But the man was a seasoned sailor! He should have known! Ah, Shit.

Jim Banks looked over at Erhart. Then he looked from person to person of his little crew. He could feel strange undercurrents, strong feelings, charged emotions within the group. What had happened in the last four hours? He didn't think it mattered. Whatever happened it would solve itself with hard work. Best thing to do was to get them working as a group again.

"People, we have maybe a couple of hours before dark. We need food. We have plenty of water. But not food. We need to scour the jungle here abouts. There has to be something to eat. Let's go find it!" No one looked up. Everyone seemed lethargic. "I am going to assign groups to go and look in different directions. Should we group together as before?"

As one, Dustin, Mary, and John yelled out, "NO!"

Ben sat in his cave high up in the mountain. He had a great view of the north end of the island. He could see the Manager's beach hut, as it was called, as well as the three northern bays. They were where the action was now. He could see down into the water of Chatham Bay. The wreck of the big yacht was clearly visible. He had an old pair of binoculars that a passing fishing boat had given him. He stared at the wreck. He could see sharks swimming in and out of the hatches and broken windows, looking, seeking for anything edible. Most of the bodies had been eaten now. Bodies of the crew, of Sam's divers, all eaten by sharks. On the beach, a group of shipwrecked sailors were standing in a circle yelling at each other. At least he guessed that they were yelling. A couple of them were waving their hands dramatically.

Three of them suddenly walked away and started up the trail to the settlement. A fourth rushed to catch up.

Why did they always climb into the island? Did they think that the sharks of the bay were the most dangerous things in the area? The two girls, they were smarter. He told them to stay put. They did. He could see them now. Them must be bored. It looked like they were building a rock path between the little cottage and the lime trees. It was a good idea. The rain often made that area slippery with mud.

The other two, the man and the woman, they were back in the barracks. Everyone down there must be getting hungry by now. Not that it mattered. The lunar eclipse of the sun was tomorrow. Tomorrow the moon would pass in front of the sun's face blocking the sun's light from
reaching the earth. Here, in Cocos, the island would be cast into darkness for almost thirty minutes; complete darkness. The whole event would take 140 minutes. Not long, but too long for the people down there. He knew that sacrifices would have to be made. Blood would have to be spilled to stop the gods from eating the sun. To make sure that the light of the sun returned.

It would look like the gods were eating the sun. The sun would look like a big cookie that someone or something was taking a bite out of. At first just a little bite, then bigger and bigger until the sun was gone, all gone. Ben was an educated man. He knew that it wasn't the gods eating the sun. He knew it.

Maybe he had been on island too long. It wasn't the same since his wife left him. Maybe he had cabin fever, no, island fever. Everything was going to hell. First the soldiers in the barracks, one day they were here, the next it was as if they had never existed. Their clothes, their gear, everything was gone. Maybe it was better that way. Maybe the soldiers offended the gods. Maybe when sacrifices had to be made, the soldiers would have interfered, so they were taken care of earlier. Then the sun might never return. Ben shook his head. Of course the sun would return. It was an astronomical event. It had nothing to do with gods. He had been on this rock for too many years, that's what it was, too many years. It was enough to drive a man crazy.

Come help me with this big rock, Mercedes. It is too big. I might break a nail!" Mercedes smiled at her friend. She was really getting into this project. A vacation was much better if something was accomplished during it. It was always that way. Something that the pair of them could remember with quiet pride. Mercedes helped with the rock. Together the two girls carried it across the slippery mud to the series of stepping stones they were building. They looked like little white islands sticking out of a sea of brown. An archipelago spanning the sea from the cottage to the lime trees. The two girls were almost finished. They just needed a few more rocks.

"Mercedes! Look! Cave paintings!" Elena dramatically pointed at the top of a boulder. The top of the boulder they had just removed a big stepping stone from, had etchings or something. Mercedes smiled at her friend.

"It can't be a cave painting if it is out in a field."

"OK, then a field painting, an etching. Prehistoric etchings! Cave man etchings, no cave woman etchings!" Mercedes looked over Elena's shoulder. It was like an etching. A three cornered hat had been carved into the top of the huge boulder. It looked like one of those hats that old British captains used to wear. Mercedes clapped her hands.

"We have our own art gallery now. Let's see if we can find some more!" The two girls cleared the tops of all the boulders in the area.

"Elena, look!" Mercedes had found another. It looked like two swords with their blades crossed.

"No! Mercedes! Look at mine." Elena had found what looked like the letter 'B' atop another boulder. "We can tell all our gentleman callers to come out here and gaze at our art with us! And once we have them out here, who knows what might happen!" The girls shrieked with laughter as they returned to their cottage to clean up after their little job of yard improvement. They failed to realize that the three marked boulders were placed in a perfect equilateral triangle. And in the middle of the triangle was a flat, stone free, grassy area.

The Prospector and Robyn stared at the open, walk in safe. It, not surprisingly, was still empty. They checked very carefully for hidden doorways or trapdoors. It was nothing but a secure room. Robyn stomped her right foot and tossed her head, flinging her hair over her shoulder.

"So what and where is whatever was in here, anyway." The Prospector smiled at her, she looked so pretty when she was frustrated.

"Most likely it is where ever the missing guards are." He waved his hand vaguely at the empty bunk beds and lockers. "Let's check the rest of the barracks. Maybe we can find a clue." Robyn was the first to hit pay dirt. On the top of one of the lockers, in a dusty shoe box, she found a mini-cam.

"Stud! Look! Evidence!" It didn't take her long to put it in replay. She had enough experience with cameras. The replay started with a lot of static, then Jackie's face appeared.

"I am now on the supply boat that services Cocos Island. There are four other passengers. Two Costa Rican girls off on a holiday and two very tough looking park rangers. The girls, or a least one of them, work for the police department. The rangers don't speak to anyone."

"My mission if I choose to accept it, sorry, an attempt at humor there, I will have to edit this! My mission is to discover if the Costa Rican Government is covering up something out in Cocos Island. All treasure hunting permits have been canceled. The island has been declared a ecological reserve and in 1997 became a United Nations World Heritage Site, supposedly for its unique endangered species. However, the only scientifically logical reports of unique species is one report of the existence of the Cocos Island Cuckoo. That might be someone's idea of a joke. No photographs of the supposed Cuckoo have been discovered by this reporter." The image broke off and was replaced with static again. Robyn turned off the camera.

"How about them apples, Stud?" Her Stud just smiled and held up another shoe box, he opened it and pulled out a satellite phone. Robyn shrieked. "A phone, a phone!" She started dancing around the room, yipping and cheering, as the Prospector was dialing a number. She quieted down as he talked on the phone. As he continued to talk his face became darker and his eyes flared like a double barreled shotgun. Finally he hung up.

"No monies have been deposited to my account. That Hawkins has been lying from day one. Fuck him!" Robyn looked up at his uncharacteristic language and the anger pouring out of his eyes. She had always thought of her Stud as the most level headed man she had ever met. Now he was showing he had a temper. One hell of an evil temper. God, he was sexy!

"Forget Hawkins. Call the mainland. Call the Coast Guard. Call the Marines! Call a caterer! I need food. I'm hungry!" The Prospector raised up the phone and extended the antenna again and then suddenly stopped.

"We have the phone now. We can call whenever we want. Before we get rescued, lets give this island a good look over, see if we can't find some of that gold. When we get rescued, there will be cops everywhere. Won't be any chance to do any looking around. I'd like to come out of this experience a little in the black." Robyn's eyes lit up at the mention of gold. She nodded.

"So where is that gold?"

He was wearing his father's skin. He had others, but this one was roomier. Last night he had carved two ten foot sharpened poles. Poles strong enough to hold a man. Or a woman.

He was very careful in dismantling his trap. There were other stakes not yet sprung. Finally he dragged the two bodies away from the bait. Stupid thing to die for. A mineral. A very common mineral on Cocos Island. Wouldn't do you any good when you were dead. Good bait, though. Always worked.

He striped the two bodies. It was easier when he found the man's knife. Once denuded, he worked the sharp end of one stake into the hole between the man's legs. It was good to do the work before the body stiffened. He pushed it in further and further, following the spine. Up through the guts, the heart. In the throat he took great care. Wouldn't do to break the skin. Had to be done right. Finally he pushed it up through the brain till the sharpened end rested against the top of the skull.

He dug the hole carefully. Had to be just the right depth. When it was ready he lifted the man's body and levered the butt end of the pole into the hole. A few rocks and dirt made sure it would stay erect. He jabbed the second sharpened pole deep in between the woman's legs. He giggled to himself which hole he would enter. Of course, in the end, he shoved it up her anus. Tradition is everything in these matters. She was easier. Body was less muscular. Throat was skinnier, however. Had to be careful. In life, one had to be so careful. In death, even more careful.

Dustin, Mary and John were walking up the hill when they heard footsteps behind them. They stopped and Erhart soon caught up. John looked at him in distrust. "So, you are going to hang out with us now? Tired of lounging around the beach? Telling hard working people lies?" Erhart didn't seem upset.

"You know John, an insult is just like a drink, it affects you only if you accept it." Dustin momentarily looked directly into Erhart's eyes with increased awareness. John kicked at a rain puddle.

"Some of us could really use extra money. I, for one, would really like to find some pirate gold. Do you really know where some is or are you just going to blow smoke up my ass and call it insight?" Erhart just smiled at him.

"I don't have the faintest idea where any pirate treasure is. What made you think I did?" John's jaw fell open, Mary looked disappointed, Dustin just smiled. He looked directly at Erhart.

"What do you know?" Erhart smiled at Dustin.

"I know, or to be more exact, I know of hundreds of treasure maps, treasure directions, death bed confessions, secret codes. What I don't know is which are correct and which are fabrications. More exactly, I don't know if any are correct. I believe that most if not all treasure maps are codes penned by the pirate to remind himself where exactly his treasure was buried. After all, he planned to return one day and retrieve his booty. Or at least some of it. It didn't do any good in those days, or indeed, these times, to walk around with too much loot in one's pockets. That was and is an easy way to the grave. Other pirates, criminals, government officials, just about anyone would kill him for the fortune in a pirate's pockets. No, it was better, in those days, to drink up all the money on your person before leaving the bar, or like some did, just throw it in the ocean and let young boys swim and dive for it.

"Now, you are asking, what do I know that will help you find some treasure. Right?" Dustin just nodded. Mary seemed shell shocked, but managed to nod her head once. John looked at Erhart in a new light. A sad new light. He looked directly into Erhart's eyes.

"Do you know where any treasure at all is?" Erhart smiled sadly.

"I speak but they refuse to listen. John, I don't know where any treasure is. None. Zero. Nada. Got it?" John's eyes were glazed over. He so much wanted to be rich. Dustin patted him on the shoulder.

"John, if it helps, it is the search for the treasure that gives it all meaning. After we find it, we will be on the run. Running from the IRS, the Costa Rican Government, other treasure hunters, modern day pirates, and believe me, they exist. It might be easier to throw it in the water for young boys to chase. Or else spend it so fast, there won't be any left. Of course, no one will believe you that you haven't stashed some away." Mary seemed to wake up. She raised a finger.

"Or, don't leave any witnesses. If no one knows you have it, you are free!" Erhart smiled sadly.

"The second anyone even hears of the Virgin, you won't have a moments' rest for the remainder of your life. This is the Virgin of Lima, people. The most incredible piece of art ever created. There are only two artifacts on earth that can restore life to the dead. The true cross and the Virgin. You know, maybe we should just look for Benito Bonito's treasures. It would cause a lot less trouble. Less money, but a lot less hassle."

"Where and what are his treasures?"

“There has been so much pirate treasure buried on this island it defies the imagination. It seems incredible that we haven't stubbed our toes on some by now. Benito usually marked his caches with a three cornered hat. Like a British Naval hat from those days, you know? He was a British officer before he turned pirate, after all. After he killed all his men. Did I tell you about that?” Everyone shook their heads while staring at him spell bound. Erhart smiled to himself and cleared his throat.

“Benito, originally was a British officer named, Bennett Grahame, who was charged by the Admiralty to survey the coast between Cape Horn and Panama. He soon tired of the work. While anchored in Acapulco he noticed a warehouse close to his ship being loaded with gold for transshipment to Spain. Late at night, he and fifty of his more greedy crew killed the guards, took the gold and escaped to sea. The rest of the crew refused to join him. He agreed to drop them off at an island he knew of where whalers called and where they could get a ride home. However, after he dropped them off, he followed them ashore and killed each and everyone of them with his swords. Leaving no witnesses, you know?” He smirked at Mary. “Quite an individual feat indeed. It helped that he had excellent night vision and a total solar eclipse occurred during his killings.

“Anyway, he buried the bulk of his gold on the island and went on to a storied piratical career. Whenever he made a big haul, if that is the right word, took a rich prize, he always returned to Cocos to bury his loot and re-water his ship. It was a perfect spot for him. His men couldn't tell stories and anyone who was giving him trouble, he killed off. In the end, he was captured by the British and hung. He never admitted being a pirate and never revealed any locations of buried loot. None of his treasures have ever been found.

“At least ten of his men were captured with him. All of them were more than happy to sing. Each, however, told different stories. It seemed that after burying his loot, Benito Bonito, as he called himself as an alias, killed off the crew that helped him bury the gold.

“Many of maps and descriptions that we have today originated from his crew. Many groups of treasure hunters have searched for his gold using these maps, none has been found. Most likely, the crew were saying anything to prolong their miserable lives. One thing they did always agreed on, was Bonito left a sign somewhere near the treasure of a three corner hat. We pirate historians have termed it Bonito's Hat. Many such hats have been found on the island, no loot has ever been recovered. Some say he used other symbols to indicate his caches. That the hats were just guide posts as they might be called. No one knows.” John was bouncing on his toes.

"Where are these hats?" Erhart smiled at his sadly.

"They have been found almost anywhere. Usually carved into rocks. Back then, no doubt, he carved them into trees also, but none of the trees have survived down the decades. It has been almost 120 years since the last of the pirates used Cocos as a bank. Trees that grew then are almost certainly long dead." Dustin pursed his lips.

"Shall we take a walk and keep our eyes open then?" Eyes flared, heads nodded, and hunger was momentarily forgotten. They followed the trail upwards, always upwards. They came to a corner in the jungle and heard something. Sounded like static on a radio. John mentioned for them to stop and then crept forward on his hands and knees. He slowly edged his head around the corner and stopped in shock. Slowly he turned back.

"We have to go another way. This is a dead end." Dustin looked at him speculatively. With three long strides he reached the turn of the trail. A man and a woman were staked out across the trail. They were dead but looked alive as the millions of insects eating them made their bodies seem to move. They seemed to be screaming as bugs crawled in and out of their mouths, their eyes, in and out their noses.

The bodies were naked. Dustin looked down between the woman's legs. He looked away quickly and swallowed back a surge of acid from his stomach. As he watched, one of the man's fingers was de-fleshed. A whitish bone was all that was left once the insects moved away. In front of the bodies, a line had been drawn in the sand of the trail with a stick. The message was clear.

Dad! I can see it! I mean, Land Ho! There, there, do you see it?" Jill was bouncing around the deck in her excitement. "And look! Oh, look! It has trees on it. Lots and lots of trees! Oh, wow!" Harv and Janet popped their heads out of the cabin's hatch, out of the cabin where they had been resting while Jill took a watch.

"Honey, how marvelous! You found our island all by yourself!" She smiled at her rapidly growing daughter. She really was such a treasure.

"Where? Where is it? Are you sure you can see it?"

"Dad, you are looking the wrong way. It is off the bow not the stern. Really, Dad. Sometimes I wonder what you would do if I wasn't there to keep an eye on you."

"Oh, is that it? That little thing? I thought it would be bigger. Its so little we won't even be able to step on it."

"Sir Daddy! That is because it is still so far away. Are you having fun with me? Trying to trick your one and only daughter? Really Dad. Sometimes I think you are the teenager!"

The trio laughed together in joy as they slowly approached the treasure island of Cocos.

Hawk was getting angry. The more he thought about how he had been embarrassed in front of that lousy Mary II, the more he wanted to punish her. In his mind he convinced himself that she had laughed at him. Laughed at him in a rare moment of weakness, all because he had some bad luck and his ship had sunk. That's why he had a once in a lifetime, wouldn't ever happen again, been under a lot of stress, kind of event. After all he had done for her, all the money he had thought about putting in her account. The more he thought about it, the angrier he became. He wanted to punish her, violently, physically, sexually. He wanted her to remember him till her last moment on earth, remember him with horror. Remember him as she tried to make love again, tried because after he was finished with her, nothing would ever work right again.

And where was she now? Gone off somewhere to look for his gold. Gone off with that Dustin. Yeah, soon as he busted his little gold hunting toy, he took off to see what he could find. Bastard. No loyalty. None. Who got him to this island anyway? And then that nerd, Erhart. Asshole didn't know where any gold was. He was just full of stories he had made up. A con artist. Sending him out on a wild goose chase. Who did these people think he was anyway? And that John! After all he had done for the boy. This is how he repaid him. There should be a law or something. Hell's Bells. He had half a mind to send his bodyguards out after all of them. Teach 'em a lesson. He gulped suddenly and glanced out at the last resting place of the *Steel Balls*. They had sunk his ship. That was it. They had tricked him into pulling the trigger on that missile. That was it.

The ex-Seal only worked for cash. Wouldn't take a check, ever. He was insistent about it. Got angry if he wasn't paid right on time. The Seal's pay was on the bottom of the sea. He wondered if he could con someone into diving down and opening his safe. It could be done. That Sam could have done it. He didn't think the Seal would be very impressed if he just pointed out in the water when he came in to get paid. Came in, God. His payday was today! Fuck! He wondered if he could get that Arab to guard him from the Seal? Fucking Arab was after his money. He could sense it. He felt it in his eyes whenever the fucker looked at him. He could offer him some. He could offer him a lot! He wouldn't even have to pay. No one could kill the Seal. He was like a force of nature or something. Death incarnate.

He wished the supply boat would come back. He needed to get away from this island and that Seal. The hell with the gold. He needed to live. He could always con someone out of some money. Money was easy to steal. Everyone put it in the same place, in the bank. Saved him the trouble of running around looking for it. Like the gold on this stupid island. Why did they have to hide it so well, anyway?

He looked over at Jim and Charlie. He was left with the worthless sailors. All the treasure hunters had left him. Well, fuck them. Naomi was kneeling at his feet, running her fingers though the sand, her head bowed. He loved to take this girl. She was always ready. For anything. She would fuck until she dropped from exhaustion. But she was worthless in finding gold. Shit. Looked like he would have to save everyone again. He raised his foot and pushed Naomi on the neck, sending her sprawling. She picked herself up and kneeled next to him as if nothing had happened. He didn't notice that her hands had formed into fists below the surface of the sand. Her head was bent downwards, so he couldn't see the rage in her eyes. He didn't know that she was thinking of her few belongings that now lay on the bottom of the sea, and blaming their loss on him. Blaming him for sinking his own ship.

It was his ship, so what if he sank it? What did they have to complain about? He lost his beautiful ship. Of course, the insurance would cover his loss. And the insurance money would help prop up his teetering financial empire. Still, he wanted that gold. He would do anything to get that gold. He would kill to get that gold. After all, this island had seen a lot of blood spilled in the name of buried treasure, what would a little more matter? He looked down at his Naomi. Sure, she was a great fuck, but, hell, she was just a woman.

Naomi's clenching fists found a heavy rock below the sand. She grasped it, hard. Her eyes, staring unseeingly at the sand below her, slipped a little closer to insanity.

Book III

How it all Ended

It doesn't matter how fast you are going,
if you are on the wrong road.

Elena saw it first. She had stood up to stretch her muscles after a hard morning of sunbathing. She was naked. She and Mercedes didn't even make a pretense of wearing clothes anymore. Up on their roof, they felt so secure. Once in a while they saw some people walking along a trail down in a valley between the trees, if they looked over their wall. They didn't know why no one came to visit them. Neither did they bother to explore to find out. Elena was raising up her arms in a salutation to the sun when she saw the speck of white on the horizon.

"Mercedes! There is a boat or something out there! A floating one, I mean! Come look." Mercedes slowly stretched her way out of her chair where she had reading a book on yoga, in between rain squalls. She looked like a Hollywood starlet. Her every move was a fluid motion of grace and style. This relaxing lifestyle was doing her a world of good. She raised an elegant hand to her naturally sculptured eyebrows to shade her eyes from the sun. Her little finger was pointed slightly up.

"Yes, I believe you are right. Unless it is a very large, non flying bird with white feathers. A particularly slow non flying bird." The girls went back to their idyllic lifestyle without another thought to the possibility of a boat visiting the island.

Robyn didn't like making love when her stomach was empty. In fact she hated it. She wouldn't do it. She refused; absolutely, totally refused. For her, a proper seduction started with a fabulous meal, preferably one featuring large amounts of steak washed down with expensive wine. She didn't mind the cost, even if she was picking up the tab, which sometimes she did if the guy was really cute. After all, it didn't cost her anything. Not with her abilities. But it would be nice if she could afford the bill. If she could just throw down a couple of C notes on the table and walk away. It would be great if she was filthy rich. If she had bars of gold and sacks of golden doubloons under her bed. And a refrigerator stuffed full with delicious food.

"When exactly are we going to eat? And when exactly are we going to find that gold? And when are you going to use that phone to call for a helicopter? And stop doing that, it tickles." The Prospector stared at her back, where he had been running his fingertips up and down, as they rested for a minute in the shade/umbrella of a bushy tree. It was a beautiful back. Somehow the rips in the cloth she got when she was trapped in that thorn bush just added to her allure. She was so sexy.

"Just a few days ago, you loved me to touch you. To touch you anywhere at all." Robyn tossed her hair this way and that. Her hair felt so dirty and her scalp itched. She thought that maybe she had a bug in there or something. Her vanity case had gone down with the ship. She felt less a woman when she was dirty.

"Well, I don't like it now. So stop it." She tried to daintily scratch her bottom. Something had bitten her there. She wiggled her toes in her shoes. She wondered if she was developing jungle rot. That thought got her worrying about her left ear. Something had crawled in there and bitten her. It was very painful. She didn't complain. She wasn't that type. Instead, she pouted.

"Why couldn't they have buried their stupid treasure somewhere decent, like Miami Beach? Somewhere with penthouses, somewhere with room service and fluffy towels and clean sheets and a decent mini-bar?" Her voice changed. "Somewhere with graveyards."

They had left Jackie in the trap with a stake through her heart. The Prospector had to pull Robyn away. She hadn't wanted to leave anyone like that. At the very least, they should have given her a decent burial. It was so sad. But the Prospector had been insistent. His grip around her wrist had been like iron. He had pulled her back to the main path and up the mountain. There, they had gotten lost. Or he had. Robyn knew exactly where she was. She was in Hell, or at least on the very bottom level of Purgatory, starving to death.

"Anyway, how can you even think of romance when we are stuck here in Hell? And we have no idea of how to get out? Can't you find a gas station attendant and ask directions or something?" The Prospector wasn't paying attention to her right now, which didn't improve her mood. He was staring at some tree or rock or something. Certainly nothing edible. She promised herself that the next time she fell in love, it would be with a cordon blue chef. Or a guy that owned a fabulous restaurant. Or at least a Daniel Boone type that could rustle her up a halfway decent breakfast in the middle of nowhere, who wouldn't get lost and who could find a waterfall with a pool to bathe in. Someone who paid attention to her when she was complaining, not that she ever really complained. Certainly not to someone who walked away, who found some stupid tree more interesting than her. Who, unless her eyes were tricking her, was actually rubbing it! If he wanted to rub something, he should rub her poor feet.

"Robyn. Come here. Look at this." He was pointing to the side of a particularly large tree. With a huff she meandered over to his side. "It's Benito's Hat!" There carved deep into the tree was a large three cornered hat. Robyn started getting excited. She forgot about pouting, about eating or taking a bath. She ran her fingers over the carved wood. Her eyes widened till white showed all around the irises.

"The treasure! It's here, somewhere, close by! We found it!"

He wasn't wearing a skin today. He decided to be himself. From high above the clouds he stared down at his kingdom and spit. He didn't bother to watch to see where his spittle fell. Wherever it landed, that land was his. His by right.

Today he wore gold. He only dressed in splendor when he was planning a great feat. A matter of great consequence. The clouds opened below him as if on command, and he gazed down at his land, especially at the two nude women far below him on the roof of the house. One was but a girl, a nothing, but the other was a princess reincarnated. He could tell she had royal blood flowing in her veins, by just looking at her. When she walked, she had such presence, such a sense of the dramatic. What a queen she would make! He wasn't much to look at without a skin. Receding chin, squashed nose, and dumbo ears were his best features. The acne was slowly going away.

This time, tomorrow, he would take her for himself. He would take her in front of Inti, in front of the minor gods sleeping in the cave behind him. Some might call them mummies brought here from the old land. Brought here to be safe in their slumber until they woke at the end of the world. He would take her in front of them after the proper rites were preformed. They would like that. He would fill her with his seed while Mama Kilya ate Inti, the sun god. Thus, his son, his successor, would be kindled. His son would grow into the future king of this land. He would teach him all he needed to know. He would carry in his genes the wonder that was his mother. Not that he would come to know her. She would be sacrificed after the birth as was always the way. It wouldn't do to have his son, the future king, coddled by a woman. Her work would be finished. He would send her back to the gods personally. He would send her friend along to keep her company. His queen would carry her friend's still beating heart in her hands as she rejoined the gods. That would wed them together for all eternity. What a great kindness that would be. He amazed himself at how considerate he could be when he wanted.

The clouds returned and veiled the women from his view. He looked farther and saw sinners strolling over his land, sitting on his beaches, fouling the perfection of his land with their disgusting, primitive ways. Paca Mama did not approve. She wanted blood. She wanted vengeance. He walked into the entrance of a huge cave. The minor gods slept along the walls. He bowed before each and every one of them. It took a long time. There were a lot of them. And they all were thirsty. He asked them to wait for the morrow. He knew they would. It was the way. To make their waiting easier, he covered them with gold.

He finally came to the one. She was not of his line. She was an alien god. But powerful she was. Even in the dark, shielded by a curtain, she shone with the light of the eternal. She shone from within, through the many gems that studded her body. She did not want the blood from a beating heart. She was the only one who didn't. She wanted a man killed before Her, thorns driven into his head, his hands and feet nailed into wood. She did not want a quick, honorable death. She wanted her sacrifice to suffer for many days, dying slowly, becoming weaker as he hung on the wood till he could not raise his chest to breathe. To suffocate, to bleed, to starve. He knew this is what she wanted. He had found many golden crucifixes depicting such sacrifices. Truly she was a most fearsome god. He had to find a strong one for her. One that would last many, many days. Maybe then she would stay out of his dreams. Maybe then she would stop haunting him with her unbelievable beauty. He reached out a hand to touch her body, but pulled it back quickly. How dare he touch such a great god!

He had tried to offer her gold. He had taken it away ashamed. Nothing he could offer could match her cold beauty. The others, they had grown old and died in the old land. They had taken the last voyage and their servants had brought them here, to this far away island, where none would ever discover them and rob their graves. The servants had gladly died to insure their masters' afterlife. Here they could sleep safely for all eternity. Many were here. True, the dead had stopped coming many years ago. Beyond his grandfather's father's time. That was not his worry. He had his duties. He walked out of the cave and stared up at the bright face of Inti. Off to the side a thin silver sliver of Mama Kilya approached him. Yes, tomorrow was the day. He shuddered. There would be so much blood.

He walked in the dark, taking the required steps by memory. It was a dance he had learned long ago from his father. When he came out to the main cave Ixtolic was waiting along with the others. He eyed him with hostility.

"They are touching the holy places. They ignore their dead. They are turning their backs on the sea. Surely they are evil. Why do you not order their deaths?" Ixtolic was his brother. They were all brothers one way or the other after so many years without any fresh blood to breed with. But Ixtolic was his brother out of the same mother, sired by the same father. Ixtolic was jealous of him. Ixtolic thought he should be King of this land. Ixtolic had many friends who thought the same. They all loved to spill alien blood. There had been so little strange blood for years and now it was everywhere, just waiting to be spilt.

"Have you no patience? The gods must be appeased at the proper moment!" It was useless. Ixtolic wanted the sacrifice for himself. He wanted to smell the fresh blood boil and steam on the hot stones. And he wanted what went before. Before when the sacrifices had to be taught humbleness, to accept their fate, to welcome their fate, to willingly want to join the gods, to flee from this miserable existence where every unseen tissue of their bodies was penetrated and tortured. The victim had to be perfect, the gods required perfection, but they had to be willing, welcoming the voyage to meet the gods. They could only be tortured where it could not be seen. Ixtolic was angry that he had killed two and used the stake. Ixtolic understood so little. Without the proper sequence, the offering would not welcome the obsidian knife. They had to start early to grow tired of this earth and to want it all to just end, to get it over with. That is what Ixtolic wanted. He wanted to teach them to want to leave this life. Ixtolic and his friends wanted to start now, this very second. He hoped he had the strength to stop them.

Hawk stared at Jim and Charlie. They were talking quietly under a tree fifty feet from him. He could hear the occasional murmur but that was all. It had all gone to hell so quickly. Two days ago he was a master of the universe, owner of a super yacht, a multi-millionaire. Today he was a beach bum, sitting on his ass as others told lies and stared at him from the corners of their eyes. Who the fuck did they think he was? A nobody? He raised his hand and signaled to the jungle. The ex-Seal appeared seemingly out of nowhere. In a few long strides he was in front of Hawk.

"Those two are talking about me. I don't like it." The Seal looked at him strangely. He turned to go and then hesitated.

"Today is the first. Is my pay ready?" Hawk sneered at him.

"Of course it is. I am a man of my word. I honor our contract. But tomorrow is the first. Not that it matters. Do you want it now?" The Seal looked into his eyes for a second.

"Tomorrow, then." He walked over to the two whispering men. That is inaccurate. He glided over. He seemed immune to gravity. His giant body seemed to create its own rules in the universe. The men looked up at him as he approached.

Jim Banks had commanded many men in his seagoing career. He had fought many times in dark corners deep in the bilges and in dark streets in stinking ports. He was a tough man. But the giant before him added a new definition to the word tough. Charlie took one look and his eyes teared up. The Seal picked up a hand sized stone from the beach and looked deep into Banks' eyes.

"Obey, the One." He squeezed the stone and it groaned and snapped as it turned into dust in his hand. The Seal opened his hand and slapped his palms together ridding himself of the dust. His clapping hands sounded like doom. Jim Banks nodded quickly. Charlie fell to his knees, crying openly. The Seal walked back to Hawkins.

"What do you want to do about the boat?" Hawk looked at him, questioning.

"What boat?" The Seal pointed a stubby finger out to sea at a speck of white sailcloth. Naomi had been kneeling in the sand under the sunshade of the shore boat's bimini. She leaped to her feet and rushed out to scan the horizon. On spotting a flash of white sailcloth she sank to her knees in relief. She turned to Jim Banks.

"It is going to stop here, isn't it?" Sudden fear filled her face. "Shouldn't we start a signal fire or something. Banks studied the distant sail.

"It is coming into Chatham Bay. All we have to do is to wait for it." The Seal took one look and faded back into the jungle.

The Prospector carefully searched all around the tree with the carved three cornered hat. He moved slowly, agonizingly slowly for Robyn, looking for any indication of a trap, a snare, a booby trap. He smelled as he went. His eyes were hard, as if he was staring at a mine and judging if it would collapse on top of him or not.

Robyn fleetingly thought he resembled a big bloodhound, seeking the trail of an escaped convict. She half expected to see him jump up and start to howl as he ran through the forest. He turned once and she saw his eyes. They weren't eyes. They were hardened steel, cold as ice, as expressionless as a robot's. She was so elated as he hunted, hunted for gold for her, but after she saw his eyes, her elation dried up. Fear of what she saw in his eyes, sobered her up. Fear, fear of why his eyes were so hard, sobered her up. She had forgotten, just for a second, what had happened the last time they found a gold cache. Suddenly she stepped back, quickly swiveling her head looking for sharpened stakes.

"Honey, Stud. It isn't worth dying for. Get away from that tree." The Prospector edged away from the tree as carefully as he approached it. "Oh, I am so happy you listened to me."

"Wasn't any gold there. Was once. Taken away many years ago." He looked around the jungle surrounding them. "It was taken that way." He pointed higher up the mountain. He turned without glancing at her and started trail-breaking up hill.

Dustin wiped his glasses again on his soaking shirt. It didn't help. The rain was worse the farther they went into the center of the island. He was trying to edge them south and east. He wanted to stay as away far as he could from the center peak of the island. There the rain would just be worse. As it was, they were all injured from slipping in mud and falling on loose rocks. He was hoping to reach the last bay of the island, Iglesias Bay. He hadn't realize that there was a second peak on the island, Jesus Jimenez. According to Erhart, it was lower than the main peak, Iglesias, by some 100 meters. He guessed the bay could only be two or three miles from Chatham Bay. Shouldn't take more than an hour. Unless you were bashing your way through an untamed jungle. What he wouldn't give for a machete! They pulled vines and bushes apart and helped each other through the maze. He called for a break and as the little group gathered together he looked over at Erhart sarcastically.

"Anytime you see some treasure, let us know." Erhart just looked down at the ground. He was very tired. He would have thought that slipping through the jungle would have been easier for a little man. It wasn't. He didn't have the strength to pull apart blocking vines. He wished he could just lay down somewhere and sleep. But he couldn't. Everytime someone sat down they were invaded by countless insects. Insects that burrowed under their clothes, into every crevice and orifice in their bodies. Mary had it worse. She continually brushed bugs off that were trying to climb up the insides of her legs. Who would have thought that the jungle would have been such a hell hole. The Virgin of Lima could be standing ten feet away from them and they would never have seen it. No wonder past expeditions had no success. This was impossible. How did those pirates ever hide their loot so well. One look at the jungle and he would have buried it close to the shore. Maybe they were iron men back then sailing wooden ships, whereas today we were cardboard men riding in aluminum planes.

Dad! I can see a house! See, on top of that hill? Someone is waving at us. Where are those binoculars? Aha! I was right. It is a beautiful woman waving and she is stark naked! I am going to, so, so, so, love this island!" She started taking off her clothes.

"Jill, put down those binoculars, put those clothes back on and climb up to the spreaders. Let me know if you can see any rocks or reefs in our way."

"Yes, Sir, Sir Stuffy Pants!" Janet picked up the binoculars. She scanned the island. Jill left a few buttons undone on her blouse.

"Harv, I think there are people on the beach, next to an old dock. Nobody is waving. I hope they are friendly."

"Friendly or not, we just need some water and we will be on our way. No one will refuse us water, will they?"

"Getting water and climbing trees. Don't forget the climbing trees part, Dad! This is going to be so great!" Slowly the *Rose Marie* drifted in towards the island on the light cat's paws coming off of the island's heights. The crew had to tack this way and that to make any headway. Progress was slow but within an hour they could make out the people on the beach without binoculars. There seemed to be five people there, but as they watched a large man walked into the jungle. The house on the hill
had disappeared within the trees as they approached. No one else could be seen.

"Dad, there is a big reef or something right in the middle of the bay. Looks like it is close to the surface."

"Thanks, Jill. Keep an eye on it. We want to anchor far enough away from it so the anchor doesn't get fouled. Doesn't look like a good place to get shipwrecked."

"Ok, Sir Daddy! And just so you know, there are lots of trees on this island. Lots and lots of them!"

At the last second, Jill dropped down from the mast and helped her mother hand the sails and then they lowered the anchor snubbing it into the sand far below with the momentum left on the boat.

"I am going swimming! I am going swimming naked! Watch me!" Her mother gave her a stern look.

"Not in front of all those people you are not, young lady." She looked ashore. Everyone was still staring at them. She happened to look down to note if she could see the anchor in the crystal clear water. "Jill, this place is loaded with sharks. Better not go for a swim."

"Ah, Mom. They won't hurt me. Besides, I'm too fast!" Just at that moment a large shark swirled in the water below, raced for the surface and leaped out, mouth gaped open and snapped at Jill as she leaned over the side of the boat. Her mother must have somehow felt what was going to happen for she raced to her daughter and pulled her away from the rail at the last second. Janet's eyes flashed black with streaks of red momentarily as she held her daughter to her breast. The ocean erupted in a fury of foam and churning red water as every shark in the area attacked the large shark that suddenly was floating around dead.

"Mom, look at all the blood! That could have been me!" Jill watched the flashing of white teeth, a bit of tail that flew into the air, the blue water suddenly turned pink. Her eyes paled and her lower lip trembled. "That could have been me."

"Honey, this isn't going to work. Out little inflatable dinghy will be eaten up in a second with all these sharks. We will have to tie up at that dock. Sorry, but let's raise the anchor again and we will have to use some of our diesel. It will be a lot easier to get water at the dock. Maybe they will have a hose instead of a bucket brigade?"

Ben stood at the opening of his cave. Another boat was anchored in the bay. He closed his eyes in sorrow and pity for the sailors on her. The bad times were coming. He knew they would be very bad. It had been many years since the last time. Many years for the urge to grow. The desire would be strong this time. During the last eclipse, he didn't have an easily barricaded cave. The last time he had to run for his life. He had run and hid and fled for a week of terror till things returned to normal, quasi normal. As he looked at the small sailboat in the bay with his binoculars, he didn't notice a dusky arm snaking its way into his cave, or the face of Ixtolic that followed it. He was looking down at the two girls' house when a hand circled around his old neck and squeezed with the strength of a boa constrictor.

Five men soon crowded into the cave. Their mouths were silent but their eyes spoke volumes. They stared down at the old man as Ixtolic stripped him naked. They shoved herbs down his throat to increase the pain he would feel. They bent him, belly down, over a rock and held him spread eagle. They took turns readying him for sacrifice. His anus ripped from the abuse, ripped up towards his spine and down towards his genitals. but they were past caring. His blood lubricated their organs making them wilder than ever. The scent of blood filled their noses, making their eyes widen, their nostrils flair, their teeth bare, and their cocks harden. They took him over and over again, one after the other. When his ass was so ripped it was of no use, they took him again, shoving themselves down his throat. When he tried to close his teeth to prevent them, they took a rock and bashed his teeth in, snapping them off at the gums. Eventually, after they were finally spent, they came to their senses and looked down at the half dead, mutilated creature at their feet. He feebly coughed trying to rid his lungs of cum. Ixtolic judged. He could not be offered to the gods. He was unworthy. He was a disgrace. He was filthy. They kicked and cut and stoned until there was nothing left of the man who had been so kind to two young women.

Hawk walked out to the end of the pier along with Charlie and Jim Banks to take the boat's lines as it motored alongside. After lines were secured and fenders deployed, Hawk caught the Captain's eye.

"Permission to come aboard, Sir?" Harv hesitated for a second then agreed. Hawk made himself at home on the port cockpit seat. He never extended his palm for a greeting. "Is your vessel for hire? Actually, let me rephrase that. Would you accept $10,000 for taking me and my friends over to a beach on the other side of the island. It isn't but a few miles away. Not more than three miles or so. We would take ourselves, but as you may have noticed our vessel was sunk by a Great White shark."

"A Great White sunk your boat? How Cool! Did it eat a hole in the bottom or what?"

"Jill, leave the gentleman alone. Mr. er, what is your name?"

"Hawkins, but just call me Hawk." He smiled slightly. "Everyone does. There are just the four of us. It'll take less than an hour." Harv looked the group over. That was a lot of money.

"We came in here for water. Is there a hose on the dock?" Hawk jumped up and took over.

"Banks, you and Charlie get that hose for the supply boat rigged and turned on. The Captain here needs water. Is there anything else you need, Sir?"

"I need to climb a tree, and I need to climb it right now!" Hawk smiled slightly and glanced at Harv. He didn't shake his head.

"Naomi, escort this young lady to the nearest tree suitable for climbing and make sure she comes to no harm. Bring her back when she is climbed out."

"Any other pressing needs, Sir? Does your cook need anything or is it just the two of you?" Janet stuck her head out of the companionway.

Hawk opened his eyes wide with shock. He had seen many women in his life and bedded most of them that interested him. Women were one subject he knew inside and out. But this one. Or rather this head in the hatch had such an allure. It was like she had a man's spirit, a man's ability to decide, a man's aggression, trapped in a woman's body. He imagined that the woman probably was one of those that looked more like a man than most men. One with no curves and muscles and hair everywhere. But as she rose out of the hatch he had to blink. She was the most sexy woman he had ever seen, and he didn't know why. She had the wisdom of age in her eyes but the body and face of a sixteen year old girl. Her face was sculptured, it contained neither baby fat nor worry lines. He had bedded women who were more beautiful, who were more sexy, whose eyes sparkled more. He had sex with so many starlets he'd lost count. But this one was different. He couldn't say how she was different. But give him a little time. Then he would know. Say one night in the sack.

Mary saw it first. The men were doing what men always do. Keeping their nose to the grindstone till the job gets done. No looking up. No recess till the bell rings. Mary always observed her surroundings. Luckily, as they were about to fall off of a hundred foot cliff and into a raging river below.

"Hey, hold up. Stop, already. Foods on the table. Half time is over. The girl is naked." The last made them stop. Then they looked back and then realized in their tiredness that they had walked into a cul-de-sac where the only way on was down. Way down. Carefully they edged their way back the way they came. Erhart was very tired. He sat down with a sigh.

"So, Mr. Dustin. This is how you guide us? Into disaster? And you have the nerve to complain about me?"

"Listen you pipsqueak. I'll have you know..."

"Oh, knock it off you two. You are like two first grade kids arguing over who gets the swing." John was just getting warmed up when Mary stood up and stepped between them all.

"Are we going to find that gold or are we just going to sit here and argue until we die of starvation?" She refused to let any of them speak. "All of you, quiet! The bay we want is on the other side of this ravine. What say the first person who finds a way down, and up this ravine, gets first pick at the treasure?" The men gazed at her for two heart beats, then they jumped up and started exploring.

They were close to the top of the mountain. The Prospector could sense it. The scent of gold had died out a while back, but both of them needed to have a look around, to take their bearings. They had been in the jungle for so long, it had become claustrophobic. They needed fresh air. They needed sky. They needed space. They got it. The top of the mountain was solid rock. The wind blew over it at near gale force. Robyn didn't know why. The sea far below her was calm and unruffled. From the top, the jungle looked the same, impenetrable. From what they could see, that is, between the flying rain clouds. The clouds didn't even have to be raining to get them wet. Just standing still as the cloud went past and seemingly through them was enough to soak them to the bone. With the wind chill factor, their body temperatures plummeted as night fell.

"Whose idea was this anyway? First, here I am starved to death in a jungle, cooked to medium rare in the heat, tenderized to near death by thousands of insects, and now I am living inside clouds and have been shoved into a deep freeze. I tell you, straight, I am going to check out the next boat I stowaway on. Really check it out. None of this, 'Oh, look. What a pretty boat. Let's go take a ride.' No way. Next time, it is going to be a Lloyds of London for me. Start at the top. Pick out the best ship in the world first. One with room service. 24 hour room service." The Prospector didn't seem to mind the conditions. But then he was a mountain man. He was happy to get out of the jungle. Worse than any hole in the ground he ever saw.

"If'n I knew you was a complainer, I never would have made love to you. If'n I knew you were a whiner, I wouldn't a rescued you in the first place."

Robyn blinked twice. Her? A complainer? A whiner? What would the gals back in cell block C say. 'You were within a mile of an incredible treasure and you spent your time whining?" Robyn straightened up and peered over the edge of the mountain. She ignored the cold and the wind. It was hard to see down with all the clouds as the sky darkened. She turned west and looked up. She nudged her Stud.

"Looks like this ain't the tallest hill in these here parts, partner." She pointed up at a faintly glowing light far above her about a mile distant. The Prospector took one look and pulled her to the ground.

'Well, if I knew it just took speaking hillbilly to him to get him started, we could have been having a real good time.' She pursed her lips and closed her eyes, just to show she was willing. He seemed to ignore her except to whisper in her ear.

"We have to get off this hill before we are seen." 'Well, there goes making love on the top lookout of the Eiffel Tower,' she thought, and obediently followed him down the hill keeping her lips tightly sealed.

The ex-Seal was feeding himself on mangos and bananas. He had found plantations deep within the jungle. Plantations with trails leading in and out. He thought about taking food back to the others. Then he thought about the Hawkins' eyes as he lied about his pay. He would not be paid tomorrow. He knew it in the bottom of his soul. He had met many men who had tried to lie to him to save their miserable lives. He knew when he was being lied to. The new boat could take him back to the world. What he needed now was pay to tide him over till he organized a new gig. Preferably in gold. And it was just up that trail. It was OK working for rich dudes, but he had to think about the future. It would be great if he had a big place of his own. Maybe an island. An island with no people.

He waited till the workers left. They were mostly women. They carried their loads atop their heads as they headed back up the trails that seemed to lead deep into the mountain. As dark approached, the Seal started to move. A moth would have made more noise. A moonbeam would have made more of a disturbance. Inside his brain he divorced himself from the Hawkins. He was the One, not Hawkins. He was. And soon he would have enough gold to make all the others bow before him. He was the One. He could see that now. It just took gold. And gold was just up that mountain. Waiting for him. The gold was his to take. This is what would give his life meaning. This is what his training had been for. This was the future. Just up that mountain.

He was giving a speech. He felt foolish. It was his job to order. It was theirs to obey. But times seemed to be changing. So he was giving a speech. They were all below him. Faces raised, watching him. He saw Ixtolic and his cohorts off to one side grinning and fooling around. What had they done now? The women, who were tired from the work in the fields, sat waiting for him, mute, like farm animals. The young were restless. They had never gone through the eating of Inti. He saw the young studs nudging their girlfriends, whispering. The whispers were always the same. 'If Mama Kilya, the silver crescent, the wife of Inti, the moon mother, eats Inti, then why would their girl friends not eat them.

He tried to count. It was impossible. They moved around too much. What happened to the discipline of years ago? He would have never dreamed of moving or talking while his father prepared to speak. He tried to count anyway. He gave up at 79. Not counting those on guard duty. Call it a hundred souls living in his mountain, caring for his gods. How many of them would gladly give up their lives to their gods tomorrow? How many would have to die if they did not corral the trespassers? The gods had to be appeased.

The weather was fine in San Jose. Dominic stared out of his window at the guards practicing their formations below. They resented being pulled from Cocos Island. They worried about where their next duty station would be. Dominic worried more about Elena. Did he really send her out there to die? True, his wife had been getting more and more suspicious. And the secret communiqué he had received from the President noted that the spat of deaths occurred only sometimes on Cocos Island during a solar eclipse. The difference was his nephew was a member of the squad presently there. And if a President couldn't protect his own nephew, he wasn't much of a president.

The helicopter had flown in at first light and removed everyone except the commandant and his servants. There had to be someone left in charge. And anyway, as soon as the eclipse was over, he would fly them back. Much better idea. He wouldn't want to lose his job because of a disaster.

He had sent those two rangers that the President had found to help out in the meantime. Just in case. It had been his idea to send Elena. He hadn't even realized what he was doing, when he did it. Thing was that now, he really missed her. The typist with the long legs hadn't worked out. Plus it turned out that his wife wasn't being suspicious, she was just planning a surprise birthday party for him. Some birthday. He ended up having to make love to his wife. Not that she was ugly or anything. Just that there was no piazzaz left in their relationship. Not like Elena. Work wasn't any fun anymore. The office was a bore. He hoped she would be all right.

The water was flowing into the tanks. Harv was happy. Jill was screaming at the top of her lungs to all who would listen to her up in her tree. Janet was speaking to the Santa Claus character. Even if he had to drop them off on another beach, it wouldn't be far off his route. He would have his water and all would be right in his world, especially if he made a few bucks in the deal. He smiled happily to himself, then the doubts started flowing in.

The last time he allowed someone else on his boat, he was pirated. By a crook on the lam. What was the difference here? He looked over at this Hawkins guy talking to his wife. Was he a crook too? Could he be getting ready to pirate his boat?

He heard the stainless water tanks below 'bonk' as the top panel of the tank changed shape from internal pressure, from concave to convex. A sure sign that they were full. He pulled the hose out and capped the tank before any flying bugs could get in. Last thing he needed was contaminated water. Or a contaminated crew. He could hear his daughter up in her tree, screeching away having a good old time. Should he give her a bit more time or take off now? It would be good to get a bit of rest after this long voyage. But this Hawk guy made him nervous. Who but a predator would name himself Hawk?

And the rest of Hawk's crew. Two of them looked like sailors. The woman seemed alright, she kept trying to make eye contact with him, as if she would like to know him better. And anyway, if it was so close, why didn't they just walk over to this bay that they wanted to go to? They had to want his boat. But why? He knew that a regularly scheduled supply boat called at Cocos. All they had to do was wait. And anyway, how was he going to be paid? By check? By a guy he would never see again? Did he look like a sucker? Maybe a year ago he might have been, but hardly likely after his recent experiences. He gave this Hawkins character an evil look out of the corner of his eyes. The guy seemed to see him do it but ignored him and continued talking to his wife. Fat lot of good that was going to do him. Janet was so disagreeable these days. She seemed to be turning into a different person. Sometimes she would be the Janet of the past. Others, she would be a complete stranger. He worried about her. Was she having a mental breakdown or something? Should he be taking her to a mental institution? More likely, she was just reacting as she went through menopause. He had read all about menopause in Playboy. They had a great article about it. It said that the kindest thing to do would be to take a mistress and to leave the poor overworked wife alone. Thing was though, he really loved Janet. He always had. Even before he knew her he had love the idea of her. Of someone who could be his soulmate.

That woman was trying to catch his eye again. Naomi, he thought she was called. The woman, was obviously trying to get to know him better. He looked back at Janet talking to this Hawk creature. He couldn't help himself. He still loved Janet. He guessed he always would. For better or for worse. If true love wasn't true, then what was the point of life?

Mary found it. It was a skinny path. Maybe a goat path, that is if they even had goats on this liquid island. Slowly they worked their way down the trail until it reached the river. Erhart was still being quarrelsome.

"Okay. We're down. Now, how are we going to get back up?" Mary ignored him and started walking down stream. "Hey, Mary, explorer girl. Where do you think you are you going?" Mary turned and stared at him.

"You want me to climb back up that hill just so we can climb down it to get to the beach? Do you have low blood sugar? Have trouble thinking on an empty stomach?" She reached a deep pool and sat down in the water, ignoring the others, and let the current carry her downstream. She kept her legs and feet in front of her to act as shock absorbers. She didn't look back to see if the others followed suit. The canyon walls sped by until the sky opened out in front of her. Mary suddenly had a bad feeling about this. Maybe she should have been more cautious. But she was so sick of this island, she just wanted it to be over. She tried to grab on to boulders as they sped past to slow herself down. They were too slippery. She tried to swim to the sides and hold on to something, but the walls of the canyon were worn smooth by the raging river. Suddenly the sky was all there was and she was catapulted out over the sea. She held her breath. She didn't know why. She was going into that shark infested ocean. What use was a couple seconds more of life?

The ocean was nice after the hot jungle and the freezing river. She plunged down beneath the surface 20, 30 feet. Instinct made her struggle back to the surface. She didn't have a face mask, but there didn't seem to be any sharks here, at least right now. Just as she was getting close to the surface, white water surrounded her.

Her eyes widened, some of her precious air left her lips in a scream, her arms and legs didn't seem to want to work anymore. She fought against her panic. Fought to regain her rationality. Finally her weakening struggles brought her the last few feet to the surface, to life giving air. After a couple of breaths she thought about sticking her head back under the water, to see what was down there. She didn't know why. She knew what was making all that splashing, all this white water. She had seen the sharks at the pier splashing, rolling, snapping as they attacked. Might as well get it over with. Death would be easier if she didn't see it coming. Much easier.

Something grabbed her ankle and she screamed. She wanted to die with peace in her heart, but she had to scream. It just came out. She couldn't help it! She was being dragged under, legs first. She closed her eyes and didn't struggle. Why bother?

It let go of her leg and grabbed her arm. That made sense. Arm meat was more tender. Better marbling. Less fat. It was pulling her back to the surface. She wished this stupid shark would just get it over with and stop playing cat and mouse with her!

"Open your eyes, Mary, and stop screaming." My God! These sharks talked. There wasn't any hope. Mankind was doomed! She tried to remember her prayers.

"Now I lie me down to sleep, I pray the lord, my soul to keep." Something was kissing her on the mouth and her eyes popped open. It was her Dustin! Her head spun this way and that. They were alone. There weren't any sharks. In front of her was a torrent of fresh water, a waterfall from the river, falling directly into the sea. Off to one side, just a short swim away, was a beautiful black sand beach with splashes of white coral sand here and there. Looking up, she noticed red earth between some trees. She quickly kissed Dustin again.

"Come on, Honey. Lets go." He looked confused.

"Go where?" With a jolt in her heart, she realized he had lost his eyeglasses in the waterfall. Without them he was very nearsighted.

"Just follow me." She looked up. No one else was coming over the waterfall.

Elena and Mercedes made themselves canned spaghetti for dinner. The box of food was getting a bit bare. They hoped Ben would return soon. After washing up, they donned their nightgowns and were getting ready for bed when the mob came for them. There were twenty of them. Twenty big burly men. They burst through the door like it was made of paper. The lock, that Ben had found for them, seemed like nothing but a popsicle stick. They treated Mercedes like royalty but ignored the girls' shouts, yells and blows. They dressed them in beautiful robes, Mercedes, in a cloak made of gorgeous bird feathers and then carried them back to the cave system through secret paths in the jungle and then to a door in the mountain that they opened by twisting an iron bar. Eventually they ended up in jail. A nice room with all the amenities but a jail nonetheless. When Mercedes, in a fit of passion, threw the feathered cloak on the ground and started to stomp on it, they returned. They ignored Mercedes. Three of them held Elena and the fourth slapped her face and he wasn't gentle about it. When Mercedes yelled at them to stop, they did, and then turned and watched what she would do next. When she gave the cloak a parting kick, they really wailed into Elena. Her cheeks were fire red now. Tears flowed down her cheeks. She was in such pain she couldn't yell or cry. It hurt too much to open her mouth. Mercedes picked up the cloak from the ground and gently lay it on the bed and they quickly released Elena. Mercedes smiled at them and spoke sweetly in Spanish.

"You dumb bozos. You can't treat her like that. Its against the law." They didn't react. Mercedes sat down quietly in a chair and the squad left the room. Elena tried the door after they left. Locked again.

There was nothing in the room to aid in an escape attempt. A small single camping bed in a corner and a canopied four poster in the center on the room. An upholstered easy chair by the luxurious bed and a small wooden stool by the cot. A wooden, leaky bucket in a corner and a covered, delicately made, china night pot for Mercedes under her bed. The girls knew it was Mercedes bed, as when Elena lay down on it the door burst open, and the goon squad returned. Before they could get to her, she fled from the bed. Elena felt her flaming cheeks from under a blanket on the safety of her cot.

"I think this is unfair," she complained bitterly through barely moving lips, "there should be a law against it. It is discrimination, that's what it is. The nuns wouldn't allow it. I am going to report all of this to Lieutenant Dominic. He will make these men suffer." Mercedes sat on the edge of Elena's cot and ran her hand over Elena's hair.

"It is OK, Chica. This is just some misunderstanding. I don't know who these people are but help will come soon. I'm sure it will." Tears of frustration flowed from the corners of Elena's eyes. She wiped them away angrily.

"This was such a wonderful vacation. Why did it have to get ruined? Why does my life always end up in the toilet? Why can't I be beautiful like you, Mercedes? They love you because you are beautiful. They hate me because I'm not. I am so sad, so sad." Mercedes continued to rub her hair. Silent tears dropped from her own eyes.

No one was in the fields, not that it mattered. The Seal, as massive as he was, could hide anywhere. He could hide in a field shorn of its crops with workers just feet away, buried in the dirt with just a stalk to breathe through. Now it was coming on to dusk and the shadows made his work easier. He seemed a ghost. Perhaps an acute observer would have seen a hand here or a foot there but that was all. Soon the cave door loomed before him and he crawled in favoring the south side where the shadows were deeper. There were guards. He didn't look at them, he didn't even acknowledge their existence in his brain, knowing that all humans retained some vestige grasp of extrasensory perception. Almost all humans felt shivers shimmy up their backs when they felt someone unknown looking at them. He moved past them. Their eyes reached outwards, not downwards, watching. After passing the guards, the Seal found a long thin tunnel slowly raising up. There were alcoves on either side that he glanced in from the corner of one eye. They seemed to be empty. A few left over stalks and leaves indicated that they were storerooms for food supplies. He saw a few booby traps along the path. He avoided them easily. He was so used to setting such traps himself, he smiled to note variations of creations developed by the Teams.

Deeper in, higher up, he felt a drumming. A low rhythmic, almost sub-audible pulse. His body felt it more than his ears heard it. His own heart tried to mimic the rhythm of the drum, as if it seeked to be one with the mountain. The drumming almost disappeared at times only to return as he traveled through different densities of rock. Ahead of him he saw a glimmer of light far down the tunnel, just a speck at first.

Figures passed between him and the light and as he crept closer he could make out that they were dancing to the drumming. Dancing was the wrong word. They were united with the drums, the drums directed them and blanketed their minds, the drums readied them for the events that would unfold the very next day. Just before the lit cave, he slid into a side alcove. He didn't realize until too late that this cave wasn't empty. Inside was another guard. A monster of a man. He held a stone knife in front of him. The Seal didn't laugh. He knew how very, very sharp obsidian knives could be, just as sharp as the finest Swedish steel.

The Seal didn't have time to pull a weapon. He crossed his forearms as the guard swept the knife down at him from above. The Seal caught the man's forearm just behind the knife in both of his hands and fell backwards. He raised one foot in a Judo move and propelled the guard over his prone body until the giant rammed his head against the wall, breaking his neck. The Seal was instantly on his feet, pulling the body out of sight from the door. He hoped the drums hid the sound of the guard dying. It was OK. They were still dancing in the main cave. He warily eyed the alcove opposite his. It seemed vacant. Only one way to find out.

He dove across the span of the intervening space and came up in a crouch, the obsidian knife in his hand. The cave was empty. There was a small window opening out on the main cave. There must have been fifty people out there dancing. Calling them people was generous. He couldn't be sure. They were dressed in a variety of costumes and masks. Some pretended to be sharks. They wore the skin of the shark over their own skin and somehow snapped the jaws open and closed. Others wore masks of some godlike creatures. He even saw a few wearing human skins, poorly closed along the spine and inseam. At the back of the cave, higher up on a stage, a curtain was thrown open, illuminating a tall woman painted in gold. She wore a mask of gigantic gems that threw rays of different colored, luminescent light all about the dancers. She held a child whose head was surrounded in light. A sparkling, gleaming, diamond like light that was hard to look at. It pierced the room as if seeking out something. Before the woman, on the floor, lay a wooden cross, a life-sized cross and a pile of five inch, hardwood spikes. The drums increased in ferocity. The dancers stomped their feet on the floor until it seemed the entire mountain shook. High above them a single source of light entered the mountain through a small hole. The light slowly faded as night came. The dancers became more rabid, more psychotic. They threw their bodies at each other in a frenzy of sexual abuse. They tore each others' clothes off. They coupled with whoever was nearest, hooting, screaming, yelling, pounding, grunting, always to the rhythm of the drums.

The Seal stared, he had never seen such a display of primitive culture. He had to stop his feet from tapping to the drums. He almost wished he was out there stomping, fucking with the dancers. He couldn't tear his eyes from the window. He didn't realize anything was wrong until he felt something touch his back. He tried to turn but couldn't. The back wall of the alcove had silently slid forward leaving him a bodies' worth of space. As he watched, struggling, rock walls slid in from the sides until they pushed against his shoulders. He tried with all his mighty sinews to shove the walls away from him. He couldn't move them. He was trapped under a mountain with a tribe of rabid aborigines. His head was next to the small window. He could still watch the sexual exploits of the masked natives and their golden queen high above them and his toes still tapped to the drums as he cleaned his fingernails with the obsidian knife.

Hawk was entranced. This boat woman, this amazing woman that had just saved his bacon by sailing in with her boat was so alluring, it was unbelievable. He had ignored her husband. No doubt he was just a drone. She had a brat running around, somewhere, some tree climbing pre-human. Shouldn't be too difficult to get rid of them both, leave 'em in the woods. Whatever. Fuck 'em. His eyes rose to the beach once and he saw Naomi staring at him from the edge of the forest. She had tears in her eyes. He had to think twice to remember her name. He didn't even bother to wonder why she was crying. He shook his head. His boat woman was speaking.

"There is no way we can accept a check for transporting you from one beach to another. That is just human kindness. However, in return for our kindness, we do expect something in exchange. What do you have of value?" Hawk smiled admiringly at her. How beautifully done. Of course, a check from him was worthless. Any businessman of any ability knew it. But what a nice way to say it. Ninety-nine percent of business is saying no and still having the customer remain loyal to you.

"The two of us could go far in business, little one. We could become multibillionaires together. With my smarts and your beauty, we could go all the way to the top." Kissing up to competitors was one skill he had never mastered. He hired people to do that for him. If they couldn't do it, he fired them without a second thought. This girl might be fun to use in his business, and for him to use in his bed. To screw as he liked, to take any way he wished, whenever he wanted. She was so young, so beautiful. Not a line or imperfection marred her skin. Yet it was as if she had all the wisdom of the ages within her. The goddess Athena reborn, just for him! For him! He reached out a huge hand to touch her. The second his giant fingers curled around her arm, all the hairs on his hand stood up and he was filled with a terrible foreboding. He pulled back quickly and slipped his hand under his leg. It was trembling uncontrollably. His eyes were confused and, to be fair, a bit fearful. He slowly raised his eyes to hers. It was if she read his mind when he made physical contact. Flames burned hotly in the back of her eyes, slumbering, smoking, cruel flames.

"You may not touch me or mine, understood?" He managed to nod. "You may not harm or caused to be harmed this boat. If you disobey, you will forfeit your life." He nodded again. He was recovering a little. Regaining his balance. Ignoring his hand. Remembering who he was.

'Who the fuck is this boat girl? She sure as hell has never met the likes of the ex-Seal or the Arab, that's for sure. Stupid cunt has a lesson coming.' The allure he had felt before disappeared. All he saw now was an enemy. An enemy to be crushed either under his feet or fucked to within an inch of her life in his bed. And right now, nursing his hand, he didn't care which.

"You are not entrancing or alluring. You are a man-eater, a witch, a demon. Keep away from me, Satan!" he whispered under his breath. Her eyes just stared at him and through him, as he jumped off the boat.

Erhart looked at John's back adoringly. He was such an Adonis. He ached to reach out and touch the boy. Just to touch. Nothing else.

But he didn't have the nerve. John was trying to break through a bit of jungle ahead of them now.

After Dustin and Mary disappeared down the river, they turned up stream and soon found a rock slide which they scrambled over to exit the ravine. 'Too bad about those two,' Erhart thought, 'but it has always been destined for me to find the treasure. Who else knows all the locations and tales? I'm the essential ingredient. Me.'

"Watch your step here, Erhart. This boulder is unstable." Erhart held his breath. 'He had said his name! John was a poet! Oh, what a great, wonderful day!'

"Sure thing, John." He turned the name into a three syllable word. Rolling the letters off of his tongue. A combination of the rain and sweat soaked John's shirt detailing each and every muscle. Erhart was gazing so long at John's back that he almost missed it. It was a white mark. A white mark made of some kind of mineral. Erhart looked around. The sea was gone. Stunned he closed his eyes and searched his memory for the clue. John looked back at Erhart standing with his eyes closed, and walked back to find out the problem, this time.

"I quote, Benito Bonito, John. Listen. 'Turn your back on the sea and then make your way towards the mountain that is in the north of the island. On the mountain slope you will see a deep brook to the west. Cross this and go twenty paces due west. Then take fifty paces toward the center of the island until the sea is completely hidden behind the mountain. At the place where the ground suddenly falls away you will see a white mark on the rock. That is where the cave is. It has a well hidden entrance covered by a stone slab and a tunnel entrance leads sideways into a chamber.' There. I think that was letter perfect." He looked at John and pointed down a steep slope to a obvious white mark, pointed all around at the lack of ocean, nodded at several stone slabs down the precipice. "Well, John, my man, we are in the south, but let's have a look shall we?"

The Prospector wasn't much fun. He wasn't even tickling her back anymore. Wasn't treasure hunting supposed to be fun? Robyn asked him about it. He just grunted. Men, they think a grunt was supposed to communicate something. No wonder they played sports. They could speak in monosyllables, then. Three, five, hike. Strike, ball, safe. Ready, set, fight. At least in tennis they said love. That had to be an improvement.

"Stud, can't we take a rest? I'm getting very tired." He didn't pay attention. He just grunted a reply in a low voice.

"We're hunting treasure, but someone is hunting us." She stopped walking and looked at him in amazement.

"Well, for god's sake, let them find us. Maybe they have hot showers and breakfast! It has been so long since I have eaten my stomach is going to jump out of my throat and eat my tongue." Her stud just grunted. This was one hell of a way to run a romance. Maybe if she was a gorilla she would understand his grunts better.

They found a trail in the jungle and were walking along it when suddenly there was this guy in a mask standing in their way, and it wasn't even Halloween. She thought she loved her Stud, or at least liked him a whole lot. Thing was, there was a lot she didn't know about him. Like now. His eyes got all cold, kind of like he was made of steel, and he tore into that masked fella like King Kong on steroids. Towards the end he was hitting the guy over the head with the guy's own mask. He walked back to her, after. The same old Stud. He took her hand, told her not to look, and guided her past the remains. He pointed at the mountain in the distance.

"That is where we are going. We have to be very quiet. Can you do that? Can you be quiet?" She nodded her head and zipped shut her lips in her very best little girl imitation, but her eyes were haunted as she looked back at the remains on the trail. There wasn't much left. A lot of red and a few bones and a broken mask. She shivered despite herself.

She was quiet ever so long. She was sure he had to be proud of her. She knew he didn't want any other masked guys to hear them, so instead of talking, she whispered in his ear.

"Do you think these bad guys have any food?" He just gave her a dirty look and they went back to tramping up the trail.

Dustin wasn't much use without his glasses, not that it bothered Mary. She was used to doing everything in the lab while Dustin sat around. Supervising, he called it. They didn't meet any sharks on the way to the beach. Dustin said he remembered hearing Sam saying something about sharks not liking bubbles. Maybe the waterfall was scaring them away.

Ashore, the beach was lovely. There were no buildings. No trails. Nothing. She tried to remember the directions they had followed back in Chatham Bay.

We have buried at a depth of four feet in red earth, cloth of gold, emeralds, rubies, diamonds, and doubloons. 28 feet to the northeast, at a depth of 8 feet in yellow sand, a bunch of gold and silver. And then 12 arm span to the west, 12 feet deep in red earth, the Virgin of Lima.

She didn't think she had it completely correct, but still, it was worth a look. It didn't seem like anyone had been on this beach for decades. She led Dustin to the tree line and walked along it hoping for a clue. The jungle was just as thick here as it was in the other bays. How could anyone ever find anything on this island? They rounded a rocky projection of the beach and on the other side discovered five men fishing in the surf. The two groups stood staring, astonished, at each others' existence for a couple of seconds until Mary, her heart in her mouth, pushed Dustin back the way they had come and yelled, "Run!"

She was a young woman who took care of her body. She doubted any man could catch her. Yoga practice exercised her joints so well she could change directions like a rabbit. Dustin was another story. She took his hand as she sped by and guided him back towards the ocean. If they stayed in the waterfall bubbles, maybe they would be safe. Maybe the locals would fear the sharks. Dustin stumbled over a rock and they had him by the ankles. A hand grabbed her shirt and ripped it off her. She quickened her pace and did a competitive dive off the shore and quickly swam towards the waterfall. The locals were left far behind. They were laughing and kicking Dustin in the ribs. Just as she reached the safety of the bubbles, something large reached out of the spray and pulled her back into the falling water. Behind the waterfall was a pitch black cave. It pulled her up onto a ledge, above water, and tied her up, none too gently. Then it frog marched her, holding onto her bra strap, towards the back of the cave and even deeper darkness, if that was at all possible. She tried to twist away. Her bra was torn off and a hand or claw grabbed her hair and yanked it back, exposing her neck. Something sharp was pressed against her throat. She stopped resisting, her eyes filled with panic. It seemed she couldn't get a full breath and her legs seemed to turn to jelly.

John found the stone slab first. He called Erhart over with a high, excited voice. They stared at it in wonder. Beneath the ledge was a three foot wide hole. A very black hole. Together they crawled to the entrance, and jostled each other for the right to go first. Erhart gave up with good grace and let John go first with a little smirk on his face. John had to lay on his belly and crawl like an Indian to make progress.

Erhart wondered what he was doing. He liked John. He might even love John. Why was he risking John's life? Was it because he had been sarcastic to him in the jungle? Or because he wasn't interested in him? Someone had to check the caves for booby traps. There were only two of them. Love is hard.

"Erhart, we should have a light, it is really dark in here." Erhart lay down on a rock outside the cave and nodded silently in agreement with his eyes closed.

"Feel your way in then. Touch everything. Make sure you don't miss a side chamber." He didn't have long to wait. A shriek echoed out of the cave, then the sound of wood hitting something, and then, nothing but silence. After ten minutes, Erhart crawled into the cave. It was much easier for him as he was so small. The first twenty feet were easy. After that he discovered John's feet. He carefully climbed over the body, feeling carefully, right and left, for triggers that might set off a snare—or worse. There didn't seem to be anything. He reached John's shoulder and felt John's muscular body below his. He had dreamed of this moment for so long. He reached one hand up to John's head, to his hair, he had such wonderful hair. He felt moisture first, sticky moisture. His hands felt a wooden stake driven down through the back of John's head. He started to retch. But before anything came out, hands reached down from above and lifted him up into another cave. There, before he could make even a token sign of resistance, his head was covered with a bag and his hands and arms bound behind him. Rough hands picked him up and he felt himself thrown over a shoulder and carried away. He shouted John's name. Only a laughing echo replied.

Hawk had strained his sore elbow, waving it at the jungle ever more emphatically. He held it by his side now, his hand in his pocket. His life was going to shit. His boat was gone, his bodyguards had disappeared, cute girls were ignoring him, glaring at him with smoky eyes and he hadn't found a single gram of gold. He could see the faces of his bank managers if he returned empty handed. The greasy smiles would be gone. He would be left waiting with the magazines, a worthless bug on the marble floor. Gone would be the million dollar loans at preferred interest rates that he had considered his due. He kicked at a nearby tree and hurt his toe. His temper raged within him. His eyes glared at the tree that had hurt him.

'Fuck this island. Fuck these people. May they all die in the fire pits of eternal damnation. Fuck them all. This is my world. I am in charge.' He spun around. The sailboat was still there at the end of the dock. Jim Banks and Charlie were talking to the woman. Naomi was sitting on a spreader on the mast talking with the stupid pre-human. The man was coiling up the water hose. As he watched, the woman invited Jim and Charlie on board. His temper raged to new heights. He felt his blood pressure surge into his brain dangerously. He could feel capillaries burst painfully from the pressure in the back of his brain. He calmed himself down as he stomped his way down the dock, towards the boat. He felt the heat of his glare, he felt the strength in his fists, he felt the conviction of his place as one of the prime movers of the world. He didn't stop at the side of the boat. He swung his legs over the rail and positioned himself behind the wheel. Jill, uttered a curse, stood up on her spreader, grabbed the backstay and slid down its length, her feet aimed at Hawk's head. Hawk reached down and turned the starter key and edged over to the left as he watched the pre-human slide past him. As the engine roared to life, he eyed the man running back down the dock after returning the water hose to its stand on shore. He glared at the man. He glared at Jim and Charlie.

"Cast off the fucking dock lines." His two men rushed to obey. Harv made a giant leap to return to his boat as it pulled away. On board, he turned to the cockpit with anger in his heart and stopped dead in his tracks. Hawk had one of his huge hands around his daughter's neck. As he stood there in indecision, Hawk tightened his grip and twisted the thin neck to one side. He looked straight at Harv, snarled with one side of his mouth and raised the opposite eyebrow. Harv sat down, deflated, like a kid's balloon poked with a pin. Hawk turned to Jim Banks.

"Get that fucking witch up here. Make sure she hasn't anything in her hands." Jim hadn't even moved when Janet appeared in the companionway.

"Mom. Make him stop. He is hurting me. I can't breathe so good." Hawk sneered at Janet and tightened his grip further. As he watched her, she seemed to change. The feminine traits of her face seemed to disappear, her shoulders seemed to swell, her biceps increase in size, her hips seemed to narrow and her waist bulk up with muscle. Her voice became lower and infinitely more threatening.

"You heard what I said about harming me or mine? Let the girl go!" Hawk measured the distance between them. A good eight feet. He could kill this little pre-human before she was anywhere near him. He knew if he did she would drop to her knees and cuddle the dead body of her daughter. He had seen it many times before. The mothering instinct was just too strong. Besides, what was she going to do, make his hairs on his arm raise up again? Oh, so scary!

"Fuck you, witch. I am in control, now. I am Captain. You don't obey, hope you got a coffin on board, as this little brat will pay with her life for your disobedience." Janet said nothing. Her eyes seemed to flare with a deep reddish hue. Hawk felt a constriction round his neck. It was like a giant hand was squeezing it. The constriction became tighter and tighter. He could barely breathe in but couldn't exhale. Suddenly his neck twisted over. He let go of the girl and felt for something around his neck with both hands. There was nothing there. His neck twisted further and further over until his ear was touching his shoulder. He couldn't stop it. He tried to pull his head up with his hands, yanking at his hair, trying to ease the pressure. His neck continued to twist farther and farther. He could hear his spinal cord in his neck popping in protest. His eyes bulged out of his head until it seemed that all that was connecting them to his head were some overstretched muscles. Everything started to go black. He felt a burning sensation, like the flames of hell, starting at his feet and moving up, searing his flesh as it rose.

"Janet! Let him go, Janet! He isn't worth it. Don't do something you will regret forever. Please, Janet, please. Let him go. Let him go for me." Slowly the pressure eased and the burning sensation eased. He fell onto the cockpit floor, looking like a misshapened lump of former humanity. The last thing he remembered was a foot kicking him in the stomach, hard.

"Take that you, you ape. I hope the sharks eat you up!" A glob of spit dripped down his face. "Mom, can I throw this thing over the side? It really is taking up a lot of space. Look at it. Just sprawled there, getting in the way! How are we supposed to sail with this thing taking up half of the cockpit?" Her Dad suddenly stood in front of her.

"Listen to me, Jill. That man doesn't live in the same world as us. We should just throw him back like some ugly fish we prefer not to eat. We, all of us, live in a world of purity and light. If we dirty our hand with this type of trash, some of him will contaminate us and slowly but surely destroy our happiness. When you kill someone, a piece of you dies with him. Understand?"

"But Dad, he hurt me. He hurt me really bad." She played her final card, a card she thought was an ace. "And I won't be able to do any school work for months and months. And it is his fault!"

"Honey, your Dad is right. We have to try to do good, if we can." Her mother looked like her mother again, a strikingly beautiful woman, with a small, tiny flare of red in the back of her left eye.

"You men," Janet glanced at Jim Banks and Charlie. "As soon as we anchor, get this thing into the dinghy and dump him on the beach." She looked back at her daughter. The woman, Naomi she thought she was called, was massaging her bruised neck. Jill seemed to be enjoying it. She turned to measure the distance to the far bay where she could get rid of this crew of misfits. Behind her she heard her daughter talking.

"That feels really good, Naomi. Don't stop, OK?"

"Your pleasure is my pleasure, Muffin."

Ixtolic laughed. All the young studs were gathered around him, asking him to teach them the secrets of preparing the sacrifices for the ceremony. As if they didn't know. They all had heard the stories. None of them knew the full extent of the preparation. But they would learn. He was in charge of the more or less harmless sacrifices. His brother, the so-called lord had them gathered into one room, to make it easier for the trainees. The important sacrifices, HE retained for himself. As if no one else could do it. He would show them. One of the idiot off islanders in the room was trying to crawl out. Stupid one! He stomped on its arm.

"Observe. This is what you may not do. These may not be harmed in any visible way. They must be honorable sacrifices, immaculate. The gods may not be offended. However, these sacrifices may not resist their fate. They must go willingly to the knife. They must lean back and expose their chests for the gods to judge. They must willingly do this.

"Look at these animals. Bah!" He spit on one. The phlegm dribbled down its face. It raised up and glared at Ixtolic. "This one will be our first subject. Bring it." The older soldiers grabbed the sacrifice and dragged it out of the cell. It resisted but they did not punish it. It would learn in other ways. They lay it on the table and stuffed its mouth full of ceremony weed, herbs that increase the pain an animal feels, a hundred fold. Ixtolic picked up a bamboo switch and swished it through the air. He hit the end on the table a couple of times to splinter the ends to make it more effective. Without warning he hit the subject on the soles of the feet. It bucked in the soldiers arms and attempted to spit out the weed, the soldiers were ready for it.

"The inflammation of hitting the feet releases a histamine into its blood. Histamine increases the perception of pain the sacrifice feels. Observe." He hit it again on the soles. It bucked and struggled far more. "A fat subject like this is far easier to train than a thin one. The fat releases more fear and dread into its blood which increases the perception of pain. Observe." Ixtolic whipped his bamboo against the feet again, the bamboo made a high pitched thwack everytime it hit. Soon the sacrifice was weeping and making sounds of cowardice.

"This is not good. Cowards are not worthy sacrifices. It must be taught to accept pain, to accept death as an end of pain, to desire death as an end of pain." He handed the switch to a trainee. "Continue." One stud in the back raised his hand.

"But Sir, when do we, you know, do it?" Ixtolic glared at him.

"Is that why you are here? To have sex with a sacrifice? To rape a sacrifice to the gods? Get out of here. You are not worthy to train. Anyone else not worthy, get out." No one else moved. "Next trainee." He indicated the switch.

Mary was openly weeping in the cage. They should have taken her. Women could bear pain far better than men. Poor Dustin. Poor, poor Dustin. He was bucking on the table, at times his entire body from head to heels would lift off the surface, arcing in pain. The bottoms of his feet were swelling up fiercely and were cherry red. Mary worried that he may never walk again. Finally, her poor Dustin fell into unconsciousness. Unfortunately, it was only for a second. They threw buckets of water over him and then ripped off his clothes. The soldiers bent him over a bench and the trainees took turns inflicting pain in another hard to see area. Dustin didn't struggle anymore. Everytime he did, he was whipped on the feet again. Suddenly Mary stopped crying. Her mouth sagged open and her bottom eyelids fell. She realized that she was probably next. They wouldn't even have to tear off her shirt or bra. She moved slowly to the back of the cage and tried to look small. She could still see Dustin jerking as he was tortured. What good was his brain now?

They fed the Seal regularly through the window. He ate the food without concern. He had to keep up his strength. He knew a chance would come. Maybe not a good chance, but enough of one to make a fight for freedom. He knew more of his captors now. He knew they prayed to pagan gods and killed humans to appease these gods.

He knew something big was coming up. He didn't know what, but the eyes shining in anticipation were easy to read.

Once an hour he worked on his cage, more as exercise than as a hope to escape. The walls were solid rock and seemed as thick as a mountain. The window offered more hope. He had to be careful. He scrapped at the stone with his fingernails where it couldn't be seen from the outside. Two of his nails had been worn to the quick. Still he continued. He didn't seem to mind his lack of success. He knew only one way to live, to the hilt. Hell, if he was going to stop now.

The curtain was drawn over the golden goddess after the dance, but the wood crucifix was still in plain sight. One little old man spent an hour sharpening the wooden nails. The Seal's eyes narrowed. Dying didn't bother him. Going out good, that was what mattered. He wanted to take as many of the little fuckers with him as he could if it came to that. Those nails could be damn good weapons. And that golden goddess, that would be nice to have. Real nice. Thing like that would keep him in the money for a long time.

Every once in a while the Prospector would stop on the trail and bash sideways into the jungle. Robyn would take a big breath and follow along behind him. Luckily, it was never far before they broke out on another trail. There he would smell the air, the ground, the leaves, and then they would set out in a new direction. Robyn was starting to blank out on occasion. Once she fell. The Prospector rushed back to her. He took her pulse, patted her arm and then rushed off.

"Oh, great. What a hero. He runs off and leaves the heroine to be eaten by wild animals, as if they would want a bag of starving bones." She was still mumbling to herself when the Prospector returned. He shoved weird things into her mouth. She chewed and swallowed obediently. It didn't taste like anything her mother used to make but she decided it was much better to die of indigestion than of starvation.

Finally they stood in front of the side of a mountain. Her stud wandered this way and that, but always he returned to the same solid piece of rock.

"The gold is on the other side of this rock and it was taken through this rock somehow. I don't know how." He sat down and stared at the mountain with such dejection that Robyn felt her heart go out to him like never before. He needed help. He needed her help. She strolled up to his back, put her palms on either side of his head and gently levered his chin up till she could see her eyes.

"Going to cost you the best steak dinner I can find in Houston. Not New York or LA, Houston."

"What is going to cost me a steak dinner?"

"In Houston."

"Fine, what is going to cost me the best damn steak dinner in Houston?"

"For me to help with your little stone wall, of course. What did you think?" Her stud just looked up into the rain, shook his head and went back to being depressed. The stone wall didn't bother Robyn. She was used to it. Wherever there is gold or other items of wealth, there is a door and wherever there is such a door there is a lock. And locks were what she knew. It didn't take her long. It helped that she knew what she was looking for. A big heavy door as big as a mountain couldn't be moved without a lever. Even if it was a little door, it would need a little lever. The lever would be disguised of course. That's what made it fun. She checked out the wall. Pure solid stone. So it had to be a tree or the ground. The earth looked solid and the rain would give away any hidden passages. She tugged at trees for a bit until she tired. It was just a few hours ago that she fainted from semi starvation. She started to fall again. To save herself she reached for a branch. It didn't work. She fell anyway with the branch still in her hand. A rumbling noise came from the mountain. She sat up. A small door had magically appeared in the rock wall.

"The best damn steak in Houston plus a bottle of the most expensive wine this little girl can find in Dallas." Her Stud just gazed at her and then jumped up and rushed for the door. He felt himself being tackled from behind.

"Hey, Stud. You can't get out of my steak dinner that easy. The place has to be booby trapped. You know like the one that got Jackie..." The Prospector gave her a quick kiss and approached the door carefully. It was just like a mine. Another hole in the ground. Fuck. But this one was sure to have gold in it. A lot of it. He eased very, very slowly in, letting his eyes become adjusted. He knew that whoever set these traps was damn good. He was about to find out just how good.

Mercedes was sleeping fitfully, despite that she had dined like a queen last night. Platter after platter was brought in for her to pick and choose from. Elena was forced to kneel by her feet, besides the small table. Mercedes tried to sneak some food to her. They were caught, or rather Elena was. They came in and slapped her across the face. Mercedes had jumped up and grabbed the hand of the guard doing the slapping. The guard fell back in astonishment. He bowed before Mercedes and then they took Elena out of the room. The door, as always, was locked. She heard an cry of agony and then sobs of pain. The door opened and Elena was thrown back inside. They had broken her little finger on her left hand. It stood up at a ninety degree angle to the other fingers. Mercedes managed to pull her finger back into the proper alignment and then tied it to Elena's ring finger with a strap she tore from the lining of her robe. Mercedes stopped eating in protest. They came back in and started slapping Elena across the face again. Mercedes gave in and sat down at her table. Elena crawled over and knelt at her feet. The guards had left. At the end of the day, a guard had brought in a bowl of thin gruel with a cockroach swimming in it. Elena had happily slopped every bit up. Except for the cockroach, of course!

At night the women had come. They had stripped Mercedes naked and searched her head to toe for the slightest imperfection. They had inspected her private most areas, jabbing, poking with their fingers. Finally a man had come in while the women had held her spread eagle and naked on the bed. He was dressed in the skin of another man, but his own sexual organs jutted out through a hole in the skin. He inspected Mercedes, his expressions hidden by the skin's face. At his signal, she was rolled over and spread eagled again. He felt the muscles of her rump. His fingers were like talons. At another signal, the women yanked apart the twin globes of her behind, exposing her. He inspected the double orifices displayed there. He poked one talon deep into her ass. Mercedes cried out in pain. He dug deeper, besides for a gasp, Mercedes was silent, not wanting to give him the pleasure of her pain. He slipped something from his pocket and secretly forced it deep inside of her. He grunted and left. The women bathed and dressed Mercedes. They seemed to be especially kind to her, for some reason. Elena remained kneeling by the bed, thankful at last that she was the underling.

Harv lowered the inflatable into the water. There didn't seem to be as many sharks in this bay. He threw in a pair of oars and told Jim and Charlie to climb aboard. Then he levered the still unconscious Hawk to the side of the *Rose Marie* and dropped him into the dinghy. He really didn't care if the man fell into the water or not. Naomi gently lowered herself into the already overloaded dinghy. Harv put one foot on the side of the boat. Water flowed over the side. The little boat was overloaded. He couldn't let them go by themselves, he wouldn't get his transport back.

"Dad, I'll take the dinghy in. That man is practically dead. He can't hurt me. I'm light enough so the boat will still float."

"Alright, but no tree climbing. Come right back, you hear? I want to get underway."

"Yes, Sir, Sir Daddy!"

Laboriously the dinghy approached the beach. There was a swell running which crashed on the beach with an audible roar. Jill did a fine job lining the dinghy up to the surf. The swell picked them up and Jill guided them in with just a touch of the oars here and there. They dragged the dinghy up on the beach and Hawk, who seemed to be recovering, fell out onto the beach and crawled up towards the forest. Jill spotted a tall tree and was off in a flash. Before she could grab the lower branches, Naomi grabbed her arm with surprising strength and whispered something into her ear. Jill looked back at her parents on the *Rose Marie* and shook her head at Naomi. Hawk who was recovering faster the farther he was from Janet, seized Jill's other arm and pulled her into the jungle despite Jill's efforts to escape. Jim and Charlie followed. Within five minutes, the beach looked like it had been abandoned for a decade save for a little inflatable dinghy left stranded on the sand.

Ixtolic tired of the fat one. He ordered him thrown back into the cage. He pointed at the little man and leered at the woman. He would enjoy doing her. He could see in her eyes that she would fight him. His brother might get the princess but he could have some fun too. The little man was already terrified after witnessing the last training. Ixtolic picked out a fresh bamboo switch and the little sacrifice started crying before he was even touched. That was no good. Inti, the sun god, didn't want weeping sacrifices. They wanted willing souls seeking to join him in the afterlife. Willing to offer themselves to the moon mother, Mama Kilya, so she would release Inti after eating him; the people needed the sun, they needed Inti to grow the crops. No weepers would get out of this room. This land had no need of cry babies. He flung himself at the small man. He switched and whipped him over and over again. Soon blood seeped out from between the toes and the arches of his feet. Tiring he gave the switch to a trainee and instructed him on the proper grip. The trainee looked at the blood splattered floor, the sacrifice who had long since fainted and the blood saturated switch

and threw up. Ixtolic howled in frustration and started kicking the trainee. The door opened with a crash. His brother
strutted in. Behind him, slaves carried a naked body, a beautifully muscled, handsome youth with a stake embedded in the back of his head.

"Why have you killed this one? He would have been a wonderful sacrifice. Look at him, or look at what you left of him. This is your idea of honoring the gods? You are pathetic. You are replaced. Go to your cave and remain there till I call for you to replace this boy as a sacrifice. Go now!" Ixtolic picked up the bloody switch and swung it this way and that while eying his brother.

"Guards, seize this impostor. He is not your Master. He is one of these sacrifices trying to escape. Get him quick!" The guards stood with their mouths hanging open, heads swinging from one man to the other. The Master straightened himself up to his full height.

"Do not listen to this man. He will allow Inti to be eaten! What will we do without sunlight? This man will kill you all! I have been your Master for years. Has life been good?" A few guards nodded. "Yes. You are right. Think what life will be like with eternal night. Nothing to eat. Mold will take over the caves. Children will be born blind. Is this what you want?" Ixtolic snarled.

"Master. Is that what you call yourself? You who allow off islanders to walk over our lands, to dirty our souls. They couple together in the privacy of their caves! Sin! Terrible sin! All know that to take a woman alone leads to the madness of possession. Soon the private couple will want a better cave, want more food, want more for themselves. All here know that Inti instructs us to love one another in the light of his face, in the sight of all. Privacy encourages rebellion. Is that your sin, Master?" The last word was laden with sarcasm. "Do you wish to run this island from the isolation of your cave?

"Guards, seize this man! He impugns the high office of Inti! He must accept Inti's grace by sacrificing himself. Seize him before he corrupts your souls and sends you to Inti's knife!" The guards still looked bewildered. The Master turned and left the cave room leaving a sneering Ixtolic behind. Ixtolic turned to his men. "You did well to resist the betrayer. For your bravery, you may have this one for your toy. He kicked the little body of Erhart in the ribs. He turned and looked at Mary and licked his lips.

The Prospector moved slower than a snail. He looked everywhere before he moved a millimeter. His feet were still hanging out of the cave mouth. Robyn was cooling her heels with her back against the rock wall.

"Damn, Stud. I am likely to starve to death out here if you don't get a move on. Snares are all mathematical progressions. If they weren't, no one could remember them." A voice came echoing out of the cave.

"Margaret, what the hell are you talking about? This is damn tricky. If you think you can do better, I would like to see you try." Robyn smiled to herself. 'Men, all balls and no brains.'

"Well, come on out of there and let an expert show you how it is done." The Prospector was only too happy to come out. He hated caves, especially caves that didn't have timber supporting the roof, like this one.

"Ok, big boy. Watch a woman do it. Be sure to follow exactly in my footsteps. Don't touch the walls and especially the ceiling. OK?" Her Stud agreed and stepped behind her. Robyn stripped naked.

"Take off all your clothes. You can control your body, but the whish of clothing might set off an unfortunate series of events." The Prospector quickly striped and thought that this was the way to lead troops into battle. The view of Robyn from behind was mesmerizing. "And Stud, watch my feet, not my derriere." She moved into the cave like a dancer. She never stayed in one spot more than a second. Her clothes were tied to the small of her back.

"It's the rhythm, Stud. It is a dance. All thieves have great rhythm. Follow my lead." The Prospector tried the best he could, he was distracted by the lure of Robyn's charms in full display. He supposed she would be upset if he took her right now, here in the cave. A cave full of snares and booby traps. But he sure wanted to. Who ever said that males were overly logical? Desire was at the core of a male. Suddenly Robyn stopped her dance in mid step. She stepped back over his then crouched body, almost protectively, and whispered to him.

"Don't move. We have visitors."

I don't care about sharks, Harv. My daughter is on that island and I am going to get her back so get out of my way, now!" Harv looked at her sadly.

"Janet, I am the better and faster swimmer. I am going for the dinghy, not you. Understand? You are going to sit here in perfect obedience until I return. OK? If not, then I will have to tie you up."

"You and what army? Get the fuck out of my way, Harv!" He saw her waist start to broaden and her eyes start to redden. He let his shoulders sag in defeat. Then he brought his right fist up from his knees in a perfect bone crushing jawbreaker. As he expected, Janet easily avoided the obvious blow but not his left hand which seized her arm and twilled her around to land on his knees butt up. He spanked her tight behind once, twice, three times. Then lowered her onto the cockpit floor.

"I'm Captain, Janet. You have to learn to obey. Stay here till I return. Got it?" Janet rubbed her right cheek lightly. It really stung. Her eyes had returned to their normal brown. She held back a sniffle.

"Why didn't you just tell me, so go already." He dove in the ocean off the side of the boat in a racing dive. He swam as fast as he possibly could.

The sharks must have been elsewhere or he thought he remembered Jim saying that it was only in Chatham Bay that the sharks were so aggressive. In any case, it was an non-eventful swim to the beach. He shoved the dinghy back into the water and rowed out to his boat and his waiting bride. He loved her so much. Well, he loved who she used to be.

Nowadays, she was becoming different, more assertive, more commanding, more male he guessed. He wondered if males really were different from females down deep where it counted. Sure they were more aggressive, and females more forgiving, but when the shit hits the fan, things seem to change. Then, males look around for something to hit or kill, while females, not having the same strength, key in on the essential connection that, if severed, send the enemies' deck of cards fluttering to the ground in complete disarray. By the time he returned to the boat, Janet had two backpacks loaded with gear and jumped into the dinghy with them, ready to rock and roll. He could see her left eye was already smoldering.

Jill kicked Naomi on the ankle and then shoved her over as she raced for the nearest tree. She didn't have to go far. They were lost in a jungle with rain pouring down, seemingly endlessly. Away from Janet, Hawk had recovered quickly.

"Let the stupid brat go. She is of no help. She will be as lost in this rotten jungle as we are and her parents will never leave without her. Fuck her. We will still have the boat." No one else had the strength to oppose him. The heat and liquid humidity of the jungle were oppressive. Jim Banks looked up at the canopy and judged the area of greater luminosity.

"I believe we have to turn slightly to the left. The slope of this hill is pushing us off course." Hawk snarled.

"Who the fuck asked you? Who wants anything from a former Captain? A mutineer? A disobeyer? Fuck you!" Jim looked shocked and then sat down on a log and let the rain run over his body unabated. The others continued on, only Naomi looked back in sorrow.

Charlie wasn't doing so well. He thought that treasure hunting would be as easy as digging up a couple of shovel loads of dirt on a beautiful sunlit beach and walking away a rich man. It didn't seem to be working out that way. He wished so much that he could be back in Key West, second in command of a major yacht. His life had been so good then.

Naomi eyed Hawk. He was returning to his former self, full of overconfidence and intolerance. He didn't seem to care that they were lost. He just kept bashing ahead like it was the jungle that was the enemy. She had seen him win many battles the same way, so she followed in his shadow hoping when the time came she could grab a few crumbs.

Jill watched them disappear in the rain and vegetation. They were going to get themselves so lost. Not that she cared. She knew where she was. She was in heaven. She eyed a vine hanging from a tall tree and without a moments hesitation, leaped off her branch, grabbed the vine and yodeled like Tarzan as she swung through the jungle to another branch. This was the life!

He didn't mind defecating and urinating in his pants. There wasn't anything he could do about it anyway. It was up to him to be in fighting trim if he ever managed to get free. And fighting trim didn't mean having to stop and take a shit. Besides, it was a good distracter. Most people, when they smelled human waste, closed their eyes and averted their heads. Perfect time for a counterattack! His feeders were careful never to get too close to him. They knew who he was, a prime male. A killing machine. Alpha to their sad little betas. They fed him carefully, never getting close enough to be grabbed. No doubt they feared he might eat them. Who knew? If it was a cute enough little tart, he just might eat her up. Tastes like honey.

It was getting dark now and everyone was busy hanging up decorations. Coffins containing nothing but a few old bones were moved to areas with good visibility. He narrowed his eyes as the coffins were draped with gold. The guy with the fake skin was everywhere. Organizing, directing. He placed guards at key locations and seemed to spend a lot of time giving them instructions. The wooden crucifix still lay of the stage, waiting.

The Prospector lay as still as the dead. Robyn knelt over him, frozen in place, and tried to ignore those ahead of them. They were locals, cave dwellers, snare setters, whatever. They seemed to be resetting all the traps at an intersection of four tunnels. A thin light of a fading sun displayed their emancipated bodies. The harvests must have been bad. Unrest, no doubt, was rampant. One was well fed, the one giving the orders. Robyn watched them carefully from the corner of one eye. She noted the placement of the new booby traps and where their triggers were. Finished, the group moved up a side tunnel and disappeared. Robyn smiled at her man below her legs, her naked tush tickling his nose.

"So, now's your chance to ravish me, if you want."

"Robyn," he whispered, "what are you talking about? Have you lost all measure of self preservation?" She smiled at him.

"Ok, I gave you your chance. Don't ever say I'm not willing. It wasn't me who said no. Just remember that." The Prospector closed his eyes and took a deep breath.

"Alright, it was me who chickened out. Now since it seems to be you leading this scouting expedition, what's next?" He raised his eyebrows as he looked up at her above him. At her face framed between a perfect set of breasts.

""Lets go see what's in those other tunnels. Might be something interesting, hmm?"

Jill was having the time of her life. For a while. Problem was, there wasn't an audience. Her mother wasn't there to smile at her. Her father wasn't around to tell her to be careful. It was boring and she was getting hungry. She swung through the trees for a bit going this way and that. It didn't help. She was getting really lonely. With a sniffle she decided to go back to the *Rose Marie*. Wouldn't her parents be happy to see her! The hugs, the sweet tears! Her father would be so proud of her for getting away from the bad guys! She looked around and realized that she was lost. She reached down the front of her blouse and pulled out her GPS that her father had given her for her birthday. She had marked a waypoint with the position of the *Rose Marie* when no one was looking. She noted the direction she had to go and returned the instrument on its lanyard around her neck. Now that she wasn't swinging this way and that endlessly, the insects started to find her, and to bite her skin.

"Arg! Jane no like bite!" And off she went again swinging through the jungle her face a study of contentment and joy.

Ixtolic had left the woman sacrifice for later. He and his men rushed out and started changing the snares and booby traps in the tunnels. If his brother, the oh, so, high and mighty 'Master', thought he could beat him, he was terribly mistaken. Who did he think had been doing the grunt work around here? Who knew the caves like no one else? Stupid brother. Anyway, he had always pushed little kids around when they were younger, including him. The big bully.

Soon, every trap was changed. Only he and his little army could move around easily. He was getting ready to head back for the confrontation when he heard a bellowing coming from the outside.

Hawk had stubbed his sore toe. It hurt. He yelled and screamed and hopped around on one foot. This jungle, the frustration of it, was just too much. He was used to fighting in boardrooms and offices, not in an unending shower while being bitten by millions of insects. It was all just too much. He let out an extra loud bellow just to get rid of some of his anger. When he looked up from examining his toe he saw a cave in a rock face. He was sure that cave hadn't been there before, but beggars can't be choosers.

"Everyone. Cave. Look. Get yourselves in there before the rain washes us away to skinless skeletons." Naomi said nothing and followed along in Hawk's footsteps. Charlie seemed about to speak up but with a

sigh descended again down the long road of despondency. As the trio approached the entrance, Hawk stopped and eyed the cave warily.

"Charlie. We need a good man here, a navigator. Here, you go first and check out our little shelter." He grabbed Charlie's arm with one of his huge hands, levered and pushed him forward and towards the cave. Charlie didn't care. He plodded into the dark entrance.

I

Ixtolic stared in amazement. He grabbed one of his men around the neck in his excitement and had half killed him before he came back to his senses. That man, the one with the white hair and beard, he had the biggest hands he had ever seen! What a sacrifice! Everyone had seen men crucified, women gang raped until their insides were torn apart and they bled to death, men arched over the altar to give up their lives and hearts to Inti. But this! Imagine! He could cut off this ones hands and pass them around to the crowd to play with, and then cut this one's heart out for the gods. He wondered if his heart was as large as his hands! What a coup! His brother couldn't offer anything half as good!

"Guards, open the door, let them come into the mountain, then close the door behind them. I want to take these sacrifices unharmed. Not a hair on their heads! Understand? Disarm the snares. I want them alive!" His men moved to obey. That is when he saw the woman behind the man. He recognized her instantly, of course. He had heard the stories. His great, great grandfather had traveled to the mainland and returned with such a one. With the same fold on the neck. That one had been offered to the gods for five days straight before she had joined Inti. His great, great grandfather had not been Master then, but after his offering all had obeyed only him. And here, offered on a single platter were two great sacrifices! Oh, this was going to be a great year!

"Guards. Take great care of the woman. After she is captured, bring her to my cave room. I wish to examine her. After that, close all portals. I want this mountain closed up tight. No one goes in, no one goes out. Got it?"

Janet was transformed. She lifted herself from the dinghy with just the tips of her fingertips. Only the tips of her toes touched the beach as she raced towards the jungle. She seemed to slip through the trees and vines as if they didn't exist. The whites of her eyes shown all around her pupils. Electricity seemed to surround her body. If the Sensei in Acapulco saw her now, he would be very frightened. Her aura was deep red with streaks of black. The blackest black imaginable. It didn't take her long to find Jim Banks. She grabbed him by the hair and lifted him up from the log he had been sitting on as easily as if he had been but a toy. He stared at her in fear as his feet dangled uselessly. Her pupils were fire red with streaks of yellow radiating outwards.

"Where. Is. My. Daughter." The words were like thunder claps. "She escaped. She ran away and climbed up a tree and we couldn't find her. The others they went that way." He pointed to an obvious trail that had been bashed through the jungle. "I, I decided to stay here. Hawkins and I, we don't seem to get along anymore. I'm sorry I don't know more. Would you like me to help you search?" Harv appeared after racing along the trail that was getting more obvious with each passage.

"Harv, you and Jim search for Jill that way. If you find her, take her back to the boat. Got it?" Harv nodded to the command. And it was a command. He could barely recognize his wife. She was so different. He wanted to touch her, to reassure himself that it was really her. But he remembered the coldness in her body he had felt in Zihuatanejo and was afraid. Deathly afraid. And then, just like that, she was gone, racing after Hawk and his tribe. Her only thought, to punish. She had told him not to touch her family. He would live to regret his error, or rather he would die regretting it.

Harv helped Jim Banks up from where Janet had dropped him and the two of them worked their way through the jungle calling Jill's name.

He wore the skin of his older sister. It was a good skin. Good elasticity. Good tone. She had gone to Inti first, he had skinned her afterwards. He had asked her if he could first. She agreed. It was like part of her would still live here on earth. He looked out over his island as the sun sank down towards the horizon. He waited to see the eye of Inti, his green eye, as he looked over his world for a last time before morning. Behind him, his workers were readying the great hall for the celebration. He hoped it would be a celebration. There was always the thought, what if their offerings were not enough, what if Mama Kilya ate Inti for good, what if she refused to give him back to the people? What would become of them, then?

Of course, the ancients said that Mama Kilya was a huge moon that traveled between Inti and their world and at times accidentally blocked Inti's light. Such rubbish. Did they think he was such a fool? One look at Mama Kilya was enough to see that she changed her face every night, just like a woman, always changing her mind. How could a huge planet change its face. Ridiculous. Absurd.

Inside, he heard them shouting and yelling at each other. It was always the way. Everyone wanted to be first. He strolled back in and instantly felt the cold eyes of the golden goddess on him. Some fool had opened the curtain, letting the Golden One see their preparations.

"Close that curtain, you fools!" The cretins rushed to obey. How stupid could anyone be. Letting one god see the preparations for another. This was a preparation for Inti, not for the Golden One. True he would crucify a man for her, but that was just because the gods could be terribly jealous. Especially the female gods. Who really knew what powers the Golden One possessed? What armies she might command? What paladin might fight for her honor? The fools. He decided to throw the one responsible for opening the curtain off the mountain in punishment, but on a second thought, he decided to offer him up to Inti the next day. The ceremonies would start at first light. They had many sacrifices. Much blood to spill. Best to get started early. Wouldn't do to still be offering after Mama Kilya had regurgitated Inti. Wouldn't do at all.

Behind him, the green flash of the setting sun momentarily lit up the cave, painting all within it in weird hues, and then the light was gone. A flash and then nothing. Such is the way of the world.

It didn't take Jill long to figure out her directions. She thought using the GPS was cheating. She tried to remember her Tarzan movie reruns. She couldn't remember Tarzan, Jane or Boy ever using any GPS instruments. As soon as the sun started sinking in the west, she swung through the jungle away from the sun, to the east. From the tops of the trees, the sun was much easier to locate. Soon, she could see the blue of the sea peaking through a few of the leaves. She found a beautiful river and as she came out of the trees, saw it falling into the ocean in a beautiful waterfall. She checked her GPS. The *Rose Marie* was just on the other side of that hill. On the side of the cliff, a series of steps had been carved out of the solid rock descending to a lookout just over the river before the waterfall. Without a thought she skipped down the steps and on reaching the lookout jumped off in a flash, curled her legs to make a cannonball dive, and yelled 'Geronimo' all the way down. The current of the river quickly swept her over the waterfall and into the sea. Jill laughed and giggled in the bubbles in the base of the waterfall.

Once in the sea she saw her home, the trusty *Rose Marie* anchored peacefully right where they had left her, next to a beautiful beach. It was only a matter of minutes and Jill was aboard drying her hair with a nice fluffy towel. She thought it was funny that her parents weren't on board. Looking for her, no doubt, stumbling around in the dark. Didn't they know she could take care of herself? She made a big bowl of popcorn and settled down to watch one of her favorite videos, one about a Volkswagen that talked.

The tunnels branched off endlessly. The Prospector carved little archaic symbols at each branching. Robyn asked him what they meant but the explanation was so long and boring that she stopped listening as he continued to speak. The sound of his voice was reassuring, but the content was, well, it wasn't very interesting. She knew she couldn't tell him that. He would get all offended. She just listened to his voice, much as she would the sound of her car's engine, reassured that all was well. They found a small, room like, cave that had some bedding on the floor.

"Let's spend the night here, Stud. Whatcha say?" Her stud studied his watch and looked at her in surprise that she knew it was getting dark. She just pointed up at the small air holes far above them where the rainy sky was fading into night.

"What, you thought I was a psychic, too? Am I able to leap tall buildings and see through walls?" He just looked at her, wondering.

He was disappointed that they hadn't found any gold. The odor was all around them. It was as if every cave they had found had been filled with gold and just moved a few hours ago. Frustrating, that's what it was.

"It's frustrating. That's all. I mean we came here for gold and we can't find any. Very, very annoying."

"Don't worry your head about it. We'll find some tomorrow. Anyway, lay down here with me and dig around. Maybe you'll find something a lot nicer than any old dusty gold thing." She lay down, still naked.

They fell into each others arms while in a cave far above their heads another woman was in torment.

Mercedes sat on her night pot, her innards in an uproar. It felt like every bit of her body was exiting into the pot. They had given her something in her food or pushed something up into her. That much seemed to be clear. Some vile evil chemical that was making her poop till there was nothing left. Her belly was so slim, both from lack of content and the convulsions her stomach muscles were going through.

Elena gently rubbed her neck and shoulders. It didn't help the pain but Mercedes treasured it for the companionship, knowing that she wasn't alone. It seemed, almost, that she was being prepared for some show or exhibition or something. In a way, Mercedes had never been more beautiful. Her beautiful tan had not faded and her washing women had continued her habit of being shaved between her legs. She was so thin that it emphasized her already well developed breasts. Breasts that had been swelling since she had been on the island. The purge had created a wan look about her that made any man want to take her under his wing and care for her. But the pain!

Elena bit her lip in empathy when Mercedes screamed as her insides all seemed to expel themselves out through her anus. After each cramp Mercedes panted like she was going through childbirth. She worried so much about what they were going to do to her friend. Nothing else was coming out now, but still the purge made her cramp and scream and sweat, till her entire body vibrated from the exertion. Suddenly Mercedes screamed so hard that all screams before seemed to be just for practice. It was a scream of horror, of despair, of sadness, of horror, of gut wrenching agony. Her entire body convulsed. Her legs were somehow forced open and between them a little six inch long perfectly formed baby emerged, dead. Mercedes, thankfully fainted. Elena did what she could as she cried for her friend.

Hawk, still pushing Charlie before him, turned a corner of the cave and came face to face with mob of spear carrying locals. They did not look friendly. He glanced behind him. Another group had snuck up and his little group was trapped. They grabbed Charlie, hit him over the head and tied him up. They separated Hawk from Naomi. They tied each up, careful to avoid sticking them with the spear tips. Once secured, a bigger man appeared before them. He carefully inspected Hawk's hands. He pulled at each huge finger as if expecting that he was wearing a glove. He laid his hand on Hawk's breast, feeling his heart beat. His eyes widened in amazement.

He sliced the ribbon from Naomi's throat and gazed in rapture at what he found there. He reached up and pinched the little fold of skin between his thumb and a knuckle. The guards gasped as the fold turned pink and seemed to swell open before their eyes. Naomi closed her eyes and felt her knees weaken. She dropped her chin trying to protect herself. Ixtolic grabbed her long hair, his fingers spread to grasp as much hair as possible and pulled her head back, exposing her neck. He signaled two big men to take her arms, another to hold her tied arms.

"Take her to the holding cave and hold her there. Do not touch her. She is to be a great sacrifice."

I

Ixtolic had the guards bend the two women before him till they were on their knees and heads on the ground. They snuck looks of compassion at each other. Mary remembered the night on the boat when Naomi had kissed her. That seemed such a long time ago now. She licked her lips and winked at Naomi. At least she knew what was likely to happen.

Naomi was still in the dark. The room was illuminated by torchlight, it cast shadows, making small things huge and the man before them small.

He picked up a bamboo switch and tapped each woman on her exposed and naked ass. He tapped the their thighs and the guards pulled their legs apart. He tapped the exposed mound of their sex, once, twice, three times. Then without warning he sliced his whip against the soles of their feet. Mary struggled to remain quiet but Naomi, unprepared, gasped in pain. He turned all of his interest towards her. He whipped Naomi over and over again until her feet swelled up grotesquely. Mary tried to signal to her to remain quiet, but the tears in Naomi's eyes blocked her vision. After a few minutes, a change came over Naomi. Her nostrils flared and she stopped her weeping. The fold on her neck became red. The guards noticed that her vagina was swelling and a hint of moisture slipped through its lips. The guards pointed and Ixtolic stopped his whipping and got down on his knees to examine her.

"It is true then," he mumbled to himself. "She is a child of Paca Mama, the earth goddess. She is endlessly fruitful, always ready for the seed of man. This will be a truly wonderful sacrifice." He indicated for the guards to return Mary to her cage. This one, however, this one with the fold, she would require further study during this long night.

"Take this one to my cave and hold her there till I arrive."

They had Hawk and Charlie in the cage in the back of the room. Dustin and Erhart were huddled in the corner. Mary pretended to be comatose. Charlie had tried to talk to them. He shook them, his hand on their shoulders. They didn't respond. It was like they had withdrawn from this world and were just waiting for the next. Hawk ignored everyone. He paced back and forth, tossing his Santa Claus head this way and that. A door crashed open and a squadron of guards flooded into the room. They held spears against the two guards already there. A man wearing a human skin entered the room. He stared at Hawk, at his hands, at his head. He indicated a spot on the floor. The guards opened the cage and forced Hawk out into the main room. They bent him down in the position of obedience, on his knees and his forehead to the floor. Two guards stood on his wrists so the Master could get a good look at the man's hands. He looked at the hands, disdainfully looked at two bodies slumped in the corners and ignored Charlie. He indicated Hawk.

"Prepare," and walked out the door.

These guards didn't waste time. They kicked him in the balls, one after the other. They stuffed a cloth down his throat and poured water down his nose. They inserted long splinters down the tip of his penis where Inti would never see the wound. Hawk held out for a long time of constant abuse, fighting when he could get a limb free, but after two hours he was a sobbing wreck. After four, he resembled Dustin. Just waiting for death, ready for it and welcoming. Thrown back in the cage, Charlie tried to comfort him. It was like communing with a rock. There seemed to be nothing left inside. The man who liked to abuse had finally been abused.

Janet was not having a good time. This island was a nightmare. There was jungle everywhere. She had thought tropical islands were supposed to be like the one on Gilligan's Island, with grass shacks, lagoons, trails and fruit trees. There weren't even coconut trees here. Probably because it rained too much. She did see a few in the bay where they refilled with water. Not here. What a hassle. There was no sign of anyone. Not that she could tell. The jungle swallowed signs of her passage like magic. But she was determined. She bashed through the jungle as night fell, ignoring the cuts she received from thorns and the prickers embedded in every portion of bare skin. Every half hour she climbed the tallest tree she could find to take her bearings. It was an hour after dark when she got her break. There was a light on the top of a mountain. She thought she could see people up there decorating. Her upper eyelids lowered down, half covering her pupils. Those were the people who had her Jill! That Hawkins had taken her there and they were going to do unspeakable vile things to her young, innocent body. Her red eyes glowed in the dark. The insects took one look at her and left her alone.

With a growl of anger, Janet surged to the jungle floor and made her way towards the mountain. They would pay. They would all pay. It was like a mantra. She said it over and over to herself, getting angrier and angrier each time. Each time she said the mantra, that which was within her became stronger and stronger. The wounds on her skin healed almost as fast as they tore. Each step she took was stronger than the last. With every breath she inhaled, she seemed to grow into something else, something more powerful, something not quite human, something either god like, or a spawn of a devil.

Around midnight, Harv and Jim gave up. They hadn't seen the slightest sign of anyone. They thought that maybe, just maybe, Jill had escaped and had returned to the boat. Jim Banks had maintained a running log of their movements and guided them back to the beach. The dinghy was still there. Harv felt his shoulders sag. He had hoped Jill had gotten away. It wouldn't have taken much in a forest. That girl could climb like a monkey. But it hadn't happened. He sank down on the sand, defeated. Jim Banks cupped his hand, creating a tunnel between his palm and his fingers and examined the *Rose Marie* by looking through it. It was a technique first developed by Bartolomeo Baretta who discovered it and built the first gun sight for rifles which he sold to Napoleon, contributing greatly to the Emperor's successes. By looking through a narrow aperture, clarity was increased. Jim lowered his hands.

"Harv, did you leave a light on down below?" Harv looked at him in surprise.

"No, we are all very careful with power. Except for Jill. She loves to watch movies." Harv stared at his boat, afraid to hope.

"It does have that flickering common to a television and the same washed out grey light." He looked at Harv from the corner of his eyes. Harv grabbed his dinghy with a curse.

"Help me, Jim. I don't want to harm the hyperlon bottom any more than it already is." Soon the two men were rowing out to the *Rose Marie*. As they got closer, Harv was convinced that he could hear a movie playing, but he refused to get his hopes up. They tied up to the back of the boat and rushed to the cabin. There, fast asleep on the settee, was the little girl they had been searching for. She had made popcorn for herself and had discovered some secret cache of chocolate, some of which was smeared over her face. Harv had to go below and touch his daughter before he could allow himself to believe. He tenderly held his child's shoulder in his hand and bent down to kiss her. She mumbled something in her dream, something concerning someone named, Jane. He turned the TV off, covered her up with a thin sheet and returned to the cockpit and to Jim Banks.

"I supposed we should try to find Janet," He mumbled to Jim, keeping his voice down. Jim looked at him square in the face with both eyes.

"Nothing could be more counter productive. Right now you have one lost crew member. If you go ashore, you will have two. Chances are, your wife will check the beach, just as we did, and seeing the dinghy missing will assume you or your daughter are aboard."

"But how will she get out to the boat? She can't swim, it is night when sharks are more aggressive." Jim Banks patted Harv on the shoulder.

"We will take turns standing watch. No doubt she will halloo when she sees our lights. I'll take the first watch. Get some rest, Harv."

Dawn found her on top of the mountain. She stood there welcoming the daylight. She didn't know how she had climbed the peak. She remembered many rock faces with tiny cracks, the only imperfections. She had inserted her nails into the cracks and kept going. She faced loose scree where for every four steps up, she slip back three. She shimmied up natural rock chimneys, worked around overhanging ledges, leaped over ravines until she found herself here, on top, with nowhere else to go. Here she waited for daylight, chanting her mantra to herself.

And now the day was coming. There was light for her to kill. She had changed during the long night. All that was Janet was gone. In its stead, stood, either, an avenging angel or a devil from the bottom rung of hell. Her aura was almost all black now, a few streaks of red the only remnants of her humanity. Her eyes were black on black. The irises the exact shade of black as the pupils. Her body was never still. Her hair seemed to be slicked back into a helmet. Her fingers could no longer be straightened. But most of all, she projected a foreboding. A feeling of death come to pay Earth a visit, finally. An avenging angel to end this disease of the earth called man. Completely.

She waited for now. The time would come. The cusp, when all was balanced, when one thrust would tip it one way or the other. The time for her appearance. The time for them to pay. For them all to pay.

Daylight came shining down from an air hole far above them. Robyn squinted, her eyes shut, and squirreled deeper into her Stud's embrace. She ran her hand over his back. He was so strong, still so virile for a man on the wrong side of 50. She felt so safe next to him. So secure.

She finally opened her eyes and looked around. They were in some kind of cave with rugs or something under them. A small door led out to a hallway. A dark hallway. She looked up at her Stud. He should sleep. She had certainly used him last night. Not that he had minded. But still he should get his rest. Who knows? She might get the urge again soon. She slipped from his embrace and as quiet as the thief she was, she tiptoed to the hallway. It was empty. She gazed down. Her Stud had marked this turning as he had all the others. She didn't understand what the marks meant. It didn't matter. Women were naturally better in spatial navigation then men. They had to be. Back when they were Cro-Magnons, women had to find their way to fruit trees and to know which tree would be fruiting when. She could find her way. There had to be some fruit around here somewhere!

She slipped from doorway to doorway. The place was empty. Everyone must be up already, preparing for some feast or something, no doubt including enormous amounts of meat and potatoes and carrots and pie and coffee.

She stopped herself from thinking about food. Her stomach was growling so loud, it sounded like an alarm clock. Ten caves down the tunnel she hit pay dirt.

It was only a leftover piece of bread but to Robyn it tasted like ambrosia. Before she knew it, it was all gone and she had guilt. She had to bring something back for her Stud. It was only fair. She continued her prowling. A faint aroma aroused her interest. It came from somewhere just ahead.

With the dawn the ceremonies began. He wore a huge mask and a skin. It was the skin of the off islander, the one called, Tugs. He wondered if it was a sacrilege to wear a nonbeliever's skin on such an august occasion. He shrugged his shoulders. It didn't matter. He felt comfortable. Some skins retained an echo of their previous inhabitants. Not this one. This skin didn't seem to care. It smelled a little, though. Smelled like death. Appropriate.

The first sacrifice was a man who had taken the rain cloak of another. Everyone agreed that he should be offered, the man included. It was the best solution. They lived in too small a community to allow rifts to develop.

He held his head high as he came out. Everyone was there, the entire population of the mountain. They tried to act dignified, to honor him, but still there was a little shoving and pushing to get a good view. The first sacrifice was so important. He lay himself down of the altar.

The four stretchers held his arms and legs, but only as a matter of form. The knife came flashing down. He saw his own living heart held high just as the first rays of light struck the altar. He died with a smile on his lips. It had been well done. The blood from his body ran in twin culverts leading to the cliff where it spurted forth to fall on the rain clouds far below and to fertilize the land for further generations. The people cried out in approval. It was well done. His body was sent down a chute and his heart thrown on a fire to burn into smoke for the gods to enjoy.

He was being shaken awake. Blurrily he opened his eyes to see two liquid pools of light hanging inches from his nose. Something shook his shoulder yet again. The twin lights spoke.

"Dad! Wake up. Where is my Mom? Dad? Dad!" He blinked his eyes several times in succession and struggled to get up. His daughter was staring at him and was half sitting on his chest. Morning light was pouring through a port hole and suddenly he remembered his yesterday. His daughter! She was alright!

"Dad!" She was yanking at his shirt now. He still wore the filthy clothes from yesterday. He had been so tired he had instantly fallen asleep the second his head had touched the pillow. He hadn't relieved Jim Banks to watch for Janet. He rose up, much to Jill's satisfaction and stuck his head out of the hatch. Jim was still awake and was sipping a cup of coffee. He eyed Harv's head with a smile.

"No action on the beach, Sir. Everything is quiet." He looked a little bit tired, but content; it was as if he was used to spending hours and hours on watch.

"You should have woken me up." Jim just smiled.

"You looked too exhausted." A hand was pulling at his shirt again. Pulling hard.

"Dad! Where is my Mommy?" He looked down to a very concerned and worried pair of eyes. He gave his daughter a hug.

"She is looking all over the island for you, Kiddo. She freaked when that woman took you yesterday." His daughter snorted.

"Her? I could run rings around a woman like that when I was twelve! But, Dad. Lets get going. We have to find my Mom. She might be in trouble. Come on. I made you some coffee and I found some granola bars for breakfast. Daylight's burning, Dad, as Jack London used to say." Every bone and muscle in his body ached, but Harv couldn't find it within himself to say no to his prodigal daughter. The three of them crowded into the dinghy and rowed to the beach of the treasure island of Cocos.

Mary moved her hand very slowly till it shaded her face. She cracked open her eyes only enough to see through her eyelashes. It was morning. Surprisingly, there were no guards outside their cage. She could hear some cheering from somewhere down the tunnel. Beside her, Dustin and Erhart lay. She had to watch carefully to be sure they were breathing. They seemed almost dead. As if their souls had already left their bodies. She nudged Dustin in the stomach with her foot. With a shock, she realized he was dead. She shook him to be sure. She felt lost for a minute. "If I am going to get out of here, I going to have to do it myself." Charlie was asleep in an opposite corner. Hawk snored in the middle of the cage.

Footsteps echoed down the tunnel. Four men crashed into the room and opened the cage. They picked up Erhart and shoved some herb in his mouth and marched him out and down the tunnel. Mary's lab tech eyes instantly noticed that the lock hadn't closed all the way. She levered herself up and gave Hawk and Charlie a shake. They were still out of it. Either way, it was time to see what was what and she slipped out of the cage and turned down the tunnel away from the direction they had taken Erhart. Everywhere she looked there were caves and branching tunnels honeycombing into the mountain. She blinked her eyes, trying to jolt herself into full alertness. This would be no time to lose her bearings.

Naomi stretched her body in pleasure. What a night! She had lost count of the number and ways they had done it. She was a little sore between the legs and her butt was welted where he had whipped her when he couldn't get it up anymore. She smiled. She couldn't believe some women turned down their men when they wanted sex. Why not do it? And especially over and over again. It was so good after the third time. Sometimes she wished she could make love 24 hours a day for the rest of her life.

High above her, a hole in the cave let in a weak daylight. Maybe he was up for a morning surprise. She glanced over at his side of the bed but it was empty. With a sigh of disappointment she tried to rise only to find that she was tied hand and foot to the four corners of the bed.

She grunted in anger. She had to pee, badly. How mean of him. She tried to break the ropes. They were too strong.

'Fuck him!' And she let herself go and peed the bed.

It was a feast! A huge glorious feast! Platters and platters of food covered every table. Fish, fried fowl, fruit, beans, potatoes, and more that she had no idea of the names, but it sure tasted good. They must have searched every corner of the island to come up with such a meal. She shoved handfuls of food down her throat until she couldn't eat any more. With a sigh of contentment she leaned against the wall. Then misgivings crept into her little head. Whoever made this feast would be back soon. Best to skedaddle before they returned. She grabbed as much food as she could carry and returned to her Stud, keeping an eye out for a bathtub with bubbles or at least a hot shower with lots of shampoo. She giggled as a few pieces of food fell from her hands, not realizing that she was leaving a trail. There was a passage off to her left. On impulse, urged on by some female intuition, she wandered up it for a few feet. The murmur of crowds echoed down to her. She danced up the tunnel, avoiding the footfalls, snares and booby traps with ease. The addition of real food into her diet helped clear her mind. She didn't notice the traps had been disarmed.

Up ahead were many coffins, most draped with gold chains and gold candle sticks. Sparkling gems flowed over their sides, pieces of eights lay on the ground ready to be swept up by an alert custodian. She stared for a second and then looked down at her still naked body. Definitely a lack of pockets. Carefully she backtracked, marked the turnoff with a squeezed guava and glided back to her Stud and her clothes.

The guard that had opened the curtain allowing the golden one to see out was next. He was not as willing but the aides talked to him, explaining things to him. Reminding him that his wife was less than faithful during celebrations, that his kids were wild, that his people needed his blood. He finally came forth to the altar in resignation. The guards had to hold him down on the table as the knife flashed, but once the black obsidian knife flashed and the heart was held high, he died well. One of the off-islanders was next. A small man. He had been prepared well. He walked slowly on his sore feet as well might a sacrifice. He kept his eyes on the ground in front of him, the weed that brought him back to alertness was working a little too well. He smelled the burning hearts ahead of him and bucked a little. The guards were ready for him. Not a step was lost. They levered him easily onto the altar, the knob on the table forcing his chest high, opening the ribs. Just as the knife flashed, the sacrifice screamed. It was just for a second, but the audience gasped. This was not good. This was very bad. Everyone looked up at the face of Inti and swallowed their fear. Off to one side the barely visible outline of Mama Kilya seemed to surge towards Inti just a little faster.

She who used to be Janet, grunted. This mountain it sat on was full of power. Many souls had died to transform a pile of rock to a living source of spiritual power. It bathed in the radiance of the mountain. It grew stronger and its spirit surged within it. Still, within, was she who once was. It required little of its attention to keep her in check. Maybe tomorrow, it would eradicate her. No hurry. A minor soul at best. Nothing to worry about. It might die by then, saving it the trouble. It flexed its mental muscles and heard the nothings below it, in the mountain, gasp. One screamed. It smiled. They would soon die, but they would die for its glory, and to add to its power, till it could regain its ability to transform elements. To create anything, say, for example, gold out of lead. Or, more importantly, to create a universe obedient to it. To command, and all would obey. To blink, and men would die in terror. To raise an eyebrow and women would tremble throughout their bodies. To, finally, completely, be a god.

Jim Banks, Harv and Jill followed the now more obvious trail towards the middle of the island. Off to the southwest they thought they could hear a thin cheering. They hacked their way through the bush with the machetes from the *Rose Marie*. When they stopped for a breather, they ate granola bars from the boat. They were well supplied by having a vessel at their disposal. It wasn't long before they ran into a well beaten trail heading towards the mountain. The mountain they had heard the cheering emanate from. Jill was grumpy.

"Why are we acting like ants? Walking along these stupid trails like some sub mammalian species? Why aren't we brachiating like the apes that we are?" Her father looked at her in wonder.

"Brachiating?" She snorted and leaped up a tree, hence to a higher limb, grabbed a vine and swung on ahead down the trail with a Tarzan like howl.

"Dad, don't be a klutz, get up here." Harv looked at Jim. Jim stared at Jill swinging with ease over the jungle they had been bashing through.

"If you can't beat 'em, join 'em." Harv took a deep breath and leaped for the first branch and promptly fell on his bum. On his second try he managed to grab a vine before he fell. Jim didn't do much better. But after a few decades of minutes, they were brachiating with the best of them, struggling to keep up with Jill as she sped towards the mountain in the middle of the island, checking her GPS now and then.

Ixtolic saw his chance. The so-called Master had failed. His sacrifice had cried out in fear. Now was his chance. He stood up and moved towards a minor altar, one used for domestic requests. Women asking for a baby or men asking for respect. He signaled to his men and they brought the one called Charlie to the altar. He looked over the crowd and shouted as loud as he could.

"Behold now how sacrifices should be preformed. Behold!" He had told Charlie, in pantomime, that he was to be in a passion play and that afterwards he would be dined and wined until he was satisfied. Upon the altar, Charlie exhibited no signs of fear or stress. He smiled at the obsidian knife as it flashed above him. After, as his heart was raised above him, he lacked the strength to speak. He tried to raise a hand to his heart, to grab it and replace it in his chest, but it was too late. All who watched thought that he was raising his hand to Inti. All applauded the sacrifice. Ixtolic looked over the crowd at his brother and smiled at the discomfort he saw there. It didn't last long. His brother had more strength than that.

He ordered the big handed one brought out. They had tied his hands out in front of him so all could see. The crowd gasped. They stared at the hands. Women cowered and covered their breasts and hid behind others. Ixtolic stared at his prisoner taken from him by his brother. 'So, it was to be like that,' he thought. The Master strode forth and stopped the procession.

"All who need help in the fields, all who need help with the children or keeping the fruit trees in order, this is your sacrifice. Here is helping hands for you. Look at them!" The Master's warrior's held the sacrifice's hands up high. "These hands will be yours if you truly believe. Your labor will be cut in half! You will be able to sleep in the middle of the day as these hands do your work for you. Watch now as I make all this possible for you, my people."

They brought Hawk to the altar, but instead of lifting him up to the projecting rock, they held his hands, wrists down, on the altar and the Master, showing, at last, the true sharpness on obsidian, severed the wrist of the left arm in one motion. He picked up the bloody hand and threw it into the crowd. The crowd fought over it. One grabbed it, staring at the hugeness of it. One man formed it into a fist and held it high. They cheered for their true Master. The sacrifice had the stub of his left arm thrust into the fire to stop the blood. The gods wanted him to die on the altar, heart held high, in front of all, nothing hidden as was the way. The sacrifice knelt on the floor and held his right hand up in a fist with the tall finger extended and stared at the master. Ixtolic laughed at the sacrifice. His brother hadn't prepared him properly at all. Then he scowled. His Brother had broken the truce. He had stolen his captive. So be it. If that was the way he wanted to play...

The Prospector was still sleeping as Robyn dropped mango pieces into his mouth. He snorted and then bit down with his teeth. He grunted, blew mightily out of his nose and came awake. As was usual with him, there was no waking up period. One moment he was fast asleep, the next he was staring at her with those eyes that sent shivers down her spine, and if the truth be told, sent shivers elsewhere also. As he sat up, she popped a piece of pineapple in his yawning mouth.

"So why exactly didn't you take me here first, instead of starving me to death?" It was just too bad his brain didn't work as well as his body. She checked him out. His Studdliness was a bit stubby. He stared at her for a second vaguely chewing his pineapple as if he was wondering where it had come from. He finished and looked at her.

"Good. Taste good." Damn, men, good thing god made women so horny or the human race would have died out years ago. She squatted, her legs apart, grabbed a mango in her palm and tossed it between his legs.

"Eat. Food make strong. Get naked. Have party. Make baby." He stopped chewing.

"Say what?" Robyn raised her eyes to Mary in heaven who had to put up with two of these chromosome deficient humans.

"Eat the food and lets go and pick up the damn gold, bury it somewhere else, call for help on the satellite phone, get rescued, buy a boat, come back at night, dig up the gold and live like movie stars the rest of our lives in total luxury with 24 hour room service." He looked at her strangely.

"Gold?" Suddenly his brain seemed to kick in with sugar molecules finally racing to his brain. "You found the gold?" She smiled at him as his eyes focused at her with the full intensity of his fully awake personality. "You really did?" Robyn just smiled.

"You expected someone else, perhaps?"

Ixtolic was surprised that his brother brought out his big guns so soon. It was a mistake. But his brother had to believe that he, his younger brother was defeated. So he called for a woman that had stolen another's baby as she couldn't conceive for herself. She came out, unbound, head held low and allowed herself to be hoisted onto the altar of the women. Her legs and arms were spread wide and her clothes carefully removed from her. A hush of anticipation spread among the crowd. Ixtolic raised his hands.

"Who among you would like to be first to fertilize our land for the coming year? Who among you is brave enough? Who is strong enough?" It didn't take long for his guards to surge forward as well as other younger men. He nodded and they took her in ever orifice. She remained silent and accepted her death and a good woman should. She might have blinked back a tear as she was taken over and over again. At the last second, when her body was torn apart inside, she welcomed the obsidian knife as it slashed down, her tormented heart was thrown on the blazing fire and she left a sad, unhappy life.

His brother, the Master, glared at him. He looked at his guards and made a secret signal. As he did, everyone in the room heard a thumping behind the curtain. A hard, almost sub-audible, rhythmic thumping. The Golden One was angry about the last sacrifice.

The Prospector could hardly move his legs. He had gold doubloons in every pocket. Gold chains and pearl necklaces rose up his neck to his chin. His arms held golden chalices and candle sticks. He had tied the ends of the sleeves of his shirt and filled the arms with diamonds and rubies the size of robin eggs. Robyn was worse. She couldn't open her mouth without displaying hundreds of diamonds, she had gold foil wrapped around her arms and legs, golden daggers pinned her long hair high on her head, pieces of eight shared her bra with glowing flesh, and each finger was strewn with rings of gold. They worked their way out of the mountain. When they reached the door, Robyn did some of her thief trickery and the mountain opened for them. They stumbled out, struggling against the weight they carried but giggled and laughed as they continued their adventure. They left the door open behind them as it was just too much trouble to go through the rigmarole to close it.

Jill was in her element. She decided she didn't like to climb trees anymore, now she liked to swing between them. She stopped for a minute to let her father and Jim catch up. She looked at them smugly as they finally joined her on the branch of a huge tree.

"You men are going to have to keep up if you want to help me save Mom." She smiled, then, as happy as a teenager can sometimes be.

"We have veered to much to the left, little one. Can you guide us more right?" Jill beamed at him. Finally a man that treated her with respect. She nodded, grabbed a vine and was off before the men had gotten their breath.

The pounding behind the curtain was stronger now. He feared the Golden One like no other god. She was so demanding. He signaled for the Golden One's sacrifice to be brought out and as he approached seemingly tame from the stone cage, he ordered the curtain opened. The Golden One was flashing her eyes over the crowd, seemingly angry at the ceremonies. As the sacrifice was led up to the stage, he heard a commotion in the back of the room. His brother, Ixtolic was bringing out another sacrifice! The nerve! The heresy! The gods will be angry. He tried to ignore his brother and gave the signal to start the crucifixion. He turned to check out what his brother was doing. He saw the fold on the woman's neck and gasped. He didn't know that such still existed. Half gods themselves, they were the embodiment of the gods of love and fertility. Such were spoken of in hushed terms, by voices filled with awe, the nymphomaniacs.

A clatter made him turn. The sacrifice had not been properly prepared. He had grabbed two of the wooden nails and had killed his guards. It stood now, breathing easily, smiling at the crowd, waiting for their next move. He noted that the Golden One seemed to have calmed down, her eyes were no longer flashing around the room, they were aimed now only on the sacrifice, illuminating him, glorying in him. The crowd, eyes staring, stood still in shock. Behind them, Ixtolic stripped the woman naked and shouted to the crowd, asking who wanted to be first? The Master was loosing the momentum of the ceremonies. He signaled for his bride to be brought out. She came, dressed in a white robe, her face scared as a bride should be. He stripped his woman naked and the people gasped. No one had ever seen such a beauty. So thin, so sexy, such curves! Every eye was drawn by her incredible beauty, drawn away from the stage where the Seal was now trying to lift the Golden One. She was too heavy. Now he was attempting to pry a diamond out of the child's halo. Suddenly the Seal was thrown backwards by some unknown force. From his new vantage point the Seal saw the Hawkins kneeling by an altar holding his wrist close to his chest. The Hawkins who had cheated him. If he was to die here, Hawk would die also. He slipped over to him, ignored by the crowd staring at two beauties at opposite ends of the cave. In the midst of all the activity a high knelling was heard by all, coming from out in the sky just beyond the main altar where hearts burned on the coals, sending their scent high up into the sky.

Harv, Jill and Jim climbed up the tunnels, past the disabled snares and bobby traps, led on by the sounds of shouting from far above them. On the way up they met Mary coming down. She shouted at them as they passed.

"Follow the food on the floor. Watch out, there are many of them and they are killing people." Harv tried to stop her.

"Did you see my wife? A woman, five and a half foot tall up there? Did you?" She turned, just for a second.

"They are killing many women. Watch out, they are going crazy." The threesome continued climbing. Jim started to lag back. Harv turned to look at him in question.

"Maybe, someone should go back and watch the boat? I mean, anyone could just take it, and there where would we be?" Harv considered. A non-committed fighter would drag him back, make his fight harder, not easier. He eyed his daughter out of the corner of his eyes.

"All right. Best to take Jill with you. Sounds nasty up there." Jill stamped her foot.

"Oh, no! You are not going to hog all the fun! I am so going up there, too. After all, who saved you last time? Anyway, just try to stop me!" With that, Jill scampered up ahead, followed by her father. Jim stood in hesitation. Finally, he turned back and returned to the jungle. He had been trained to try to avoid storms if he could, to always save the ship and to send out rescue teams when anyone was in danger. The captain never was a member of such a team. Who, then would save the ship? For a sailor, the ship was all, without a ship, all was lost.

Naomi was enjoying herself. This was the life! One guy was fucking her while one was spurting in her mouth. She had two other cocks, one in each hand and was jerking them off. Two women were sucking her tits, two others, of unknown sex as yet, were rubbing her sore feet as they waited their turns. The guy fucking her finished and another took his place. He took the cream flooding out of her cunt and lubricated her ass. She forced herself back towards him as he entered her. It felt so good when he was in deep, but men always put it in halfway. They loved it when the sphincter muscles squeezed them. Very painful for the woman. In deeper, the cock released the sphincter, allowing the anus to stretch wide. In deep, he filled her insides with vibrating love that she felt throughout her body. Another, a woman was licking her clit. God, this was great!

The altar was clear and then, suddenly, this Being stood there. There on the altar. It had flown in from the sky. Few noticed the rope hanging from above. The Being eyed Hawkins. He was slowly, painfully, being throttled by a large male. It pushed this male away with the power in its mind. The Seal was tossed into the crowd who hammered and yanked at him and tried to force him back towards the cross. He looked back at the altar. The thing up there had easily tossed the Hawkins onto the altar with one hand. Hawk's chest was forced high by the mound on the altar. The thing up there didn't even look for a knife. It forced its hand through the belly muscles, up under the ribs, grabbed Hawk's heart and tore it out of his chest. It looked at the heart for a instant, half expecting it to be black and then shoved in down Hawk's mouth and throat. Thus died a man that had been so cruel to others. He died meekly and without a fight. With a sarcastic snort, It looked around the cave and, not seeing a small girl, turned to leave.

Ixtolic signaled to his guards. What a sacrifice! He had to have such a one. He wasn't sure if it was male or female. It had the body of a female but moved and acted male-like. An offering to Inti and Mama Kilya both at one time! He spotted his brother. He was trying to make love to his new bride but he couldn't get it up with all the disturbances! What a joke of a leader! He would show everyone how it was done.

The Seal easily killed everyone around him, anyone who tried to restrict his motions. A ten foot circle, empty of anything living surrounded him. He moved towards the coffins, eyeing the piles of gold draped over them.

A hush came over the cave. All looked up into the sky through special viewing holes. It had started! Quickly, it grew dark. Keen eyes could see that much more than half of Inti was gone. They had been fighting among themselves as their god was being devoured!

In the dark, the gems of the Golden One shone from the reflected light of hundreds of torches set up for the celebration. The Golden One seemed to enjoy her sacrifice as he killed and maimed those who did not honor her below her feet. Ten well armed guards moved in and surrounded the Seal. Up by the altar, that who once was Janet leaned against a wall and watched the coming battle with a faint smile on its face, might as well enjoy the show, now that it was here.

Jill and Harv came around the last corner of the tunnel to a bloody free-for-all where there seemed to be no rules. Jill saw the most beautiful woman in the world held down on a bed by ruffians as some old guy was trying to stick it in her. In the middle a huge, very well built guy was defending himself against ten guards plus a few civilians. In the back a woman was being gang raped by a huge crowd. Here and there people seemed to fight with each other over nothing more than the ability to see the different shows. Far across the cave she saw what had to be her mother. The person there looked a little like her mother but didn't act like her. Right now her mother was laughing as the big guy grabbed two of the guards and smashed their heads together.

Her mother had her thumbs stuck in the front of her trousers, fingers curled down towards her crotch, she leaned against the wall by keeping her back as stiff as a board and with only the tops of her shoulders touching the stone. Her legs were spread open, knees locked, bracing her. When she looked from here to there she moved her head to change her view instead of moving her eyes within their sockets. Her eyes were strange. It looked almost like they had turned black with red streaks. Jill turned to her father but he wasn't there. She looked around her wildly. Finally she saw him working his way through the mob towards his wife.

It was hard going carrying all the gold. It was very heavy and the jungle was thick. Luckily, they had found a trail that seemed to lead towards Chatham Bay. After a while it petered out and they were back to bending and pushing their way through. The Prospector called for a stop by a huge tree. Robyn sat down gladly.

"Babe, we have to bury some of the treasure here. We will never make it to the beach with this much weight. Keep the gems, bury the gold. Besides, we really don't want to bury everything in one spot. This treasure is just too big to put into one basket." Robyn was eager to obey. She didn't have her Stud's strength and she had picked up as much treasure she could carry standing still, too heavy to carry while forcing herself through a jungle. As they dug the Prospector seemed to become more interested in the digging.

"This is deep enough, Stud, don't you think?" The Prospector didn't stop. He continued to scooping dirt out of the hole with his hands.

"Just a little deeper, Babe. I feel something, its vague but I can sense it, somewhere here." The deeper they dug, the more excited he became. Finally their hands hit wood planks. It was only a matter of minutes for the excited couple to clear the dirt and yank off the cover. There under their unbelieving eyes was a casket full to the top with golden doubloons! The Prospector held one up and smelled it with great pleasure. Robyn came form an older school, she bit one with her eye teeth and gazed at the dent her teeth had caused with glee. Only pure gold was soft enough to dent with teeth. They stared at each other in astonished pleasure until Robyn picked up a double handful of coins and let them shower over her face. Her Stud forced his hand down through the coins trying to judge the amount of gold before him. His arm was elbow deep before he hit the bottom. With a feeling of regret, he replaced the top, added their paltry bits of gold on top of the lid and buried the whole lot. He and Robyn took great care disguising the treasure spot. Finally, when they were finished, they stuffed their gems into their pockets and continued down towards the beach.

Elena wished she could do something. Her friend Mercedes was being tormented. This old guy couldn't get it up and he was blaming Mercedes! First he shouted at her, telling her that everyone was watching, that it was her duty to help him perform. Her sister-in-adventure, Mercedes was so tired from pooping all night, and then giving birth, there was little she could do. When he started to spank Mercedes on the bum, Elena moved. She had been kneeling obediently by the side of the bed as she was told to do. When he started to hit Mercedes, Elena shuffled over to the man and before he could complain, took him into her mouth.

She had never liked oral sex in this world of aids and STDs, but now she just wanted to save her friend. The man seemed ready to slap her face, but then he had started to grow. He smiled down at the little slave girl then and snaked his fingers through her hair and forced his limp cock down her throat. She swallowed in surprise and as her throat convulsed against the foreign object, he grew to full length finally. He kept her poor face jammed against his belly sending his growing cock deeper down her throat. As she started to throw up he pulled out and gazed in happiness at his erect organ. He started to mount the body of Mercedes and the Golden One started to thump against the floor again. She shone in all her glory in the torchlight while the sun was hidden in the eclipse. He felt his organ deflate again. He heard a man laugh. Laugh at him! It was the sacrifice! The one to be crucified! No wonder the Golden One was in such a foul humor. He shouted out to all in the cave.

"Crucify the big stranger, quickly before Inti is gone forever." His people obeyed. They might have their squabbles, but they always came together in times of danger. The man was still laughing. Laughing as he killed right and left, laughing as he drove his wooden nails into skulls. Finally there were too many of them and they bore the Seal down under their weight. They called for the cross and dragged him on top of it. The nails and the hammer were retrieved and his arms held by the weight of fifty. One jabbed the nail into his wrist and another raised the hammer. A sudden coldness flooded into the cave. A fearful wave of terror seized each and every person.

It strode away from the wall. It walked on the tips of its toes, lightly like a ballerina, balanced like a sumo wrestler. Everyone crabbed sideways to stay out of its way. It raised its hand and the nails and hammer were thrown against the far wall. It flicked it fingers in a shooing motion that one might use for flies. All fled involuntarily, to cower against the far wall, far from its eyes, from its fingers, from its spirit. All save for one that walked towards it. It was an off islander. A stranger. Not a sacrifice, he walked with alertness and courage.

It raised its hand and the stranger was thrown against a wall. He picked himself up and walked back towards it. The air was freezing. Icicles started to form on the walls in the moisture laden cave. The closer he came to it, the colder it got. His skin started to turn blue, ice froze covering his eyebrows. Still he walked closer. He bent towards it, like walking against a high wind. It raised its hand and the man was forced back. The people against the far wall started to freeze. It was so cold in the cave now, people started to sneeze, they who had never seen ice in their entire lives. Slowly, then more rapidly, they began to cough. They didn't know what was happening. None of them had ever been exposed to germs, ever. They had lived in isolation for over a century.

The Seal had picked himself up off the floor, off the cross. He spotted a coffin, covered in gold, against a wall. He stretched his muscles and walked well around the thing in the center of the cave and grabbing a gourd container, started filling it with gold.

Harv was within ten feet of it which used to be his wife. He couldn't get any closer, he hadn't the strength. It couldn't kill him. Something within itself, forbid it. They stood eyeballs locked, frozen in place when off to the left came a strange sound.

"AHHHhaaahaAHHHA." A small body, swinging on a tapestry, zoomed in screaming to her heart's content. She dropped to the floor and rushed in and hugged it which used to be her mother. It lacked the time to stop the child, and something within stopped it from killing with its mind. The little girl hugged and hugged it, binding up its arms and legs.

Ixtolic was coughing badly now. He could hardly get a breath. His brother was dressed in the skin of Tugs, a skin riddled with the diseases of the slums of the world, activated by the cold, spreading out its microbes, killing all in the room. Ixtolic's thought his last as he lay dying.

"Who now would care for the minor gods and for the treasures of the gods? Who now would pray and sacrifice for Inti?" He decided it didn't matter. The proper sacrifices had not been made. Inti was consumed. He looked around him and all was black. Even the torches had gone out. He had failed. His brother had failed. All were dead.

Elena helped Mercedes get out of the bed. she wrapped her in a sheet and cuddled with her trying to keep warm. Naomi was alone. Everyone around her lay dying on the floor.

"Damn, I hardly got started and they are all worn out already. Shit." The Seal had filled his gourd to the top and was suddenly drawn back to the center of the room. The thing there was calling him.

"Kill this girl and this man and I will reward you beyond your wildest dreams." The Seal just stared at it. He only worked when payed in advance. And anyway, after his last employer, he might take a breather, especially after seeing all this gold. The Seal looked down at the little girl.

"She is my mother, Sir. She is lost. She can't get back. Could you please help?" Fuck, he would love to help but what did he know about lost women? Killing them sure, but saving them?

It sensed that the Seal was not an ally. It reached out to control him also, and in doing so, it lost a little of its control over the one called Harv. He was forcing himself closer and closer to its body. The little female, it knew suddenly, somehow that her name was Jill was hugging it ever tighter. She pulled the Seal in closer hoping to get him to remove the girl.

The man had reached it. He was kissing it on the mouth. Its eyes flared at him and with a last bit of strength, it threw him from it. It was of no use. This one, it knew now it was called Harv, came back, fighting against its power. Its weakening power. This Harv was kissing it again. He was crying out to someone called Janet.

"I know you are in there, Janet. I know it. Fight against this thing. You are a strong, powerful woman in your own right. You can do it. I know you can! Don't give up. Fight Babe. Fight!" It felt weak. It started to sag. Its black on black eyes faded to blue, but still within, it struggled to survive. It released the one within and let her rise to consciousness.

"Oh, Harv! Jill! I have missed you so much, so much! She kissed her husband on the mouth. Within her, it felt the moment was right. It gathered its power and surged towards the mouth. It needed a new body.

This one was too self willed for it, it resisted too much. This husband, he would be better. It got along better with males anyway. Time to switch homes! As its old body kissed, it surged towards the mouth.

Janet felt it coming. She remembered when that Larry had kissed her, how the thing had gotten inside of her then. She couldn't let it have Harv! Not Harv, not her lover and husband. No! It couldn't have her Harv. In a smooth motion, she rose her body, turned and kissed the Seal who was right behind her, square on the mouth. He seemed surprised to be kissed by a beautiful woman. He didn't complain. Hell, he enjoyed it. He closed his eyes to get right into it and didn't notice the pale smoke that slipped from the woman into to him. Janet fainted. Harv and Jill carried her out to the light of the sun just returning from the depths of the eclipse. The threesome looked up and smiled as the warmth of Inti glowed into them. They ignored the cauldron, now extinguished, topped by human hearts. They gazed instead, past the jungle, over the hills, out to the ocean, where in a little bay the *Rose Marie* was anchored, patiently waiting their return.

Epilogue

We live not for gold or fame,

we live to pursue them.

It is not your house, your job, your car, your wife. It is not your accomplishments, your deeds, your successes.

The reason to live, is to experience joy.
That's it.
That is why we are here.
Cool, huh?

It took the Prospector some time to get anyone to even talk to him. No one seemed to care what happened on a small island in the Pacific.

He eyed the phone battery level worriedly. He looked out at the ocean from the beach at Chatham Bay and turned off the phone to think for a second and to let the battery recover. A shout came echoing down from a hill high above them. It was Robyn that spotted them. Two women were waving at them.

They had already buried their gems in a great but well hidden spot close to the bay, they climbed up the hill and found a side trail where one had never been seen before. A little while after, they were greeted by the smell of cooking and by two showered and freshly clothed women.

"We saw that you have a sat phone, how wonderful! But first, come, sit down, have something to eat."

"Yes! Absolutely! How wonderful!" The Prospector gazed at Robyn in amazement, she should weigh over 200 pounds with the food she ate, but he doubted she tipped the scales at over 118. After the meal, Elena called up Lieutenant Dominic Ferer in San Jose on his private line. He promised to send a helicopter immediately, especially after Elena told him they had found tons of gold and the Virgin of Lima.

Mary met Jim Banks at the beach in front of the *Rose Marie.* She wanted to go aboard right away, to get off this cursed island, but Jim wouldn't let her.

"It isn't my vessel. We must wait for the Captain to return. It is the law of the Sea." Luckily it wasn't long before they heard a Tarzan yodel coming closer and closer. Jill landed lightly on the tips of her toes in front of the couple.

"Hi! If you are waiting for my Dad, he will be a few minutes more. But if you are waiting for my Mom, then you are in luck!" From out of the tree tops a sexy shape dropped to the sand. Jill rushed to greet her.

"Mom, you are so, so cool!" Janet, with eyes of blue, with an aura of violet smiled down at her daughter and hugged her with laughter seeping out of every pore. If the Master from Acapulco was there, he would have told Janet that her aura was now violet. And that violet auras belong to visionaries of the highest level, souls who can change the world by just envisioning clearly a better way and telling others how to travel the path.

Harv finally broke out of the jungle where he had been traveling along on the ground much to the dismay of his daughter. His heart soared seeing his family and his boat well and sound. Janet smiled at him and molded herself to him in a long passionate kiss. As he broke the embrace, she looked at him, her eyes tearing up.

"Thanks, Honey. I can never repay. Ever. You are so noble, so wonderful." She reached out and grabbed her daughter around the shoulders and gathered her into their embrace. "Both of you saved me. Thank you. Thank you ever so much. Thanks. Words are so inadequate. I am yours, my family, my heart and soul are yours for all eternity." The three were united in love, experience, and most of all in shared moments of joy.

The five of them rowed out to the *Rose Marie*, weighed the anchor, set the sails and departed Cocos Island for Costa Rica and restaurants, grocery stores and a DVD parlor to buy Tarzan movies.

On the trip back to the mainland, Janet occasionally glanced in the mirror and an echo reflected from her eyes. A thought came to her that given the ability to kill, a person can't stop him or herself from falling down into a pit of despair and unhappiness.

The Seal had found love late in his life. Naomi had found paradise in her lover's arms. He was such a great lover, finally a man that could satisfy her in every way. She only needed to do it ten times a day now. If sometimes his eyes turned red and he was violent and aggressive, that was just the way it was. She was used to living with violent men. The two of them closed the rock doors, built by the Incas, now all dead. They sealed up the mountain and lost themselves in their love and passion for each other. They had all they needed. And if they ever wanted anything else, they had all the money in the world.

Lieutenant Dominic Ferer couldn't find any of the treasure. The mountain was just a mountain, the jungle just a jungle, no different than thousands of others. When the hospital reported that Elena and especially Mercedes had ingested a variety of mind blowing herbs on the island, he discounted everything they said. He had to report ignorance, to his superiors. He was in enough trouble for authorizing the secure treasure room with an unbreakable lock. His superiors had just asked where the treasure was that the room was built for. He had no answer to that as well as to the disappearance of the two rangers he had sent to the island. No doubt the sharks had eaten them as they had so many others. The other two, the man and the woman he had taken off the island, they had disappeared soon after the chopper landed in San Jose. He put out an all points bulletin, but it was as if they had disappeared from the face of the earth.

They had seemed like normal people, but they seemed to be able to cross international borders with ease, to avoid the authorities as if they didn't exist. He had sent bulletins to surrounding countries. Nothing. He did get one report from Goa, India, but that was so far away and the description so vague, that he doubted it could be true.

In the aft cabin of the *Rose Marie*, at sea, Jill pulled gemstones from every pocket, every sock, even from her training bra and laughed, eyes
ablaze with joy as she played with her treasure, running the gems through her fingers. Responsibly she set some away for college or her own boat, whichever came first.

High in the highest mountain of Cocos Island, the Virgin of Lima still resides, waiting for someone to rescue her. Even today, in the light of the full moon, the gems embedded in her body and in her child's brow, still reflect light throughout the interior of a mountain. Whether she is just a statue or if she has gained some power through the released psychic energy of human sacrifices, is yet to be determined. Future treasure hunters should be aware that she isn't simply gold to be dug up. She will decide whom will survive to reintroduce her to the world. Future hunters should pack more than shovels and picks, metal detectors and sonar sets. A priest might come in handy.

Author's Afterward

Chatham Bay on Cocos island is blessed with numerous hammerheads. They are not as aggressive as written herein. I based their behavior on the sharks in Palmyra Atoll in the Line Islands. There in milky water, making them hard to see, the sharks are as aggressive as stated. They truthfully do jump out of the water, on to the beach, in attempts to grab and eat people.

The Treasures described to be on Cocos Island really do exist. They are there somewhere. There are far, far more on the island than I related. None have ever been found despite many repeated attempts.

It is a matter of Spanish historical record that the Incas used Cocos as a burial site for their high born dead. Absolutely no evidence of this has ever been found on Cocos Island.

This is a work of fiction. Even though veins of truth run through out the story, the author retains the moral right to describe this work as the product of his imagination. In other words, I ain't telling.

www.ingramcontent.com/pod-product-compliance
Lightning Source LLC
LaVergne TN
LVHW020530100826
845148LV00010B/1406

* 9 7 8 0 9 8 2 8 2 4 7 5 7 *